Sherry Ashworth ... radio broadcaster. ... novels: *Just Good Friends, A Matter of Fat, Personal Growth, The Perfect Mother, No Fear* and *Money Talks*. She lives in Manchester with her husband and two daughters.

Praise for Sherry Ashworth's previous novels:

Just Good Friends
'Wickedly funny' Maeve Haran
'Perceptive and entertaining' *Manchester Evening News*

The Perfect Mother
'Wonderfully, sharply funny. All imperfect mothers will love it' Penny Vincenzi

A Matter of Fat
'In *A Matter of Fat*, Ashworth has retained a wicked sense of humour, while raising some very important questions. Does she have the answers, though? You'll have to read the book if you want to find out!' *New Woman*

Money Talks
'Sherry Ashworth examines the effect of money, and lack of it, on people's lives and relationships with well-crafted characters, spot-on locations and her trademark humour' *Manchester Evening News*
'This is a warm-hearted tale with some amusing observations on human foibles . . . Good fun' *Big Issue*

Also by Sherry Ashworth

A Matter of Fat
Personal Growth
The Perfect Mother
No Fear
Money Talks
Just Good Friends

Otherwise Engaged

Sherry Ashworth

CORONET BOOKS
Hodder & Stoughton

Copyright © 2000 by Sherry Ashworth

The right of Sherry Ashworth to be identified as the Author of
the Work has been asserted by her in accordance with the
Copyright, Designs and Patents Act 1988.

First published in Great Britain in 2000
by Hodder and Stoughton
First published in paperback in 2000
by Hodder and Stoughton
A division of Hodder Headline

A Coronet Paperback

10 9 8 7 6 5 4 3 2 1

A CIP catalogue record for this title is available
from the British Library.

ISBN 0 340 75019 7

Printed and bound in Great Britain by
Clays Ltd, St Ives plc

Hodder and Stoughton
A division of Hodder Headline
338 Euston Road
London NW1 3BH

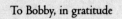

To Bobby, in gratitude

I am indebted to Barbara Levy for our tours of Leeds, Ann Evans for the bridal wear, Geoff Barlow for the taxis, Elaine Griffiths for showing me Gorton Monastery, Maria for her memories, and Colette for her support.

Chapter One

━━━◆◇◆━━━

Ruth reflected that it was a measure of her love for Dan that she had consented to spend Saturday afternoon in B & Q. Musing among the cotter pins and annular ring shank nails she tried to imagine what it must be like to be excited by screws, nuts and their possibilities. Not that Dan was the DIY type; he just needed a new roller blind for the bathroom, and had asked her to come with him and help him choose.

Being with Dan was pleasure enough. In his smart Gap jeans and T-shirt, he was the sort of man who drew envious glances from other women, distracting them from the wallpaper samples and tile grout. The odd thing was Dan wasn't in the slightest bit aware of it. He was the most modest, unaffected man Ruth had ever known — it was one of the primary reasons she loved him. Though what he saw in her was a mystery. She linked arms with him as they passed a stack of Teletubbies wastepaper bins.

The trouble with B & Q was that it was confusing; the aisles were arranged in such a way that you kept arriving back at your starting point. This was a problem, as every time they passed them, Dan stopped to look at the covings and artificial ceiling roses, then began examining other packages, regressing, no doubt, to the atavistic shelter-provider that lurked in all men. Being a psychologist, Ruth knew all about that sort of thing.

As they passed the light fittings she suddenly felt as if she'd forgotten to do something vital. What was it? Lock the front door? Get some food in for tonight's meal? No – at least twenty minutes had gone by since she'd wondered about the fate of their relationship. This was much longer than usual. She was slipping. Time for a quick fix.

Although Ruth had been going out with Dan for almost a year, she had known him much longer than that, from her first year at university, in fact. She had begun to notice him in her second term, propping up the student bar she and her friends frequented, and then occasionally on the steps of the union when she was going to meetings. Or she would see him pushing a very empty supermarket trolley in her direction at Safeway's. She couldn't help but notice him because of his striking good looks. He was so blond and so beautiful that she'd placed him right out of her league.

Then, as if to torment her, she kept bumping into him in the most unexpected places. His bike came to rest next to hers at the traffic lights, he was working at the next table in the library, and sat in the row behind her at the lecture on child development: Nature versus Nurture. Which was odd, given that his degree subject was mathematics. Ruth found that out a week or so later, when Dan finally plucked up enough courage to accost her at the bar.

It was heaven being chatted up by him. He was intelligent, he was funny, and he listened to her. No one had ever listened to her like that except her dad. Ruth was vain enough to appreciate the fact that her friends were watching from the table over by the juke box, consumed with envy. She discovered that he had fancied her for weeks — *he* had fancied *her*! She wasn't going to give the game away at this early stage by saying that she fancied him too, but suspected the grin plastered over her face was all too eloquent.

And so they started to go out together, sickening everyone with their established coupledom. Ellie used to tease her about it continuously, and that taught Ruth to make it a little less obvious when they were in company that she was totally besotted with Dan. When they eventually went to bed together, it was like nothing Ruth had ever known. Until that point, Ruth had allowed boyfriends to do things to her; there was some pleasure to be got in their pleasure. But now — it was as if everything he did was for *her*. Sex with him was so unbearably exciting she couldn't wait to be with him at the end of every day. Sometimes she couldn't even wait that long, and nor could he.

But it wasn't just sex. They talked; she told him the story of her life, and he told her about his. Then they swapped views on politics, favourite bands, religion, football, careers, fashion, the people they knew and the meaning of life. She felt so comfortable with him that it seemed inevitable that they should be together.

It was that feeling of inevitability that finally prised them apart. They acknowledged how young they were, and how little they knew of other people. They worried how each could pursue a career if they had to move around the country as a couple. Ruth wondered how much she was in touch with herself and her own needs; she noticed she had begun to think for two. That was when Dan began to spend more time with his mates, fooling around in an uncharacteristic way, getting drunk and stealing traffic cones. Ruth had concluded it was either the pressure of finals or the pressure of their far-too-serious relationship.

Parting was a joint decision. They decided they needed breathing space and time to grow. They were only nineteen when they had met, after all. Leaving Dan was like having a major amputation, Ruth felt. It had been the same for him, and each fought the temptation to ring the other frequently. Gradually work took precedence. Dan started his accountancy training in London, while Ruth settled in Leeds. She tried going out with other men, and she managed after a fashion, but Dan was always there in the shadows, a backstop, a safety net.

Then last year he was transferred to Leeds. The night she met him for a drink in the Calls and saw him walking towards her, that feeling of beautiful inevitability returned. This, she was certain, was the beginning of the rest of their lives. They would end up together. He was utterly familiar to her, and yet so totally opposite – the yin to her yang. How could she have been so stupid as to risk letting him go for all those years?

Yet she kept her feelings to herself, and proceeded cautiously, as did he. Bit by bit they resumed their relationship, more soberly, more wisely, but every bit as passionately. Ruth had forgotten sex could be that good. She felt complete again, happy, fulfilled, secure. Life had shape and pattern and meaning. She and Dan were made for each other; this was a fact recognised by all their friends. They were as much a pair as Laurel and Hardy, fish and chips and – Ruth strained for another simile as they passed the electric drills – and Black and Decker.

They spent most nights together. Not all nights; Ruth had her own flat near the hospital, and when Dan had arrived in Leeds he had invested in a two-bedroomed house. Having two places helped when parents came to visit, and gave each an illusion of independence. Dan had said to Ruth that she could move in with him; she was surprised to discover she was slightly disappointed when he'd suggested it. Moving in with someone seemed so casual; secretly she had been hoping for more. Since then Dan had said nothing and Ruth had said nothing. The absence of comment about the matter had become so palpable as to constitute a presence. The question – what ought they to do about the rest of their lives? – seemed to Ruth to be printed as a subtitle at the bottom of each frame in which they appeared. It obsessed her because it seemed so all-important.

Yet, as with most obsessions, there were temporary respites. This afternoon was one such. B & Q had an anodyne effect on Ruth. It obviously affected the alpha waves in her brain, and made her indolent and lazy. She was content to trail after Dan and live in the present and wonder what B & Q actually stood for. Big and Question? She was only teasing herself, she knew.

Dan had his back to her, examining rows of packets of curtain fitments. Whatever turns you on. She could hardly complain; his patience in Dorothy Perkins the other week was so exemplary that the assistant commented on how lucky Ruth was. In his absorption with hinges and brackets Dan hadn't noticed that the roller blinds were right opposite them.

'Wake up, handsome. We're here!' Ruth tugged at his arm, and Dan turned round.

'Oh, great!'

She nestled up to him as he lifted individual blinds and scrutinised them.

'What do you think of this?'

'Looks like a deckchair covering. It's gross.'

Dan slid it back into the rack. 'I like orange. It wakes you up.'

'Orange is the colour of insanity,' Ruth intoned. 'If every time I used your bathroom I was confronted with an orange roller blind, I'd go MAD!'

He laughed. 'Something more muted then.' He lifted a marbled, lilac blind.

'Too nothing-y.'

'There's no pleasing you.'

'What about that one over there, on the top? The blue checked one with the yellow flashes?'

'I don't know. It's a bit common.'

'Common? You go to B & Q and you don't want common?'

Dan grinned. 'No, we can do better than that. I like the plain green blind with the faint stripe. It'll go with the bath.'

Ruth picked it up. 'It's quite nice, actually. Green is a healing colour.'

'But what if we decide to get a new bathroom suite eventually?'

Ruth looked ahead to the bathroom section where four bathroom settings were displayed in front of a line of shower cubicles.

'Those are quite nice.'

They wandered over. Then something occurred to Ruth as she replayed Dan's last comment through her mind.

'You said "we". You said if *we* decide to get a new bathroom suite.'

'Well, yes,' Dan mumbled. 'I meant, one day, when we get married, we'll have to think about renovating the whole of the upstairs. I think it could do with it.'

'Hold on. Run that past me again. Did you say, "When we get married"?' Ruth felt her pulse zoom into overdrive. The whole of B & Q seemed to recede into the distance. It was happening at last. She was breathing rapidly and her knees seemed as if they might give way.

'What do you think?' Dan said. 'Do you want to get married?'

'To whom?' she hedged. 'Is this a general question, or does it refer to one person in particular?'

'Do you want to get married to me?'

Ruth was drowning in a tidal wave of momentousness. Quick, before it swept her away.

'Yes,' she gasped. She was afraid to look at him. Then she had a thought. 'I've said I want to marry you. Do you want to marry me?'

'It's the only thing I want.'

Now she looked at him. His eyes were full of happiness. No one had ever looked quite like that at her before. An utter conviction possessed her that Dan ought to be her husband.

'So we're getting married, then,' she said in a small voice.

'Seems like it,' Dan said.

It was the most solemn moment of her life. It was commemorated by the family with a trolley full of planks and house plants and rolls of wallpaper, who edged past them.

'Dan. I think I'm going to have to sit down.' The nearest seat was the toilet in the bathroom setting. Ruth eased herself down on to it. Dan came and knelt by her.

'Here,' he said. 'I've got something for you.' From his pocket he took a packet of curtain rings and, fumbling, opened it. He withdrew a medium-sized brass ring. 'Give me your left hand.' He placed the ring on the fourth finger. 'Of course, I'll get you something much better later on. But we might as well make it official now.'

As he slipped it on, Ruth felt the irrevocability of her choice. It was both terrifying and exhilarating. On the bath there was a notice saying 'Please do not sit in this bath' and Ruth wondered whether anyone ever did. Perhaps children did. Or toddlers. But most toddlers couldn't read so the notice was fairly pointless. She knew that for the rest of her life, whenever she thought of Dan's marriage proposal she would see the words 'Please don't sit in this bath'. She smiled to herself.

And then she felt incredibly happy. She knew she had always wanted to marry Dan, right from the time she saw him at the student bar in Reading. And it had come to pass. She was the luckiest girl alive.

'I love you,' she said to him. 'I want to kiss you.'

'Not here,' he said. 'Somewhere private.'

Ruth got up. 'I have an idea.'

She led him by the hand to a shower cubicle, pushed open the folding door and pulled him inside.

'This will do nicely,' she said.

They lost themselves in their embrace. Ruth closed her eyes so as not to see the Triton shower attachment in front of her. Their bodies fitted perfectly. It was a match made in heaven – and B & Q.

When Ruth emerged from her state of bliss, out of the corner of her eye she saw the security guard standing just outside the cubicle. She opened the door.

'It's all right,' she explained to him. 'We're getting married.'

Fours hours later. A September evening, with a persistent drizzle over most of Manchester. Away from the city centre, semi-detached houses nestled shoulder to shoulder, bricks glistening wet. In Oakhill Road, Crumpsall, stood a comfortable, compact house, an elderly garage nudging against it. From behind the curtains there was the glow of a light, the hum of a television and then the sudden illumination of a room upstairs. Below the ground, travelling faster than thought, pulsed an electronic signal. And the telephone rang . . .

Sylvie Collins heard the ring, and thought it was probably her mother. She closed the book she was reading, marking the pages with a money-off coupon that was lying fortuitously close by on the carpet. With mild irritation, as she had been enjoying herself, she lit a cigarette and took her ashtray with her to the kitchen, where the phone was sited. In one movement Sylvie lifted the receiver and settled herself down at the kitchen table.

'Hello?'

'Mum? It's me.'

So it wasn't her mother. 'Me' was the appellation which all of her three daughters used when they rang home, and Sylvie was supposed to know instantaneously which one it was. Such is a mother's intuition. This evening, however, she didn't have to think too hard. Sharon, her second daughter, the hairdresser, was in the shower, grooming herself after a day spent grooming other women. Rachel, her baby but now unaccountably nineteen, was home from college and upstairs in her room listening to some distorted sounds she called music. So, by a process of elimination, the phone call had to be from Ruth, number one daughter, the psychologist and know-it-all.

'Ruth? We haven't heard from you for a while.'

'Yes, but you'll forgive me. I have some incredible news!'

'Incredible news?' Sylvie's voice was doubtful, questioning. She knew Ruth had a streak of grandiosity. She couldn't imagine in a million years who she'd got it from.

'Mum, prepare yourself. I'm getting married!'

'Oh!'

Sylvie could have kicked herself for her inadequate response. She'd been a mother for twenty-five years, twenty-two of those being sentences running concurrently, and all she could think of to say was 'Oh!' The standard Jewish mother, she knew, would be dabbing at her eyes with tears of joy. That made her a substandard Jewish mother. Sounded about right. Sylvie inhaled again on her cigarette.

'Mum? Aren't you happy for me?'

'If you're happy, I'm happy.'

'I am. I'm so happy that the Oxford English Dictionary is going to use me as the classic definition of the word. Listen to how it happened. Dan and I were in B & Q this afternoon as he was looking for a roller blind for his bathroom, and he didn't actually propose as such, but just said, *when* we're married, and I picked him up on that, and I said—'

'Take a breath, Ruth.'

'I asked him what he meant and he said, did I want to marry him, and I asked him if he wanted to marry me, and that was it – and so we're engaged!'

'I wish you *mazeltov*. He's not Jewish, you know.'

'Don't be so daft, of course I know he's not Jewish! But it was you who always said you'd prefer me to marry a nice boy rather than a Jewish boy who wasn't nice.'

'I never said that!'

'You did, sort of. Anyway, we're going to have a fairly short engagement because there's no need to save up as Dan has the house and I can just move in. Is nine months long enough? Sharon and Rachel can be bridesmaids but Rach must get rid of her dreadlocks first – tell her from me. You were twenty-five when you married Dad, weren't you? It's strange how history repeats itself. Is Dad there? Can I speak to him.'

'Yes. You'd better tell him your news yourself. I'll get him.' Sylvie clutched the telephone to her ample bosom. 'Ivan?' No response. He'd probably fallen asleep in front of the television. '*Ivan!*' Sylvie was surprised to find her voice was a little unsteady. 'IVAN! There you are. It's your daughter Ruth. She has something to tell you.' Sylvie passed over the phone as if it were a smoking gun.

There was no saying how Ivan would receive the news. He adored Ruth, and generally this meant that everything she wanted was all right by him. But did this include a non-Jewish husband? She watched him closely, while helping herself to another cigarette. And then there was her mother, Renie. How would she react?

'Congratulations,' Ivan said. He flashed a look at Sylvie, the purpose of which was to find out what she thought. She raised her eyebrows expressively. Ivan, bemused, grinned as Ruth chatted on. Sylvie could tell he was as stunned as she was.

She had no objections to Dan. He was polite to a fault, good-looking, and a trainee accountant, no less. If it wasn't for his ash-blond hair, he could almost pass as a nice Jewish boy. He made Ruth happy; it was more than evident she made him happy. But marriage! Ruth was still a baby, bossy, impulsive, set on having whatever she wanted. The concept of compromise was as foreign to Ruth as good table manners to a wolf. Come to think of it, Dan was so much of the gentleman that he'd probably let her walk all over him. Poor Dan. Perhaps he was a good choice after all. And yet there was something about Ruth Collins, Anglo-Jewess, born and brought up in Crumpsall, a working-class kid for all her education, and Dan, blond, British and no doubt raised on cricket and cucumber sandwiches. An expression of her own mother's came to mind. *Oy vey!* It was Yiddish, untranslatable, doom-laden and utterly apt.

Ivan put down the phone. 'He's not Jewish.'

'I know.' Sylvie attempted to cheer him. 'But I always said to her, better marry a nice boy than a Jewish boy who isn't nice.'

'Did you tell her that?'

Sylvie shrugged.

'One down, two to go,' Ivan quipped. 'Do we have enough money to marry her properly?' Sylvie held the purse strings. It suited them both.

'I've been putting some aside. How many people do you think we can fit in the living room?'

Ivan looked aghast.

'I'm only joking. We can manage a small reception some-where. But if Ruth offers help, I'm not going to say no.'

'With David being president of the synagogue, I'm sure he'll let us have the hall.'

'Are you mad? For a non-Jewish bridegroom? We'll be lucky if David and Lila come to the wedding.'

'Do you want Lila at the wedding? You can't stand her.'

'She's my sister, of course I can't stand her. But she must be at the wedding.'

'I can arrange the taxis,' Ivan said, with a touch of pride.

This was true. Ivan drove a black cab, and had done ever since the girls were small. Transport was one issue they didn't need to worry about. And then it hit Sylvie. Marriage was one thing, and that was hard enough. But the wedding would be infinitely worse. Where did you begin? There was the reception, the caterer, the wedding dress, the guest list, the band, the speeches, new clothes, announcements in the news-papers . . .

Sharon chose that moment to walk into the kitchen in her bathrobe with its Ralph Lauren logo. Her hair was towel-wrapped in a turban and her face was pale blue with a face mask. She picked up a biscuit from a plate on the table and nibbled at it. With three of them, the kitchen was crowded.

'Who was on the phone? Was it for me? Did you take a

message? When's dinner? I need to eat something before I go out. The water pressure in the shower isn't very strong, Dad.'

'It was Ruth,' Sylvie said. Sharon wiped some face mask away from the corner of her mouth where it was interfering with the enjoyment of her biscuit. 'She rang to say she's getting married.'

'Married!' Sharon gave a scream of delight. 'Married! How cool is that? There'll be a wedding and she'd better let me be a bridesmaid or I'll kill her. I'll have to get a new dress. This is so cool. We'll have to go down to London — you can't get anything halfway decent up here. Tell her I'll do her hair for her and Louise will do her make-up. Can I tell everyone at the salon? Can I invite some of my friends? I'm going to tell Rachel.' Sharon ran out into the hall and shouted up the stairs. 'Rach? Rach! Come down, we've got some news!' Sharon re-entered the kitchen. 'It's going to be just like *Four Weddings and a Funeral!*'

'My funeral,' Sylvie muttered.

Rachel appeared in a huge T-shirt emblazoned with the word 'Verve'. Sylvie thought it was singularly inappropriate. She looked heavy-eyed, as if she'd been asleep. Sylvie still hadn't accustomed herself to the dreadlocks and pierced eyebrow.

'Yeah? What?'

'Ruth's getting married,' Sharon announced.

'Is that all you called me down for?'

'Listen to her, Mum! You could show a bit more feeling, Rachel!'

'Shut it, Sharon. I just assumed she was getting married anyway. It's, like, the sort of thing she would do. Like get a job and get married and a mortgage and all that boring stuff. Yeah,

I mean, that's great. Dan's quite fit, really. Are we going to have a drink to celebrate?'

'Tea?' Sylvie suggested archly.

'I didn't mean *tea*.'

'You drink too much, for someone of your age.'

'Oh, Mum, *everyone* drinks.' With that, Rachel went over to her mother, cuddled her, and buried her face in her neck. Sylvie secretly enjoyed the physical contact. Rachel was her baby, and that was why she still demanded hugs.

'Rachel's right,' Ivan said. 'We ought to do something to celebrate.'

'I'll go and have a look in the drinks cabinet,' Sylvie said, disentangling herself from Rachel.

She entered the living room. Years ago they had knocked through, and later had a small extension built, so the room was long, but rather narrow. The extension was full with Sylvie's sewing machine and a rail of clothes that she was altering. The rest of the room exuded shabby comfort. The settee was begging for a new cover, and Ivan's armchair sagged in the middle. The dining-room table was cluttered with newspapers, Sylvie's library books, Sharon's hair magazines, a vase of wilting flowers, some of Rachel's textbooks and letters that needed answering.

Sylvie fought a war of attrition with the mess. Every so often she'd attack it, but a few days later it would be the same as ever. It was the reverse of the story of the Elves and the Shoemaker; in her family, there were little sprites who came out at night and created mess mysteriously. There had to be; Ivan and the girls claimed they never left anything lying around.

But what do you expect? Sylvie argued to an imaginary adversary. In a house this small with four adults? You want me to be constantly nagging everyone? As if I haven't got enough to do. And with this wedding as well. Huh. I don't even have time for myself. It's the story of my life.

Sylvie glanced regretfully at the book she had been reading. It was an unusual choice for her – *Hard Times*, by Charles Dickens. Normally she picked contemporary novels or Jane Austen, two or three a week, but she'd seen a notice in the library about a reading group that was starting this term, and the first book they were to look at was *Hard Times*. Sylvie wasn't at all sure about the reading group, but she borrowed the book anyway, just as she'd borrowed the Weight Watchers diet from Lila without going to meetings. The title had appealed to her. *Hard Times*. That was the story of her life.

It was a slow read but more meaty than the last book she'd read, and there was more to think about. That Gradgrind fellow wanted shooting. Although maybe her own kids would have turned out better if she'd brought them up according to a system. She chuckled to herself, and prised open the door of the drinks cabinet in the wall unit, and started. It was so long since she'd opened it she'd forgotten that Ivan, in one of his DIY phases, had fixed a mirror to the inside of the door, and Sylvie was faced with herself, looking aghast. Her hair was a mess and needed dyeing again, and her lips were pale and needed lipstick, and the only reason she didn't have any wrinkles was because she had the full features of a woman who'd given up the battle of the bulge years ago. And this apparition was the mother of the bride. Heaven forbid!

She decided she did need a drink after all. The Collinses

were not great drinkers (except for Rachel) and all she could find was the bottle of cherry brandy bought two years ago when Lila and David last came round. It would have to do. She found four thimble-sized glasses and prepared to take them to the kitchen, but the rest of the family trailed one by one into the living room. They always followed her about.

'We have cherry brandy,' she announced.

'What's that?' Rachel asked. She picked up the bottle, unscrewed the top, and sniffed the contents.

'Ugh, Rachel, don't! No one will want to drink out of there now,' Sharon complained.

'Tell you what,' Ivan suggested. 'I'll drive over to the off-licence and get a bottle of wine. And a Chinese. You shouldn't have to cook on the night your daughter announces her wedding!'

Sylvie was touched.

'Get me chicken and cashew nuts in yellow bean sauce with boiled rice and prawn crackers. *I'll* pay for my own.' Sharon walked over to the TV where her Moschino bag was lying on the floor and opened it to get out her purse.

'I'll have boiled rice and sweet and sour sauce,' Rachel said, 'just in case they don't fry in vegetable fat. Someone will have to treat me – student grants don't run to takeaways.'

'God knows what you spend it on – not clothes, that's for sure,' Sharon remarked.

'At least I don't parade around like some overgrown Barbie doll.'

'Girls!' Sylvie shouted warningly. But they were out for blood.

'Mum, she is *so* rude! Do something about her!' Sharon's

eyes were small and hard and murderous. Cracks appeared in her face mask. 'It's so peaceful when you're not here, Rachel. I wish they'd make university terms longer. Like fifty-two weeks.'

'You're jealous. It's not my fault that you bummed around and flunked your GCSEs.'

'Rachel!' Sylvie shouted.

'I'm going now,' Ivan announced. No one paid him the slightest attention.

'And you're not just jealous of me, Sharon. I bet you're jealous of Ruth. You'd love to get hitched – except that no one in his right mind would have you.'

'Mum, just listen! Shut her up!'

Sylvie entertained a delicious fantasy of banging their heads together. When they were smaller she used to drag them to their separate rooms for a spot of solitary confinement. Now she was the one who chose the solitary confinement.

Leaving them to it she picked up her book and went back to the kitchen, shutting the door tightly behind her. At least these days it was only Sharon and Rachel who argued. When Ruth was at home, any permutation was possible. There was Ruth and Sharon, Ruth and Rachel, but mainly Ruth and herself. Sylvie had wondered about establishing a league table, and the winner of the greatest number of arguments could take the others out to dinner once a year.

It was just her luck that all her daughters should turn out so differently from each other. Ruth was the ambitious one, the driven daughter. She had brains, too. And with her interest in people – she got that from me, thought Sylvie – she had become a clinical psychologist. It sounded good. Sharon was her material girl, interested from a tender age in fashion, make-up, money and little else. She was now a senior stylist in a Manchester salon, hoping one day to have her own business. Rachel saw herself as the alternative sister, walking on the wild side. Sylvie prayed the body-piercing and strange music and incense-burning was just a phase. Rachel was in her first year of taking media studies at university.

Who would have thought they would all turn out so well? Sylvie knew she had hardly been a role model for success. She had left school at sixteen to start work, and had always promised herself that she'd catch up on her education. But it was like running for a bus that was putting on speed. First there was Ivan's business that went bust, then the girls to bring up, and the necessity to earn money. And now there was the wedding to prepare for. All she had time for was her reading, and even that was prone to interruptions, such as the odd marriage proposal. That was life for you. Life was crisis management with time off for good behaviour. It was her daughters who had the aspirations, not her. Sylvie was reasonably content with who she was; two stone lighter, and three thousand pounds per annum heavier, she would be perfectly content.

Away with such vain daydreams! Now she had the wedding to think about. She hoped Dan's family weren't too stuck up, and would take her as they found her. And if they didn't? Sylvie reached for her cigarettes again. Then they didn't. She wasn't putting on airs and graces for anyone. Even Ruth's new in-laws. Especially Ruth's new in-laws.

*

Easington, just outside York, seven o'clock on Saturday evening. There had been a slight breeze earlier, but otherwise the day had been fine. Some light traffic was moving towards the city on the A98, but it did not disturb the spacious, detached houses strung out along the road, hiding coyly behind the expansive front gardens. The Hollies was typical, a white-painted, double-fronted house, with three cars in the drive, a new Saab, a Cinquecento and a Skoda. In the L-shaped kitchen at the rear, three people were sitting round a large, pine table, finishing their evening meal.

Heather Blake was about to suggest to her husband and elder son that they should finish off the fruit salad with some of the Greek yoghurt when the telephone rang. Luckily Heather had remembered to put the answerphone on as they did not like to be disturbed during family meals.

'Hello. If you have a message for Kenneth Blake, Heather or Timothy Blake, please speak after the tone. If you leave your name and telephone number we will get back to you as soon as possible.'

'Hello, everyone. It's Dan here.'

'Dan!' Heather exclaimed and rose immediately from her chair. She turned off the answering machine. 'Hello, Dan! We were eating — it's seven o'clock.'

'Sorry, Mum. It's just that I've got something rather important to tell you.'

'Good or bad?' she said anxiously.

'It's good. Very good.'

She wondered what it could be, and happily anticipated a promotion, or Dan returning to work in York.

'Mother, Ruth and I have decided to get married.'

'Married?' She was taken by surprise. What ought she to

say? 'That's wonderful, darling! Ken! Tim! Dan and Ruth are getting married.'

'I know I should have come round with Ruth to tell you face to face, but I just wanted you to know immediately.'

'Of course. You've done the right thing. Oh, Dan, I am excited. Tell me how it happened. I hope you proposed properly.'

'Yes, I did. I asked her to marry me in the middle of B & Q.'

'In the middle of B & Q,' Heather repeated doubtfully.

'And we got thrown out. But I'm very happy.'

'And I'm very happy for you. The police weren't involved, were they?'

'No, everyone was very good-natured. We're hoping to get married in May. Ruth and I don't want to wait too long. There's nothing to stop her moving into my house—'

'When you're married,' Heather interjected.

'When we're married, and we don't see any point in waiting as we're both sure this is what we want.'

'Are you having an engagement party?'

'We hadn't thought—'

'I think we ought to. We could have a small affair here, just family, and the vicar, some close friends, and I think it would be nice to invite Ruth's family too. We ought to meet them.'

'Great. I'll tell Ruth. Listen, I've got to go. We've booked a table.'

'You mustn't be late. Give Ruth all our love, and warmest congratulations to you both. 'Bye!'

' 'Bye.'

Heather replaced the receiver carefully. So Dan was getting

married. She hoped she had reacted properly. Quickly she reviewed what she had said to him. That it was wonderful, that she was excited, that she was happy. That sounded OK. Was there anything else she should have mentioned?

In fact she was still in a mild state of shock. She paused and scrutinised Ken and Tim. How had they taken the news? She hoped Tim didn't feel too put out. He was the elder brother, after all, and by rights should marry first. It was essential to soothe his ruffled feathers.

'Aren't we lucky, Ken?' Heather said swiftly. 'One son has his contract renewed at the university, and the other is getting married.'

Tim smirked slightly and Heather was relieved. Now for Ken. She wondered what he was thinking. Did he have misgivings about the marriage? Or, worse still, would he be annoyed at Dan for telling her rather than him? By rights, Ken ought to have been informed first. There was a protocol to be observed.

'Are you happy, Ken?' she asked with trepidation.

'Delighted,' Ken said. 'I have to say, I'm not entirely surprised. I had a feeling he was keen on this one.' He beamed at her.

So it was all right. He hadn't noticed the irregularity. He maintained his characteristic air of kindly authority, befitting the ex-headmaster that he was. Tall, greying, benign, he looked every inch the part. With him, Heather often felt as if she was a sort of honorary head girl.

'I think this calls for a celebration,' Ken announced. 'I don't think we have any champagne in the cellar but there's a nice Chilean Chardonnay from the *Sunday Times* Wine Club.'

'That would be lovely.' Heather meant it. She wanted a drink now more than anything.

She watched him make his way to the cellar. Now it occurred to her that there would be a wedding. There would be guest lists to plan and new clothes, and decisions about honeymoons and hymns for the wedding service. Her heart sang. She loved having things to do.

Ken returned swiftly and uncorked the bottle with accustomed ease. Heather watched him covetously. Soon the three of them held a glass of wine aloft. Ken proposed the toast.

'To Dan and Ruth!'

'To Dan and Ruth,' Heather repeated.

'Dan and Ruth,' Tim mumbled.

Heather drank deep, revelling in the coolness of the wine and anticipating the rush of pleasure it would give her. She liked the way that wine bathed everything in a roseate glow.

Ken addressed Heather. 'I'll see to the notice in *The Times* on Monday. I'll need some details from you. Ruth's from Manchester, isn't she?'

'That's right. Her surname is Collins. I think her parents are Sylvia and Ivan. Did Dan ever mention to you that her family was Jewish?'

'Jewish! I daresay that rules out St Luke's for the wedding.'

'Do you think so? Are Jews fussy about that sort of thing? I'd always imagined Dan walking down the aisle at St Luke's. I don't know a lot about Jews. Of course I'm familiar with the Old Testament and Maureen Lipman.'

'There was a massacre at Clifford's Tower in the thirteenth century,' Tim remarked, picking the grapes out of the fruit salad. 'Or rather, they all committed mass suicide.'

'Tim!' Heather was shocked. 'I don't think you ought to say things like that, and especially not to Ruth. Actually I think it must be wonderful to be a Jew. Such an old religion, and they have such strong, happy families. I think Dan is lucky to be marrying into a Jewish family.'

'What does her father do?' Ken asked.

Heather was glad she had remembered, 'He owns his own taxi. And her mother is a seamstress. Perhaps she'll make the wedding dress. If so, I'll ask if I can see to the flowers. I can grow some orchids in the greenhouse and make a display. And then there are the table decorations. I wonder which hotel the Collinses will have for the reception? Do you know any nice hotels in Manchester, dear? You go there from time to time.'

'There's the Midland,' Ken said, 'and the Ramada. And quite a few others.'

'I'm assuming Ruth and Dan will get married in Manchester – it's only right. But if he does want to have the ceremony at St Luke's, perhaps we could have the reception over here. Oh, there's so much to think about!'

Ken smiled at her, and it seemed to Heather for a moment that it was the kind of smile he might have given to a class of eleven-year-olds who were all busily at work on their Latin prep. She really ought to get out of this habit of thinking that Ken was judging her all the time, or that at any moment he might hand her a school report commenting on her perform-ance as a wife or mother. It would probably say, 'Tries very hard.'

'Do you know what class Ruth's degree was?' Tim asked. He had been awarded a first, and it was the defining moment of his life.

'I don't think I've ever asked her,' Heather replied, swiftly finishing her wine. She glanced at Ken's glass. His was empty too. This gave her permission to fill both again, generously.

'I think I'll go upstairs,' Tim commented. 'I want to play around on the computer.' Tim was one of the rising stars in linguistics at the University of York. His reputation was considerably greater than his salary, and so he lived at home with a state-of-the-art computer.

'Would you like me to bring you up some coffee later?' Heather inquired.

'That'd be nice.'

'Shall I put some on now, Ken?'

'Not quite yet. I think I'll take my wine to the study and sort through some papers for Monday. I'm OFSTEDing again next week, and I don't want to leave all the preparation for tomorrow. I'll join you for coffee in about an hour. We can have a chat then. Wonderful news, isn't it?'

'Wonderful.'

In a few moments the kitchen was Heather's again. She could hear Ken moving about in the study. She decided to top up her wine glass. Then she examined the bottle and saw that it was almost empty. No matter. Tonight was a special night, and she had every right to drink a little bit more.

Her younger son was getting married. The prospect of telling everyone delighted her; thoughts of the wedding excited her. No doubt, as she got to know Ruth better, she would see in her what Dan had seen in her. No; that was unfair. Ruth was a lovely girl, just a bit colourful. And loud at times. And unconventional. That was the word. Unconventional. She could see why Dan might be besotted with her.

But would she make a good wife? Ruth was educated and had a demanding career; she wouldn't do the things for Dan that she herself had been able to do for Ken. Theirs was a text-book marriage. Ken had risen quickly through the ranks in his school, and had got a headship before he was fifty. She had given up work to support him and bring up the boys. She had rather enjoyed attending school functions as the headmaster's wife, being escorted to a seat in the front row at prize-giving or a concert by fresh-faced, acne-prone schoolboys.

She was grateful to Ken for providing her with a lovely home and some status in her community. She felt duty bound to repay him with social behaviour that would never discredit him. He was unfailingly kind to her and made few demands. Nevertheless she was obscurely pleased when he went on one of his little jaunts as an OFSTED inspector, or to study medieval church architecture. It gave her a break from the pursuit of perfection.

She reprimanded herself. She was wrong to resent him. He was the acme of kindness. She had a duty to strive to meet his standards. She only hoped that Ruth would do the same for Dan. She'd always imagined Dan marrying someone like herself. She caught her reflection in the darkening kitchen window, and patted her hair straight as she did so. She was greying gracefully, and maintained a well-cut bob. Today she was dressed in some trousers from Marks and a Jaeger sweater. It was her gardening gear.

She looked out into the garden, and saw the outline of her greenhouse. She rather wished she was there right now, seeing to the seedlings and checking the moisture levels of the various plants. She was good at gardening. But then gardening was so much simpler than life. Plants, by and large, did what you told them. When they didn't, there was always a book to consult.

Rather like church, she decided. In church, instead of Dr Hessayon, there was the Bible. In church there were certain rules, and it was easier to know if you were doing things correctly. Just the other day the vicar had asked for her help, and she had been about to mention it to Ken because she thought she ought to get his permission first, but this business with Dan had put it right out of her mind. Over at St Jude's John Foster was hoping to start a drop-in centre for the unemployed, and that was what he wanted her help with. She was flattered, and gratified by the look of pleasure and approval in his eyes when she said that she would think about it. Not that she had many skills to offer. She was trained as an infants' schoolteacher, and had taught until she married Ken. It helped her as a mother, but really that was all there was to her – she was a housewife and mother.

She sipped some more wine, relaxing. It was funny, really, that feeling she always had – that disquieting feeling that even as a housewife and mother she was a fraud. The trick was to get the details right, then no one need ever know. It bothered her that her future daughter-in-law was a psychologist – all the more reason to try harder than ever.

Heather decided to finish the Chardonnay as there was so little left in the bottle. She would make a note of the label as it was rather nice. She hoped there was some more in the cellar.

As the wine warmed her, she felt a glow of optimism. She would make absolutely sure this wedding was going to be a huge success, a triumph for them all. She would start by planning the engagement party. It would be a charming affair; she thought it was only right to put herself out for the Collinses, so she could make the best possible impression. A cold buffet, perhaps, with paper napkins printed with the entwined names of Dan and Ruth. And at least a case – or two – of the Chilean Chardonnay.

La Bella Pasta wasn't very busy yet – it was only eight o'clock – but there was sufficient privacy for the clientele as most tables were placed in intimate booths. Towards the rear of the restaurant an attractive, dark-haired girl in a turquoise satin blouse was leaning forward, eagerly talking to the young man with her. He was fair, clean-shaven, good-looking, and obviously very much in love.

Ruth took Dan's hand and held it firmly. 'Are you sure your mother was pleased?' she asked.

'Yes. She was delighted. I'm sure she likes you very much.'

'I like her too. Although in the beginning I was a bit frightened of her. No, not her so much as the house. It was so immaculate I didn't dare sit on the sofa in case I displaced the cushions. But that was my fault really. I'm not used to living so elegantly – but I want to, if that's what you want. I think your mother has lovely manners.'

Dan lifted Ruth's hand to his mouth and kissed each fingertip. In between kisses he spoke. 'She doesn't mean. To be fierce. She's just so. Determined. To please you. I expect you find her different to your mother because she's the only female in a house full of men. You've only met her two or three times.

When you get to know her better you'll find you have a lot in common.'

'So who would you say you were closer to? Your dad or your mum?' Ruth looked at Dan's hand lying on the table, and admired the long, strong fingers and the definition of his joints. Knuckles to die for!

'It's hard to say. I talk to them about different things. School was always Dad's area, and rugby, and the big career decisions. Mum just liked to know generally what was going on. She was around all the time. Dad always had to travel a lot.'

'As a headmaster?'

'Oh yes. You'd be surprised. There's the HMC and QMA courses and conferences and hobnobbing with university departments. Here's the waiter. What are you having?'

Ruth realised she hadn't been listening, lost in contemplation of Dan's hand. The waiter brought her to her senses. She lifted the menu to look at it once more.

'What's linguine? It's not a kind of seafood, is it? I'm allergic to most seafoods.'

'It's a sort of pasta.'

'Oh, all right. I'll go with the linguine.'

'Two linguine,' Dan said, 'and the Frascati.'

'Will you be having a starter?' the waiter inquired.

Dan glanced at Ruth who shook her head.

'Just the linguine.'

'Right you are,' said the waiter, who made some notes and disappeared in the direction of the kitchen.

'If he's Italian, then I'm a member of the Sacred Heart Missionary Society.'

Dan laughed.

'Pure Manchester,' Ruth continued. 'Wonder what made him cross the Pennines. Love? Or maybe a desire to get as far away as possible from his family.'

Dan's legs tangled with Ruth's under the table. 'Your family aren't that bad,' he said. 'I've met them, remember.'

'They were on their best behaviour. Before you came I had Mum at gunpoint to force her not to have a go at me in front of you. I didn't have to bribe Sharon. That night she was as pleased as punch because she'd got a cheap Baby G watch from a client of hers. Rachel was sulking in her room because she'd had her navel pierced and it went septic. Dad's all right, though.'

Dan nodded enthusiastically.

'I hope you're going to be half as good a husband as he is! No, my dad's only fault is that he can't see the faults in the rest of us. He thinks we're all wonderful.'

'You are.'

The lovers shared a gaze of such intimacy that the couple at the table opposite, in glancing at them to see if their food had arrived yet, looked away again, embarrassed.

'My dad's the sort who's hard to please,' Dan said. 'At least he was with Tim and me. He always made us feel as if we ought to be doing just that little bit better than we were.'

'The Critical Parent,' Ruth said, ad-libbing from her knowledge of transactional analysis. 'We'll soon train him out of that. Right. We've done our dads. What d'you think of my mum?'

'She reminds me of you.'

'Take that back immediately or the wedding's off. We argue

all the time, as well you know. She thinks I'm bossy and obstinate and like to have my own way. I can't stand how she's so cynical about everything – do you know what she said when I told her we were getting married?'

'No. What?'

' "Oh!" She said, "Oh!" As if I'd told her I was working for a day in London next week. Oh. I'm having a French manicure. Oh. Whenever I try to impress her, she belittles me.'

'I'm sure she doesn't mean to. Perhaps she's bothered about me not being Jewish.'

'As if! The last time she set foot inside a synagogue was for my cousin's Bar Mitzvah fifteen years ago. My grandad was a member of the Communist Party and she was brought up an atheist. Sometimes I think she's taken a personal dislike to God. She complains about him almost as much as she complains about me.'

'I can't see why.'

'She thinks I'm her problem child because I answer back. Dan, I don't want to sound mean about her. I do understand why she's like she is. It comes from frustration. She's quite bright but she never had an education. She failed her eleven plus and ended up on the scrap heap. I go on at her to do something with her life, but she just scoffs and tells me she's getting on, and it's too late. To be honest, I get frustrated with her. She is *so* unambitious. Or maybe she's scared of change. Perhaps that was why she sounded so lukewarm on the phone. Ever since I was a kid she's never behaved as I wanted her to. She—'

Dan placed a finger on her lips. 'Ssh. Try me. I'll behave just as you want.' He leant forward and kissed her. Ruth responded so eagerly that the couple opposite felt quite awkward and could not meet each other's eyes.

'Let's talk about us,' Dan said, when the kissing had stopped. 'Tell me where you want to get married.'

'Somewhere dead romantic.'

'Where?'

'You choose.'

'No, you.'

'Oh, all right. On the Manchester Ship Canal. On a barge strewn with flowers. And you must dress up as a Venetian waterman.'

'I love you.'

'I love you.'

'Why do you love me?'

'Because I fancy you like mad and you're so good and I love you so much I want to *be* you. Why do you love me?'

'You're so different,' Dan said, 'and you bring everything to life. And you're sexy. And . . .'

The conversation of lovers is never very original, but endlessly fascinating to its makers. The waiter brutally interrupted it with two plates of linguine and a bottle of Frascati.

As he twisted his pasta round his fork, Dan had a thought.

'My mother said she was going to throw a party for us. She wants to invite all of your family.'

'*Oy vey!*' Ruth said.

Chapter Two

Ruth glanced at the interior of her flat, saw that it was a mess, and decided that yet another advantage of being engaged and moving out was that she could throw away all of this clutter without ever having to actually tidy it up.

The flat was nothing special. It was modern, and in a small three-storey block in Chapel Allerton. It was the third property Ruth had rented. When she moved to Leeds she had shared a large, Victorian terraced house in Harehills with some friends, but it was so near St James she felt she was never away from work. Then she moved over to Headingley and found the travelling annoyed her. Ironically, when she moved back to north Leeds to her present flat, the job came up at Chapel Allerton Hospital, and so she was back living virtually a stone's throw away from work.

She liked Chapel Allerton, however. It was just south of Moortown, so when the urge took her, she could go and feast on bagels. Jewish bakers lived cheek by jowl up there. It was also reassuringly multi-cultural, with a new Sikh temple down the road, should she ever decide on a change of faith. There was an excellent launderette, a Safeway's, no end of takeaways, and even a decent Italian trattoria where she could have met Ellie this evening, but Ellie had naturally suggested a cafe-bar by the Corn Exchange. Ruth had given in gracefully. This evening would be a tough one for her friend and the least she deserved was first call on the venue.

Ruth's Fiesta was in the car park, and she quickly got into it. There wasn't a great deal of petrol left, but there was enough to get into the centre and to the Street Lane general practice tomorrow. Then it was the weekend, and Dan was driving them both home to Manchester. He was to be welcomed officially into the family. Ruth had told her mother not to make too much of a fuss but secretly hoped she would. Her family was so much nicer when they made an effort. It was important to her that Dan should love her family every bit as much as he loved her. But then, she thought, turning right down the Harrogate Road, that was asking for the moon. Lovable was not exactly the adjective she would apply to her family, except for her father. He was lovable; the others were . . .

Ruth struggled to find an adjective as she cruised through Chapeltown. Her mother was cynical and deflating, Sharon had made superficiality into an art form, and Rachel was a creature from another planet. She supposed they weren't very much worse than other people's families, and certainly when she listened to the tales of woe delivered by her clients, she had to concede they were probably better than many. Yet at times in her life she had been vouchsafed glimpses of other people's families, seen vistas of calm, fresh vases of flowers on occasional tables, mutual support, gleaming ornamental coal scuttles, sophistication, Classic FM on the radio, space, and, above all, good manners. She'd had a friend at school, Barbara, whose mother had laid the table for dinner when she visited, and even put out little bread rolls, and there were napkins in napkin holders, and apparently she did this every day. When Barbara's father came home from work, Barbara's mother had actually kissed him, and said, not exactly have you had a good day at the office, dear, but some approximation of it. Everybody was unfailingly polite to each other.

Later she stayed with Elspeth in Surrey, when she was at university. Elspeth's father was a university professor, and her mother wrote novels. She trailed around the house in kaftans and there were books everywhere, and in the evenings they played concertos and opera highlights on a CD player enthroned in a mahogany bookcase. They had meaningful conversations and Elspeth's mother actually drew her out – what a delightful sensation to be drawn out, to be listened to, acknowledged, and best of all approved of. Approval for Sylvie Collins was just the period of time that elapsed before you had to pay for the goods you ordered. Ruth reflected that she had not been in touch with Elspeth for some time; she was in London, teaching in a secondary school. She really ought to invite her to the wedding.

Ellie never liked Elspeth, saying she was rather insipid. Ellie didn't have a family, as such. She used to live with her divorced mother and had lost touch with her father. She was quite open about her broken home and even made jokes about it, which Ruth had thought was very brave. Now she wondered whether humour was just Ellie's defence. Despite a surface cynicism,

Ruth knew her friend was capable of real affection. She was dry and often quite dismissive in manner, yet needy for love, like everyone. Ruth was fond of her. It was great that she should end up in Leeds too.

One would almost think it was too much of a coincidence that both Dan and Ellie should follow her to Leeds from Reading, but not if you knew Leeds. It was the boomtown of Yorkshire. Many financial institutions, including Dan's own KPMG, had come here recently, and a whole new yuppie culture had sprung up to support the young employees. There was even a Harvey Nichols. Ellie's firm, which was a PR consultancy, was home-grown, however. Her boss, Adam, was a Bradford lad, and had started the business himself. Ruth was not particularly fond of Adam.

She drove slowly along the Calls, hoping to find a parking space, and as luck would have it, there was a gap just outside Sparrow's Wharf. It was only a stone's throw from the Corn Exchange, where she had arranged to meet Ellie. Manchester had had a Corn Exchange too, once, she reflected, until the IRA blew it up. Even then, it was just a shade sleazy and disreputable, whereas in Leeds the Exchange housed some very fashion-conscious outlets. She felt guilty at her sneaking preference for her adopted city. Leeds was thriving, solid, going places. Manchester was somehow dirtier, wetter, and more comfortable in an insinuating, suggestive way. And a dangerous way. They said if you fell into the Manchester Ship Canal, you'd have to have your stomach pumped.

Ruth guessed that the reason why she was filling her head with these interesting but pointless comparisons was that she was a little nervous of meeting Ellie, for Ellie did not know that she was engaged to be married to Dan. The point of this evening was to tell her.

Ellie was bound to be surprised for the simple reason that Ruth had deliberately misled her. In order to protect herself should Dan never mention marriage, she had convinced Ellie that marriage was the last thing on her mind. Ruth had told Ellie that she was marking time with Dan, that he was OK for now. How was she going to convince Ellie that *now* had suddenly become *forever*?

Ellie, who was always early for everything, was standing outside the Corn Exchange, wearing a short, pale blue dress, with a black jacket draped over her shoulders. She'd tied her hair into two plaits, squaw-style, with blue ribbons at the ends. The whole effect was rather striking and made Ruth feel a touch dowdy. She had slipped on some baggy trousers before she'd come out, with a matching grey silk blouse, which still had a memory of Dan's after-shave adhering to it. She greeted Ellie and they hugged enthusiastically.

'Please can we go to the Terra Firma?' Ellie begged. 'I adore their pizza with pepperoni and black olives.'

'That's fine by me. I prefer to go somewhere where we can hear ourselves speak.'

They took a table by the window and Ruth enjoyed the preliminaries of settling down, choosing food and wine, and absorbing by osmosis the select, fashionable ambience. Ambience, she thought, was a more appropriate word than atmosphere. The ambience of the Terra Firma seemed to infuse her engagement and made her feel surprisingly grownup. The place was airy, modern and minimalist, with black and white prints on the walls, which were ugly but eye-catching.

They sat on wooden chairs, and on their stainless steel table was one thin vase with a yellow rose slouching in it. Some bluesy music thrummed in the background.

Ellie was talking work, and Ruth half listened as she debated yet again how exactly to introduce the subject of her engagement. On the one hand, she knew she had to be careful not to make Ellie envious, but on the other hand their friendship would be so much less a friendship if she falsified the excitement she felt. Marriage was a difficult subject for Ellie, she knew. It would be necessary to tread very, very carefully. She would have to—

'You haven't been listening to a word I've said,' Ellie remarked.

'Yes, I have,' Ruth bluffed. 'Sort of. Sorry.'

'My fault. I was being boring. It's just that I've come straight from work and I need to offload. Oh, good, here's the wine.'

The waiter filled their glasses and Ruth summoned all her courage.

'Actually,' she said, 'we've got something to celebrate tonight.'

'Cool. What?'

'Me and Dan.' Ruth reflected that the conversation was getting as minimalist as the decor.

'You and Dan?'

'We've decided . . .'

'You've decided,' Ellie prompted.

'To get married.'

'Married! But you said . . . I mean, that's wonderful! Married? You told me you wouldn't contemplate it until you were at least thirty-five. But, hey, congratulations! You'll be a wife. That will seem so weird. Really weird. Mr and Mrs. You're going to keep your own name, aren't you?'

'Well, I thought I'd be known as Dan.'

'Oh, I want to kiss you. Except if I lean over now people will look – oh, what the hell!'

Ellie leaned over and kissed Ruth. When she'd recovered her balance and emotional equilibrium, Ruth could see that her eyes were moist. She thought she knew why and felt distinctly uneasy.

'So when's the wedding?' Ellie asked, taking a long draught of her wine.

'May, we thought. I mean, I can move into Dan's house but I suppose there'll be a lot to do beforehand.'

'Too right. Masterminding a wedding can be as bad as planning an invasion of France. You know something? I don't have any married friends. Well, except one.'

Ruth deliberately ignored the last comment. 'It's not going to make the slightest difference to our friendship that I'm married. I can't stand those couples who are joined at the hip. Look, I've known you longer than Dan. We're virtually sisters. Better than sisters,' Ruth added, thinking of Sharon and Rachel.

'You're right. Women count more than men anyway. I remember the first time I met you at uni. You were all red-eyed. You'd been crying in your room because you were home-sick.'

'And you took me straight to the bar for a drink.'

'And we chatted all evening, and we were both so glad to find someone we liked.'

Ruth enjoyed recalling the past. 'Then we shared a house for the rest of the time – do you remember number six Ragdale Road?'

'Where the bathroom flooded regularly and a garage band held its jamming sessions in number eight! How could I forget?' Ellie cheered up. 'And now you're getting married. Ruth – why are you getting married?'

The question threw her. Ruth had to collect her thoughts. 'I love Dan. I want to spend the rest of my life with him.'

'You can do that without getting married.'

'I know. But I want to stand up in public and tell everyone my intentions. And not getting married is like saying you expect the relationship to end one day.'

'OK. Look – you don't mind me playing the devil's advocate, do you?' Ellie looked questioningly at Ruth.

'No. But you can't change my mind.'

'I don't want to. But marriage is a big step. The biggest step. You might lose your individuality. And if things go wrong later, it's tricky getting out.'

'Not all marriages end badly. My parents' didn't.' Ruth could have kicked herself.

Ellie was the child of divorcees.

'One in three marriages end in divorce.'

'Two in three marriages don't.'

'Are you saying that for the rest of your life you'll never fancy anyone else?'

'What is this? A public interrogation?'

'No. A very large pepperoni and black olive pizza.' The waiter had arrived with their food.

End of round one, Ruth thought, as they helped themselves to slices of pizza. She felt nicely invigorated. Ellie hadn't said anything that had really disturbed her. It was true that not all marriages lasted and she was perfectly aware of that, but she and Dan weren't going to be part of the statistics. She knew that. She was the marrying sort, and he was the marrying sort. If you like, they were both a little old-fashioned. There was nothing wrong with being old-fashioned. Not if it made you happy. And she was happy. What else had Ellie said? she mused as she ate her pizza. She supposed it was true one might fancy other people once one was married, but then one simply wouldn't do anything about it. Fanciable men would become, as it were, pictures at an exhibition. Look, don't touch.

'Delish,' Ellie said, her mouth full of pizza. 'Now, I'm not satisfied yet. Don't you and Dan qualify as being a mixed marriage? With you being Jewish and him a Christian? Is that going to be an issue?'

Ruth had a twinge of guilt as she swallowed some pepperoni. 'Not at all. I'm not observant or anything. I don't deny I'm Jewish, but that's as far as it goes. Dan's not religious either.'

'Hmm.' Ellie emptied her wine glass. 'That's as may be. But I suppose you'll need some differences, otherwise you'll get terminally bored with each other. Don't you ever worry that you'll run out of things to say?'

'No,' said Ruth staunchly. 'I can't think of anything nicer than being with Dan every day. And we do other things apart from talk . . .'

'I'm sure you do.'

Ruth found herself blushing. She was closer to Ellie than any of her other female friends, but still she would never dream of telling her about her sex life. That was utterly private. It was assumed rather than asserted. Once when Ellie had started a conversation about the more physical side of their relationship, Ruth had headed her off. Ought she to do so again?

Ellie saw the blush and just laughed. 'Look, I'm really very happy for you, Ruth, and it's only because you're my best friend that I can talk to you like this. You know what I'm like, leading member of the awkward brigade. I could bite my tongue, some of the things I ask people.'

'I know – but that's what my mother likes about you,' Ruth said loyally. 'She says you always speak your mind, and that's rare.'

Ellie raised her wine glass again. 'To you and Dan, and all the little Ruths and Dans who'll result from this happy union!'

'Not yet, please!' Ruth felt that harmony was restored, and she was relieved. Only one point was still bothering her, and she knew she had to bring it up.

'Ellie, I'm happy for you to bring Adam to the wedding, you know.'

'That's if his wife will let him come.'

Ruth shrugged. She found it hard to know exactly how to handle the great love of Ellie's life. Adam Eastwood was Ellie's boss. He was quite old, around forty, she supposed, slightly greying around the temples. He was tall, athletic, wore Paul Smith trousers and bright, joky ties. He was a good business-man and artistic too. He was, apparently, generous, good in bed, capable of real passion. He was so much more grown up than twenty-something men. He was also married with a small daughter.

Ruth thought, if she were Ellie, she would never have let herself get involved with him. But Ellie was Ellie, and she *had* got involved with him. Ellie was her friend and her role was to be there for Ellie, wanting what she wanted for herself. Or should she? Sometimes Ruth had tried to argue that Ellie would be better off breaking up with him; at other times she had seen why it was that Ellie needed to continue seeing him. Adam's wife was a shadowy figure, blurred around the edges, someone who had let this situation happen. For all they knew, she had a lover herself. It was a convenient fiction.

Ellie claimed that Adam was on the verge of leaving her anyway. It was only a matter of time. And besides, she preferred to have a man who had other ties. It left her free. Yet every so often a bitter remark would drop from her lips, as it had just now. Ellie before Adam was slightly wild, affectionate, pleasure-seeking. Ellie with Adam was well on her way to a first-class honours in cynicism.

'Look, whatever you're thinking, Ruth, I'm not jealous of you. I am not jealous. We're just different, that's all. I'm perfectly happy right now. Marriage isn't for me, under any circumstances. Imagine living with someone, day in, day out. Watching him grow old, trying not to look as he sniffs his socks in the morning to see if they'll last another day. Refusing to acknowledge that his endearing habits are annoying the hell out of you.'

Ruth just grinned. Ellie sounded for all the world like someone who was trying to convince herself. She noticed that the bow of one of her ribbons had come adrift and was skimming the surface of her empty plate.

'Your ribbon,' she said.

Ellie rescued it, retying it swiftly. 'And your parents?' she quizzed Ruth. 'Are they glad you're getting hitched?'

'I daresay they'll be relieved to see the back of me. Well, not Dad. In actual fact I'm taking Dan home this weekend. We're staying over.'

'Sharing a bedroom?'

'Imposs. My mother's a prude, and anyway I share a bedroom with Sharon when I'm at home. Dan gets the settee.'

'Will you be celebrating?'

'Oh, yes,' she said stoutly. 'It'll be Dan's official welcome to the Collins clan Let's hope he still wants to marry me when it's all over.'

Chapter Three

———————

Dan was at the wheel because he preferred to drive, and Ruth liked it that way. It made them seem like man and wife already. And what was wrong with a little role-playing? she asked herself and an imaginary audience of angry, hatchet-wielding feminists. Especially if it made you happy. She was happy now, Dan by her side, a ribbon of M62 stretching out in front of her, the dark, bumpy hills of Lancashire massing in the distance.

She stole a sideways glance at Dan. Her Dan, his straight nose, firm, well-defined mouth, that slight cleft in his chin. His blue eyes, fine lashes, almost transparent, his square forehead, that scar above his left eyebrow from when he fell in the playground when he was six. His hands on the steering wheel. Her hand on his knee. Her hand moving up from his knee and along his thigh. And up to the very top of his thigh, and – dare she? Not at seventy miles per hour on the M62. Instead she traced the muscles of his thigh with her fingers and watched him try not to smile. She squeezed his thigh.

'I'll be a good girl now, honest.'

'Don't try too hard.'

She smiled to herself, brimming over with satisfaction. Her parents couldn't fail to love Dan every bit as much as she did. It was true that on the several occasions they had met before, everyone had held back a little. This was, she assumed, because her parents didn't know what his intentions were. Now Dan had proved himself, so to speak, he could be welcomed into the bosom of the family.

Ruth had taken certain precautions. At the end of the week she had rung her mother to explain what sort of celebration might be in order. Not a full-scale engagement party, obviously, she'd said. But I do think we ought to do something nice. Like what? her mother had asked. Ruth had chewed her lip, thought a little. Invite some of the family round, she'd said. You mean Lila and David? Sylvie did not get on with her sister. Yes, Ruth insisted, Lila and David. I don't want Dan to feel I'm reluctant to show him off to all of the family. And what about your sisters? asked Sylvie. Make sure they're there, and that they dress properly. Does Rachel have anything but jeans? And get Grandma over – I know she'll be thrilled. And don't make a meal as such but get something nice in – a few bridge rolls, some gateaux, some cheesecake – Any excuse for cheesecake, her mother had put in. And just tidy round a bit – you know the house can look really lovely when we all make an effort. We? Sylvie had remarked. I know it's a lot to ask, Mum, but it means so much to me. I really want Dan to feel welcome, as if we want him in our family. And if I were there I'd do all the work. Please . . .

She'd used the tone of voice that she knew her mother

found irresistible. And Sylvie had caved in. Ruth had not mentioned to Dan that they would be having a bit of a party.
Rather, she had given the impression that this was to be a
private gathering just to discuss the wedding arrangements.
Then, when he saw the fuss that had been made, he would
realise how much he meant to her and to the Collinses. It was
a brilliant idea. If it was manipulative, then, OK, she was
manipulative. Being manipulative was a better way of getting
your own way than being aggressive. Ruth knew that, she was
a psychologist. Being a psychologist, she also knew that it took
two to have an argument. If she decided she would not react
to any provocation, then peace would be maintained. Her
family did have a tendency to row, using conflict as a means of
communication. She and Dan would show them that it didn't
have to be that way. She would stay calm and happy.

And who said there would necessarily be any arguments?
Sometimes her family could have fun. On Mum and Dad's
twenty-fifth, she and Sharon had arranged a luxury meal to
arrive at Oakhill Road, and the five of them had had a great
evening. Dad was always kind, Mum had a sense of humour,
Sharon certainly wasn't a shrinking violet and Rachel was only
a baby. Most of all, they were *her* family, and when they pulled
the stops out and made an effort, they could beat the world.
That was all she was asking for, that they should make an
effort for her. She was perfectly aware that there wasn't a lot
of money to spend on the wedding, and that was fine with
Dan too. All she wanted was a little effort, to make things go
with a swing. Her parents greeting them, standing waiting at
the door, maybe, a few flowers in the hall, Grandma in her
posh frock, and maybe a card or two. And some champagne or

even an Asti would do, as long as it didn't have a supermarket label. Automatically she looked to the left as they reached the roundabout at the end of the M60 slip road.

'It's OK,' she said. 'It's clear.'

And now they were almost in Crumpsall. Ruth was a little nervous, and became chatty.

'Ah, Crumpsall,' she said. 'Lovely Crumpsall. The best thing about coming from Crumpsall is that it charges you with ambition. You can't wait to get out.'

'It's not that bad.'

'No, but it could be anywhere. Just look! On your left, a garage, a chemist's, a newsagent's, a tanning salon, and a Chinese takeaway. And on the right? A Chinese takeaway, a newsagent's, a garage and a Victoria Wine. Nobody actually chooses to live here. It's where you go when you can't afford to live anywhere else. When I visit your parents in York, it's so different. York is full of history, and tourists and culture. North Manchester just sort of happened by accident.'

'I'm glad it did,' Dan said.

'I can't believe we're getting married,' Ruth said. 'I feel like I'm acting all of this, as if there's an audience out there, getting ready to applaud. First left, then second left. I'm talking too much, aren't I? I suppose I'm nervous. Don't know why. It's not as if you haven't met them before, only its different now. You'll be their son-in-law.' And Ruth looked at him once more as they drove into Oakhill Road and the sheer impossibility of this handsome, Anglo-Saxon, Aryan hero being the son-in-law of Sylvie and Ivan Collins hit her with a force that made her gasp. Then as suddenly as the overwhelming feeling of unreality arrived, it departed, leaving in its place just Dan, her old front door, and the vanishing chimes of an ice-cream van as she got out of the car.

Sylvie picked up the sodden bath towel from the carpet and decided that Sharon must have thrown it there because she thought she was in the salon. She hung it up carefully on the rail to dry, trying not to inhale the fumes of the latest Calvin Klein concoction.

Sharon had overslept, then crashed through the house like a whirlwind as she had to go over to Bolton to pick up her new beau. She'd apologised profusely for not being able to help. That was why the lounge still needed tidying, and Ivan hadn't been able to do it as he was out getting the bridge rolls, which meant that the food wasn't ready either. Sylvie was beginning to feel hot and bothered. She decided it was time to wake up Rachel. She gingerly pushed open the door of her bedroom, seeing clothes and other possessions strewn on the floor, looking for all the world as if her daughter had been packing to go somewhere and had fallen asleep halfway through.

'Rachel! They'll be here in half an hour!'

A snuffle, a groan. Rachel had come home at three thirty last night, watched TV until five, and then made her way to bed. No wonder she wasn't up yet.

'And put on something decent. The family's coming round.'

These words, as she spoke them, filled Sylvie with dread. The reason she knew Rachel had come in so late and watched TV till five was that she had been lying awake in bed hating the thought of today. For Sylvie, her house was a retreat, the one place where you could be yourself, relax, not have to bother. Ivan felt the same. She wasn't one of those women who used their homes as status symbols, as reflections of material prosperity. A home was where the food was. That was all. Her home was her security blanket, frayed round the edges, comfortable, in need of a good wash. The idea of it being invaded was a nightmare.

It had always been the case. The girls' birthday parties had been ordeals for her, the frenzied preparation, giggling little girls filling the house and robbing her of her fragile sense of control, and the eagle eyes of the mothers collecting their off-spring, noticing that she didn't have a fitted carpet in the hall, that the banisters needed painting. Today was not quite as bad in that she knew everyone who was coming. No, no, she thought, it was far worse. Lila would be there.

Lila was her elder sister, her wealthy sister, president of the Ladies Guild at the synagogue, chairlady-elect of the Bernstein Friendship Circle, wife of David Cohen, partner in Mansell Cohen Textiles, whose refurbished headquarters were a stone's throw from Piccadilly Station. Lila was the sister who had made it. Sylvie had given up trying to make it years ago. One of them, she had joked to her mother, just had to be the milkman's daughter, they were so unlike. Renie had not been amused.

Privately Sylvie thought Ruth was mad to want them all round. Or perhaps she was having second thoughts about marrying Dan and was trying to put him off gently. She smiled to herself as she made her way downstairs. As she did so, the telephone rang. She hurried down the final few stairs.

'Hello?'

'Sylvie? It's me. Ivan. I can't speak long, I'm in a call box.

The bridge rolls won't be out of the oven for half an hour so what I'm going to do is collect your mother from her flat, go back to the bakers', get the bridge rolls, and—'

'But they'll be here in half an hour!'

'So? It's only Ruth and Dan. We can all muck in. Tell Ruth I'm looking forward to seeing her. 'Bye.'

Sylvie shook her head. It wasn't that Ivan didn't try to get things right, but disasters seemed to crowd in on him. She knew she should have got up early to get the food herself, but she'd had to scrub the toilet, vacuum the hall carpet and repair a dress of Sharon's. Sylvie presumed that Ruth would not mind that Sharon was bringing her new boyfriend too. Ruth had seemed to imply the more, the merrier, and from what Sharon had said, this Henry certainly sounded merry. What she would do, she thought, was to tidy round before getting changed, then get the food ready, and if she was in the kitchen when Lila arrived, so be it. Ruth could do the entertaining. Which was only right and proper given that the whole show was for her, and typically Ruth, she rings with a list of instructions as long as your arm! Sylvie tingled with resentment, then felt guilty for feeling resentment when it was her first daughter's engagement party. Perhaps she should have invited Dan's family too. Perish the thought! And still Rachel wasn't up!

'Rachel! Get out of bed or I'm coming up there to drag you out!'

Ruth froze as she heard those words. Surely Rachel wasn't still in bed? It was one o'clock! What were they all doing in there? And why wasn't her father's taxi in the drive? She was filled with foreboding, but then dismissed her fears. It was imposs-ible that her family would let her down on such an important occasion. Dan stood by her side with a large bouquet of flowers for Sylvie. Ruth rang the bell.

'Ruth!' exclaimed her mother. 'Thank goodness you're here. We're nowhere near ready. Come on in. Rachel! I'm warning you!!'

Ruth quickly assessed the situation. The house looked exactly the same as ever. She could almost think that her mother had forgotten why she had come over. Dan thrust the flowers at Sylvie and kissed her on the cheek. She sensed her mother stiffen a little; theirs was not a kissing family. She held the bouquet awkwardly in front of her, as if it might go off. Then Ruth saw a figure at the top of the stairs – it was Rachel, with just an old T-shirt on, a T-shirt that barely skimmed the tops of her legs.

'Rachel!' Ruth shouted. 'Dan's here! Make yourself decent,' and hated herself for sounding like her mother. Calm, calm, she told herself. She took a deep breath.

'Stop screaming!' Rachel screamed, 'I've got a headache!'

'A hangover, I daresay,' Sylvie commented. 'God knows where she was last night.'

There was the sound of the bathroom door slamming shut.

'I'd better go and put these in some water, then,' Sylvie said, a little nervously, as if she was checking that that was what you actually did with flowers.

'Where is everyone?' Ruth cut in. 'Where's Dad? I thought we were going to, you know . . .'

'Sharon's gone to pick a friend up, and your father couldn't find any bridge rolls and had to go all the way to Whitefield where they—'

There was the sound of a key in the front door and Ivan appeared, bags of food in each hand. Ruth's face lit up when she saw him and, despite the bags, she gave him a hug. Ivan grinned at them both delightedly and was soon vigorously shaking hands with Dan.

'*Mazeltov* to both of you. Someone take these bags. I've got Grandma in the car and she needs a hand getting out.'

Sylvie relieved him of the food and vanished. Ruth felt her spirits rise again. Grandma had never met Dan before, and that she was doing so now gave the afternoon the feel of an historic occasion, which was what she had wanted. Checking the lounge wasn't too untidy, she ushered Dan in there to await Grandma. She straightened the Sunday papers, and whisked away an old coffee mug. Ivan helped Grandma with her coat, and then she entered in state on his arm. She glanced at Ruth, then settled her gaze on Dan.

'Well, he's good-looking, I will say that.'

Ivan settled her in his armchair, then, slipping a little, she slouched rakishly, like a sack of potatoes thrown down in a hurry. Ruth felt like giving her a good shake to tidy her up, but the combination of arthritis and obesity were invincible. She wore a flowery green and white dress that didn't suit her. Still she didn't take her eyes off Dan.

'So they tell me you're not a *yiddishe* boy? There'll be trouble when you have children. If your first one's a boy, you'll have to have a *bris*.'

Dan nudged Ruth for a translation.

'A circumcision,' she murmured.

Dan just nodded.

'The royal family have all been circumcised. Do you like this dress? They brought round a rack of dresses, dirt cheap; it's from when they die at the Home. They sell them off. Dirt cheap. I bought three of them. We all die sometime.'

'But not yet, I hope,' Dan said manfully.

'I haven't been too good lately,' Grandma said reproachfully. Her look swivelled to Ruth. 'And when they told me you were marrying out, I said *oy vey!*'

'Untranslatable,' Ruth said quickly.

'*Oy vey*, I said, these mixed marriages never work. But he's good-looking, that's for sure. But looks aren't everything. I hope you've got some backbone, some get up and go. That's what a man needs. It's what your father never had, Ruth.'

Ruth tried to think of a way of shutting her up without sounding rude. She was saved by Rachel who made her entry then, dressed this time in torn jeans and what looked like one of Ivan's old shirts.'

'I feel wretched,' she said.

'You don't look so good,' Grandma said, suddenly attentive. 'She doesn't look so good. Are you sure it's not meningitis? I was reading in the paper. Have you got a headache?'

Rachel nodded pathetically.

'She ought to see a doctor. Tell Sylvie she ought to see a doctor. They get it at university, from too much kissing. Have you got a stiff neck? Does the light hurt your eyes? Do you feel sick? All of last week I couldn't eat a thing, and he says it might be a high-up hernia.'

Ill health — her own and other people's — was Grandma's

passion. Now there was no stopping her. Ruth could see the glint in her eye. Like a retired military general recounting campaigns lost and won, Grandma was preparing to launch into the siege of the gallstones, the battle of the grumbling appendix, the shootout at OK North Manchester General Hospital. She had to be stopped.

'Dan's been looking forward to meeting you, haven't you, Dan?'

'What does he do? Is he a doctor?' Grandma looked hopeful.

'He's an accountant.'

'Hymie — you know, Yetta's Hymie — he was an accountant.' She was silent for a while, sucking her teeth. Ruth began to relax. 'Yes, he was an accountant, and he ended up in Strangeways. Embezzlement. Five years. He was thin as a rake when he got out. I hope you eat. I hope he eats, Ruth. I wouldn't trust the thin ones.'

Ivan reappeared.

'Dad, look, why don't you take Dan out for a walk? It'll give us a chance to get things ready. Please!' Her voice vibrated with urgency. Ivan, always attentive to her needs, took the cue immediately.

'An excellent idea. You'll need to stretch your legs after the journey. Let's give the women a bit of space.' Ivan ushered Dan out as quickly as he could.

All was not lost. If she helped her mother in the kitchen, arranged the flowers, forced Rachel to put a dress on, they could still have a proper reception for Dan. Rachel groaned.

'She's not well! It's the meningitis!' croaked the raven Grandma.

'She's ill like this every weekend,' said Ruth, her voice laced with satire.

'Then maybe it's not the meningitis. It's the ME.'

'Well, you tell Rachel all about ME while I go and give Mum a hand.'

Ruth left the room and paused for a while in the hall. It frustrated her that her family hadn't tried to rise to the occasion. She knew they were capable of it. She reminded herself that it was important not to get angry with her mother, or with anyone. She didn't want to spoil her special day. But it was hard. And you'd have thought that someone would have had a word with Grandma to tell her to keep her mouth shut. Ruth took a deep breath and entered the kitchen.

At least there was a lot of food. In fact, all over the kitchen there were buttered bridge rolls, cakes and an assortment of cups and saucers. Sylvie, looking slightly flushed, was pouring peanuts into bowls. Ruth went to the sink to wash her hands.

'What shall I do?'

'Put some chopped herring on the bridge rolls.'

'Did you get any smoked salmon?'

'At two ninety-nine a packet?'

'But Dan might not like chopped herring. It's an acquired taste.'

'So are you, my dear.'

Ruth bridled. She knew her mother was making a joke, but it wasn't a nice joke. Sylvie had a habit of doing this, of puncturing her every so often, making little barbed comments which pricked at her self-esteem. And why couldn't she have pushed the boat out a bit for Dan? Ruth was hurt, but reminded herself that she wasn't to get upset. She set to work on the bridge rolls.

'And how have you been?' she asked her mother civilly.

'Busy as ever. There never seem to be enough hours in the day.'

'But it's good if you're busy. At least there's money coming in.'

'But never enough.'

If only her mother could cheer up. Perhaps it was no surprise she was a pessimist, having the doom-laden Renie as a mother. Ruth felt sorry for her. Perhaps it was the daughter's role to be a beacon of hope for the mother. She decided to be unremittingly cheerful.

'Come on,' she said. 'We're all healthy, even counting Rachel and her hangover. And I'm getting married and this afternoon will be fun.'

'Did I tell you Sharon is bringing her new boyfriend?'

'I didn't know she had a new boyfriend.'

'Nor did I till yesterday. Henry, she calls him. She's gone to pick him up.'

'You've not met him?'

'No.'

Ruth frowned to herself. She hoped he would get on with Dan. With luck he would be a little out of his depth, meeting Sharon's family for the first time, and therefore stay completely silent. Or perhaps he'd keep Sharon under control.'

'I think,' Sylvie said, 'she's a little jealous of you. In her own way, she admires you.'

It didn't feel like that to Ruth. Sharon was her arch competitor, the potential usurper. Her constant refrain when they were small was that she wished *she* was the older sister. She'd wished it so much that she'd grown taller than Ruth, and revelled in the fact. Was that admiration? Ruth thought not. She decided to change the subject, but before she did so she stealthily helped herself to a bridge roll. She was getting hungry.

'So what have you been doing with yourself lately?' Ruth asked Sylvie.

'Nothing. Reading.'

'Reading what?'

'Dickens, would you believe.'

'Dickens!' Ruth was surprised and delighted. She knew her mother enjoyed books, and also suspected she was able to get more out of them than most readers. 'Why Dickens?'

'They're starting a reading group at the library. *Hard Times* was the book they recommended. Have you got a decent knife? This one isn't cutting properly.'

'No, hold on. So you're going to a reading group?' This was getting better and better.

Sylvie laughed. 'Me at a reading group? You must be joking.'

'No, I think it's a wonderful idea. You'll get so much more out of what you read. And you could even go on and study. And make friends. Oh, do it!'

'I'd stick out like a sore thumb.'

'No, you wouldn't. And then you could have an interest you could talk about to people. Like when you meet Dan's parents. His father's a retired headmaster, you know – and he taught history. His mother – that's Heather,' she tried the name on her tongue, 'she's very nice, and she used to be a teacher too.' If only her mother would join this reading group!

She could imagine them all talking about nineteenth-century literature. She would be so proud of her! 'Please give the group a try.'

'What is this? Educate your mother week? I'm perfectly happy reading by myself. Aren't I good enough for you?'

Ruth felt hurt by that comment. Nothing could be further from the truth. 'It's for your sake. Everyone needs some intellectual stimulation.'

'Shut up with your intellectual stimulation and take the bridge rolls into the lounge. I've got to go and change before Lila gets here.'

Sylvie popped into the lounge to say hello to her mother. 'Are you all right?'

'*I'm* all right,' said Renie, 'but your daughter Rachel isn't.' Rachel had her head in her grandma's lap and Renie had placed a protective, gnarled hand on her shoulder. 'You should call the doctor.'

'Somehow I don't think so,' Sylvie said.

'At her age she should be running around and laughing, and look at her!'

Sylvie sighed, sandwiched between her mother's disapproval and her daughter's disapproval. Neither would be satisfied until she was on-message at the doctor's surgery, while creating a cordon-bleu buffet single-handed and taking a postgraduate degree in English literature. It was hard being a mother, it was hard being a daughter, but infinitely worse was being both a mother and a daughter. She hurried up the stairs, into her bedroom, and opened her wardrobe to get out the dress that she wore for her twenty-fifth wedding anniversary, the navy dress with the white collar from Big 'n' Beautiful on the Bury New Road. Her mother was being ridiculous; perhaps she should tell her after all about Rachel's alcohol habit. But Ruth . . . Ruth unfortunately had a point.

It was a shame she didn't have the kind of mother who would have put on the right sort of spread for her and Dan. Ruth liked everything to be just as it ought. Sylvie smiled as she remembered the first time she saw the diary that Ruth had been keeping at primary school. The opening page had a drawing of 'My Family', and Mummy had been depicted as having blonde, curly hair a smiley face, and the classic trian-gular skirt. Below it Ruth had written, 'My mummy looks after us.' Sylvie had pointed out to the six-year-old Ruth that she had dark hair, lanky, some of which was falling out after Rachel's birth, was on a permanent short fuse, and wore trousers. And she didn't so much look after them as run around after them. The pleasantry was lost on her infant daughter.

Sylvie stretched her mouth to apply some lipstick and decided she would do. Just in time, for there was the sound of the door opening. Ivan and Dan were back. Guiltily she thought she should have been more grateful for the flowers. They were still propped up in the kitchen sink. Sylvie vowed she would try a little harder.

Another key in the door. This time she heard Sharon's voice. Curious to see her latest acquisition, Sylvie made her way to the top of the stairs and looked down. This Henry was dressed very casually; he wore a Manchester City shirt, joggers, and possibly he hadn't shaved, or perhaps it was just the light. No; he hadn't shaved. Strange, he wasn't Sharon's type at all. He had an arm round her and was grinning fit to burst. What an abnormally wide mouth he had, Sylvie thought. She wondered again what Sharon saw in him.

She came down the stairs in time to see a rather stiff Ruth being introduced to Henry.

'So you're the blushing bride?' he said. 'Nice one. And where's the lucky man?' Dan came out. Henry slapped him on the back. 'Rather you than me, mate.'

Sylvie observed the expression in Ruth's eyes. It would have turned Medusa herself to stone.

The door opened a final time, and there were Lila and David. Sylvie fought an impulse to run back upstairs and pretend all this was not happening. Ivan helped divest Lila of her jacket, revealing a smart, tailored suit beneath. Lila's gold-framed glasses looked larger than ever, her neck redder than ever, and David stood by her, self-satisfied, corpulent, bestowing himself upon the gathering.

Sylvie approached her sister and kissed her on the cheek.

'Ought I to say *mazeltov*?' Lila asked.

'Of course you say *mazeltov*!'

'*Mazeltov*!' said Lila, to no one in particular.

The cattiness was not lost on Sylvie. Lila had deftly pointed out that Dan was not Jewish, right at the beginning of the afternoon. Should she be surprised? Hardly. It was Lila who used to banish her, in the years when she still smoked, to the toilet if she wanted a cigarette. Lila, whose own daughter couldn't stand her so much she'd emigrated to Israel. Sylvie ushered everyone into the lounge.

Every available surface was covered with plates of food. Lila looked at the food, raised her eyebrows, and then rested her glance on Henry.

'Congratulations,' she said to him.

'Yeah, too right. I've been trying to land her for ages.'

Lila smiled uncertainly.

'That's Sharon's boyfriend,' Sylvie explained, amused. 'This is Dan.'

Ruth didn't blame her aunt for the misunderstanding, although it didn't reflect well on her perceptiveness. She blamed Sharon. She knew precisely why Henry had been invited; it was done deliberately to upset her. Sharon had made sure that he hadn't even bothered to dress up for the occasion. He was obviously one of Sharon's reject admirers, brought here simply to redress the balance of power. Ruth felt her poise, her Leeds self, deserting her. Instead she was being drawn into that familiar, magnetic, obsessive hatred of Sharon. She loathed Sharon's black PVC hipsters, the way her hair was piled on top of her head, her talon-sharp lilac-painted nails, and most of all the fact that she seemed to be enjoying herself. Ruth could hardly concentrate on the introductions, on Dan explaining how they had met at Reading, on Uncle David's remark that he had been to Reading once, on business, and Grandma muttering about Rachel's temperature.

With a deep breath, Ruth tried to step outside her temporary madness. *I will not succumb*, she told herself, her jaw clenched tight. She reached out for Dan's hand and held it, smiled, and tried to find a way into the general conversation. On the surface all seemed to be going well. Although they hadn't been ready on time, there was sufficient food and a sense of occasion. Lila and David might be rather right wing, stuck up, opinionated and hated by her mother, but at least they had a bit of class. They looked smart and prosperous. Lila, David and Ivan were lined up on the settee, Sharon was actually perched on Henry's knee, Sylvie was standing by the door ready to bolt, and she and Dan were sitting side by side on the kitchen chairs which had been brought in to make up numbers. Grandma, still nursing Rachel, saw Ruth's attention was unengaged.

'I'm thinking maybe it's not ME. Have you thought of a brain tumour? Has she been acting strangely lately?'

All of her life, thought Ruth. She would have shared that remark with Dan, but he was still listening to Uncle David, and was on his best behaviour. She wondered what her fiancé could be thinking. She regretted having arranged this get-together, but then swiftly dismissed that thought from her mind. Sooner or later Dan would have to get to know them all, and provided he could see she was nothing like the rest of them – her glance was drawn to Sharon again – no harm would be done. Auntie Lila gave a deliberate cough, the sort used to attract general attention.

'So,' she said, 'tell me all about the wedding plans. It's ages since we've had a family wedding. But of course you won't be getting married under the *chuppah*. A pity. There's nothing quite like a proper Jewish wedding.' Ruth glanced at Sylvie. Was her mother having a hot flush?

'We were thinking of either a register office or somewhere a bit different. You can get married in lots of different venues now,' Ruth explained.

'What about a hotel? We had Ben's Bar Mitzvah in the Midland. A lovely place.'

'I don't think we can quite run to the Midland, Lila,' Sylvie said. Ruth saw her mother had one hand on the back of Dan's chair. Her knuckles were white.

'A shame,' said Lila. 'It would be nice to get married and have the reception in the same place. But I know money is a problem. Tell me, how big will the reception be?'

'We haven't decided—'

'Because these things need to be worked out as soon as possible. Do you have a large family, Dan? We must be fair about allocating invitations. Of course when Rochelle was married in Israel there weren't so many of us as there were of his side, but it was a lovely affair. Which reminds me. Do you have a caterer? I'd book soon if I were you, the best ones get taken well in advance. I daresay you've left it too late already. When you start looking for a dress, have a word with David. He's the expert, he's been in the trade for years. And are you having a photographer? I know young couples these days prefer to be more informal, but I think there's nothing like a proper wedding photographer, Sylvie, and you ought to get a videographer too. Think how your grand-children will feel if you don't. And you might start thinking about getting the invitations printed – I know a very nice man—'

'Auntie, we haven't really begun thinking about the details yet.'

Lila raised her eyebrows. 'Your mother's dreadful,' she said playfully. 'She leaves everything to the last minute.'

Ruth prayed Sylvie wouldn't rise to the bait, at least not in front of Dan. Sisters could be annoying, as she knew only too well.

'So are you having a stag night?' Henry said to Dan. 'Mate of mine had a do at Bernard Manning's Embassy Club. Got plastered. He woke up in the morning just in his boxers in a luggage van on the way to Rhyl.' Henry guffawed. Sharon giggled.

'You are funny,' she said. She mussed his hair playfully. He put his arms round her and squeezed her tight. She placed her head on his shoulder; he twisted round and then kissed her full on the lips, for three seconds at least. Ruth could not believe her eyes. Her sister seemed to be deliberately acting out some crude parody of her and Dan, upstaging and debasing her all at once. It was their old game, anything you can do, I can do better. Usually Ruth's move was a sharp kick administered where it would hurt, and if Dan hadn't been there, she would have done it. No, she would not give way to temptation. She would not be dragged down to her sister's level.

'So, Sylvie,' Lila continued, 'have you decided what you are going to wear for the wedding? Navy does suit you, I suppose. It hides a thousand sins.'

'I'm actually thinking of getting something new,' Sylvie said.

'Of course you are. Listen, I have a good idea. Maybe we could join Weight Watchers together. We must diet for the wedding. I could do with losing a few pounds and you could certainly. The meeting's on a Wednesday.'

'Sorry. That's the same night as my reading group,' Sylvie came back, quick as a flash.

'That'll be good for her,' said Lila to the company in general. 'She missed out on her education. I passed for the grammar school, but Sylvie went to the secondary modern.'

'Only because I refused to go as you were there.'

Lila looked surprised.

'And can you blame me?' Sylvie continued. 'After you've sat here, insulted my children, laid down the law, and—'

'Stop it!' Ruth was aghast.

'Not bloody likely. I've finally had enough.'

'David,' Lila said haughtily, 'I can tell when I'm not wanted.'

'So why are you still sitting here?' Sylvie shot back.

'Mum!' Ruth shouted frantically. 'It's my engagement party!'

'I can't help it. My sister drives me mad.'

Ruth was blind with fury at her mother. 'My sister drives me mad too but *I've* kept control.'

'What do you mean, I drive you mad?' said Sharon. 'What a horrible thing to say! I've made all this effort, bringing people to your party, I'm the only one who's bothered to get dressed up, and you insult me! Mum! Tell her off!'

'Sharon, you be quiet.'

'Me? She started it. God, I can't stand the way she's so stuck up, and you're always on her side.'

Ruth's anger was like a tidal wave gathering force. It swept through her, breaking up her sanity, fragments of which bobbed helplessly on a surge of unstoppable fury.

'I've had enough,' she shouted. 'This is the most awful day of my life. All of you squabbling like animals, and Sharon dressed like a lap dancer, and Rachel with the world's biggest hangover, and Auntie Lila taking over everything and nobody paying the slightest attention to Dan, which is just as well given the kind of things people say to you in this house when they do pay you attention. I mean, I'm getting married, and nobody's happy! I want to be happy, and I damn well want you all to be happy!' Then she sobbed hysterically.

'I'm happy,' said Grandma. 'I like a good argument.'

Sylvie finished off the last bridge roll. It was a shame for good food to go to waste. She had offered a box full to Ruth and Dan but Ruth had said she had no appetite and didn't want to see another bridge roll in her life. By that time, she had calmed down. Half an hour sobbing upstairs, with Dan outside the bedroom door begging to come in, had helped her get back to normal. Lila had left in high dudgeon, threatening not to come to the wedding. Every cloud has a silver lining, Sylvie reflected.

Sharon had been contrite, but it would be some while before Ruth spoke to her again. This did not disturb Sylvie, on the contrary, it felt normal. The chopped herring was giving her heartburn. That felt normal too. And it was as well for Dan to see Ruth in her true colours. If he loved her as much as ever after today's outburst, then he was the right one for her.

Which, Sylvie thought, he probably was. There were certain ways in which he reminded her of Ivan, both of them being the gentle, unassuming sort. It was essential that fire-crackers like herself and Ruth were partnered by the gentle and unassuming sort. No one else would be able to get along with them, that was for sure. She imagined that once Ruth got back to Leeds and talked it all through with Dan, she'd see the funny side of it, as she herself was beginning to now.

One unexpected outcome was that she'd publicly committed herself to this reading group. Perhaps it would be no bad thing. It wasn't entirely true what she had said to Lila about the secondary modern. She had opted to go there because she was a little scared of the grammar school. She often wondered what would have become of her had she gone there. And the reading would take her mind off the impending wedding. There were decisions to be made and venues to be visited. Even though the wedding would be a modest affair, the complexity of it overwhelmed her. Perhaps she could do with Lila's help after all.

She hoisted herself to her feet to go and get some Rennies from the bathroom cabinet. Tomorrow she would have to ring Lila and apologise, and then have a chat with Ruth. There was no point holding on to grudges. Not with a wedding coming up. These arguments they had, they were like storms, loud and frightening but soon over. After all, they were a family, and all families fought. Even the royal family. And a family that didn't just wasn't natural.

Chapter Four

'No, my family doesn't fight,' Dan said. 'Everyone gets on pretty well.'

Ruth half-closed her eyes in bliss, and opened them again to see the tree-lined avenue where Dan's parents lived.

'It's lovely here,' she said.

As indeed it was. It was a sunny, mellow afternoon, and the trees had not yet lost their leaves. Sunlight irradiated them and threw lazy shadows on the pavement. The sky was blue with clouds like trails of smoke moving slowly across it. The houses in the avenue looked as if they belonged. It was the gentle harmony of the bricks and trees that appealed to Ruth, that, and the undoubted air of propriety and comfort that exuded from every nook and cranny.

Dan's parents' house was towards the bottom of the avenue, on the right. A tall hedge obscured most of it from view until you were right outside it and could glimpse its white-painted double front. Bow windows announced themselves on either side, and the door was of some dark, ancient wood, with a brass knocker placed centrally. The slate roof had two terracotta brick Tudor-style chimneys which rose up from the rear. A low, modern double garage was at one side. Dan pulled in and parked in front of it.

Ruth noticed that the front garden was immaculate, the lawn not so much groomed as shaved, and small plants were ranged neatly along the borders. By the side of the front door, where she was now standing, was an old whisky barrel varnished to perfection, with a small evergreen standing proud in it. The quarry tiling of the front doorstep was clean, so clean Ruth was afraid to place her feet on it, and surreptitiously wiped them on the gravel.

Dan rang. In a moment Heather opened the door.

'Dan! And Ruth!' Heather beamed at her. 'Come in, come in.'

Ruth followed Dan who carried in their cases and placed them in the hall by the hat stand. Ruth glanced up the pale-carpeted stairs in front of her, glimpsed the sitting room on her left where a huge vase of flowers sat on an occasional table, then saw the same scene reflected on her right where there was an oblong mirror, giving back to her one rather nervous, dark-haired young woman in a belted grey jacket.

Heather kissed her. 'So glad you were able to come and stay this weekend. I want you to know I'm thrilled about everything.'

Ken arrived from the sitting room, in casual trousers and a fawn sweater. He also kissed Ruth, shook Dan's hand and held it for a moment. Ruth was touched by the unspoken emotion in the gesture. Jackets were removed, and Ruth and Dan were ushered into the sitting room where Ken moved swiftly to the drinks cabinet.

'What will you have?' he asked, pouring himself a whisky.

Ruth looked at Dan who grinned at her. This was the acme of civilisation, to have drinks in the middle of the afternoon.

'Whisky, gin, sherry, Pimms?' continued Ken.

'Pimms,' said Ruth.

There was some to-ing and fro-ing with ice and cucumber from the kitchen and Ruth felt a little embarrassed that she had put Heather and Ken to so much trouble, except they assured her that nothing was too much trouble and they looked as though they meant it. Soon Ruth was perched on a hard-backed chair with a mustard-coloured velvet seat, and she crossed her ankles demurely. She was presented with her Pimms, and delighted in the sight of all that ice and lemon and orange and cucumber crowding together at the top of the tall glass. Ken proposed a toast to the happy couple, and Ruth remembered to say thank you before taking a sip of her drink. She thought it tasted a little like cough medicine, then reprimanded herself for being so uncultivated. To punish herself, she took another sip.

'It's wonderful to have you both here,' Heather said. 'And I'm so glad Ruth can see York on such a lovely day. The weather hasn't been too bad this week; it rained a little on Wednesday, but that gave me some time in the greenhouse. Thursday was doubtful although you still managed to get on to the golf course, didn't you, dear?' Ken nodded. 'I've seen quite a lot of Daddy this week,' Heather said to Dan, 'though he has an inspection in Wilmslow in ten days or so. That's near Manchester, isn't it dear?'

It was lovely to be called 'dear' by her mother-in-law. 'Yes, rather to the south. More in Cheshire really.'

'And is it true what they say? Does it always rain in Manchester?'

'We have our fair share,' Ruth said. 'That's partly why I moved to Leeds.'

'And how has the weather been in Leeds?'

'Not at all bad, especially yesterday. It was quite sunny in the afternoon.'

It occurred to Ruth for the first time what a blessing it was that the English had weather. It was the perfect small talk, general, democratic, personal yet impersonal, and it helped her to begin to get to know Heather. She admired the way the older woman directed the flow of conversation, making it so easy for her to find the right things to say. In fact Pimms wasn't so bad after all. Drinking in the afternoon was fun. She was quite thirsty, and took some more, noticing that on a low diamond-paned cupboard was a little saucer of nuts. In her house those would be gone in five minutes. It was a sign of the Blakes' class that they could leave small bowls of food out and no one wolfed them down.

'I'm making something rather special tonight, Ruth. Halibut in a shrimp sauce. Now I'm going to be quite busy in the kitchen and, Dan, I thought it would be nice for you to take Ruth into York and show her round. Perhaps you might like to go too, Ken. There aren't many tourists at this time of year. Tim will be joining us for dinner. Do you know York, Ruth?'

'Only slightly. I've been here a few times but never for very long. It's a beautiful city.'

'One of the finest in the country.'

'I think it has more character than Chester,' Ruth continued, her tongue loosened by the alcohol. 'I adore York

Minster.' She was delighted how quickly she was picking up the rules of this situation. First, you talk about the weather. Then you praise everything indiscriminately. Nice people emanate niceness, which curls and wraps itself around all it meets.

'What a beautiful garden!' Ruth announced, glancing through the French windows at the back of the dining room, which stretched beyond her.

'It is rather nice,' Heather said. 'I have to admit I'm fond of it, and spend more time there than I ought.'

The next rule, apparently, was that the women did all the talking. That was comfortably familiar. And then you could begin to be a little self-deprecating.

'I wish I knew more about gardening,' Ruth continued, taking another sip of Pimms, a slice of lemon bobbing dangerously close to her nose. 'I'm hopeless at anything to do with the outdoors. It's the downside of being an urban Jew. All plants look the same to me.'

Silence. She'd said something wrong. What was it? That gardening was a mystery to her? That she was Jewish? Surely not. She drained her Pimms. How could she salvage the situation?

'Though I do recognise that gardening is an excellent therapy. We recommend it to our clients, particularly those who are recovering from breakdowns. There's also been a study recently showing that the best way of socialising adolescent boys is to give them something useful to do, like mowing the lawn. And talking to plants might be one way of dealing with multiple personality disorders!'

Heather looked blank, and although Ken continued to

smile at Ruth, he said nothing. They hadn't realised she was trying to be funny. Obviously jokes were out, or had she transgressed some taboo by referring indirectly to her work? It could have been that, or maybe she was just talking too much. She knew she had a habit of talking too much and it came from nervousness but presented itself as empty-headedness. Or was it – God forbid! – that she had implied that Heather, because she enjoyed gardening, was in some way suffering from a multiple personality disorder? She'd better put her straight immediately.

'You didn't think that I was suggesting that gardening was only a pastime for the disturbed, did you? I think gardening must be great fun, even when you're feeling well. What I mean is, I'm sure that for you it's just a hobby . . . Ruth felt herself drowning, her words curling their tentacles round her and dragging her down. Then she noticed that by the side of the settee was a Folio Society edition of *Hard Times*. A heaven-sent coincidence and a life raft. She lunged at it.

'*Hard Times!* My mother's reading that right now. She was telling me about it. Who's the character in it that pretends to be a self-made man but isn't, and won't acknowledge his own mother?'

'Bounderby,' said Ken.

'That's him. My mother can't stand him. A real hypocrite.'

'The halibut!' Heather announced suddenly. 'I haven't taken it out of the freezer yet. Dan, take Ruth to her room, she's sleeping in the pink bedroom, and I've made up your old bed for you in your room. Don't be back any later than six. We have so much to talk about.'

Heather rose; Dan rose with her, and Ruth followed. She felt obscurely dissatisfied, rather as if she'd just taken an examination and was uncertain about the result. She looked longingly at the drinks cabinet and the bottle of Pimms, but followed Dan into the hall. He took her case and carried it up the stairs. As they reached the landing she saw there were two bedrooms in front of her. Dan entered the smaller one to her left, next door to the bathroom. It was a pretty guest bedroom with a single bed covered by a pink counterpane. There was a plump, folded pink towel on the bed. A window looked out to the side of the house. There was a chair, a dressing table, and white curtains with sprigs of flowers, running chiefly to pink. Ruth thought she could smell lavender. She felt utterly out of place.

'It's a nice room,' she said to Dan.

'I'd prefer it if you were sleeping with me, but I didn't feel it was worth making a fuss.'

'Absolutely!' Ruth agreed.

Then he took her in his arms and began to kiss her. Ruth was unaccountably tense. She craned her neck a bit to check that no one in the house across the way could see them kissing, and realised that the room Heather had allotted her reeked of virginity. As Dan's kisses increased in intensity, she almost began to feel as if he was forcing himself on her, and she, the young maiden, in her pink bower, was struggling to resist him. She broke away.

'Do you think your parents like me?' she asked.

'Of course.' Dan kissed the tip of her nose. 'Just ignore it if you think they're being a bit stuffy. They can't help it.'

'Where's your bedroom?'

'On the other side of the house, next to Tim's. Do you want to unpack, or shall we go straight out?'

'I'll unpack,' Ruth said, wanting time to orientate herself.

Dan withdrew, and she picked up her case and put it on the bed. She noticed that by the bedside table was a glossy book called *English Houses and Gardens*. A dried flower arrangement sat in a little cut-glass vase in the centre of the dressing table. She would have felt more at home in Mongolia.

But the main point was, did Heather and Ken like her? Ruth realised, as she took out a dress and opened a wardrobe with padded hangers and a faint smell of mothballs, that she didn't have a clue. As she reviewed her reception, her only recollections were of how *she* felt, what *she* said and did. Heather and Ken were just a blur. She winced as she acknowledged her awkwardness. She could see now that she had hardly paid any attention to her parents-in-law-to-be at all. Her self-consciousness had risen like a heat haze and obscured everything. She reprimanded herself for being so childish, and resolved to do better. Heather was the last word in good manners, and she had much to learn from her. The truth was that men always thought of their mothers as the definition of womanhood. She knew that it was up to her *not* to be like Heather for things such as sex but to be like Heather for things such as cooking and manners. She told herself to be more observant and less shy, more deferential and less wisecracking.

Finishing her unpacking, she left her room and decided to use the bathroom. There was much pristine, gleaming white porcelain, a number of gold-plated taps, and a mahogany toilet seat. Ruth felt she could hardly use the room for the purpose intended. She did, however, and then washed her hands very carefully in the basin with a small bar of pink soap smelling of roses. Then she noticed there was no towel. Her hands wet, she looked anxiously around. Then she saw that on the cabinet in the corner of the room was a beautiful display of little hand towels folded into roses. Were you actually supposed to wipe your hands on them? But if she didn't, she would leave smears on the gilt doorknob of the bathroom. She extracted one of the towels, careful not to dislodge the others, wiped her hands, and then realised she had nowhere to put it.

'Ruth!' came Dan's voice from downstairs. 'We're ready!'

Quickly she opened the cupboard and shoved the damp towel in there.

'Here I am!' she announced, and ran down the stairs.

Heather closed the front door, then paused to listen. She heard the scrape of tyres on the gravel as Dan turned the car to take Ruth and Ken into town, and she breathed deeply. She was on her own again. Tim was at the university, working overtime on some problem with his research. She had all of her house to herself.

It felt particularly good because having Ruth here was obviously going to be a strain. No, not a strain, she was going to become part of their family and they all had to get to know each other and anyway she was a lovely girl and if Dan loved her, then that was all that mattered.

She hurried into the sitting room and picked up the empty glasses. The ice in Ruth's glass had melted now, and Heather recollected her sipping at her Pimms rather awkwardly. She did not mind the awkwardness, it was fitting, in a way, but she was less sure of Ruth when she was confident. The girl was so definite. So *there*. It was hard to look at her and think that perhaps her son had slept with her. Of course she accepted that they did sleep together, she was quite modern in that way, but on the other hand she didn't want them to sleep together in her house. Sex was essentially a very private thing.

One by one she placed the glasses rims down in the dishwasher. She had brought Dan up to be such a lovely boy and he was always so tender with her and sweet to everyone. Naturally he'd had a few fights and escapades in the playground – what boy didn't? – but he wasn't keen on fighting and in the end he was made deputy head boy. He would have been head boy if it hadn't been for that other boy – she had forgotten his name deliberately – who had all those grade As and went to Oxford. He was always the teacher's pet and too clever for her liking. It was true Tim was very clever, but he was clever in a different way. A rather eccentric way. She was proud of him too.

It was Dan, however, who was her chevalier. He fussed over her, made her tea, always asked how she was feeling. Ruth was very, very lucky. Heather hoped she appreciated how lucky she was. She feared for her son. She had little sympathy with all this feminism business, because the truth was that women did know more than men and were more skilled than men in just about everything. This left men utterly vulnerable. That was why you had to let them have their way in certain things and bow deferentially in certain matters such as cars, computers, finance and suchlike. Was Ruth the kind of woman who knew this, or was she one of those young have-it-all girls who would play with Dan and spit him out? Was her son at risk, and Ruth a predator?

She thought about Jane Thompson from church whose son had recently told her that he was homosexual. There had been lots of whispering and the vicar had been consoling her and everyone had said poor Jane, thinking how lucky they were that their sons were not like that. Heather thought for a moment that it might be quite nice to have a gay son, and perhaps Jane was the lucky one. Matthew Thompson would never get married and bring dark-haired beauties home – well at least not dark-haired female beauties – and he would always be there for his mother.

She opened the fridge and saw the halibut sitting there. The half-truth about the freezer had served its purpose and terminated their little conversation. It was hard, losing a son. The vicar had given a sermon the other day, which had affected her quite profoundly, because it had seemed so relevant to her. *You must give your children roots and wings.* She knew about roots, because of her work in the garden. Roots were easy. Wings were a little harder.

Did one necessarily have to lose a son? Dan was the dutiful type, and provided Ruth didn't make unreasonable demands, all might still be well. Perhaps the thing to do was to somehow absorb this Jewish girl into the family in every way, make her part of their circle. Heather resolved to make a splendid meal tonight, and to be at her most charming and motherly. She would draw Ruth in and show her the Blakes at their best. True, it was a little disconcerting to know that her daughter-in-law-elect was a psychologist, and that she was analysing them all the time. All the more reason not to let anything slip, not to let the side down the tiniest amount.

She reached over the sink to where several little pots of herbs sat in line. She took one of them and looked around for the kitchen scissors. There was a lot of work to be done. She would even forgo her usual cook's sherry. She hoped that Ken was excelling himself in showing Ruth around York. He knew so much about the city's churches because that was his special hobby. He had always spent much of his time travelling around, observing and noting church architecture. He wasn't religious as she was, but sufficiently reverent and a mine of information about rood screens and flying buttresses and Romanesque arches. His favourite periods were medieval and Victorian Gothic. Since he had retired he was keener than ever, travelling miles to see particular churches.

She smiled to herself. She had foolishly imagined that after he'd retired he would spend more time at home. As a head teacher he was always at conferences, meetings and courses; now he was OFSTEDing and collating information on churches. Perhaps it was why their marriage had thrived; he was hardly here. As quickly as the thought came, Heather banished it. She admired Ken enormously, admired and respected him. She hoped Ruth admired and respected Dan in the same way, although she feared she didn't. There was something a little too playful in her manner. Her own marriage was based on mutual respect and demarcation, and hard work. You had to work at marriage, and she feared Ruth might not know this. Yes, marriage was hard work. Suddenly she decided she might have a small sherry after all.

*

'Holy Trinity dates from the first half of the twelfth century, although as you can see here the stained glass is obviously later, fifteenth century, in fact.'

It looked pretty old to Ruth. It was chilly in the church, and a little damp, and all the empty pews and very polite notices about coffee mornings and service times exuded an air of faded gentility. She had her arm tucked in Dan's and only half listened to Ken's commentary.

'If we go back to Goodramgate now,' he continued, 'we can make our way to the Minster.'

Yet more churches. Ruth had never seen so many churches. Every corner she walked round, there was another. They were more numerous, even, than the pubs in Liverpool. She found it oddly disconcerting. So many reminders of morality and mortality. They had been along the river, and that was very pretty. There was an air of quiet grandeur, and even the pleasure craft and people eating sandwiches and ice cream didn't detract from it. The pale York stone buildings congregated along the river and Ruth felt she had never seen anything so quintessentially English. Of course as they left the banks of the river and made their way through the town centre, there were all the usual W. H. Smiths and Nexts and McDonald's, but around any corner there might be a little medieval street or another church.

'And this is St Jude's,' Ken announced.

'Isn't that where Mum's drop-in centre is going to be?' Dan asked.

'Yes, I believe so. You see, Ruth, there is quite a problem with disused churches in the city, and whereas one accepts that they can't all be used as places of worship, one is reluctant to lose them, and so—'

'Mum was saying,' Dan interrupted, 'that her vicar is on the committee to turn St Jude's into a drop-in centre for the unemployed. I think the idea is they're going to train them, or start job clubs, or something. I know she's been talking about getting involved.'

'Really?' Ruth was quite interested. 'What will she be doing? Counselling? Or will it be more like CAB work?'

'I don't really know,' Dan said. 'Dad?'

'I'm not sure.'

Ruth thought they both seemed rather vague. She resolved to ask Heather about the scheme later on. She made a mental note to do so by fixing the sight of the blackened little church in her mind, with its scaffolding along one side, its Gothic windows and air of dilapidation. An unemployed church for the unemployed. It seemed appropriate. And yet she could see that when the scaffolding was removed and the little arched windows let in the light, and the stone was cleaned and restored to its original creamy yellow and it was thriving with righteous activity, it would be a lovely place. A place of hope for the future.

They walked along Low Petergate and came to the Minster. It soared massively in front of them and Ruth found herself craning her neck to follow the spire to the top. The pale stone and the intricate carvings awed her and made her feel once again like a tourist. It was exciting to think that this was Dan's stamping ground, and she tried to measure the distance between it and the little synagogue off the Bury Old Road that she had been to on a few occasions, and failed.

Ken strolled in as if he owned the place. Ruth stole a glance at him and thought how upright he was. His back was straight and he walked with a slight spring in his step. There was something of Dan in him; he was a good-looking man, his face weathered a little now, with pouches under his eyes, but he had a certain presence. Ruth could just imagine him conducting prayers at school, or gowned for Prize Day. Just now he seemed fully enthused by his surroundings.

'The nave is thirteenth century. The stonemasons were concerned about the weight of the stone vaulting, and that was why they spanned the ceiling with wood. And if you look over there . . .'

Ruth did not pay attention. His words were distracting her from the place itself. The space and height opened up something in her, and the vertical lines that rose up everywhere, the fluted pillars and the high, stained-glass windows thrilled her. I'm marrying this, she thought joyously.

'If we move along to the north transept,' Ken said, 'you'll see it's Early English style, again thirteenth century.'

'Those windows look very old.'

'The Five Sisters. Also thirteenth century, built at a time when coloured glass was prohibitively expensive.'

He talks like a guidebook, Ruth thought. Yet she appreciated his geniality and impersonal conversation. It was so restful. In her family, everything was charged and barbed. With the Blakes, life was as spacious as the interior of the cathedral itself. She squeezed Dan's arm, and he squeezed her back. Would she ever be worthy of him?

'This is the Great East Window,' Ken announced. 'The alpha and omega of everything. Now, Ruth, if you look at the very top you'll see your own ancestors.'

For one moment she thought he was talking about the

Greenbergs, her mother's family who came from the *shtetl*, but no, it was, as Ken explained, a select few of the Old Testament characters. Ruth could barely make them out. They were too high up and dwarfed by the scale and complexity of the window. Ruth shared their insignificance and as she did so that feeling of not quite being right, of being on the outside, not *bona fide* English, came back and she wondered what she was doing here. I'm here because of Dan, she told herself. Suddenly she wanted to be out of the Minster and somewhere safe like the food department at Marks and Spencer.

'Oughtn't we to be getting back to your mother soon?' she whispered to Dan.

'There's no hurry.'

Ruth felt a little guilty then. Perhaps she ought to have volunteered to stay at home and help Heather, rather than joining the men. Poor Heather was probably as sidelined as her father was at times. He had to exist in a house of women, and Heather lived among men. The cheering thought occurred to her that probably Heather was delighted to have a quasi-daughter at last. It was possible that her needs had been suffocated by having to be at the beck and call of three men. Ruth remembered how little Dan and Ken seemed to know about her new venture with the centre for the unemployed. Ruth realised she was in an ideal position to show Heather some female solidarity. She tried to imagine what it must be like, living entirely with men, and had visions of rugby kits and toilet seats left up and lots of hearty eating of square meals. There would be none of the chatty evenings and leg-shaving and joint chocolate binges she'd enjoyed in her house. Poor benighted Heather. Having a mission, Ruth felt revived.

It was wrong to think, as she had done earlier, that she needed to be more like Heather. While conceding a few points, perhaps, she ought to be herself and take Heather with her. She was positively looking forward to the meal tonight, and smiled to herself as at last they made their way out of the Minster.

Chapter Five

———⟢⟢⟢⟢⟢———

A few hours later, pushing the very last morsel of halibut on to her fork and anticipating the way it would melt in her mouth, Ruth thought she might have been wrong, thinking that she had anything to teach Heather. The meal had been delicious, the table laid even more elegantly than in a restaurant, and everyone, including herself, had shared in the ease and grace created by Heather. Like a shuttle weaving back and forth, Ruth couldn't decide whether it was better to commit to being a good, old-fashioned wife and mother, or to be a woman who found herself rather than a role. More worryingly, would Dan expect her to cook like this? So far he hadn't, which was a relief.

Heather was telling everyone about the problems with the upkeep of the church hall, and giving amusing accounts of some of the members of the Buildings Committee. It was all very restful. Ruth was sitting diagonally to Heather, and opposite Tim. She had said very little to Tim all evening. He didn't really look like Dan; in fact his rather full lips and heavily lashed

eyes made him resemble his mother. There was nothing effem-
inate about him, however. His reddish complexion and round
face reminded her of an overgrown public schoolboy, a Billy
Bunter of the fifth remove. His social graces seemed under-
developed too. He said very little and ate a lot, but when he did
speak it was with an argumentative emphasis and an expression
somewhere between a shy smile and a smirk. Ruth had asked
him a little about his work at the university but couldn't properly follow what he said. Still, he had seemed glad to be asked,
and bringing him out in that way was the sort of thing Heather
would have done. In fact, Ruth was aware of Heather's approval
as she had chatted to Tim over the asparagus and arugula salad.

Ken was at the head of the table, in front of the drawn
curtains concealing the French windows. The soft gold of the
curtains and the light thrown from a standard lamp lent him
an almost regal air. It was interesting the way Heather seemed
to defer to him, asking him if he would like a little more to
eat, or to drink. Ruth found it alternately sweet of Heather
and irritating. Her mother cared about her father but never
paid very close attention to his needs. Sylvie took it for
granted that Ivan was grown up and could ask for whatever he
wanted. Ken was talking now, addressing her, in fact. Ruth
schooled herself to pay attention.

'Do your parents come from Manchester originally?'

'Yes. Dad was born in Cheetham Hill and Mum in Higher
Broughton. But my great-grandparents came from Russia and
Poland. They came over during the pogroms. I think they'd
have all liked to have made it to the USA but they ran out of
money or something.' Ken looked fascinated. Feeling a little
nervous, Ruth drained her wine glass.

'Have you ever researched your ancestors?'

'Would you like to finish off the potatoes, Ken?' Heather interrupted.

'Just one or two.'

'I don't think I'd get very far if I did. They were all peasants, woodcutters, that sort of thing. Most of them were illiterate.'

'It's sad how much history has been lost to us,' Ken pontificated. 'What we study in schools is generally the history of the middle and upper classes. The lower classes are all but forgotten.'

Ruth nodded sagely from this classless vantage point.

'And yet if we bothered to look for it, the evidence is still there. Take place names, for example. Through them we can trace the spread of the Vikings.'

Ruth replied brightly, gratefully accepting the wine that Dan poured into her glass. 'We did the Vikings at school. They came in from the eastern seaboard. They didn't get as far as Manchester.'

'Ah, no!' said Ken. 'The Vikings were very much in evidence in Manchester. In fact there was quite a bloodthirsty battle south of the city, in Gorton. Just beyond Richard Peacock's house, Peacock the engineer. There's nothing there to hint of it now but the Gortonians—'

'I'm sure Ruth doesn't want a lecture on the Vikings when she's enjoying her engagement dinner,' Heather cut in. Ken did not seem abashed by this reprimand; rather, he appeared happy to deserve it. He listened pleasantly as Heather took the reins of the conversation.

'How far have you got with the wedding plans?' she inquired.

'Your mother was saying,' Dan looked at Ruth, 'that we could get married in the register office in the centre of Manchester, and that she'd hire a hall near the house.'

'And we could probably get away without a Beth Din caterer if we stick to fish. My sisters will be the bridesmaids, and Dan was wondering if Tim . . .' Ruth's voice trailed away because she didn't know if Dan had asked his brother yet.

'Yes, I'm best man.' Tim assented.

'You didn't tell me,' Heather said. There was a moment's awkward silence, which Ruth attempted to fill.

'We haven't really made any firm plans yet because we were waiting to talk to you. My mother's a bit overwhelmed with it all. But we don't want a big affair. The marriage is more important than the wedding, if you see what I mean.'

'Of course, but you only have one wedding day, and it would be a shame to skimp in any way. It's something you'll remember for the rest of your lives. It's your chance, Ruth, to be a princess for a day. Didn't you used to play at weddings when you were small?'

Ruth wanted to be able to say yes but the truth was she preferred being She-ra, Princess of Power. She didn't know how to explain to Heather that although the wedding was important, she didn't go in much for show, rather like her mother. Dan was the important thing. She moved her leg so that it adjoined his.

'Yes, of course, it will be lovely to be the bride. But it's always seemed to me there was an aura of primitive sacrifice about it, the maiden all dressed up in white like a meringue, passed on from one man to another. I don't mind the celebrating angle, but—'

'I don't agree,' said Heather very pleasantly. 'The wedding is the two of you making a public statement about your love and your new status. The ritual represents what you feel for each other.'

Ruth felt her own beliefs slipping away from her like discarded undergarments. Naked she came blinking into a new reality where the wedding was both metaphor and expressed the reality of her love for Dan. Heather was right. The day ought to be as special as they could make it.

'I suppose I see what you mean.'

'It's just that I've had some ideas. How set are you on getting married in Manchester?'

'I just assumed I would be.'

'Look, I don't want to trespass on your mother's territory, not in the slightest, but now they've nearly finished renovating St Jude's I'm sure we could arrange to hire that, and we could have a civil ceremony in the church.'

'You mean St Jude's, where the unemployed . . . ?'

'Yes. I'm sure we could arrange for a civil ceremony there, given that these days you can even get married in football grounds! And the church is as secular now as, oh, a hotel, since the Bishop performed the deconsecration ceremony. A Jew, a Muslim, anyone could safely get married there. Oh, Ruth, it would mean so much to me! And you could have both ceremony and reception in the same place. There's both the basement area and the hall itself – plenty of room.'

'But my family live in Manchester.'

'They could stay with us – no, we'll put them up in a hotel, wouldn't we, Ken? We'd be happy to foot the bill.'

'Of course we would,' Ken agreed.

Heather's eyes were shining. 'But first we must meet your parents to discuss it all. It would be lovely to have a proper engagement party for you both. Give me your parents' address and I shall write to them. Yes. And we shall invite the vicar, and I'm sure we could ask him to give a blessing and, Ruth, if you knew a rabbi who would do the same, I'd be only too happy.'

Ruth felt as if she was on a runaway train that was gathering speed. Had she actually agreed to a wedding in St Jude's? Heather seemed to think she had. What would her mother say? Perhaps she would be pleased to have the whole thing taken out of her hands. Then she remembered the little blackened church in the centre of York, and how she had imagined it transformed, just as she would be on her wedding day. They were a pair. And she would be married a stone's throw from the glorious Minster. Married in St Jude's? It sounded lovely. She wondered what St Jude was the patron saint of. It didn't matter, the church was a pretty little place, and she imagined Ellie arriving in a hat, and Lila and David, and it would show them all what she could aspire to. She wasn't certain that she wanted to say no to this idea just at present.

'There's a lovely bridal shop along Micklegate,' Heather continued. 'I popped in the other day and they have some beautiful dresses. They arrange a number of services from there too. Have you been shopping for dresses yet?'

'No, but I thought it would be nice to go into Manchester with my mother one weekend.'

'Yes, but if you don't find anything you like, you could both come over here. Do you know, Dan, I'm getting ever so excited!'

Heather certainly looked excited. Ruth was pleased. She seemed to have gained ground this evening, and was glad she had conceded to Heather's reception plans. The more she thought of them, the better they seemed. Heather refilled Ken and Tim's wine glasses with the Beaujolais, then poured the rest of the Chardonnay into Ruth's glass.

'I'll go into the kitchen and get some more wine,' Heather said, 'and if everyone's ready, I'll fetch the dessert.'

'Do you want any help?' Ruth asked.

'No, it's quite all right, dear.'

Ruth felt uneasy. She wasn't used to being waited on hand and foot like this. Since none of the men were going to get up, Ruth decided that she would assist her future mother-in-law.

'I'll take the empty plates,' she said, standing up, straightening her dress and beginning to stack the crockery. She realised she felt a little light-headed. The effort of being on her best behaviour had made her discount the effect of the wine. She must have drunk well over half a bottle. She concentrated on getting everything safely into the kitchen. She found Heather opening a new bottle of wine.

'No more for me!' Ruth announced.

'This is dessert wine,' Heather explained. 'Just put the plates near the sink, I'll pop them in the dishwasher later. I've made a tiramisu and a lemon tart. They're both in the fridge.'

The kitchen was spacious and very well-equipped. Ruth sat by the table in the L-shaped room, feeling more at ease in this traditionally female environment. Perhaps it was time for her to get to know Heather a little better.

'You haven't told me much about St Jude's,' Ruth began. 'Tell me how you're involved there.'

'Try this Sauternes,' Heather said. 'It's one of my favourites.' She poured her a small glass and took one herself. 'Yes, John Foster, our vicar, has been one of the chief movers and shakers in the St Jude project. We've been fundraising for ages to renovate the church and then when we won a Lottery grant, we were able to go ahead. The idea is that the long-term unemployed can come in and get help with job application skills, presentation skills, or even befriend someone. John asked me if I would like to be one of the volunteers, because of my teacher training. He said I was very good with people. I said that teaching infants was hardly a preparation for counselling the unemployed but he said it was more a matter of empathy, and he was sure I had empathy. I will receive training of course – I've never done anything like this before – and then go in one or two half-days a week.'

'You don't work at all, do you? I mean, you don't have paid employment.'

'Oh no, what with a busy husband and Tim at home and a son getting married!'

'Don't you feel, well, a bit of a spare part at times? I could never imagine not working. I can see that when children are small it might be different, but afterwards . . .'

'No. I'm perfectly happy staying at home.'

Ruth could have bitten her tongue off. A haughty tone had crept back into Heather's voice, and she was certain she'd upset her. Ruth cursed herself for being so impulsive, and yet she wanted to understand how Heather could be happy just ministering to the needs of others. Sylvie said it drove her mad.

'So you don't get bored?'

'I have my garden and my greenhouse, the church and its committees, and a hundred and one things to do. I wouldn't have time to work. Running a home is a full-time occupation when you do it properly.'

Ouch, thought Ruth. Not for the first time, she tried to imagine what her and Dan's married life would be like. At first she had simply imagined them both coming home from work and revelling in each other's company. Then she imagined them sharing domestic tasks. But had Dan been trained to share domestic tasks? A chilling thought. He might have feminist sympathies in theory, but not in practice. Yet sitting here with Heather she could see the attraction of the domestic life. No rushing out to work in the morning, no permanent exhaustion, but instead good food and good wine. She desperately wished she was the sort of person who could have a set of convictions and not keep trading them in for another set as regularly as she changed her knickers. Then she remembered the disregard Dan and Ken had shown for Heather's interests. To keep a man's respect, you *had* to have a life of your own.

'But don't you feel it's important to have a life of your own, apart from being a wife and mother?' Ruth asked her.

'The desserts!' announced Heather. 'The men will be wondering where we've got to. I think we've chatted long enough. I made the tiramisu especially for Dan – it's one of his favourites. I have a super recipe which I'll let you have, as well as my Yorkshire pudding instructions, which Ken's mother gave me. If you take the tart in – here, the dish is quite cold – I'll fetch the tiramisu.'

Like an iron bar approaching a negative magnet, Ruth felt

herself subtly repelled. But no matter. The dessert wine was delicious, and she looked forward to Heather bringing that out too. It was good, having spoken frankly with Heather. Nice to see Dan again. She entered the dining room and almost caught her breath as she saw her fiancé sitting there. Her heart contracted with love for him. He was so handsome, beautiful, even, with eyes that were so kind, and she imagined him as he appeared to her when they made love, intent and passionate both at once. She ached from wanting him, knowing that in this situation, in his parent's dining room, she had to abandon all thoughts of Dan as her lover and go back to the formal role-playing that ensured she'd fit in with the Blakes.

'Shall I serve the tart?' Ruth asked Heather as she entered. At her assent Ruth began to cut into it.

'Do you remember, Dan, the time I baked you a birthday cake – I think it must have been your fourth – and because I said it was yours, you helped yourself to a big slice before your party?'

Dan laughed. 'You were so upset as you'd spent hours icing it.'

'You always had a sweet tooth,' Heather continued, spooning out tiramisu, smiling. 'I'm surprised you never put weight on. The amount of Danish pastries you used to get through! Now there's a tip, Ruth. If you want to get round him, buy some Danish pastries.'

Ruth held out her glass to Ken who filled it with more Sauternes.

'I suppose you needed all that food because you were always so active,' Heather mused. 'I think you must have been in every team at school at some time. Do you remember that awful occasion when you dislocated your shoulder in a swimming tournament? You were so brave, but I insisted we went to casualty, and the X-ray proved me right. It was an awful time, Ruth. Ken was away on a school visit and we couldn't locate him anywhere. The problem with boys is that they're always injuring themselves. Tim broke a leg when he was little, tripping over a football.'

Tim smirked.

'But with Tim it was more a matter of clumsiness. Dan was a shade reckless and enjoyed taking risks. It doesn't surprise me he is the first to get engaged. Tim has always been the independent type. They always commented in his school reports about how good he was at working on his own. Dan was more of a team player, and always very sociable, rather like Ken. Whenever we went on holiday it would always be Dan who would make friends with other little boys. Do you remember the summer in Newquay when you played five-a-side football on the beach? Didn't your team win a tournament?'

Dan laughed, Ken nodded vigorously, Tim emitted a noise that could have been laughter, and Ruth felt as if she was marooned on a desert island and the Blake family were all together on a boat sailing away from her. She was a newcomer; Heather had borne Dan, nursed him, nurtured him, shared all his early years and formative years and adolescent years – would she ever catch up? Under the table she took Dan's hand and began to stroke his fingers. He squeezed her hand, and she felt a little better.

She was quite tipsy now, and wished she could give in to the languor that was stealing over her. Yet she knew she was still on parade, under inspection. She assumed a bright smile, and hoped no one realised that it was false. All she wanted now was to be alone with Dan, to debrief and comfort herself with him, her favourite cure-all and stress remedy. When Heather returned to the kitchen to make coffee, Ruth decided to stay put, and was glad when Ken opened up the subject of the cotton industry in Lancashire. She even asked him little prompting questions, so he would continue talking indefinitely. She successfully stifled a yawn, propped her chin in her hands, and assumed an interested expression.

It was only later, when Ruth was about to take off her make-up at the little dressing table in the pink room, that she realised she had presented to Ken two dark half-circles beneath her eyes where her mascara had smudged. Not that he would have noticed, or if he had, he was too polite to say anything. She proceeded to dab eye make-up remover cream on to her eyelids. She could hear sounds from the bedroom next door, which was Heather and Ken's room. Someone was in the bathroom too; she could hear running, splashing water. She also thought she could detect the distant clacking of a keyboard. Tim? It was lucky she'd had so much to drink, it would help her to get to sleep. Without it she would have been sure to have lain awake in bed, listening to alien sounds and revolving everything that had happened.

All that was left in her consciousness now was the fact that she was going to get married in a church with a vicar present. She had better explain that one very, very carefully to her parents. Ken was charming in a headmastery sort of way, and

Tim was all right, she supposed, and Heather . . . How desperately she wanted to please her, and yet at the same time she felt so different from her, and rather resentful of the way she had prowled around Dan, staking her territory. The fact was that boys grew up, and Dan now belonged to her, and she knew things about Dan that Heather would never guess at. Or perhaps she had guessed at them, and that was why they had been put in separate bedrooms.

Ruth sat on the edge of her bed in her silk nightie and listened carefully. There were no more sounds from next door. The person in the bathroom had gone now, and there was silence everywhere. The bed she sat on was soft and yielding, and she knew once she lay in it she would be cocooned by its virginal whiteness. It subtly instructed her in purity. She turned back the coverlet and prepared to get in. There was a soft rap at the door. She started.

'Ruth?' came a whisper.

It was Dan. Ruth tiptoed over to the door and whispered back, 'Yes?'

'Can I come in?'

Guiltily, like a boarding school pupil about to commence a midnight feast, Ruth turned the porcelain knob with its circlet of pink flowers and opened the door. Dan slipped in, wearing paisley pyjamas she hadn't seen before. They didn't suit him.

'What do you want?' she said.

'Just curious if you enjoyed yourself this evening.'

'Sure.' Neither of them was speaking above a stage whisper. It was farcical and embarrassing.

'Are those your pyjamas?' Ruth had to ask.

'No. They're my dad's. I forgot mine.'

Dan sat down on her bed and beckoned her to him. She felt a little hesitant. What if Heather or Ken weren't really asleep and heard them? She could never look them in the eye again. Gingerly she went to sit by Dan, and began to talk.

'Your mum's a good cook. She must have gone to a lot of trouble. I feel quite flattered that—'

He stopped her mouth with a kiss, and gently eased her on to the bed, moving on top of her. Ruth felt herself stiffen.

'No, not here!'

'Ssh – relax.'

'Hey, stop it, you!' She laughed and extricated herself. 'We can't. They'll hear the bedsprings.' To demonstrate her point, Ruth bounced up and down on the bed. Sure enough, there was an audible rhythmic creaking.

'The floor then?' said Dan.

Ruth glanced at the cerise carpet. 'Uh – no.'

'Hey, what's wrong?' His hands had pushed up her night-dress and were confidently claiming their familiar territory.

'No!' she said a little more sharply.

Now Dan looked hurt. She tried to explain.

'I just can't, knowing your parents are in the next room. It's not polite.'

'I won't make a sound. They'll never find out.'

'But that isn't the point.'

There was silence. Ruth realised this was the first time she had ever refused him. She owed it to him to try to explain why.

'Look,' she said, 'I just can't be sexual in the earshot of anyone's parents, yours or mine. Especially mine. I don't feel at ease. And you don't seem like you in your father's pyjamas.'

'I'll take them off.' Dan proceeded to do so.

'No!' She forcibly buttoned up the jacket again. 'This isn't the time or the place, but I promise I'll make it up to you. In duplicate. In triplicate, even, but somewhere else, all right?'

'You drive a hard bargain.'

Breathing easily again, she kissed him chastely on the forehead, as his mother might have done.

'I love you,' he said.

'Love you too. See you in the morning.'

'In the morning,' he repeated, and got up off the bed. She watched him open the door, check no one was around, then leave and close her door silently.

Quickly Ruth got into bed, her heart thumping. How strange that Dan should want to make love to her under his parents' noses, so to speak. It wasn't like that in her house. In fact, whenever anyone even kissed on the telly and Dad was in the room, she, Sharon and Rachel all exchanged embarrassed glances. She was surprised at Dan, but pleased, too, that she should have such power that he would come to her even in his mother's house. In his father's pyjamas. Gross!

She realised it was the domestic connotations that made sex an impossibility. For her, sex had always been an act of rebellion. It was what you did when you played away from home. It was why she had never really wanted a Jewish boyfriend – the Jewish boys she had known reminded her too much of her father. Sex was naughty, wild, faintly disgusting, an assertion of independence. Tonight she was not in the mood for it.

She wriggled down into the tightly made bed, inching her legs between the cold sheets. There was no way she could make love here. Here she was not herself. Heather had skilfully turned her into a construct of her own – the polite, respectable, Anglo-Saxon fiancée of her younger son. Such people never had sex; they produced offspring by immaculate conception, or at the best by lying back and thinking of England.

Ruth thought of England. She thought of Yorkshire, York, York Minster, St Jude's, gardens, St George, St Michael's, Marks and Spencer – no, they were Jewish, or at least one of them was. And Tesco's – they were Jewish too. But not Sainsbury's. And then she shut her eyes to see if she could think of any more supermarket chains with Semitic origins, and soon she was asleep.

Heather and Ken lay in bed back to back, forming a curling V-shape. From the soft exhalations close to her, Heather could tell that Ken was asleep. She knew all of his habits intimately, and could tell to the second when he began to slumber. She, on the other hand, was not asleep. She was listening intently to the sound or lack of them coming from the pink room. It was too quiet. Surely if Ruth was in there, she would hear something. The mattress was an old one, and creaked when you turned on it.

Taking all things into consideration, the evening had gone well. It was something to have got Ruth to agree to a church wedding, and on all points the girl seemed quite amenable. That was good. At times Ruth was very sweet and Heather even had to admit she was good company. And yet . . . And yet . . . There was something about Ruth that frightened

Heather. She was a little too forthright, a little too inquisitive, an Alice in Wonderland character who asked too many questions and didn't quite realise that there were certain things that were better left unsaid. She'd actually suggested that being a wife and mother didn't amount to much of a life. That was positively rude, although Heather was sure that Ruth didn't mean to be rude, it was rather that she couldn't help it. A bad upbringing? Heather wondered what her mother was like. Intelligent, because she read Dickens. But apart from that?

She tried to imagine what Dan really saw in Ruth. Of course, she was very pretty, and vibrant too. She was his intellectual peer and easy to talk to. Heather heard the bed next door creak, and she relaxed. Ruth probably was quite a nice girl, and Heather resolved to be charitable. Still, it was hard losing a son, especially a baby son. And what if Tim was inspired through this to find a fiancée himself? The thought chilled her. Without her sons, she would be almost on her own. Husbands weren't the same thing at all. Ken gave a little snort, as if in agreement. Roots and wings, said the vicar. Don't you feel it's important to have a life of your own? asked Ruth.

Tomorrow, perhaps. Tomorrow is another day. Now who said that? Scarlett O'Hara? Resembled Ruth in a way. *Gone With the Wind*. Mammy and that red petticoat.

And with a rustle of red petticoats, Heather was asleep too. And Tim tapped away into the night.

Chapter Six

Sylvie opened the door of the cab.

'Be here at nine,' she told Ivan.

'Enjoy yourself.'

'Huh!' Sylvie hurried along the path that led to the library, wondering what on earth she was doing here. She was not a joiner, never had been. She was happier paddling her own canoe. Alone, or with her immediate family, she was quite content. When she was forced to belong to a larger group, she felt that part of her was in danger of being sucked away, and she became even more aggressively herself. The aggression masked shyness, although Sylvie would have guffawed at the thought of herself as a shrinking violet. But for now, with a city dweller's wariness, she just hoped that no one would emerge from the shadows and make off with her handbag.

Reaching the library doors safely, she found a notice with an arrow pointing upstairs to the reading group. The library was familiar territory to her. She had almost come to associate the smell of disinfectant and the old posters of young black women who had their lives turned around by a college course with the pleasure of the reading experience. This evening, however, she was not feeling her accustomed anticipation. God knows what this group would be like. Intellectuals? Show-offs? She rather hoped no one else would turn up, then she could go home. Or so many people would turn up that she could sit at the back and say nothing, think a little, and then go home.

She found herself finally in a little oblong room with some computers that had been put to bed for the night, a circle of easy chairs, and closed vertical blinds on the windows. Several other women were already seated, looking embarrassed and expectant. Sylvie shrunk from joining them, in case they began to talk to her. Mind you, she thought, this was better than Weight Watchers, which is where Lila was right now. Better also than ringing Ruth up yet again to discuss wedding plans. She hoped Ruth realised there was only a limited budget for the reception, unless she wanted to contribute herself. Not that Ruth had a great deal of money either. Sylvie realised that part of her reason for coming to the reading group tonight was to get away from the wedding. Please God, there would be no talk of weddings. She took a seat between two empty ones, smiled freezingly at the other participants, and looked around the room.

One by one other women came in – no men, Sylvie noted, without surprise. The women conformed to the usual Manchester stereotypes. There were the earnest, round-spec-wearing, cropped-hair feminist ecologists who lived in Longsight or Chorlton or Didsbury and travelled everywhere on bicycles. There were the mumsy-looking, rather overweight, slightly anxious thirty-somethings, obviously escaping from little children and feeling guilty about it. There were several grey-haired older women who seemed more confident, obviously doyennes of adult education, filling their spare hours by attending every course going, from African pottery to Spinoza for beginners. There was no one like herself. Feeling isolated, and a little annoyed at both the situation and herself, Sylvie grouched at the fact that this class was organised by the Workers Educational Association and none of them looked like workers.

From another door a young girl, no older than Ruth, walked in. She had long, curly hair, tied back, wore jeans and a hand-knitted sweater, but the most noticeable thing about her was that she was carrying one of those detachable baby seats with a very small baby slumped asleep in it. Fancy bringing a baby to a reading group. Sylvie supposed she was a single mother, and admired her enterprise in getting out of the house. Then, as she covertly watched her prop the baby up at right angles to her, open a battered briefcase and get out sheaves of notes and a well-thumbed copy of *Hard Times*, she realised this young girl was probably the teacher. So young! Sylvie felt sorry for her and a little impatient of a system that let a group of mature women be taught by someone barely out of college.

Observing the teacher so closely, she didn't notice that someone had taken the seat to her right. Suddenly alert to her presence, Sylvie turned to see a woman of about her own age, dyed blonde hair with roots showing, a plump face and lipstick. She smiled easily at Sylvie. She defied all stereotypes. She didn't have the faux-middle-class look of the other students, and wasn't old. She was large-busted, and wore a black sweatshirt with a diamante poodle stitched on it, over black leggings hugging swelling thighs. She kicked off her shoes to reveal painted toenails under stockings, then brought one leg up and tucked it under the other. Sylvie was baffled. She couldn't place her at all. A cleaner? She looked as if she'd had to work for a living. A madam from a brothel? She was tarted up just a little too much for a reading group.

'I'm Linda.' the woman announced to Sylvie. 'Never been to anything like this before in my life.'

'Me neither,' said Sylvie, taken off her guard.

'And I wouldn't have come tonight except that Suzie was worried no one would turn up, and then she'd be out of a job. Not that they pay much, but it's something.'

'Who's Suzie?'

'My daughter.' Linda pointed to the girl with the baby. 'And that's Phoebe, my granddaughter. You wouldn't think I was old enough to be a grandmother. We are a grandmother!' she announced, mimicking Margaret Thatcher rather cruelly.

Sylvie liked that. Any critic of Thatcher's was a friend of hers. Linda's easy manner soothed her. She sensed that Linda wasn't sizing her up at all. Sylvie felt a little guilty for trying to pigeonhole her.

'She made me read the book and it wasn't bad in places. But to sit here and watch her teach – don't give me embarrassing! You never feel as if your own kids can ever do anything on their own. D'you have any kids?'

'Three daughters,' Sylvie offered.

'Her,' said Linda, pointing at Suzie, 'and another. A lad. Sorry!'

The apology was directed at Suzie, who was glaring at her mother. The session was about to begin. Sylvie felt a little more drawn into things, glad in a babyish way to be selected by the teacher's mother as a companion. Her nervousness now was not so much for herself but for the teacher. Imagine if it was Ruth in charge. Linda was right, you never really trusted your own children. She wondered why. She listened with interest as Suzie introduced herself.

'I'm Suzie Miller, your leader. I'm finishing a dissertation on the depiction of the working class in nineteenth-century British fiction, and that's why I chose *Hard Times* to start the course. But other things in the book might have interested you. I'm happy for you to say what you want to talk about.'

So this is teaching? Sylvie thought. In her days, teachers told you things. She waited to see what would happen next.

'I was interested in Louisa,' said one of the ecological feminists. 'I found it hard to believe that she would agree to marry Bounderby, just on the wishes of her father. I find Dickens's treatment of women a little hard to take.'

Sylvie thought about that remark. It was true, come to think of it. Mrs Gradgrind was horribly put upon – no real woman would accept the treatment handed out to her. But was it Gradgrind who was the bastard, or Dickens? She'd have to think about that. Or were Victorian women different from women today? Considering this new idea, she lost the thread of the discussion, and schooled herself to pay attention.

'Phallic symbols,' Suzie was saying. 'That's what the mill chimneys are. Implacable manhood, indomitable will. It's a sign that there was no way Louisa was going to be able to get her father to understand that Bounderby was totally wrong for her.'

One of the blue-rinse brigade chipped in now. 'I think it's unusual for a lass to know her own mind. In my experience, it's the parents who usually have a better idea of what's what. That's why arranged marriages work so well. I was reading that in the papers.'

'I know just what you mean,' said her companion. 'My friend Betty's girl Sandra married when she was nineteen, no one could talk her out of it and it only lasted four years.'

'Betty who worked at Levinson's before it shut down?' asked another.

'That's the one.'

Sylvie hoped Suzie had the confidence to bring the discussion back on track. She hoped the reading group wasn't just going to be a place where women got together and gossiped. She wanted more than that. Also the last thing she needed was all this discussion of failed marriages and girls not knowing their own minds. It was unsettling her. She whispered to Linda, 'Is your daughter married?'

'That'll be the day,' she remarked, as her daughter glared at her.

Sylvie couldn't help but feel a little envious. There certainly was something to be said for living together. Marriage was such a huge undertaking. Once again she saw Ruth in her mind's eye, turbulent, temper-ridden, hysterical, excessive – she devoured nearly a whole box of Dairy Milk once while watching TV. Then she visualised Dan, polite to a fault, well-groomed, restrained – what was she about to do with herself? She shook her head. She had come out tonight to get away from the wedding, and here she was, worrying about it again. Perhaps she had these premonitions only because she was dreading getting the juggernaut of the wedding preparations under way. How much easier if they'd just decided to live together. She looked at the baby in the travel seat who didn't have a proper father, and changed her mind. Still, the wedding arrangements massed ahead of her like storm clouds, or pre-packaged insomnia. Once again she had to tell herself to pay attention to the discussion.

Which was getting more interesting. They were talking about Bounderby, whom she particularly loathed. He claimed he was abandoned by his mother simply so he could get all the credit for being a self-made man. In fact his mother was loving and worthy and visited Coketown in secret to see how he was getting on. But it wasn't just that. He refused one of his workers the means to get a divorce, but got one himself. One law for the rich, another for the poor. That kind of thing infuriated her. But she wouldn't say so. She was happy just to listen to the others.

'Slackbridge, the trade union leader. What did you think of him?' Suzie asked.

A grey-haired lady answered. 'A rabble-rouser. Reminded me of Arthur Scargill.'

'Stirring them all up,' said her friend.

'It's a good job we got rid of the unions.'

'D'you remember the three-day week, Elsie?'

'Always out on strike, they were.'

Sylvie was irritated beyond control. Seeing the two old harpies clutching their handbags, their lips pursed tight in disapproval, she could take no more.

'If if wasn't for the unions we wouldn't be having this reading group. Unions, and education for people like us – it comes from the same thing. What are you suggesting, that the workers should sit there and say sod all?'

Well, that was telling them. There was a tense silence, until Linda broke it.

'She's right you know. The bosses aren't any better than us. There's no harm in speaking up for yourself.'

Suzie intervened. 'Dickens also presents working-class life positively in the circus scenes.'

Linda nudged Sylvie. 'That's me. I would have run away and joined the circus.'

Sylvie appreciated her support, and warmed to Linda. In fact, she was warm all over. The heat was not a stray menopausal flush but the exhilarating energy of an argument. She realised then that her love for a good argument extended into the public domain. From that moment the class stopped intimidating her. She listened attentively, waiting for another opportunity to strike. Fuelled with adrenaline, she absorbed easily everything Suzie explained. In her mind, the class was still divided into friend and foe, but she knew she was enjoying herself. She was almost sorry when the caretaker popped his head round the door and Suzie nodded and began to wind up the proceedings. In a fortnight they would be talking about Elizabeth Gaskell's *North and South*. Sylvie had already got that from the library.

Everyone dispersed quickly. Sylvie looked at her watch and saw that it was just on nine. She overheard Linda talking to her daughter.

'I'll ring for a taxi. You don't want to be lugging that thing on a bus at this time of night.'

'Didn't you come by car?' Sylvie asked them.

'Oliver dropped us off,' Linda said, 'but he can't pick us up.'

'Where do you live?'

'Gorton.'

It wasn't far from Piccadilly. Sylvie felt certain Ivan wouldn't mind the detour. 'We'll give you a lift,' she said. 'My husband's got the cab outside.'

There were the usual protestations of it being too much trouble, but Suzie and Linda seemed grateful, and the baby had woken up, which could prove ominous. Together they made their way down the library stairs and out into the night. Dependable Ivan was there in the cab, and as Sylvie had anticipated, didn't turn a hair when she told him they were going to Gorton first.

'A good night?' Ivan asked, his back to them.

'Very interesting,' Sylvie said, aware they had the teacher with them. Then she explained who Suzie was, and who Linda was. Ivan nodded.

'Handy to have a husband who's a cabby. My fella can't do anything useful.' Linda laughed.

'Is that Oliver?' Sylvie asked, mildly curious about Linda's home life.

'No. Oliver is Phoebe's dad — Suzie's bloke.' Linda didn't volunteer any more information.

'What part of Gorton?' Ivan asked.

'Down the Hyde Road,' Linda said, 'past Belle Vue.'

'Belle Vue,' said Ivan reminiscently. 'We used to enjoy going there.' Sylvie remembered Belle Vue as it was, with its zoo and circus rides. Shame it was all pulled down. Now there was just a multiplex cinema and a Deep Pan Pizza.

They sped through Manchester city centre, dark buildings glistening in the rain, people scurrying into cafes and bars. They passed old warehouses near Piccadilly and the station itself on their right, dirty white but purposeful. They stopped as a tram clattered past them to be swallowed into the underbelly of the station.

'Do you work?' Sylvie asked Linda.

'I have my own business,' she replied. 'I run a bridal shop.'

Not more weddings! Then in hot pursuit of that thought, came another. Here was a woman – a no-nonsense woman – who actually knew something about weddings. She could be useful – very useful.

'My daughter's just got engaged to be married,' Sylvie said.

'How lovely. Did you hear that, Suzie?'

Sylvie did not notice Suzie's reaction. She pressed straight on. 'What exactly do you do in your bridal shop?'

'The usual. I sell wedding dresses, bridesmaids' dresses, and all the bits and pieces – veils, headdresses, shoes, hats.'

'So someone could come to you and get kitted out from top to toe?'

'That's right.'

'And you're based in Gorton?'

'I live on top of my business premises.'

Sylvie almost started believing in God again. Here, in her husband's cab was someone who could guide her through the maze of the wedding. And living in Gorton, she wouldn't be too expensive.

'My daughter hasn't got her dress yet.'

'Bring her over,' Linda said.

'I most certainly will.'

It was even possible, Sylvie thought, as the cab sped along, that Linda would be able to recommend a good caterer. She might even know of some halls. Or a cheap stationer.

'Do you have a card?' she asked.

Linda clicked open her handbag and felt inside. She handed Sylvie a business card with a lacy border and the copperplate words, *Wedding Bliss*. It was Sylvie's passport to peace. Back in the library, she had felt an instinctive liking for Linda. The liking was ripening into something like true love.

'I'll ring you,' she said.

They were on the Hyde Road now. They passed the occasional large public house, calling itself a hotel. There were council maisonettes and warehouses put to new, temporary uses, the flash of a neon-lit all-night garage, then a parade of shops, with a Chinese chippy and off-licence.

'Not far now,' Linda said. 'On the right. Along the next parade.'

Checking the road was clear, Ivan swung the cab round and came to rest where Linda indicated. The shop window was hidden behind metal shutters, but Sylvie could see the painted sign above, Wedding Bliss. There was a door on the side that she presumed was the entrance to the house. The redbrick premises seemed quite large, there were three floors, the top floor having black-painted gables that gave the building a rather Gothic feel.

Linda, Suzie and the baby got out and said their goodbyes and thanks. Sylvie watched Linda extract the keys from her handbag, open the side door and switch on the light. She could see nothing of the interior as Ivan chose that moment to pull out and drive back to the city centre.

She settled back comfortably in the cab as Ivan drove off, and began to tell him about her evening. He listened patiently as ever. When she had finished, he started a new subject.

'Ruth rang,' he said. 'I don't know what you'll think about this.'

'About what?' Every muscle in her body tensed. Ruth had that effect on her.

'About the wedding. She's found a place in York she likes. She's wondering about having the reception there.'

'In York? She wants us to schlep all the way to York?'

'She says Dan's family are offering to put us up.'

'And so where is this place that she's set her heart on?'

'It's called St Jude's,' Ivan said, moving carefully from word to word, like a man crossing a raging torrent on stepping stones. 'It's a disused church, apparently.'

'A church! She's getting married in a church!!'

'She only wants to know what we think of the idea.'

'Does she want me to have a heart attack?'

'I think she was sounding you out.'

'Why not invite the Archbishop of Canterbury and do it properly. A church!'

'I know. I'm not happy either. But I said we'd go up to York and meet Dan's parents and have a look round.'

'You said we're going to York?'

'Yes. They're having a party for Ruth and Dan.'

'Oy vey!'

Chapter Seven

Heather liked the effect of the gauze veil over her face, but conceded that it wouldn't do for the photographs. But then . . . She smiled through the gauze into the mirror and thought how flattering gauze was to the complexion. But no, it wouldn't do. She knew that a large, down-turned brim would be wrong too but she couldn't resist trying a cream number with a delicious arrangement of flowers and lace. It was just a little expensive, but had it been right, Heather decided, she would have brazened it out. There was a navy hat with an up-turned brim, and everyone recommended up-turned brims for the camera, as they revealed the face. She tried it, peered at herself, but thought it was a little too plain and sober, both for her and the occasion. She would have to have cream, or something similar. She spotted a pale green hat on the very top of the hat tree, and stretched to get it down. It was pretty and young looking, but it would mean committing herself to green, and they hadn't got as far as colours yet. She tried the hat anyway. It perched jauntily on her head, and Heather decided it was a little too small. It was such fun, trying on hats, and she was glad she had come early into the city centre for her morning at St Jude's. She was a little nervous about what the vicar had in mind for her, and trying on hats was calming. In fact, she thought, she had discovered her own new therapy, hat buying. Pleased at the idea, she replaced the green hat, catching a glimpse of its price tag.

It was much more than she had been prepared to pay. It brought her up short, and the Sunday church-going Heather felt chastened and subdued. Here she was, off to meet the jobless and homeless, and she had been contemplating buying a hat that cost upwards of two hundred pounds. It was a little difficult to reconcile, but she tried. No doubt hat factories gave employment, and employment was precisely what the jobless needed. Also, she would defend to the death a jobless person's right to wear a hat. In fact, she wanted the jobless to have jobs so they could buy hats, or buy their wives hats. So the enjoyment that she got from trying on hats wasn't at all opposed to helping the jobless – on the contrary, they were part of the same thing. In fact, if the unemployed were bored, there was nothing to stop them coming into the store and trying on hats, just as she was doing. And she would not object – far from it!

Feeling much better, Heather left the shop, smiling at the assistant, and vowing that when the time came for her to buy The Hat, she would go somewhere a little more upmarket. She smiled brightly at the man selling the *Big Issue* and stopped and hunted in her handbag for some money to give him. She took the magazine and carried it rolled in her hand as it was given to her, like a baton of philanthropy. The *Big Issue* man wished her a nice day, and she wished him one back.

The reason she was off to St Jude's today was that John Foster had decided to hurry along renovations by getting the unemployed themselves to do the work. He had been in negotiations with the Job Centre, and having come to an agreement about wages, some young men were going to start today, cleaning the interior. John had arranged this morning's informal meeting between the St Jude's Committee, the helpers and the workers, to encourage friendship, shared purpose and a bit of publicity in the local papers. Knowing she was going to be photographed, Heather had dressed with particular care. She had chosen some dark brown trousers and a check shirt, so she would look as if she was ready for business.

St Jude's was still partially masked by scaffolding but that would be removed as soon as the stone cleaning was complete. The church would be looking pristine well before the wedding. Of course, she had yet to speak to John Foster about her idea, but she imagined it would be relatively easy to get the registrar to give the place a licence for marriages. There was a fee involved; Heather knew this because she had taken the precaution of ringing the marriage registrar and asking. Six hundred and fifty pounds was too much for the St Jude's Trust to afford, but she and Ken could foot that particular bill. It would be a small price to pay. Still, she wasn't here to think about the wedding and her own, selfish needs; it was important to think about others too. Especially those less fortunate than oneself.

The wooden door was shut, and gingerly Heather pushed it open. It swung slowly inwards, revealing the dim interior of the church, one single light bulb hanging temporarily from a beam, a flex snaking from it. The dusty, musty smell was overlaid with the welcome aroma of coffee. Heather saw that someone had brought an urn and was boiling water in one corner. She recognised Margaret Pearson from the committee, an elderly widow, fond of dogs. John was with her, as well as a few other women, and around a trestle table sat a few young men — the unemployed. Heather felt a little nervous. She smiled shyly at the unemployed and went to join John and Margaret at the refreshment area. They exchanged greetings, and Heather volunteered to make coffee, or butter scones — anything to be useful.

John explained that the press were coming shortly and really it was just a matter of getting to know each other until then. The women nodded vigorously at that. John Foster was a young, athletic-looking man, with a dog collar and cropped hair. He exuded enthusiasm, and was forever patting people on the back, clapping them around the shoulders or picking up children and whirling them around. With the ladies of the parish he was a little more restrained but was singularly successful in coercing them to new ventures. Because he was so much younger than they were, they indulged him as they would a favoured child. At the same time, because he was their vicar, each of them imagined a special relationship with him, saw him as their mutual arbiter, wanted him to know whenever they had done something particularly Christian. They wanted to mother him, and be fathered by him. It was a powerful combination. Margaret was telling him about an elderly neighbour who was going into a home, and how she had been clearing out her cupboards. Heather nodded approvingly but was a little impatient. She wanted to ask John about St Jude's and Dan's wedding. To her annoyance she noticed that a couple of the other ladies were massing nearby, also hoping to have a word with John.

She decided to fill in time by putting the biscuits on plates. Someone had brought a supermarket cream selection, and there was a box of the church crockery. As Heather made herself useful, she kept one eye on the vicar. It was surprising how much room there was in the church, now the pews had been taken out. The stained-glass window at the west end looked rather bereft without the altar beneath it. She hoped they would leave the window intact as there was a moving depiction of Christ on the cross, with angels beckoning him from nearby clouds. Irradiated by sunlight, she could imagine it as a centrepiece at her son's wedding.

She arranged the biscuits in concentric circles, the most appealing in the centre. She wondered whether to take them to the table where the men were sitting, or simply leave them beside the urn so when they came for a hot drink they could take one or two. She would have liked to ask John, but he was still fully occupied with the other women. They were all quite needy in their own way, she supposed, either widows, or ladies with health problems — churches did seem to attract people who were a little more demanding than most. It occurred to Heather then that a good thing to do might be to go and speak to the unemployed. John would be bound to notice, and be pleased. The other women clearly lacked the courage to make the first move, but she was much more accustomed to men, and now she came to think of it, she was the obvious person to go and talk to them. With a mixture of apprehension and excitement, she approached them, brandishing the plate of biscuits.

'Would you like to help yourself to some of these?' she asked brightly. 'Tea and coffee will be served in just a moment, when the water is ready.'

There was a murmur of thanks. Heather looked round the group of men. Several of them looked around Ken's age, but with slightly cowed, puppy-dog faces. Heather imagined a lifetime of unemployment for them, and felt pity. She sat down by one of them and asked, 'How long have you been out of work?'

'Out of work? I'm the builder, come to give the lads here some instructions.'

Heather blushed. It served her right, she shouldn't have jumped to conclusions like that. She stood up. 'I'll fetch some drinks.'

Margaret was pouring them out beside the urn, and Heather busied herself as waitress, carrying mugs to and fro. She took the final mug to a young man of around Dan's age, but of a very different type to Dan. He was dressed casually; he wore jeans that had seen better days, a blue check shirt and a grubby denim jacket. His white trainers were dirty too. They were a brand Heather had not heard of – Nick, rather than Nike. It occurred to her that although she had passed many men like him in the street, she had never spoken to anyone of that type. Or if she had spoken to someone like that, it was a tradesman or delivery boy. She was unsure how to approach him but felt that she ought to approach him because a good Christian did not make social distinctions and anyway John Foster was watching her. Gingerly she took the chair next to him and tried to think of a polite conversational gambit.

'Are you one of the builders too?' she inquired, playing safe.

'No, I've been sent here by the Job Centre to get the place in order.'

'So you don't have a proper job – I mean, are you . . . ?'

'Out of work? You could say that.'

At last. A real unemployed person. Heather looked at him with renewed interest. His eyes seemed intelligent. You wouldn't guess he was unemployed. His hair was long, dark and reasonably clean. He was almost reminiscent of a painting of Christ, except for his eyebrow ring, but Heather tried not to look at that, out of politeness. He was of that age – Dan's age – when you could still see the boy in the man. There was even a dimple in the cleft of his chin. Heather tried to imagine the feelings his mother would have about him. She would feel disappointed, but she would never stop believing in him. That was how a mother would feel.

'What's you name?' she asked him

'Dawson. Richard Dawson,' he replied. His voice was a little low and gruff, almost as if it had recently broken. He didn't have much of a local accent. 'What's yours?'

'Heather Blake.' She was a little taken aback at the directness of his question, and a little flattered at his interest too. Perhaps they were becoming friends. 'Do you live in York?' she continued.

'I've got a mate in Dringhouses and I'm sleeping on his floor until I can afford somewhere better.'

'Oh dear!'

' 'S not too bad. I've lived rough for a time, and that's worse.'

'Lived rough,' echoed Heather. She hadn't spoken to anyone who'd lived rough before. She was enthralled and horrified. 'Why was that?'

'It was after my dad kicked me out. We never got on. He couldn't get over me mam leaving him.'

'Why did she leave him?'

'She found someone else. He was selling Timeshares in Gran Canaria. She went over there when I was nine.'

'You were only nine, and your mother left you?'

'Yeah, well, it happens. So, yeah, I lived rough, then the council got on to me and I was put in a home. That was even worse.'

Heather did not dare ask him what he meant by that. She had read enough about abuse in children's homes. Her heart went out to this poor chap. She admired his frankness in talking to her like this, and his courage in having assimilated his experiences and accepted them. How many of us could look our misfortunes in the face and say, 'Yeah, well, it happens'? Heather became embarrassingly aware of her sheltered existence, and increasingly in awe of this young man, an adventurer, someone who had done things she could not imagine. She wanted him to carry on talking. Yet she was conscious that the conversation shouldn't be one way. She ought to tell him about herself too.

'I live in York,' she began. 'I've been married for just over thirty years — my husband is retired now — but he's very busy and travels a lot. I have two sons, and I think the younger one must be about your age. He's getting married in the spring.'

'Congratulations. It must be hard for you, seeing him fly the nest.'

'Yes.' She was struck by his insight.

'Who are you exactly? The vicar's wife?'

Heather was pleased at his mistake. 'Oh no! I'm far too old for that. No, I'm a St Jude's volunteer, that's all.'

'You look younger than the other women.'

She was warming to this young man. He might be semi-homeless, but he had excellent manners. He was perceptive, too.

'So have you had building experience?'

'None at all. I knew a bit about motors, but nothing much else. I ended up in Burnley with some mates, and while I was there I got a job working for this man with his own garage in his back yard. Then one morning I comes in and everything's locked up, and I knock on the front door, and his wife is in floods of tears, he's had a heart attack in the middle of the night and she'd woken up and found him dead in bed. I stayed around for a bit, helping her, like, but then she went to live with her sister in Harrogate. So I came back here and signed on.'

Heather noticed the unassuming way in which he spoke of helping the widow.

Richard did not deserve his misfortunes.

'How long have you been unemployed?' she asked him.

'How long do you think?'

'Three, four years?'

'That's right.'

'You must feel so despairing.'

'You said it.'

'But don't give up hope. You look like a nice young man to me.'

'Thank you.' He smiled at her directly. Heather found herself blushing, delighted at the impact she was having. John

Foster was right. She clearly had a knack for this sort of work.

'Do you want to get back into motor mechanics?'

'No. Not really. It's dirty, and the pay's shite.'

Heather flinched at the word, but then had to admit his vernacular had a certain glamour. It reminded her of actors in serious dramas on Channel 4.

'I'm not surprised the money's poor. Is there anything else you could do? Do you have any qualifications?'

'No. And I'm not very proud of that.'

Heather was touched. He'd been around, suffered, and probably strayed from the straight and narrow – she glanced at his eyebrow ring again. Now he was ready to reform, and here she was, ready to help him.

'Do you mind if I smoke?' he asked.

'Please do,' she said.

Heather watched, fascinated, as he extracted a tin from his jeans pocket, opened it, and took out a cigarette paper. In the tin was some tobacco. He placed a line of tobacco along the middle of the paper and rolled the paper expertly with his yellow-stained fingers.

'How old are you, Richard?'

'Twenty-seven.'

Twenty-seven. Dan's age. She knew it. Her heart went out to him. Two boys of the same age, but such different lives. Here was Dan on the brink of marriage, with a first-rate career, and here was Richard, caught in the poverty trap, a victim, preyed upon by the unscrupulous, and heaven knew what he'd experienced in his short life. She felt an exquisite pity for him. With her pity came a sense of purpose. This was no coincidence, her choosing to sit down next to this young man. This was meant. Here was a boy in need of help, in need of someone to look out for him. Here she was, about to lose a son – well, not lose – but nevertheless, the symmetry of the occasion was awesome. She glanced at the stained-glass representation of Christ on the cross. She looked at the martyred Richard. It might not be possible for her to save the world, but she would save this young man.

'Are they giving you a good wage for your work on St Jude's?'

'Reasonable. But it won't go far.'

'Look, I hope you don't think this is patronising of me, but I need some help in the garden, it's a little too big for me to manage, and though I have two able-bodied men at home, neither of them seems to want to lift a finger. I have a greenhouse, and that takes up a lot of my time, then there's the lawn, and I've always wanted to establish a rockery. I daresay I could offer you about ten hours a week, when you're not here. It would be practical experience for you too.'

His face lit up. There was an expression of genuine interest in his eyes. Heather was delighted.

'I'm game for that,' Richard said. 'Do you know, I've always fancied taking up gardening. It's supposed to be good for the soul, making things grow. That's what I'd like – landscape gardening. Or working in a greenhouse.'

At this delicious moment John Foster approached and came to sit with them. Heather's happiness was complete.

'This is Richard Dawson,' she said to John. 'A very nice young man. We've arranged for him to come and help me in the garden – he wants to be a landscape gardener one day.'

'That's wonderful!' said John. He clapped Richard on the back, and beamed at Heather. All three smiled awkwardly, not sure where to take the conversation from there. Heather thought this might be as good a time as any to bring up the subject of the wedding.

'I have a question for you, Vicar.' She preferred to call him Vicar. John was just a little too informal. 'Ken and I were wondering whether it would be possible for Daniel to get married here.'

'In St Jude's? No, it's been deconsecrated.'

'I know that,' she said quickly. 'No, I meant, could Dan and Ruth have a civil ceremony here? Do you think it might be a nice idea for the St Jude's Trust to apply for a licence for civil ceremonies? It could be quite a money spinner.'

John Foster stroked his chin. 'I see what you mean, but my guess is St Jude's would be turned down. It's still very much a religious building. Licences are only given to buildings with no religious connections whatsoever. What's more, the Trust is committed to the Christian ethos, so the activities that take place here ought to be Christian in nature.'

Heather was not pleased. She didn't understand why John was raising objections. Everyone stood to profit from it.

'A wedding's a Christian activity, isn't it?' Richard said. 'The Christians started weddings. There wouldn't be any harm in applying for a licence and then seeing what happened. If you're turned down, you haven't lost anything.'

An ally! Heather almost reached out to squeeze his hand to say thank you.

'Wouldn't it be expensive to acquire a licence?' John asked.

'Six hundred and fifty pounds. But Ken and I would offer to pay that, as our contribution.'

'I suppose I could put it before the committee. When is Dan hoping to get married?'

'In around nine months, but nothing is fixed yet.'

'Hmm.'

Sometimes John Foster could be annoying. These modern vicars could be so indecisive, blowing this way and that, even in matters theological.

'You know, even if they didn't grant a licence,' Richard said, 'there wouldn't be anything to stop you having a reception here.'

This was a singularly intelligent young man. This time Heather did reach out and pat him on the arm.

'That's true,' John said. 'It's an interesting idea.'

At that point the church door opened to admit a photographer accompanied by a young woman with a notepad — obviously from the local press.

'This is the bit I don't like,' Richard said. 'I don't mind being offered the opportunity to work but I don't like being made into a sideshow.'

Heather fully understood. 'Come with me, then. I'll show you the basement. There's a lot of work that needs doing there.'

Richard followed her down some steps into the chilly, desolate basement. Folding chairs were stacked together, boxes littered the floor and paint was peeling from the walls. For a moment Heather felt vulnerable, alone down here with a strange man. She was taking a risk.

Richard interrupted her thoughts. 'I just want to say I appreciate you taking me on to help in your garden. It's not so much the dosh, it's the fact you trust me. I appreciate that. I do.'

'Don't mention it! Of course I trust you. I might be only a housewife and mother, but I'm a good judge of character.'

'I'm sure you are. What's in here?' Richard peered into one of the boxes. 'These are old pew cushions! I reckon they could be cleaned up.'

'Let me see.' Heather said.

Together they crouched down and examined the pew cushions, dusting them off, deciding which ones needed throwing, and which could be regenerated. Heather loved the conspiratorial feel of it, herself and her new friend downstairs, and all the rest upstairs with the vicar. She felt as if she was having her own adventure and the novelty was exhilarating. So was the presence of Richard. She could hardly believe what narrow-minded preconceptions she'd harboured about the unemployed. In one short morning, she had learned so much. Richard was every bit as thoughtful and sensitive as her own sons. Class didn't come into it. She suspected that despite the difference in age and sex, they might prove to be kindred spirits.

Getting him past Ken would be relatively easy. All she need say was that she was employing a part-time gardener, and the question of references would be swallowed up by the fact that he had come via church. Not that Ken would ask. He was so tied up with his own concerns, it was only right that she should have a real, live concern of her own.

'Would next Monday suit you? To come and have a look at the garden?'

'That would be ace.'

'Ace, then,' Heather replied.

Chapter Eight

Sharon opened the door to Ruth.

'You're in trouble,' she said.

'Tell me something I don't know.'

The girls did not kiss. It was enough that they'd established an uneasy truce. Ruth took off her jacket while Sharon stood there examining her nails.

'Where's Mum?' Ruth asked.

'At Grandma's. Dad's gone to fetch her back. I'm watching telly.'

'Is she really angry?'

'Let's just say I'm pleased I'm not you.'

Sharon returned to the living room, called back by the siren song of the opening bars of the *Coronation Street* theme tune. Ruth took a deep breath, inhaling the last traces of the Collins' dinner, the tang of cooked meat, a warm smell of potatoes. It made her hungry. She flung her jacket over the banister and entered the kitchen. Her mother had cleared away, and there were just pans drying by the sink. She opened the fridge and mused over its contents, hoping to find something – anything – she could put in her mouth. The slice of cold pizza looked distinctly unappetising, as did the little pots of fat-free yoghurt. Cheese . . . a row of eggs . . . skimmed milk . . . Nothing worth noshing ever lasted longer than a minute in this house. She closed the fridge. No biscuits in the biscuit tin either. The biscuit tin still had words on it that she had scratched on with a compass point when she was small – *you are not hungary* – meant to be helpful advice to Sylvie when she was on one of her perennial diets. Ruth saw a jar of real jam in the pantry – not the sugar-free variety – took that, found some low-fat spread, and began to make herself a jam sandwich.

Eating would take her mind off the coming ordeal. Sylvie had insisted she had to explain herself in person about the church wedding and Ruth, fearing fireworks, had decided to leave Dan in Leeds and drive down herself. Coming over the M62, she had rehearsed the key principles of assertiveness and had resolved not to shift her ground. She wanted to get married at St Jude's, if it were possible. It was her wedding, not her mother's. That's what she had said to Ellie, and Ellie had agreed.

On the kitchen table was a copy of the *Daily Mirror*, and Ruth sat down with her sandwich and began to turn the pages. Celebrities were getting up to all manner of things of which she, a *Guardian* reader, had been completely unaware. She greedily consumed story after story of loathsome neighbours and sex scandals and soap updates, luxuriating in the sticky sweetness of her jam sandwich. She got up to put the kettle on, spooned some coffee into a mug and made another sandwich, thinking that her old life was like an ancient sweater that should have been thrown out years ago but was just too comfortable.

Coffee, sandwich and *Mirror* balanced precariously, she made her way to Sharon to watch telly.

'You could have made me one,' her sister commented.

'Make one yourself,' Ruth retorted companionably.

Kicking off her shoes, she settled into her dad's armchair. It was almost as if she'd never been away. Work had been demanding recently, and even the intensity of her love for Dan could be draining. It was nice to take time out.

There was the sound of a car engine outside. Sharon looked at Ruth and Ruth looked at the TV. An extreme reluctance to make any effort swept over her, although she was conscious of a nugget of resistance about the wedding, which she polished and cherished and held close to her. She would not be shifted.

Ruth listened to her parents coming in and waited for the moment when Sylvie should enter the living room. She didn't have to wait long.

'So there you are, young lady!'

'Love you too, Mum.'

'Look,' began Ivan.

'You're fired,' said Mike Baldwin.

'Shall I turn the television off?' asked Sharon.

She didn't wait for an answer, and clicked on the remote. Ruth took a deep breath and tried to summon to her mind the sight of St Jude's, the refined, quintessentially English atmosphere of the Blake household, Dan, the soaring arches at York Minster — everything that had so recently become dear to her.

She dreaded being sucked into the abyss of home and Mum and the familiar pattern of accusation and counter-accusation and—

'So explain yourself,' Sylvie said as she took off her coat and sat in her armchair. Ivan joined Sharon on the settee.

Ruth decided to be conciliatory. 'You've probably got the wrong end of the stick. All it is, is that Dan's mum is very involved in renovating a city centre church — which isn't a church any more, in no way is it a church, it's a centre for the unemployed—'

'So you want to get married in a dole office?'

'No, listen. It's a very pretty building, or rather it will be when the cleaning is finished. York is really lovely, and it would just make it special for me to be married there. It would still be a register office wedding. And anyway, Heather rang Dan and said we might only be able to have the reception there — there might be a difficulty over the licence. So really I don't see what the fuss is about.'

'You don't see what the fuss is about.'

'No.' Ruth lifted her chin in defiance. Sylvie had her arms folded beneath her chest, a formidable opponent. They were two boxers facing each other in the ring, each waiting for the other to make the first move. Ivan stood back, the referee. Sharon was in the front row.

'So what is wrong in getting married from home, like most other girls?'

'Nothing. But I think I would like to get married in York.'

'As far away from your family as possible.'

'No. That's not true! I want you to be there.'

'I'm honoured.'

'Stop being so sarcastic. You're only doing that because you know you don't have a leg to stand on.'

'My daughter the psychologist.'

'Let's both calm down here. All I'm asking is to have a reception in a place of my own choosing. I'm not rejecting you or what you have to offer. This is just something I would like to do.'

'Why? Has Dan's mother been talking to you?'

'No!'

'So where would she like you to get married?'

'Well, at St Jude's, but—'

'So get married at St Jude's, but Ruth, remember who you are.'

'What on earth do you mean by that?'

Sylvie shrugged.

'Because if you mean I'm just a working-class girl with ideas above her station, you're quite wrong.'

'That wasn't what I meant.'

'So what do you mean?'

'Think.'

'Oh, you mean because I'm Jewish, and St Jude's is a church.'

There was silence. It made Ruth uneasy, all the more so because she could feel her father participating in the silence. She became defensive.

'Yes, I know we're Jewish, but you've never made out that it's important before. We don't eat kosher, you never go to synagogue, you don't light the candles on Friday night.'

Still that awful silence.

'And you never complained when I said I was marrying Dan.'

'It's not for us to complain,' Ivan intervened gently. 'But that isn't to say we haven't had to adjust.'

Ruth was cut to the quick. She could never bear to disappoint her father.

'You don't mind, do you?'

'Of course we don't mind.'

'I'm in love with him.'

'I know.'

So her parents were actually hurt that she wanted her reception in a church. Her parents, who had spent their life in retreat from their Jewishness, who had worked through the festivals, mocking Lila and David for their show of observance while they secretly ate non-kosher in restaurants, who cited the Holocaust as their reason for non-belief, who had given her to understand that she was free to make up her own mind on these issues — these two people were upset that she was marrying out and didn't want her to have the reception in a church.

She took some time to absorb this. It was strange, being Jewish. When she thought about it, she felt Jewish too, though it was difficult to say what those feelings comprised. Maybe it was that sense of being slightly different to everyone else, an outsider. Or the way she seemed to live on an emotional knife edge. Or her haunting sense that she was not quite as good as everyone else, while also feeling apart, and better. She remembered times when she had been in the synagogue for weddings and Bar Mitzvahs, men swaying in prayer shawls, women strutting like peacocks in the gallery, the buzz of conversation and prayer in competition, heavy perfumes and the sweet thrill of the *kiddush* wine on a small tongue unused to alcohol. She was about to say goodbye to all of that and she felt strangely reluctant, unsure of what she was about to do. St Jude's no longer seemed an English idyll, but a shoddy selling-out, a denial.

Her parents were still silent and as she raised her eyes to look at them, she saw as if for the first time her father's full lips and dark eyes, her mother's nose with that bump in it, her Semitic features. Still, this was no time to be sentimental. She had shifted her ground but still did not want to lose the argument. Losing arguments was against her religion.

'I just want to get married somewhere special,' she said.

'I know what she means,' Sharon intervened. 'Like, it's the most important day of your life. If it were me, I'd want the works. 'Cause I was thinking, Ruth, you and me could go down to London and get a dress. Now that would be fabulous. Or there's the bridal shop in Chester — dead posh, that is. A mate of mine went there, and it's like you're a supermodel, you get your own big changing room and they bring dresses to you. Then you could have the reception in one of the big Manchester hotels. What about the Ramada? Maybe your in-laws would help out with the money if they want a decent spread. And I could do your hair and that would help!'

Ruth was touched by Sharon's enthusiasm, and felt an unwonted rush of love for her sister. At the same time, she felt a profound distaste for her particular brand of showiness. The distaste, however, was reassuringly familiar. Ruth was the clever, ambitious daughter, Sharon was the opposite — non-academic, materialistic — and Rachel was different again — a slob, and arty. Sharon had described the sort of wedding she would like, and it made it very clear to Ruth what sort of wedding she wanted.

'We'll forget St Jude's,' Ruth said, still not wanting to make eye contact with her mother. 'It's not me, anyway. But neither do I want anything too showy. I'd like to get married in Leeds, maybe at a small, country hotel that has a licence for weddings, so we can do the whole thing all in one. Then everybody would feel at ease, and you wouldn't need to get a separate caterer. And you needn't invite Dan's family back to the house or anything. Dan and I could choose somewhere, a nice place in the country.'

This time the parental silence had a different quality. Ivan began to nod slowly, as if Ruth had something there. Sylvie's eyes were narrowed in thought.

'I suppose that could work,' she said. 'Your father and I would have to stay overnight.'

'You could stay in the hotel. Dan and I would be off on honeymoon.'

'Hmm.'

Ruth knew her mother was going to relent. She felt a wave of euphoria. She realised that Leeds was in fact the perfect and most appropriate place for them to marry. It was where she and Dan had courted, and it represented a compromise between Manchester and York. She couldn't wait to get back to Dan and tell him. Of course there was Heather to deal with, but here in Oakhill Road Heather seemed more idea than reality. Besides, she was Dan's mother and his responsibility.

'Leeds,' Sylvie said ruminatively. 'I could go with Leeds.'

'We could go to Harvey Nichols for the dress,' said Sharon.

'Forget your Harvey Nichols,' Sylvie said. 'I know someone who has a bridal shop who will help us out.'

'Who's that?' asked Ruth, relaxing, and feeling disposed to humour her mother after her climb-down.

'Linda – someone I met at my reading group.'

'So you're going to the reading group!' Ruth said, delighted.

'She's the mother of the tutor. She has her own bridal shop in Gorton. I thought we might begin by taking a look at her stock. She does all the other paraphernalia – shoes, veils, head-dresses.'

Ruth was flooded with relief. Everything was back to just as she wanted it. Her mother was actively enjoying the wedding preparations.

'Why don't we go down and take a look – as soon as Dan and I have booked a venue?'

'I'll speak to her next week.'

'Excellent, excellent,' Ivan declared. 'Shall I put the kettle on?'

'I wouldn't,' said Ruth. 'It never suited you.'

Everyone groaned good-humouredly and Ruth breathed a sigh of relief. Harmony had been restored.

Dan had a sixth sense when it came to Ruth. A moment before her key turned in his lock he knew it would be her. He had missed her last night when she was in Manchester, all the more because there was something he'd wanted to talk to her about. Tonight would have to do. In a moment he'd risen to meet her, she'd flung her jacket on the armchair and they were luxuriating in a long, warm, nuzzling hug.

'Parents OK?' he asked her.

'Fighting fit,' she said. Then, 'Hey, you smell of the out-doors.'

'I came back early from work and walked.'

'Why? Are you stressed?' They sat down together on the settee. Dan realised that he probably was rather stressed, although the explanation wasn't necessary to account for his walking. He loved being outdoors, and increasingly he appre-ciated how good it made him feel to be away from the city, being active, not tied to a desk. It amused him how Ruth was always drawn to find a psychological reason for his pleasures. Although today she was probably right.

'Listen. How would you feel if I had to travel a bit?'

'Travel? What do you mean?'

'I've been asked — well, told is the right word — that there are a few audits they'd like me to do around the country. It means I'll be away quite a bit in the next few months.'

'But the wedding!'

'I know.'

'Oh, Dan!'

Dan hated upsetting Ruth. Her disappointment mani-fested itself as a dull ache in his body.

'I've been put in a difficult position. If I say no, I'm being uncooperative. The maximum I'll be away at any time is four days, and never on weekends. You can try to get time off and I'll sneak you into my hotel room. If you need me, you can always ring. I'll leave my mobile switched on.'

'I'm not as helpless as that!'

No, you're not, thought Dan. It was one of the reasons he loved her. He never understood why so many of his acquain-tances were drawn to women who were basically airheads.

Ruth was intelligent, strong, independent, and still chose him. He grew in stature in his own estimation because she'd chosen him. Her strength meant that when they encountered problems, he knew he could trust her.

'It'll be as bad for me as it is for you. Worse,' Dan added.

'I know.' Ruth pouted. 'Mind you, I daresay we can leave the wedding preparations to the mothers. There shouldn't be that much to do. But I'll miss you.'

'When we're married, you'll look back on my absences as a golden age.'

Ruth laughed and snuggled up to him. 'Listen, you. I've got an announcement too.'

'Fire away.'

'The wedding. Now, how can I put this? You know we were looking into getting married at St Jude's? My parents weren't too chuffed. It's the fact it was a church and they still see me as a nice Jewish girl.'

'But you are a nice Jewish girl.'

'Jewish maybe, but not so nice. Anyway, I felt bad about insisting on it and so,' Ruth began to stroke Dan's wrist gently, 'I had another idea. A kind of compromise. What if we get married in neither York nor Manchester, but tie the knot here in Leeds? We could book one of those hotels with a licence to have civil ceremonies and do it all in one. So what do you think?'

It seemed an excellent idea to Dan. Pleased that Ruth had taken the news of his impending audits so easily, he wanted more than anything to repay her reasonableness.

'Brilliant! There were all sorts of problems with St Jude's, not the least that it still needs renovating. I can see a York wedding wouldn't have been fair on your parents. Maybe we can make investigations this weekend. What do you say?'

'You're on.' She kissed him.

'And I'll take you up to Ilkley Moor too,' he added.

'What's with you and the great outdoors?' she teased him.

Dan just laughed. There were some things that were cheapened when you put them into words. Or perhaps it was that he couldn't find the words to express what he felt sometimes when he was in wild moorland, or he'd climbed up high and looked around at a world that was suddenly still and tranquil. There was peace up there, proportion, and the beginning of some meaning. What could he say to Ruth that would encapsulate all that?

'It makes me feel . . . spiritual. I guess.'

'Spiritual! Perhaps we should get married on the moors, like Cathy and Heathcliff!'

'No.' He laughed. It amused him how they were so different, and because they were so different they fitted perfectly, like two pieces of a jigsaw puzzle. 'But I want you to come and walk with me. It'll do you good. We're bound to get overwhelmed with this wedding and we'll need to get away from it all.'

'You're right. You said you'd take me to the Yorkshire Dales.'

'Definitely. We'll—'

The doorbell rang. He exchanged a puzzled glance with Ruth and went to answer the door. It was Ellie.

'What have you done with her?' Ellie joked.

'Ruth? She's in the living room. Come in.'

He made Ellie welcome and offered to make coffee for

everyone, leaving Ellie with Ruth. He presumed Ellie had been round to Ruth's flat first, and needed to see her so badly that she had driven to his house. Ought he to disappear for a while? He knew something of Ellie's situation and reckoned Ruth was the best person to deal with her. He couldn't quite get his head round Ellie. He wondered what drove her to persist in a relationship that was bound to end unhappily. It seemed logical to him to pursue happiness. Yet he felt sorry for Ellie and sensed that she would feel envious of him and Ruth. He carried mugs of coffee into the front room.

He was right. Ellie's voice was breaking as she explained to Ruth.

'I didn't bring the letter because I ripped it up as soon as I read it. He says he feels as if he's torn between us, like he's continually being pulled two ways. He says it's me he wants to be with but he feels responsible for her. It isn't love any more, he was certain of that, but there was a tie. I wish it was a noose – I'd strangle him. So he won't see me out of work for a fortnight to give himself time to reflect. And he forgot he'd promised to help me decorate the kitchen next weekend. I don't mind that he's not helping, but the point is, he forgot.'

Dan watched Ruth shake her head slowly and sympathetically. Personally, he would have told Ellie to leave Adam, but prudently he waited to see what Ruth would say.

'You're unhappy, aren't you?' Ruth commented.

'You have a nice line in understatements.'

'If he doesn't make you happy, Ellie—'

'I'll force him to make me happy!'

'Is he worth it?'

Silence.

'Yes, he is worth it. I love him. I'm willing to wait. I have no option.' Ellie took down her hair and then scooped it back into a ponytail.

Ruth shot Dan a quick glance which he immediately interpreted as : 'See what a fool she is? But what can we do? And by the way, make yourself scarce.'

'I've got some work to do – upstairs,' Dan said and exited.

He came down later when Ellie had finished unburdening herself and was amusing Ruth by acting out a client with whom she'd been having difficulty. Apart from a certain brittleness, she seemed to him like the old Ellie. He said little, hoping she'd leave before too long. He felt the need for some time alone with Ruth.

His patience was rewarded. Ellie remembered that *Whatever Happened To Baby Jane?* was on and she hadn't set her video. She told Ruth she'd cheered her up a lot, and soon they listened as her car engine purred into life and she drove away. Ruth and Dan were silent.

'She ought to finish with him,' Dan said.

'Yes, but it's not as easy as that. She gets a pay-off. All she ever talks about is Adam, so without him she'll feel as if no one is interested in listening to her. She likes a cliffhanging relationship, all that excitement and the ups and downs. It feels right to her. It's all she knows.'

Dan added a thought of his own. 'In a way, she's trying to upstage you. She could have rung you, but came all the way round here.'

Ruth frowned. 'I don't think so. She says she isn't jealous of us.'

'How can she not be?'

'I think you're being mean to Ellie. She doesn't compare our relationship with hers and Adam's.' Ruth's voice trailed away and she mused for a while. 'What she says makes me think she sees us as boring.'

'That's what she needs to believe. I'm not bored. Are you bored?'

'Only when you're not with me,' Ruth replied.

Ellie slipped from his mind as he approached Ruth and responded to her statement with a long searching kiss. Love, he thought, is selfish, and—

'Dan,' Ruth said, breaking away. 'I've invited Ellie to the engagement party. Your mother won't mind, will she?'

Damn the engagement party, he thought, his mind on other things.

'The more the merrier,' he said. 'Now, how does this bra unfasten?'

Chapter Nine

This time Sylvie arrived at Gorton in daylight. Saturday afternoon daylight, to be precise, in the passenger seat of Ruth's car. It had been a relaxing journey as Ruth had prattled all the way about the country hotel she and Dan had found on the way to Harrogate. The reception hall was airy and modern although the hotel itself was an old post house, and therefore full of character. Outside were beautiful gardens where peacocks roamed. The staff were extremely friendly and professional and they had a Saturday left in May.

Apparently Dan had been wonderful with his mother, driving her over to see it and carefully explaining the advantages of the Three Tuns Country House Hotel, as well as the disadvantages of St Jude's, where the kitchen facilities were far too limited for the kind of reception they had in mind. Ruth had said that Heather was surprisingly easy to shift. Dan could only think that her mind was on other things – she was taking a very active interest in the clients at St Jude's.

Not for the first time, Sylvie wondered what Heather was

like. A do-gooder? Or an animated version of *Good Housekeeping*? She had spoken to her on the phone, and was glad it was on the phone, as she had been overcome with embarrassment and rather intimidated by Heather's fruity middle-class voice. Heather had been as polite and correct as if she was reading from a textbook for mothers of the groom. Faced with good breeding on that scale, Sylvie was at a loss. She had muttered some clichéd pleasantries and knew she sounded as inadequate as she felt. The forthcoming engagement party in York filled her with dread, and she was delighted when Ruth told her it had to be postponed as Dan was working in London for a week. It gave her a chance to prepare for the meeting. But how ought she to prepare? Lose some weight? Take elocution lessons? Start reading the *Daily Telegraph*? Over her dead body.

On Sylvie's instruction, Ruth parked the car down a side street, and together, huddling under the same umbrella, they made their way to Wedding Bliss. Linda had advised her to come in the late afternoon as she was always less busy then. That suited Sylvie. Ruth would be able to try dresses at her leisure and she would be able to take a peek at Linda's home life. Although they had sat together again at Suzie's reading group, there had been no time for any personal conversation; they just talked books. From this Sylvie had deduced that Linda had little formal education but was an astute judge of human nature, and didn't care very much what people thought of her. That was the quality that Sylvie admired most in her. It was rarer than one might think. And yet this free thinker, who had said that the only reason that the mill-owner Mr Thornton in *North and South* had appealed to her was that he made her think of chocolate, was the proud owner of a bridal shop, and nothing could be more traditional than that.

Ruth shook out the umbrella as Sylvie pushed open the door and a bell rang inside the shop. Linda was on her knees, putting some headdresses back in a glass-fronted cabinet. She grinned at Sylvie and got to her feet, leaving the headdresses on the carpet.

'I've not had a chance to tidy all day, I've been that busy,' she said. 'And so this is your daughter?' She looked with frank curiosity at Ruth who smiled tentatively back. Meanwhile Sylvie surveyed the shop. It was small and square. In front of her was a rack of wedding dresses, a mass of white satin and lace and tulle. To the right were bridesmaids' dresses, a riot of sapphire blue, burgundy and forest green. To the left were diminutive outfits for little pageboys and bridesmaids, and on shelves above the racks was a profusion of hats, posies and veils. The shop floor was empty except for a cheval mirror. To the right beyond her Sylvie glimpsed a half-open door giving on to a living room, where a TV set flickered in front of a turquoise satin-effect settee. Near the headdress cabinet was a red velvet chair, and Sylvie gratefully lowered herself on to it.

'A nice shop,' she said.

'It's not bad,' Linda conceded.

Sylvie looked round again, appreciatively. In these compact, almost familiar surroundings, she began to feel as if the wedding wasn't going to be such an impossible feat to engineer. The venue and caterer were booked, and Ruth and Dan had seen to the registrar. Once the dress had been bought, there were only the minor details to attend to. She could almost imagine herself enjoying the wedding, but then, perhaps not. Better not be too optimistic. Yet just the sight of all these beautiful wedding dresses stirred something in her. She had worn a dress like that once, in a synagogue in Heaton Park in 1968. Her dress had an embroidered bodice and a satin-effect gown. She had worn a veil too, although even before she had set off towards the *chuppah* there were little holes in it from the cigarettes she'd been chain-smoking. She couldn't remember much of the ceremony now – Ivan had been trembling with nervousness, the rabbi had grinned from ear to ear, there had been flowers twined round the poles holding up the *chuppah*, then there was the smash of the glass and cries of *mazeltov!* Her mother had dabbed at her eyes with a lacy handkerchief throughout. Later, at the reception, little children skittered around the synagogue hall in patent leather shoes that clicked on the wooden floor, and she and Ivan sat in state at the top table, apart from it all. It was sad, the way that memories faded. Sad, too, that you never appreciate your own wedding. It was as if she had dreamed it, she remembered so little, and yet it was undeniably one of the most important days of her life. And now Ruth was about to take the same step. Her own daughter was getting married. A chance to relive her own wedding and this time she would remember it, and enjoy it too.

Linda was encircling Ruth with a tape measure.

'A fourteen in the bust, maybe a twelve in the hips.'

'She's never had my weight problem,' Sylvie commented, rather proudly.

'So what do you have in mind? Have you seen anything in the magazines you like?'

Ruth glanced at the rack of wedding dresses and looked rather baffled. 'Something simple,' she said. 'Not too fussy.'

'They all say that,' Linda remarked. She rifled through the rack of dresses and pulled out an off-white matt satin dress with a scoop neck. Apart from some piping on the neck, it was quite plain.

'That will do,' said Ruth. She vanished with it into the changing room on the left.

'Do you need any help?' Sylvie shouted from her chair, not moving.

'No, thank you.'

Sylvie hoped Ruth would take her time; she was glad of this chance to chat to Linda.

'Is business good?' she asked.

'As good as it will ever be. I do it all myself, you know, the buying, the fitting, the alterations. And you wouldn't believe the outlay for the stock. I've got upwards of twenty thousand pounds worth of stock here.'

'Have you?'

'I wonder whether it's worth it sometimes.'

'What made you go into the wedding business?'

Linda smiled, then knelt down to tidy the headdresses. She picked up one lovingly, then put it down again. Sylvie noticed that her chocolate-brown blouse had a surprisingly low cleavage. Her black skirt was rather short, and revealed two chubby, dimpled knees. Her legs were bare and her toenails were painted purple.

'At one time I trained to be a machinist,' Linda said. 'I found I had a knack with clothes – I could see how to alter a dress and the other machinists couldn't. I liked the work but I didn't want to slave in a factory all my life. I thought I'd like my own shop, and I fancied something a bit different. I've been here for six years now. I have to say I do it for love rather than money. I work a seven-day week. I also do alterations. I—'

At that moment Ruth came out of the changing room. She moved awkwardly to the mirror and regarded herself, her brow wrinkled in concentration. She stood stiffly, looked at Sylvie and gave an embarrassed smile.

'It's not really me.'

'It's loose around the bust,' Linda commented. 'Look.' She gathered a handful of satin to demonstrate what she meant. 'That's why it looks strange. Do you want to try it in a smaller size?'

'I don't know.' Ruth turned slowly in front of the mirror. 'To be honest, I feel a right prat.'

'Language!' Sylvie admonished her.

Linda removed another dress from the rack and handed it to her. 'You might like this. It's plain and off the shoulder. A twelve will probably do.'

Ruth took it back to the changing room. Sylvie watched her go then turned her attention to Linda.

'What was your wedding like?' she asked her. 'Did you have all the works?'

Linda guffawed 'I've never been married.' She laughed again. 'No, we're not the marrying type in this family.'

Sylvie was intrigued. Linda had two children. Were they both accidents? Or did the father live with her? She needed to probe further.

'Did you *want* to get married?'

'I'll tell you something. It was the wedding I wanted. To dress up in one of those,' she gestured to the rack of wedding dresses, 'and to walk down the aisle like a queen. I try on all the stock that fits me and parade around at night when no one's around. I can dream, can't I? But I tell you what. I'd have the wedding, the reception, and even the honeymoon, and then I'd get rid. A wedding is all well and good, but as for marriage!'

'So your – he wanted to marry you, but you didn't want to marry him?'

'Not exactly,' Linda said. 'He—'

Ruth came out of the changing room. She held her arms a small way from her body. 'I keep thinking the whole thing's going to slip off.'

Sylvie looked on approvingly. Ruth had good shoulders and exposed like that she looked positively glamorous. It was true that the sleeves looked floppy, and she didn't understand why the manufacturers hadn't inserted some boning to make them stand out a bit, but nevertheless the total effect was pleasing. The bodice was corded and embroidered with little pearls, and the dress fell smoothly from Ruth's hips. She was beginning to look like a bride.

'I like it,' Sylvie said.

'Do you think it's a touch long?' asked Linda. She got down on her knees with some pins in her teeth and began pinning up the hem.

'That fits a lot better over the bust. I like the bare shoulders,' Sylvie continued.

'I feel so exposed,' wailed Ruth.

'No, not at all. You'll be wearing a veil anyway.'

'A veil?' Ruth sounded outraged.

'Of course you'll have a veil. You won't be a proper bride

without one. You'll wear your hair up, and we'll sit the veil on top.'

Linda, responding quickly to Sylvie's remarks, fetched a veil and headdress and put them on Ruth.

'Lovely,' said Sylvie.

'So romantic,' said Linda.

There were scattered pearls in the gauze of the veil. Ruth looked doubtfully at herself in the mirror.

'I hope nobody comes in,' she said. 'I feel daft.'

'But you won't feel daft on the day,' Linda said. 'When you're walking down the aisle, you'll want to look as wonderful as you possibly can. You'll regret it if you cut corners.'

'Try her with a longer veil,' Sylvie said.

Linda fetched a floor-length veil from a hanger and arranged it carefully, its train sweeping the floor behind Ruth.

'She needs shoes,' Sylvie commented.

Linda found some beneath the bridesmaids' dresses, and pushed a pair of white satin court shoes towards Ruth, who slipped into them.

'Do you know,' Sylvie said, addressing her comments to Linda, 'I think she could take something a little more fussy. She has striking looks. She takes after Ivan's side physically, but the Greenbergs in character. Ivan is a good-looking man.'

'Try this,' Linda said to Ruth. She shook out a crushed princess-line dress in raw silk, with little imperfections in the material.

'I quite like that,' Ruth remarked.

'It's a similar material to Princess Diana's wedding dress,' Linda remarked.

'Well, we're not having that, then,' Sylvie declared. 'I'm not as superstitious as some, but—'

'Mum!'

'What about this?' suggested Linda. She was holding up a dress that seemed to go on forever. It had a satin bodice with a shawl neckline, and a gathered skirt in tulle, embroidered with flower motifs.

'I'd like you to try that, Ruth,' Sylvie deliberated.

'But Mum! I'll look like a dog's dinner!'

'You won't know until you've tried it on.'

Ruth sighed and tutted. 'Do I have to?'

'You have to.'

She emerged in a few moments, swamped by the white extravaganza.

'Lovely,' said Sylvie.

'Beautiful,' said Linda.

'I have never looked so stupid in my life!'

'Nonsense, Ruth. Now you're looking like a real bride. Put that long veil on her again, Linda.' Linda did so. 'Try the gold headdress – the one that's on the floor.'

Eagerly Linda did her bidding, fixing the comb neatly into Ruth's hair and adjusting the band so that it sat straight.

Sylvie was thrilled at the result and blissfully happy. She had not had this much fun since an aunt had bought her a second-hand Sindy doll with its own wardrobe. Ruth was a good-looking girl; it was a shame not to make the most of her. The next best thing to having a good figure yourself was having a daughter with a good figure. Again Sylvie regarded Ruth appreciatively. She could give any bride you'd care to mention a run for their money.

'So how much is that?' Sylvie asked.

'Five hundred and fifty,' Linda said.

'Five hundred and fifty,' Sylvie echoed.

'If you don't mind,' said Ruth, 'I'm getting changed now.'

Five hundred and fifty, thought Sylvie. It was more than she'd envisaged paying, but you only get married once. Now that she'd accepted the wedding as reality, she was acutely aware of the figure she wanted Ruth to cut on the day. These Blakes had to see her at her very best; their son wasn't marrying just anyone, he was marrying Ruth. And there were Lila and David to think about too. She wanted Lila to be lost for words. The more eloquent the dress, the better.

'I said I'm getting changed now, Mum.'

'We'll put that dress on one side,' Sylvie said.

Ruth rustled her way back to the cramped cubicle that served as a changing room. Her jeans and sweater were in a mound on the threadbare carpet. She looked at herself in the spotted mirror in front of her and grimaced. She had never been one for dressing up, and as a child had even avoided fancy-dress parties because she found them embarrassing. This charade of having to dress up in white was not just embarrassing but humiliating too. She looked like a sacrificial victim, a confection, a gift-wrapped Ruth, a present from father to groom. The thought made her shudder. It was such a falsification of what she and Dan meant by getting married. They wanted to spend the rest of their lives together, to make a public commitment. That was all. She wanted to exchange vows and have a party. All this parading around in satin and tulle was a nightmare. It wasn't what she'd intended at all.

Anyway, she thought, as she wriggled out of the dress,

careful not to rip anything, it was a bit of a joke getting married in white. She was hardly a virgin. She smiled as she imagined coming to the ceremony in something shockingly scarlet. Scarlet would suit her far better than white, and it was more appropriate. She regarded herself again in bra and pants and thought how lovely it was to be cherished and lusted after by a man — by Dan. That was what it was really about. The wedding itself was an absurdity, an event that was too late to mark what had happened, an ill-suited to expressing the closeness and tenderness they felt. The ceremony was ridiculous. In fact she could see now that one got married only for other people, for one's mother in particular. Sylvie's enthusiasm for the dress-buying had surprised her, and she rather resented being used as a grown-up doll. Yet she ought to be grateful that her mother was now entering into the spirit of things rather more. Only she had another think coming if she honestly supposed that she was going to walk into the Three Tuns looking like Cinderella at the ball.

She stepped into her jeans. She debated whether to eat with her parents tonight or get straight back to Leeds. Dan was travelling down to London on Sunday so he could start work first thing on Monday. She wanted to have time to say goodbye to him properly. Perhaps they could drive over to Bradford for a curry. She pulled down her sweater, still deliberating. But then they would be too full afterwards, and an evening of eating wasn't exactly what she had in mind.

The wedding dress lay limp on the hanger in the changing room, abandoned. Ruth had resumed being her real self, Dan's girlfriend. Even the word *fiancée* embarrassed her sometimes. It was so Frenchified and so not her. At that moment the wedding seemed unreal to her, like a game she had innocently started to play. In truth, it was impossible to imagine it ever taking place. She smiled at herself in the mirror and shrugged.

Then she took the dress and carried it out to the shop.

'Here we are. I don't think this one is for me.'

'Tell you what,' said Linda. 'I'm parched. Why don't I make a brew for us all, and then you might like to try on some more.'

'Good idea,' said Sylvie.

'As long as we're not too long,' said Ruth. 'I've got to get back to Leeds tonight. I know. Why don't I try on some more dresses while you have a natter? I'll shout if I need any help.'

'That's fine by me,' Linda said. She indicated the dresses that were Ruth's size, and then she turned the notice on the door so that passers-by would read the word 'Closed'.

'Let's leave her to it,' she said to Sylvie. 'I'm all in.'

Sylvie followed Linda into the back room, glad to be able to satisfy her curiosity. While Linda hurried into the kitchen to see to the tea, Sylvie took in the room.

The settee was placed diagonally to the television, which Linda had not bothered to turn off. Sylvie had to put some magazines and a copy of *Howard's End* to one side to find herself a seat. The room was untidy but not dirty. There was an Afghan rug in front of a square fireguard, which sat in front of a coal-effect gas fire. A brown corduroy carrycot lay on the floor, with tousled blankets. There was a box of Pampers in one corner. On a sideboard was a chrome tray with a bottle of single malt whisky and Gordon's gin and some glasses. Over the fireplace was an abstract painting comprising squares of various shades and hues; not the sort of thing Sylvie would imagine Linda liking at all. The painting seemed to be an original. A dining table covered with clutter sat by some narrow French windows giving out on to a small yard with a tall wheelie bin, a statue of the Venus de Milo and a rusting fire escape. Sylvie also noticed a sewing machine, an exercise bike and a pile of books, on the top of which was a tube of Pringles.

'Is Suzie at home?' she asked through the kitchen door.

'Not this afternoon,' Linda called. 'She's visiting a friend. Gives me a bit of peace and quiet, a chance to put my feet up.'

'Is she coming back tonight?'

'No. She's away quite a few weekends. The girl's got to have a life. I'm out of milk. Do you know what I fancy? A sherry. Someone gave me a bottle as a present. It's in the fridge. Here we are.'

Linda brought it out and Sylvie thought, why not? Linda poured out two small glasses, opened a drawer and extracted a box of After Eight mints.

'We'll open these too.'

'Another present?'

'It was my birthday recently.'

Sylvie accepted her sherry and sipped at it cautiously. Out of the corner of her eye she glimpsed something stuffed down the end of the settee. It looked like a man's tie. Interesting. She looked around the room again to see if there were any photographs, but there were none.

'It's nice having you here,' Linda said.

'It's nice to be here. I hope Ruth finds something she likes.'

'She's a beauty,' Linda said. 'What's her fiancé like?'

'Also very good-looking.'

'Do you have a photograph?'

'I don't. I'll have to get Ruth to give me one. People often ask. But we don't go in for that sort of thing much. I'm ashamed to tell you how few pictures I have of the girls.'

'And they grow up so fast.'

The two women smiled at each other. Linda was a remarkably good-looking woman herself, despite her age and size, and that made Sylvie feel more comfortable about herself. Linda's blonde hair and dark brown eyes were striking, and her ever-so-slightly sluttish appearance suggested a woman who was happy to let herself go. Again an insatiable curiosity about her swept over Sylvie.

'So you've always been a machinist?'

'Not always. I've had more jobs than you've had hot dinners. I could never settle to anything, I'd get bored – you know how it is. I wouldn't give you two pence for a nice, steady job. I've been a chambermaid on a cruise ship, I've done bar work, cleaning, had a spell in an office but it didn't suit. Five years ago I got a GCSE in maths at night school,' she said proudly.

'Did you?'

'I got a grade B.'

'Well done!'

'I needed it for the business. He helped me quite a bit, it's right up his street.'

'Who? Your son?'

'No. Me fella. I owe it to him.'

'Does he live here?' Sylvie thought not. There was hardly any signs of a male presence.

'No. There's just me, Suzie and the little one, and my lad when he's at home. The house is bigger than you'd think. We've two bedrooms upstairs and the attic.'

Sylvie nodded and tried to visualise it. She wondered if Linda owned the house and shop. If it was true that she didn't make much money, and Sylvie could well believe it, she wondered what she lived on. Suzie wouldn't bring home much. Perhaps the boy earned a decent wage.

'Your son,' Sylvie began. 'What does he—'

'Da-da!' Ruth appeared in the door wearing a simple bridal dress, empire line, with a long train. Ruth lifted it and swept it to one side, and it cascaded into a pool at her feet.

'That's lovely!' cried Linda. 'I've never seen it look as well on anyone before.'

Sylvie was about to say something, but she realised she simply didn't have anything to say. Her daughter looked remarkable. Was that tightening in her throat and at the back of her eyes the beginning of tears? Surely *she* wasn't going to be the sort of mother who sits and sobs her way through the ceremony? She pulled herself together.

'You'll do,' she said brusquely.

'He's a lucky fella,' Linda remarked.

'He certainly is,' said Ruth.

Chapter Ten

Heather arranged the buttered scones on the plate with great care. She did so as quietly as possible because her attention was focused on the sounds she could hear. These were: Classic FM playing softly from her kitchen radio; the drumbeat of steady rain at the window; and a vacancy, shortly to be filled by either a ring at the doorbell or a knock at the door. He was already seven minutes late.

Not that Richard would be able to do anything worth speaking of today. The weather was execrable, as one would expect for mid-November. For the past two days it had rained relentlessly, although not in Carlisle, Ken had assured her, ringing from the Crown and Mitre where he was staying while he undertook his inspection. Perhaps it wasn't raining in Manchester either. She hoped it wasn't, because she had been working hard for days planning this weekend's engagement party, and if the weather put off the Collinses, she would be devastated. Devastated and, to tell the truth, relieved.

However, the real problem with the rain was connected

with Richard. What on earth did you do when you had arranged for your gardener to come and repair some fencing and dispose of some rubbish when it was like the Deluge out there? It would be the height of bad manners to expect him to work outside in these conditions. Last week when he had visited, the rain had held off, and he had dead-headed some roses, mowed the lawn and seen to the compost heap. They had discussed the feasibility of a rockery and even mentioned a water garden. A water garden! Heather smiled to herself. Never had a truer word been spoken, although waterlogged might be the more accurate description.

She supposed she could have rung to put him off, but she imagined that the money she paid him was helpful, and it seemed thoughtless to her, and unchristian, to make his salary weather-dependent. She would have to find something for him to do. It was almost like when the boys were small, and it rained, and they couldn't go out; she would make pastry so they could cut out shapes, or teach them how to play chess, or let them re-enact the Grand Prix all over the lounge carpet. It was always the woman's job to be inventive. Just recently she had felt a little redundant. Her menfolk didn't seem to need her quite as much. But now there was Richard.

He was a find, there was no doubt of that – the proverbial rough diamond. He may not have had much of an education, but he was quiet and well-mannered and appreciative. He treated her and her house with respect. He worked efficiently in the garden and even Ken was impressed with the amount he'd got through last week. Heather couldn't imagine why he was unemployed at all – a lovely boy! she had told her friends – and for the first time in her life she began to be dimly aware of the reality of social injustice. In the past week she had bought not just one but three copies of the *Big Issue*. Not that one read them, of course. It was the charity that mattered.

She had dressed down this afternoon, in her old M & S jeans and a grey sweater with a cowl neck that was surprisingly flattering. She only put on some light make-up, left off her earrings but compensated with a quick squirt of Estee Lauder's Beautiful. Her green wellies were standing to attention by the back door, in case she should need them. In fact they were blocking the door. As Heather bent to move them to the side, the sound of the doorbell startled her. He's here! she thought.

Pulling down her sweater and tidying her hair she hurried to the door and opened it to reveal a soaking Richard. She quickly ushered him in, wondering for a moment what the neighbours might be thinking.

'I'm dripping wet,' he said. 'What shall I do with my stuff?'

Heather insisted he take off his donkey jacket and she hung it up, and agreed when he offered to leave his shoes in the porch. He walked into the kitchen in his socks, red woollen socks with a hole near each big toe. His olive-green pullover was dry, but his jeans had two tongues of damp down the front of his thighs.

'Come and have some tea first,' she said, feeling a frisson of simultaneous excitement and apprehension. He smelt of cold, damp, fresh air and masculinity. 'Let's give the rain a chance to stop.'

'I could do with a brew,' he agreed.

Heather bustled around the kitchen, as excited as a child presiding over a doll's tea party. She wasn't sure whether one was supposed to make such a fuss of one's gardener, and she felt rather daring and unconventional for doing so. Usually she would make tea for workmen and take it to them, and they might retreat to their van to drink it – one didn't really inquire. Richard deserved more. She sat him at the kitchen table, placed the buttered scones in front of him and carefully filled the teapot. The rain came down with increased vehemence, effectively trapping them indoors. She was delighted. It provided her with an excuse for Ken should she need one – it was raining, what else could I do? She pulled out a chair at right angles to him and sat down.

'What dreadful weather!' she exclaimed. 'They're saying that the Ouse has risen tremendously.'

'Aye, it has that. I were – I was having a drink down there, like, last night, with my mates.'

'Were you?' she said brightly.

He nodded. She noticed that he wasn't wearing his eyebrow ring; there was a little mark where it usually sat. His face was ruddy from his walk through the rain but otherwise he seemed to look cleaner than usual. Heather dared to hope that he might be trying to impress her in some way, that he was making some kind of effort. It was touching.

'Well, I don't know what we can do in the garden if this continues. I didn't cancel you coming in case the rain slackened off but it doesn't look like there's any chance of that happening now.'

'I can go, if you like, and come back when the weather improves.'

'No! You must stay. I know I'll be able to find you something to do. I'm so grateful really that you're here. You see, I have a big function on at the weekend. Dan — my son who's getting married — it's his engagement party. We're having it in the house, and there'll be quite a few guests — my son's fiancée, all of her family, some friends and my Aunt Dilys — and I'm catering myself. Well, me and Marks and Spencer, that is.'

'Sounds like you've taken a lot on there. Do you have a cleaner, like, or someone to help you?'

'Well, no.' Heather felt proud of herself and a little sorry for herself too. 'There'll be sixteen of us altogether. I have to make a supper as Ruth's family is coming all the way from Manchester.'

'Ruth is your daughter-in-law, right?'

'Future daughter-in-law,' she corrected him. 'She's a lovely girl — a clinical psychologist. She works in Leeds which is where Dan is based. She's Jewish, actually. She's . . .' Heather paused. She felt the urge to tell Richard more. It was the way he sat there, his dark brown eyes lambent with empathy. He was so much younger than she was, and from a different class, but she felt that if anyone could understand her, it was Richard. And these confidences, exchanged over a stolen cup of tea on a rainy afternoon, would be soon forgotten by him. She might as well give in to temptation.

'She's very different to Dan,' Heather continued. 'She's very . . . assertive. And Dan is the sweetest boy. I fear for him a little. I think he's rather besotted with her . . . she's a good-looking girl, I will say that. You feel sometimes — I feel — that she could manipulate him. It's not just my imagination, Richard. You know how I wanted them to marry at St Jude's, or at least hold the reception there? Well, somehow, and I don't quite know how, they're not. They're having a civil ceremony and reception at a little country hotel just outside Leeds. She detailed Dan to break all this to me. She wouldn't tell me herself!'

'I'm surprised. It's not as if you're not easy to talk to.'

'Quite. I feel she has a hold over him, you see. Once they are married, it can only get stronger. And do you know, my other son, Tim – the university lecturer, he got a first, you know – he's met someone too!'

'How do you feel about her?' Richard drank some tea and wiped his mouth with the side of his hand.

'Oh, I haven't met her yet. To be honest, I don't know what to make of this. She's someone he's been writing to on the Internet. He hasn't met her yet either – that is, in person. But he told me the other day he was becoming . . . involved.'

'That's all right. It gives you your independence. Both sons off your plate.'

'I know,' she said sadly. She attempted a smile at Richard. How could he possibly understand her sense of loss? She was in the process of being made redundant – and then she thought that was precisely why Richard seemed to have so much fellow feeling for her. They were both facing the spectre of long-term unemployment.

'Now let's talk about you,' she said.

'What do you want to know?' he laughed.

'Oh, how your work at St Jude's is going. Has anything come up at the Job Centre?'

'I'm managing four days a week at St Jude's and that's OK. But it's only a stopgap. Otherwise things haven't changed much. The prospects aren't brilliant. I need to get myself some training.'

Heather nodded very sympathetically. 'Do you have a girl-friend, Richard? Have another scone.'

'Don't mind if I do. No, not at present. Too hard up. Women aren't interested in you when you've no dosh.'

'That's not true! I'm interested in you!'

Richard flashed a smile at her and for one awful moment Heather wondered whether he thought she was flirting with him. Surely not! Then she became aware of how there were only the two of them in the house and how she hardly knew him, and she saw his rough, calloused hands round her china teacup and knew she had to do something to dispel the sudden unasked-for intimacy she had created. Otherwise he would think she was one of those ageing, desperate house-wife-temptresses from the *Carry On* films.

'Now, come on!' she cried, in her best infants' teacher manner. 'Drink up your tea and we'll make a dash for the greenhouse. I never got round to showing it to you before. It's my pride and joy. Ken always says I ought to have a camp bed put up there, I spend so much time in it!' Ought she to have said the word 'bed'? But no matter. Already she was pulling on her wellies and reaching for her Burberry which was hanging on a peg on the back door.

'I'd better get my outdoor things,' Richard said, and made for the porch.

'Rightio!'

Richard glanced upstairs, wondering how big the house was. It must have cost a packet, at least two hundred thou, he reck-oned. With his toes he felt the springy close weave of the carpet, and was more than a tad pissed off that they had to go and see the greenhouse just when he was getting comfortable. Still, who knew where that might lead?

His boots were giving off a rather unpleasant aroma, but he hardly noticed as he tried to assemble the clues Heather had given him. She was lonely, that much was obvious. But then what did she want? A bit of rough? When she'd said she was interested in him he could have sworn she was after his body. That was fine with him. It wouldn't be the first time. She wasn't so bad to look at and generally these older women knew what they wanted and he wasn't averse to giving it to them. But then she leapt up off her chair like a scalded cat. Had she changed her mind? Was she embarrassed to have given the game away so soon? Was she as innocent as she seemed?

She wanted to talk. That was fine. He had no problem with being a listener. He took a comb from his jeans pocket and ran it through his hair, calculating, assessing, deciding that he was right to pursue this and see where it would take him. In a funny sort of way, he felt sorry for her. These older women always got to him – they were so helpless and grateful. He remembered Sadie whom he'd picked up in a pub one wet afternoon. She hadn't had a lover for twenty years. Dorothy was going through a messy divorce and hated men, so he made out he was gay and she had been his meal ticket for well over a year. Helen was a failed member of Weight Watchers and all she needed was someone to tell her how gorgeous she was. All this, and he was able to draw dole money too. It was a life, and it wasn't a bad life. He made a lot of women very happy, and if they paid him for the privilege, so what? They paid their hairdressers, cleaners, masseurs, therapists, and they probably did them less good than he did.

He turned to go back to the kitchen. Nice pad, he thought again. Anyway, she was all right, this Heather. She fed him, paid him, made a fuss of him. He'd bide his time, get his feet under the table, so to speak. And when he had worked out what it was she was after, he'd give it to her. And then he would take his wages.

Carrying his jacket and boots he moved silently through the hall and back into the kitchen.

Heather closed the door behind them. In the greenhouse the rain was even louder, thudding on the glass roof, enclosing them in a rhythmic cocoon of sound. It was dark too, so Heather switched on the fluorescent light, and now it almost seemed as if it was night outside.

'Well, this is it!' she announced.

'Ace,' he said, looking around with interest. Heather followed the direction of his eyes and saw her begonias and chrysanths afresh, a mass of pink, gaudy petals. They were a riot of colour and she was proud of them. Then there were her New Guinea Busy Lizzies with their multicoloured foliage. Best of all were the Jacobinia, their stems ablaze with scarlet flowers dipped in yellow. They were her alter ego, wild, untamed, exotic. She was glad that Richard had seen them.

'It's a shame you missed the tomatoes,' she said. 'I had a glorious crop this year.'

'I'd like to have tasted one.' He continued surveying the premises.

There was a line of concrete slabs under their feet. On their left was an old Gro-bag that needed throwing, and some empty flowerpots and a trowel. Her larger plants lived there. On the shelves to their right were her smaller plants, some green matting over a polythene sheet, massed together, giving off that familiar, yearned-for smell of soil and damp. Heather shivered. Perhaps she ought to switch the electric fan heater on. She had asked Ken about year-round heating but he'd um'd and ah'd and she'd let it drop because she didn't want to make an issue of it. She began to remove some dead flowers while Richard edged past her to look at the pots at the back of the greenhouse.

'What have you got growing here?' he asked.

'Just herbs,' she said. 'I really ought to give them a drink. They need constant attention in the winter. I brought in the chives and mint from the garden, but I grew the basil and thyme from seed.'

'Did you?' He sounded impressed.

'Yes — this is my propagator.' She brought it forward to show him. 'It was a birthday present from the boys. Such fun.'

'So you can propagate any seeds in there?'

'Within reason.'

'That's something I've always fancied doing. Like, taking a seed, and watching it grow.'

'Absolutely!' (They were kindred spirits!) 'This is why I love the greenhouse so much. You can watch things growing right from the beginning, and you can give them so much more care than if you had to leave them in the garden all year. This is my nursery, really.' She laughed. 'I have to tell you no one else ever comes in here. It's not Ken's thing at all. And the boys have so much more to occupy them. It's my little kingdom, really.'

'I bet you're the sort of person who talks to your plants.'

Ouch, thought Heather.

'Because that makes sense to me,' Richard continued. 'Plants are living creatures too. They need attention and love. We all need attention and love.'

I do, thought Heather.

He began to examine the propagator with interest, lifting off the plastic cover and picking up the clean, tiny pots that Heather had ranged there. She tingled inwardly as he fingered things that were so private to her, but she relished the intrusion.

'So you could germinate any seeds in here, even seeds from a hot climate?'

'Oh yes, if you get the temperature right.'

'Hmm.' He replaced it. 'What else do you want to show me?'

'Oh dear, there's not really a lot at this time of the year. November is a quiet month in the greenhouse. If it wasn't pouring with rain we could make a start on the clean-up – with a greenhouse, you do your spring clean in the autumn. We need to scrub it all down with disinfectant but first we'll have to move all the plants outside, of course.'

'We could do that on my next visit. But what about now? What do you want me to do?'

There was silence as Heather thought.

'We could go upstairs.'

'OK,' he said levelly.

'I was thinking that you could help me get some folding

chairs down from the attic. I'll need them for the weekend and I'd like to give them a good wash before then.'

'You're on,' he said.

Heather locked the door quickly, and they scurried back to the house. They removed their outdoor clothing and then Heather led Richard up the stairs. She opened a narrow off-white door,

'Up here,' she announced, switching on a light.

She arrived first in the attic. It was a large space with a grimy skylight window. Around the sides were the trunks that the boys had used when they went away to university, old furniture, boxes of records, keepsakes and ornaments from her parents' old house, painting equipment, a ladder and, in the middle, a threadbare carpet. Heather had occasionally fantasised about converting the attic into something or other but now the boys were grown-up it seemed pointless. The next family who came along to the house would no doubt do something to it. The thought made her a little melancholy. She indicated the folding chairs to Richard.

'Those,' she said. 'They need bringing down.'

Richard seemed interested in the attic. 'So what do you do up here?' he asked her.

'Nothing,' she said. 'It's wasted space.' She felt suddenly guilty. Richard had no home of his own, and she had a whole room, for the attic was room-sized, just sitting here. Though heaven knew what Ken would say . . .

'You know what you were saying before,' Richard said ruminatively, 'about this being a quiet time in the greenhouse?'

'Yes?'

'Well, I reckon you could carry on growing things up here.'

'But there's not enough light.'

'No sweat. I could fix you up something.'

'Could you?'

'Yeah. And the skylight would give you ventilation. It would be like a hothouse. Your central heating would rise up, wouldn't it?'

'Yes. It's quite warm up here already. But why would I want to grow things up here?'

'Because then you can have a year-round hobby, can't you? On days when you can't even get out to the greenhouse, you could come and hide away up here. I'll help you set it up. It'll give me something to do.'

'Flowers in the attic!' Heather laughed.

'No, I'm serious. Everyone needs something to be getting on with. It's the worst part of being unemployed – you have no sense of purpose.'

'I know what you mean. Since Ken – my husband – retired, he hasn't given up work. He still does school inspections, and he's compiling a book about churches in the north of England – he's thinking about approaching a publisher – and that's why he's away such a lot—'

'Hey, Heather! Let's think about you here.'

It was the way he used her name that made her blush. And the fact that someone was thinking about her. She felt flustered and shy and thrilled.

'We'll get something going up here,' he said. 'And it'll help me too. If I bring in seeds and grow them, and pay you for the space, I could sell them, start a business. You'd be helping me.'

'Would I?'

She could see it all. She could easily get another propagator or two, and work up here in the winter, Richard by her side. They would talk and strike up a real relationship. He could grow seedlings and sell them and one day he would open up his own garden centre, saying he owed it all to her, just like in *Pygmalion*. She would be constantly busy and he would be calling in every day. Richard would become devoted to horticulture and never marry . . .

Of course they would need to go through all of this rubbish first and no doubt he would help her with that.

'I'll help you sort through all this rubbish,' he said, as if reading her mind.

'It's not all rubbish,' she said. 'A lot of my parents' things are valuable. I really ought to decide what to do with them. Perhaps Dan and Ruth might like some ornaments.' At the thought of cleaning up and giving Ruth that appalling ormolu clock, she couldn't suppress a smile. And that heavy dinner service . . .

'I think you've had an excellent idea, Richard,' she said.

'I knew I'd be good for you,' he replied.

Their eyes met in the intimacy of conspiracy. Heather knew she had found a friend. She filled with affection for him, and yearned to express it. Then she had an idea, and before she could live to regret it, she acted. She walked towards him, placed a hand on his shoulder, and spoke.

'Richard. I would love it if you'd come as my guest to the engagement party. I want you to meet everyone.'

'Well, I . . .'

'Don't worry if you don't have anything to wear. It's awfully informal. I want you to be there.'

'I'm not sure that's my scene, I don't think . . . But if you needed help, that would be another matter. What would I do?'

'I know! You could be barman and see to the drinks. That would free Ken to mingle, which would be just as well since it's such a delicate social occasion. I'll pay you, of course. Is five – no, six pounds an hour OK?'

'Sounds great to me.'

'Wonderful. I'll be so interested to hear what you make of everyone. I have this feeling that you're a good judge of character. And your help will be invaluable.' Ken, she thought, might wince a little at the extra expense but she would explain herself by saying that she thought she could help Richard best by introducing him to polite company, therefore improving his social graces and etiquette. Ken would be sure to understand, coming, as she did, from an educational background. And having one's own domestic staff was bound to impress the Collinses. Perhaps this engagement party would not be quite so bad after all. She smiled warmly at Richard.

'Right. Let's get on with shifting those chairs!'

Chapter Eleven

'How am I bloody well supposed to read out the numbers when there aren't any numbers on the houses?!'

'All right, all right,' said Ivan. 'I'll park the cab and get out and walk.'

'Dad, that one over there is sixteen, so it must be on the other side.'

Sylvie knew she should have realised that the Blakes would live in the kind of street where numbers on the door were considered vulgar. It was just about the last straw. The traffic had been terrible on the M62, they had come the wrong way into York and then got lost in an interminable one-way system. Ivan knew Manchester like the back of his hand but he was hopeless in any other city, and if there was any chance of a wrong turning, he could be relied upon to take it. Rachel had sulked all the way because she didn't really want to go to the engagement party — Nor do I! Sylvie had screamed at her — and Sharon had dressed up as if she was going to Ascot. Only Renie had enjoyed the journey, predicting they would never reach their destination and she didn't like the sound the engine was making. Now they were three-quarters of an hour late, Sylvie was dying for the loo, and the only consolation she could think of was that at least she'd be obliged for social reasons to break her diet.

'I'm sure it's that house,' Sharon said. 'It's just like Ruth described. There's the white door and those funny chimneys.'

Ivan slowed down and Sylvie spotted Ruth's car in the drive. Ruth had travelled with Dan and Ellie from Leeds.

'That's the one,' Sylvie confirmed. *Oy vey*, she thought. It was a mansion, bigger even than Lila's place. She knew there were some Jewish mothers who would *kvell* with pride that their daughter had netted such a wealthy husband but Sylvie wasn't one of them. If anything, these surroundings were bringing out the working-class Jew in her. It was why she was thinking in Yiddish.

They got themselves out of the cab, Ivan assisting Renie, and Sharon clutching the cellophane-wrapped plant that was a present for Heather. It was Sylvie who rang the bell, and Heather opened the door. Sylvie was momentarily stunned.

'Hello! You must be Ruth's mother. I'm *so* glad to meet you. Come in!'

Sharon thrust the plant at her, and Heather cooed and fussed and said they shouldn't have. Sylvie was swollen with self-consciousness, then self-hatred on account of her self-consciousness. Then the self-hatred became detached and wrapped itself round this elegant, horribly middle-class woman dressed in a designer suit it would have taken Sylvie a year to save up for. She watched Heather shake hands heartily with Ivan and then to her horror, Heather approached her with arms outstretched. Did she want to kiss her? She did. Placing her arms lightly round her, Heather placed a butterfly kiss on Sylvie's cheek.

'I'm so thrilled,' she said.

'Yes,' Sylvie agreed, aware her reply wasn't properly grammatical. Heather's heady perfume clung to her and combined with the sound of clinking glasses and laughter, the opulence of the house and an insistent pain in her bladder. It was all too much.

'Would you like to wash?' Heather inquired.

What was this? Was Heather suggesting she looked dirty? 'No, thank you.' Sylvie said frostily.

'Mum!' cried a flushed Ruth, who had clearly been drinking. She emerged from the lounge and embraced her. Dan followed and shook her hand. Then Sylvie spotted Ruth's friend Ellie, to whom she was rather partial. But first there was another matter to attend to.

'Ruth,' she whispered urgently. 'I need the toilet.'

'Then why didn't you go when Heather suggested it?'

Sylvie then understood the euphemism and cursed the middle classes for their maddening coyness. A wash, indeed! Ruth shooed her upstairs, gave her brief directions, and before long she found herself in a palatial bathroom, blinded by snow-white porcelain, dazzled by gold-plated taps and fascinated by the range of skin care products ranged on shelves. Feeling as if she was desecrating a sacred space, Sylvie quickly saw to her needs and went to scrub her hands in the sink with a bar of dusky pink soap that stank of roses. She looked around for a towel and was surprised to discover there wasn't one. Was she supposed to go down with her hands wet? Or were the guest towels those little face cloths that somebody – Heather? – had arranged into mock roses? She eyed them for a moment, her hands dripping. Tough, she thought, removed one from the display on the cabinet and dried her hands. Then she hesitated. What was she supposed to do with it now? Throw it into the wastepaper bin? Hardly. Nervously she opened the cupboard that the towel display sat on and to her relief saw a crumpled towel already in there. A strange place to put them, but there we go. She placed her towel beside it and prepared to make her way downstairs.

Ruth took her grandmother from Ivan and led her to a high-backed Queen Anne chair that she had been saving for her.

'I'm so thrilled you could come, Grandma. There's someone here I'd like you to meet. This is Dan's Great-Aunt Dilys. She's eighty-one.' Ruth helped to arrange Renie on her chair, next to a lady with hair like white cotton wool and thick pebble glasses.

'This is my grandma, Aunt Dilys. She's eighty.'

'But very nearly eighty-one,' Renie cut in, 'if I make it, that is. I have arthritis and high blood pressure. I take tablets.'

'I'm waiting to have my gall bladder removed,' said Aunt Dilys.

'Ach, that's nothing these days. They do it through the keyhole. But I had a cataract removed—'

'I had both mine done, but one didn't work. There were complications.'

Ruth didn't want to hear about the complications. Let them battle it out, she thought. She turned and surveyed her engagement party. There was a comforting hubbub of voices, guests mingling happily, a table laid with plates, cutlery and bowls of fresh salad, and the barman Heather had hired to serve drinks. He was wearing a little white apron tied round his middle. It was all too perfect. Heather's spacious living room could have been created with just such a function in mind. The chandelier glittered, the rosewood display cabinet glowed, and the elegance of the surroundings conferred elegance by association on the guests.

She saw her mother sneak in and go and join Ellie. Tonight Ellie looked a picture. She had arranged her hair in two top-knots and looked like a German fräulein. She wore a royal blue satin dress, knee-length, but slit at the side. She whispered something to Sylvie that made her laugh. Ruth knew that Ellie and her mother shared a somewhat cynical take on the world. In the past few days Ellie had moulded her cynicism into a rock-hard shell to help her cope with working alongside Adam while their affair was in abeyance. She had taken to drinking too much and ringing Ruth at all times of the day and night. Tonight she seemed rather manic, and had talked nonstop in the car on the way here. At least, Ruth thought, someone could star as the life and soul of the party.

Ruth sought Heather with her eyes. First she saw Rachel uncertainly looking around her, and then she found Heather who was being entertained by Sharon. Best leave well alone there. Meanwhile Tim was guarding a bowl of nuts on the mantelpiece, eating steadily like a grazing cow, and Dan was in a group with some friends of Heather's and the vicar. Ivan and Ken were each holding a glass of amber-coloured liquid, talking.

Ruth watched them all, an observer at her own festivities.

As she did, she began to feel apart from them all, quite unnecessary. They could all have been performers in a play, while she had temporarily stepped into the wings. But what kind of play? Perhaps one of those Ayckbourn-inspired social comedies beloved of amateur dramatic companies. It was all artificial in a pleasant sort of way; there would be laughter, a little drama, no doubt, and then they would all go home at the end of the evening. She couldn't think what it had to do with her and Dan. She sought Dan with her eyes and found him still surrounded by that knot of middle-aged women, Heather's friends, with the vicar presiding. He seemed at ease and was smiling, looking smart, relaxed, at home. Which he was — at home, that is. She was the one who was acting; he wasn't. The discovery made her feel a little uneasy.

No; that was an illusion. It was this whole wedding phenomenon — it was running away with them. It was taking them over. The odd thing about deciding to get married was that it destroyed intimacy rather than creating it. Before, her love life was private. Now it was public property, a theme for celebration and merriment and macadamia nuts in bowls and flower arranging. And champagne. Talking of champagne, she badly needed some more.

Ruth made her way to the makeshift bar where Heather's gardener-cum-barman was presiding, polishing glasses. She thought he had a rather self-contained look that changed as soon as he spotted her to a conspiratorial smile.

'A top-up?' he asked in an accent which she could have sworn had a trace of Geordie in it.

'A new glass,' she said. 'I've left mine somewhere.'

'Easily done,' he said, and began to pour champagne for

her. Apparently Heather had adopted him from her church's unemployment project, but he didn't come across as a fore-lock-tugging member of the deserving poor. He was quite self-possessed, almost insinuating.

'Enjoying yourself?' he said to her.

'I will do,' Ruth said, 'when I get this down me.'

'So introduce me to the barman!' Ellie declared suddenly arriving at Ruth's side.

'I'm Richard,' he said, his eyes taking her in appreciatively.

'I'm Ellie. I'm fed up with drinking champagne. What else have you got for me?'

'You name it.'

'Well, let me see. I'd like something with a bit of body, a bit of muscle. Not too sweet, not too smooth. What are you dong after—'

Suddenly Ruth was aware of Heather's presence. 'Do you know, pet, you haven't introduced me properly to your friend Ellie. Dan has told me so much about you, Ellie. Come over to the piano where there's a little more room and tell me all about public relations. I want to know exactly what it is you do.'

Before Ruth had time to react, Sharon was at her side.

'This place is amazing,' she said. 'You see that settee? There's one just like it in John Lewis's in Cheadle and it cost three and a half thousand and that's without the matching chairs. And look at that painting of a castle over the piano. That's signed, that is, so I reckoned it must be worth a packet. I asked Dan's mum how much they paid for it and she said a few hundred. That carriage clock is antique and she paid four hundred and fifty for that, and the carpet is real Axminster and she spent five thou on that three years ago.'

'Sharon! You didn't ask her all of—'

'Yeah, well, people like the opportunity to show off. I know I do. And the music system is Bang and Olufsen but what I don't get is why their TV is so small. If I had as much money as them, I'd go for one of them wide-screen models with stereo. Or do they have another room with a bigger set? What's the sitting room like? Do you think they'd mind if I took a peek? How many bedrooms do they have? Do you know where Rachel is?'

Ruth looked around her but couldn't see Rachel anywhere. She presumed she was in the loo, and told Sharon so.

'I must have a look up there too. Don't tell me where it is – I daresay I'll open some bedroom doors by mistake.' She dug Ruth playfully in the ribs and vanished.

Ruth drained her champagne and felt it wasn't so much more alcohol she needed as Dan. She made her way to him, edged past Heather's friends and linked arms proprietorially with him.

'So when exactly is the happy day?' the vicar asked her.

'May the tenth,' Ruth replied.

'Are you marrying them, John?' asked one of the ladies, with a pudding-bowl haircut and buck teeth.

'No. I believe Ruth is Jewish.'

There was a murmur of interest. Immediately Ruth felt herself bridle defensively. It was a knee-jerk reaction.

'So you're getting married in a synagogue?'

'No,' said Ruth. 'That would only be possible if Dan converted. Judaism doesn't encourage intermarriage.'

'I knew a lovely couple and she was Catholic and he was Methodist but they married in Our Lady of the—'

'No,' the vicar intervened. 'There's no comparison. Judaism is quite distinct from Christianity, as much a separate religion as Islam is.'

'Yes, but Jews are so much more anglicised,' another of the women said. 'You're not so different from us. You go to church on Saturday instead but we have the same Bible.'

She means I'm white, Ruth thought, and was furious. She bit her tongue. This wasn't the time or place to have a row. Instead she tried to explain.

'There are fundamental differences,' she said. 'Theological ones. You believe in—' Jesus, she was about to say, but changed it to Christ in the nick of time, 'Christ, and we don't.'

'So what do you believe about him?'

'Well, nothing, really. That is, he doesn't come into the frame.'

The lady with the buck teeth looked taken aback. Ruth felt she ought to make a concession.

'I suppose we accept someone called Jesus lived, but we don't believe he's the Son of God.'

The *froideur* in the atmosphere made her decide to back-track further.

'But I'm sure he was a very nice man. And inspirational. Very inspirational.'

'What do you do at Christmas?' another lady asked.

'Eat turkey and slob out like everyone else,' she joked, then remembered that the vicar was listening. 'But we don't go to church.'

'So you go to the synagogue,' said a lady in a check two-piece suit who was getting the hang of this.

'Well, not at Christmas, obviously.'

'But at Passover and the Feast of Tabernacles,' she persisted, showing off.

What the hell is the Feast of Tabernacles? thought Ruth, and for the first time in ages regretted her truncated Hebrew education.

'We're supposed to go to synagogue on Saturday, but not everybody does.'

'Do you eat pork?' came another question.

Ruth was beginning to feel like a sideshow, and not a very entertaining sideshow at that. She didn't really know the first thing about her religion. She had taken it all for granted, as one would a loved parent whom you could safely ignore in the knowledge that he or she would always be there for you. One day, she thought, she ought to make an effort to find out more.

'If you're staying for the weekend,' the vicar said, 'you must come to church tomorrow. We'd love to have you.'

'Dan's driving us back tonight,' she explained, relieved at the thought of returning to the secular no-man's land she inhabited with Dan, where they would set up home and maybe start a family one day, strictly on their own terms, forward-looking and free. Right now the deadening respectability of the Blake Christian ethos was making her feel claustrophobic. She pecked Dan on the cheek, all the ladies smiled, and one of them said, they don't eat prawns, you know.

That remark was the last straw for Dan. He couldn't stand another moment of Ruth being cross-examined by these so-called Christian harpies.

'Pigs,' he said, 'are now thought to be one of the most intelligent mammals. Did you see the film *Babe*? The Israelites were ahead of their time in banning the eating of pigs. They also banned the eating of cats and dogs and insects. In fact, strictly speaking, since Christianity is only a modern offshoot of Judaism, good Christians should observe the Israelite food laws too. Do *you* eat pork?' he concluded, to the church brigade.

'Only from Sainsbury's,' one falteringly replied.

Dan shook his head despairingly and steered Ruth away from them in the direction of the French windows at the back of the room.

'Hold on a minute,' she said. 'How did you know all that about eating kosher? I never told you.'

'I picked up a book in Waterstone's the other day, *An Introduction to Judaism*. It's interesting.'

Ruth's eyebrows shot skywards.

'But you can eat locusts,' he said.

'Yeah. Right.'

Dan squeezed her hand. 'Are you enjoying yourself?'

'Are you meant to enjoy your own engagement party?'

'I'll have to consult the rabbi,' Dan joked. 'It'll be over soon,' he added to cheer her. 'These things are for the parents anyway. We just have to endure them. See, there are our fathers deep in conversation. You go over and join them and I'll find some other wheels to oil.'

'So you're thinking of a career in the diplomatic service?'

'Off you go,' he said.

Dan was philosophical about the strain of the whole occasion. Parents liked to make a fuss, and his mother, he knew, had been planning this party eagerly. Now he was on the verge of finally untying himself from her apron strings, he felt it was the least he could do to fall in with her plans. He knew it was necessary to jump through certain hoops before he could have Ruth to himself. Men used to fight dragons for their women; at least he only had the church flower committee. He smiled to himself and rejoined the fray.

Ivan was still talking to Ken, or rather Ken was talking to him.

'. . . a fascinating cathedral. The wall paintings were whitewashed during the Reformation and only rediscovered very recently. The ceiling has been restored to its original medieval splendour and there's a medallion of Our Lady in the very centre.' Ken nodded to acknowledge Ruth. 'And what might interest you is that Sir Walter Scott got married there, although there's a charming story about his little jaunt over the border to Scotland so he missed the banns being read, and the wedding had to be postponed until Christmas Eve.' He beamed at them. Ruth willed her father to say something.

'Sir Walter Scott,' Ivan repeated. 'Didn't he invent porridge?'

Ruth nudged him. 'No. He was a Scottish writer. Remember *Ivanhoe* and *The Bride of Lammermoor*?' She could see her father was none the wiser.

'Do you travel much?' Ken asked Ivan.

'All the time,' Ivan quipped. 'I'm a cabby. But if you're talking about holidays, I took the wife for a week in Bournemouth in August. Very relaxing.'

'We spent the summer in the Dordogne.'

Ivan could not think of a reply to this. Nor could Ruth. A pall of silence descended and threatened to envelope them all. Despite the background chatter, the silence was audible and palpable. As Heather approached them, with Sylvie in her wake, Ruth breathed again.

'Sylvie!' Ken said warmly, as if she was a long-lost relation. Sylvie's unease transmitted itself directly to Ruth.

'Ken, dear,' said Heather, 'it's time to eat. Can you tell everyone?'

In a booming, headmaster's voice, Ken announced that dinner was being served.

'Would you like any help?' Sylvie asked Heather.

'Absolutely not,' she replied. 'Everything is under control.' Then she raised her voice. 'If people would wander into the kitchen, there's salmon and cold meat. Salads are in here.'

Ruth noticed that no one seemed to pay the slightest attention. Evidently this was polite behaviour too. She saw Heather and Sylvie smile at each other, but the smile in each case was plastic.

'Sylvie will have heard of Sir Walter Scott,' Ivan said suddenly. 'She goes to a reading group.'

'Do you?' said Ken sounding impressed.

'Just in the local library,' Sylvie explained while Ruth bristled at Ken's condescension.

'And what are you reading at the moment?'

'*Howard's End*,' Sylvie replied.

'Oh yes, that splendid description of Beethoven's Fifth.'

'I don't know about Beethoven's Fifth. I'll tell you who I can't stand — those blasted Wilcoxes. And as for Mr Wilcox, don't ask me what Margaret sees in him. He's old enough to be her father for a start. I wouldn't trust him further than I could throw him.'

With a sinking feeling Ruth realised that her mother had been at the champagne with a vengeance. The tips of her ears were red and her face was flushed. Normally she would never have been so aggressive with someone as intimidating as Ken. Ruth felt for her.

'Does your reading group lead to any qualification?' Ken asked.

'What's the use of a qualification at my time of life? But that's not to say we aren't well taught. She's only young, our tutor – she brings her baby with her to the classes – but she knows what she's talking about. Her mother comes too. She owns a bridal shop and we're getting Ruth's dress from there. It's a beauty.'

Ruth glanced at Ken so see how her mother's champagne-inspired narrative was being received. The expression on his face was glazed, almost horrified, she thought. The bastard, she thought. She'd never realised he was such a snob. If Sylvie had been a university lecturer discussing colleagues, no doubt he'd have been fascinated. From that moment she turned against him.

'I think someone had better start the buffet, Sylvie,' Ken said, and led her by the elbow in the direction of the kitchen. Sylvie did not seem to realise that she had been sidelined. As she was manoeuvred out of sight she called to Ruth, 'Where's Rachel?'

Ruth looked around. There was no sign of Rachel. Sharon was back downstairs again and chatting to Tim. Renie and Great-Aunt Dilys were still sitting together but each looked stolidly in different directions. It was as if the Cold War had broken out. Ruth was puzzled about Rachel, and decided to find her.

She glanced in the kitchen where some people were beginning to help themselves to food, but no Rachel. The sitting room was dark and empty. She ran lightly upstairs and noticed the bathroom was free. She hoped Rachel hadn't popped out and tried to find the local boozer, but why should she with so much free booze available here? Then Ruth spotted a light coming from Tim's bedroom. Curious, she approached it. She could hear the tapping of computer keys. As quietly as possible she opened the bedroom door and saw Rachel intent at the computer screen.

'Rachel!' she exclaimed.

Rachel turned and saw her but seemed unperturbed. 'Tim said I could,' she explained. 'I wanted to check my e-mail, and I got involved in a chat room. Come here.'

Ruth advanced, having a quick peek around Tim's room. It was tidy and smart and inscrutable.

'Here. Look at this,' Rachel said. She clicked on an icon that opened Tim's mailbox. 'Six unopened messages from Samantha.'

'You mustn't read them!' Ruth said, horrified.

'I won't, but he must have known I could access them because he told me his password so I could log on. It's *yhtomit*, that's his name backwards.' Rachel exited his mailbox. 'But hey, check out this.' She opened the bottom drawer of his desk.

'Rachel!'

'Take a chill pill! I was only looking for a pencil to write down an address. I found these pictures.' She giggled. Ruth found herself looking at some colour prints of an extremely buxom blonde spilling out of a very tight dress. They were signed, Samantha.

'The original Wonderbra girl,' Rachel said. 'And that's not all.' She rifled through the sheets of paper and found another of Samantha clad only in the briefest of underwear. This one was addressed to Tim. Ruth's hand flew to her mouth.

'I reckon she's obviously someone he's met on the Net,' Rachel said. 'Sad old geek. I wonder if she knows what he's like.'

'Don't be so cruel.'

'Don't be so soft.'

Ruth looked at the pictures again and was caught between laughter and pity. And how would Heather react when she discovered her treasured older son was Internet-dating a would-be porn star?

'Come on,' Ruth urged Rachel. 'You've got to come downstairs and eat. Mum was wondering where you were.'

Rachel picked up the glass of whisky she had by her on the computer table and followed Ruth.

'Do you think I should say something to Tim?'

'Don't you dare!' said Ruth.

Dan was waiting at the bottom of the stairs and as she came to him she took his hand and squeezed it hard. He returned the pressure. She wondered if he had been suffering as much as she had been. More than anything she wanted to be alone with him and distance herself from Tim's bizarre love life, Ken's rudeness, the vicar and his acolytes, and all the social machinery that clicked and whirred and ticked around them.

'Dan,' she said urgently, 'can we—'

'Dan!' Sharon called. 'Your Auntie Dilys said could you bring her something to eat.'

'I'm sorry,' he said, looking at Ruth regretfully. He hurried into the kitchen and Ruth was suddenly alone. Ellie materialised by her side and pulled her into the sitting room, switching on the light as she did so.

'The barman's tasty,' she said, 'but I think he might be gay. He's holding back. Dan's brother blushes every time I look at him. The only decent man here is your old dad.'

'I know,' laughed Ruth, and then remembered Dan. 'And Dan,' she said.

'Oh, and Dan. Are you enjoying yourself?'

'Yeah.'

'Yeah?' Ellie raised her eyebrows in mock surprise.

'Well, as much as can be expected. The two families meet. Like the *Titanic* and the iceberg.'

'That's my girl,' said Ellie. 'It's not too late, you know. Call it off.'

'Call it off?'

'While you still can. Do you really want all this?' She gestured at the Georgian-style sitting room they were in, with its chintzy furniture and badly painted portrait of the Blake family. 'It's Dan you want. So have him. Move in with him if you must, but why tempt fate?'

'I want to make a commitment,' Ruth said mulishly, but her words sounded like jargon to her.

'Why?'

'I love him.'

'Well, love him, then. Only don't get married. Marriage is a complication you can do without.'

Ruth ignored the comment. Ellie was talking about her own situation – it would be much less complicated for Ellie if Adam were not married.

'Marriage is OK,' Ruth said. 'It's the wedding thing which is a pain. I just need to be alone with Dan. Then it'll be all right again.'

'So it's not all right?'

'It *is* all right.'

Just then the tinny notes of the cancan struck up from inside Ellie's handbag.

'My mobile,' she said unnecessarily. Ruth listened to Ellie's one-sided conversation.

'Oh, hi . . . I'm in York, actually. At a party . . . Yes, me too . . . Yes, a lot . . . An hour and a half. Shit! I've been drinking. I'm not safe to drive . . . You'll come and get me? OK, do that. It's a big house called the Hollies, near the racecourse . . .'

Ruth tried not to listen to any more. For all Ellie's flippancy with men, Adam only had to call for her and she was at his side. Ruth was conscious, too, that she felt as if Ellie was deserting her. She tried, and possibly failed, to look pleased for Ellie when she came off the phone.

'It was Adam. He said he can't stand not being with me any longer. His wife's staying with her mother. We can have the night together. He said he's learned that it's me he wants. Well, I could have told him that weeks ago. You don't mind me leaving, do you? It's not for another hour or so at any rate.' Ellie flung her arms round Ruth and hugged her. Ruth was surprised at how hot she felt.

'Shall we go and eat?' Ruth asked her.

'Food? My appetite's vanished. But I'll escort you into the kitchen, my dear. He loves me, he loves me not. He loves me!'

Chapter Twelve

Ruth had to admit the food was good. Her enjoyment of it was only marred by the fact that she and Ellie were collared by Heather's buck-toothed friend who, having established that Ellie wasn't Jewish, proceeded to regale them with the details of the arrangements for the Christmas craft fair in the church hall. Ellie's attempt to distract her by asking what she did for a living elicited the potentially interesting information that she was a retired police officer, but with steely determination she frog-marched them back to the problems with the white elephant stall. Deciding to leave Ellie to it, Ruth excused herself in order to sample the chocolate mousse. This was Heather's own concoction and was lying in state in the kitchen.

She noticed on her way back to the kitchen that her parents were sitting together and alone. For all the Blake hospitality, Sylvie and Ivan had been left stranded. Did the Blakes consider they weren't worth the effort? Ruth scanned the room for Heather and Ken and found Heather giving some instructions to the barman, while Ken and the vicar were standing by the bookcase deep in conversation. Sharon and Rachel were giggling together by the piano, Tim was eating alone, and Dan was entertaining Renie and Great-Aunt Dilys. The families had met, mingled, then separated again like oil and water. Ruth didn't know whether to be sad or angry.

The kitchen was deserted now, so Ruth spooned a great dollop of chocolate mousse into a cut-glass dish, parked herself on a kitchen chair and ate. She wondered whether she ought not to have tried harder to get her family to mix with Dan's, but then reflected that it would have been a wasted attempt. She might be marrying Dan but that didn't mean their families had to tie the knot as well. The Collinses and the Blakes had nothing in common. She knew she should be philo-sophical about this and not mind too much, but she did mind. She was in love, and wanted everyone else to love each other too. She helped herself to some more chocolate mousse. If only her mother hadn't had too much to drink, if only Heather would relax from her role of the perfect hostess. If only—'

A figure appeared at the door.

'Dan!' she cried, delighted and relieved. She put down her mousse, no longer hungry. He came to her and they kissed. Dan led her into the utility room and closed the door. There they kissed again more urgently and Ruth felt her anxieties slowly dissolving.

'Having a good time?' he asked her, playing with her hair.

'Well, not exactly,' Ruth confessed. 'It's all a bit of a strain. Families and all that.'

'I know,' he said. 'But it doesn't really matter. Anyway, I think your parents are enjoying themselves.'

'Are they?'

'Of course they are. My mother's really pushed the boat out for them.' He kissed her gently on the lips. 'Everyone's having a great time.' He ran his hands down her body and she clung more tightly to him.

'I just feel,' she murmured, 'that nobody's got much in common.'

'It might seem like that on the surface. Sure, there are differences. I think everyone's trying too hard to please each other, that's all. In some ways our parents are very alike.'

'What?'

'They're loving parents, they're excited about the wedding, they're shy of each other, wanting to create a good impression.'

'I know, but it still isn't working.'

'I don't get you.'

Ruth felt impelled to explain herself. She ought to tell Dan everything she was feeling. He was her fiancé, after all. It was natural to have doubts and fears as well as hopes and dreams.

'It's – like – if our families are so different – and they are different and you know it – then what about us? We won't grow apart, will we?'

'No. We'll grow more like each other. Married couples always do.'

'Yeah, maybe. And that's not all. Sometimes I feel I'm not good enough for you.'

'I'm the one who's not good enough for you. Don't be so negative. Come here and I'll make you feel better.'

He kissed her tenderly. Ruth knew he meant well, and had to be satisfied with that. Like a blanket, his kiss stifled the flames of her discontent. Perhaps it was best that way. Some things were better left unsaid. Of course there were social differences between her and Dan, but they had been swallowed up in the one exciting and unforgettable difference that he was male and she was female. Now things were settling, she was beginning to be aware of their secondary differences. Their relationship was simply entering a more mature level. That was all. She began to kiss him back with more fervour.

'You think too much,' he said breaking away to kiss her ear. 'You worry too much. Relax.'

'You're analysing me,' she said playfully. 'What is this? I'm the psychologist.'

'No, I'll be the psychologist tonight. You do worry too much. It's because you're the oldest child and you feel responsible for your parents, but they're quite capable of looking after themselves. Just separate yourself from them. Be with me.'

Ruth shut her eyes to the sight of Heather's washing machine and spin dryer and the basket of jeans and shirts and the red woollen socks on top of it and gave herself to Dan. He was wiser than she thought.

'Hey,' he said, after a time. 'We'd better be getting back. I think my father's hoping to give some kind of speech. We don't want to miss that.'

'Yes we do,' she said, kissing him again, her hands cupping his bottom and pulling him to her.

He freed himself and kissed her forehead. 'We have to be there. We're an engaged couple. We're part of the establishment.' He smiled at her, teasingly.

'No!' she said suddenly. 'Let's do a runner! We can sneak out the back door, drive off somewhere and make love in the car.'

He laughed at her. 'Not tonight,' he said. 'Come on, Mrs Blake-to-be. Enough of your lurid sexual fantasies. Duty calls.'

She allowed herself to be led by the hand out of the utility room. Mrs Blake. Hadn't Dan remembered that she wanted to hang on to her maiden name, at least at work? She ought to remind him at some point. But not now. All she wanted was to feel close to him again, to be part of him. She hated any kind of disagreement with him and boasted to her friends that they had never argued. She got some kind of kick out of being consciously submissive sometimes; there was a strange satisfaction in letting him have his own way. She had only one request now.

'Can I just pop upstairs? Comfort break!'

'Go on, then,' he said, and his eyes lingered on her as she ran lightly up the stairs.

In the bathroom, she rationalised her feelings still further. This ability to analyse and blow fears away by the force of reason was one of Ruth's main gifts. Her doubts and discomforts came from a rooted inadequacy. She decided it was her old enemy, low self-esteem. It was why she was so driven to do well at work, why she wanted to impress people, why she was such a perfectionist. In her quest for perfection, she had wanted too much from the party. Of course her parents were bound to feel ill at ease, there were bound to be social awkwardnesses. She had over-interpreted them. She must not be so harsh on people. She must expect less.

But why should you expect less? came a voice. Ellie's voice? *He didn't understand what you were talking about in the utility room. He thought it was all right, when it was all wrong. He didn't know how you felt.*

Then it's my responsibility, Ruth thought, to make my feelings clear. Or perhaps not. Perhaps things are best left as they are. She laughed as she washed her hands. He was right, she worried too much. She was lucky to have him. He was too good for her, that was the only problem. Unthinking she took a rose-shaped towel, dried her hands, and put the towel in the cupboard. She noticed there were two others there. At least she was getting something right.

'And there wasn't even a towel to dry your hands in the bathroom,' Sylvie said to Linda, taking another sip of tea. 'So posh, and they didn't even have that.'

Linda shook her head in amazement. It was the interval in their class on *Howard's End*, and the two women had settled down together in a corner to catch up. The rest of the group had dispersed around the room, and Suzie had gone off somewhere to feed Phoebe. Their easy chairs were comfortable, and Sylvie had to confess to herself that she enjoyed these little chats with Linda as much as the class itself. Especially tonight, when she had so much to tell her. Linda was always an excellent audience.

'And believe me, I'm not the drinking type. Only at weddings and *simchas*. But for the first time in my life I felt I needed a drink. Talk about feeling like a fish out of water. One thing I do have to say, they'd bought in good quality champagne. They're not short of a penny or two. There was no expense spared. They even had their own barman. The whole thing must have cost a packet.'

'If you have the money, you might as well spend it.'

'Granted. But could I think of anything to say to his mother? I could not. A very nice lady, I'm sure, but . . .' Sylvie's voice trailed away. She remembered Heather's voice like the tinkle of china, her immaculate grooming, her air of false intimacy, and didn't know how to convey all that to Linda in one word. 'And as for the father!'

'Not your type.'

'Not my type.'

Each woman reached for her cup of tea and took another sip. Then they put their cups down and re-crossed their legs.

'Poor old Ivan – Dan's father lectured him for half an hour.'

'Maybe he was nervous too.'

'Nervous? You should have heard his speech. Twenty-five minutes! Talk about liking the sound of your own voice. Ivan began to nod off.'

Linda laughed, and Sylvie laughed too. She reflected that now, at a distance of five days, the whole evening seemed funny, and she rather enjoyed reliving it and milking it for its entertainment value. At the time, it was anything but entertaining. All the forced social intercourse and effort to say and do the right thing had been torture for her. Hating herself for her own inadequacy, she had been in a foul mood all the way home, screaming at the girls, nagging Ivan and showing scant patience with her own mother. Not that Renie had had such a wonderful time. She couldn't stand the old lady they'd parked her next to. She bolted her food, Renie complained, and it kept repeating on her. Linda interrupted her thoughts.

'Did your daughter enjoy herself?'

'My daughter? Which – oh, you mean Ruth! Ruth? She

lapped it up.' Sylvie recalled her face, flushed with excitement at the beginning, chatting to Heather's friends, and blushing with pleasure at Ken's speech. 'My Ruth loves being made a fuss of,' she added.

Again both women lifted their cups and each drained the contents.

'She's a funny girl, our Ruth,' Sylvie went on. 'She's always running away from herself.'

'Running away from herself? What do you mean?'

'She always has to be someone different. Someone better. At her fiancé's house she's in her element. Sometimes I think we're not good enough for her.'

'That's normal. All kids are like that. Take my Suzie. She had me as an example, so what does she do? Works harder than anyone else at the comprehensive, goes to university, and even gets a postgraduate degree.'

Sylvie picked up Linda's pride, and smiled. 'And my Ruth the clinical psychologist.'

The women enjoyed a moment of rapport as they reflected on their daughters' achievements, which were, in a sense, their achievements. Sylvie felt that her narrative had reached its natural conclusion, so she was not at all put out when Linda changed the subject.

'I'm having my roots touched up tomorrow,' she said.

'They don't look as if they need doing.'

'Ah, but I've got to look my best this weekend as he's coming over.' She threw a slight emphasis on the word, 'he'.

Sylvie was immediately curious. 'Is he? Haven't you seen him for a bit, then?'

'Two or three weeks ago. He comes over when he can.'

'So you don't see him regularly?'

'He's otherwise engaged,' Linda laughed.

So he was married. Trust Linda to have a married lover. Sylvie was surprised more at her own reaction; she was titillated rather than shocked. In her old age she was growing broad-minded. Maybe all this study of literature was having some kind of an effect on her.

'Do you mind?' Sylvie asked. 'Not having him to yourself?'

'Oh no! In some ways I prefer it like that. It fans the flames. Lucky it's one of Suzie's weekends away.'

'Does she know you've got a lover?'

'Oh, yes. Like mother, like daughter. We both have a fella. In that respect, she's like me.'

Was her boyfriend married too? Sylvie wondered. She had to admit she did feel a little shocked now. She supposed it was true that these things ran in families. Now, she and Ruth were the marrying types. Looking back, she could see that her choice of Ivan as husband was a wise one. He was faithfulness personified. And she could never imagine herself wanting to have a fling, not at her age, and she had never wanted one previously. Life was easier like that. She didn't particularly envy Linda. She'd always valued security and affection rather than the roller-coaster that illicit passion brought. Ruth, she presumed, was the same. Hence her choice of Dan. He was a nice boy and would offer her just the same kind of marriage that she had: safe, enduring, impervious to storms and hardship. For all the Blakes' airs and graces, Sylvie recognised in Dan the sort of bloke who'd stand by you, who'd make a woman the centre of his world. Suddenly Sylvie began to reconcile herself to the match. She turned her mind back to Linda. She wanted to hear more about Linda's lover.

'So tell me about your fella,' she said. 'Have you been seeing him a long time?'

'On and off,' said Linda, 'for over twenty-five years. A local lad. Came from Hyde originally but they moved to Sheffield. Sheffield was where I caught up with him. I was doing some cleaning at the time and—'

'Are you ready?' Suzie said, calling her class to attention. 'Tea break's over now. I want to carry on looking at what Leonard Bast represents in the novel.'

Sylvie could have cursed her, interrupting them just as things were getting interesting. She had broken the spell. Despite what people thought, women didn't speak that easily about their personal lives to each other, especially at their age, and Sylvie knew there was no guarantee that Linda would bring up the subject again. Oh well, she would just have to use her imagination. It pleased her to think of Linda and her lover, although she did admit to feeling slightly uneasy about the wife in this love triangle. Still, for all she knew, the wife could be a cow. Women weren't always angels.

Suzie was explaining who Ruskin was, and Sylvie decided he sounded rather boring. She sneaked a glance at Linda and could immediately see that a man would find her attractive. Fifty-two was no age. Sylvie felt that Linda's escapades lent a lustre to her life; at fifty-two, you weren't past it. She thought briefly of herself and Ivan and allowed herself a quiet smile. It was true, she wasn't past it. She was not in the habit of thinking too much about matters she considered private, and she and Ivan had a very nice private life, thank you very much.

The trouble with today's society was that sex was everywhere except where it should be.

She knew she was a bit of a prude, but what was wrong with that? OK, so she'd chickened out of telling the girls the facts of life, but at least she gave them books to read. It was more than most mothers would do. She let them buy the sort of magazines that filled in the details, and watched all of her daughters meet and go out with boys, and appear perfectly normal. And now Ruth was getting married, and she guessed she was sleeping with Dan, but Sylvie didn't want to know about that either. That was Ruth's business As long as she was happy, it stayed her business.

And she was happy, there was no doubt about that. Being engaged was one of the best times in a woman's life. Everything to look forward to. So what if Dan wasn't Jewish? The children would be Jewish, Sylvie told herself. And with that comforting thought she brought her attention back to Leonard Bast and his umbrella.

Chapter Thirteen

The sun had made a feeble attempt to shine all day, but it was now fading away in a burst of glory, like an opera diva dying of consumption. Or so Ruth thought as she turned into the car park at Regency Court.

Spring seemed a long time coming. There had been snow in the first half of February, and even now there was a bitterness in the air. Despite that, the first few crocuses were beginning to show their heads, dubious little dots of lilac and yellow and white assembled on roundabouts and on verges. First crocuses, then daffodils in March, and after March it was April, and after April it was May, and in May was the wedding.

The forthcoming wedding was a huge magnet, controlling everything. Soon Ruth would have to spring-clean her flat, prior to leaving it forever. She and Dan were spending nearly every weekend now looking at furniture, testing beds, making plans, listening to Sylvie on the phone explaining who had accepted invitations and who had declined, what reasons they had given, whether those reasons were convincing or not, and why she was pleased they weren't turning up if they had that attitude. Ruth had visited John Lewis's to set up a wedding list, and felt greedy and manipulative in doing so, but Dan had patiently explained that otherwise everyone would buy them the same things and they might end up with a cupboard full of casserole dishes. She had been buying all the brides' magazines on the market, and read them obsessively over breakfast and in the bath, looking for the elusive secret that would make her wedding and married life proceed flawlessly.

So Ruth unlocked her front door, ever conscious of the wedding. It was no longer something she and Dan had chosen out of their own free wills, but a rite of passage established by society to test them. If they could survive the wedding, they could survive anything. Ruth felt as if the wedding defined her, at least in the opinion of friends and colleagues, who often asked her how the arrangements were getting on, but then she saw their eyes glaze over as she began to answer them. She was Ruth Collins, bride-to-be, and not herself at all.

Christmas had offered a brief respite. She'd spent Christmas and Boxing Day with the Blakes at Dan's request. A festive garland hung on the door; a Christmas tree stood massive and proud in the front room, tastefully decorated with white fairy lights and immaculate bows in red and gold, with matching baubles. Beautifully wrapped presents were exchanged in the morning, books for Ken, a leather document case for Tim and a hydroponics kit for Heather.

Ruth had bought Dan a watch and placed it on his wrist herself. He gave her a silver pendant with two tiny silver hands clutching a turquoise crystal. She was thrilled and admired it for ages, yet restrained herself from too great a show of delight because this exchange of presents seemed to be only a Christmas peripheral. In her family, where they celebrated Christmas guiltily, behind closed doors, the presents and the food were everything. There was inevitably a problem with the presents. Someone was bound to look slightly disappointed when receiving a gift, and the giver would be hurt, would accuse the recipient of ingratitude, and this was the prelude to the first of the Christmas arguments. At the Blakes', the gifts were a pleasant formality rather than a coded statement of what the present-giver thought of the present-getter. This was a relief.

With her parents, Christmas dinner was always later than planned because the oven was playing up and the turkey was undercooked, or because Sylvie threw a wobbler to highlight the fact that no one was helping her. In York, despite Heather's trip to church, Christmas dinner appeared at the scheduled time, and Ruth was interested to observe there was less of it than at her house. Chez Collins, the table groaned with the weight of turkey, stuffing (two kinds, including the recipe from the Florence Greenberg book of kosher cookery), three kinds of vegetables, roast and boiled potatoes, Tesco's Christmas pudding, a Yule log, apple strudel for Ivan, peanuts, chocolates, and mince pies from the Feinstein bakery round the corner. Ruth had always assumed this was how Christians celebrated Christmas too – what was a religious festival for if you couldn't overeat?

It fascinated her to see how moderate Heather's preparations were. There was sufficient food, all the trimmings, but everyone declined seconds and so Ruth did too, wanting to fit in, though she eyed the stuffing regretfully. However, the Blakes knew how to drink. From midday she had been regaled with offerings from the drinks cabinet, and by half past four she ached to sleep it all off. In the end she could fight the desire no longer and nodded off in front of the television, waking to find herself alone, and felt embarrassed that she had caused everyone to vacate the sitting room. In the evening they had a jolly game of Pictionary, and drank some more

She got back to Manchester just in time for the last night of *Chanukah*, Dan went with her. Lighting the menorah was one of the few rituals her mother still followed, or attempted to follow. She never managed the full eight nights. She started on the second because she didn't know the exact date the festival began, or forgot to buy the candles, then skipped the evenings she was out, but always caught up by the last night. Ruth had invited Dan to watch her mother recite the blessings. The family gathered round the kitchen table, and a rather flustered Sylvie assembled menorah, candles and matches and a tray to catch the dripping wax. Embarrassment making her clumsy, she snapped two of the candles as she was trying to jam them into the menorah.

'Jesus!' she cursed. 'They don't make these as well as they used to.'

Then she mumbled some Hebrew quickly over them, realised she'd said the Sabbath blessing by mistake, backtracked and completed the prayer with no further mishaps. Ruth saw that Dan was fascinated and wanted to impress him further. His dawning interest in Judaism both amused and flattered her.

'Let's sing *Mo 'oz Tsur*,' she declared.

Ruth loved the tune of this traditional *Chanukah* song and waited for her parents to start it off.

'You sing it,' Sylvie said to her.

'I don't know all the words.'

'Has anyone got a *siddur*?' Ivan suggested.

Sylvie went to look on the bookshelves, but by the time she found the prayer book, and Ivan had located the song, Sharon and Rachel had drifted away, everyone was overcome with self-consciousness, and Sylvie protested she'd forgotten all the Hebrew she'd ever learnt. Ruth hummed the tune for Dan's benefit, then Sharon turned on the TV as there was a Johnny Depp film she'd been looking forward to all day.

Occasionally Ruth glanced at the candles and thought they looked pretty. She spent the rest of the evening working her way through the Christmas dinner leftovers, and chatting to Sylvie and Ivan. She noticed that Dan seemed increasingly at home. She accused him of that when they popped into Manchester one evening for a drink.

'You get on well with my parents, don't you? But they're nothing like your parents.'

'Well, there's your reason. There's none of that keeping up appearances with your family.'

'You can say that again.'

'In your family, it's like everyone has permission to be themselves. It feels natural. I love my parents, of course, but they have this thing about propriety. I reckon it was the effect of Dad's job. Remember, I was brought up by two teachers. I kind of wish my family had been more like yours.'

'You cannot be serious.'

'Sometimes I worry you find me too straight.'

'Too straight?'

'I don't know why I said that.' Dan finished his drink. 'Sometimes it comes over me what a big step we're taking. You don't feel jealous of Sharon, do you, still free and clubbing it?'

'Dan! Don't be so ridiculous! I'm nothing like Sharon!'

Ruth had been quite put out. His comment had shaken her. How could he think for one moment that she wasn't anything but perfectly happy with what she had chosen. In fact, as she grew older she found it a relief not to have to make the effort to go out and be seen. Funny how people changed. At twenty-five she'd finished with all that man-chasing, not that she was so bad at it in her time. If she did sometimes feel a twinge of envy at Sharon's social life, she understood it was because transitions were always difficult and uneven, and it wasn't surprising that, like Lot's wife, she should occasionally look back from where she had come.

The best part of the holiday had been the time she'd spent alone with Dan. They'd decided to go up to the Lakes and see the New Year in there. They managed to find and rent a charming slate cottage just outside Keswick, with two bedrooms, a cosy front room with a fire that roared when Dan could get it to roar, and a compact little kitchen. They'd bought in provisions and Ruth amused herself trying to cook tempting meals for Dan from the River Café cookbook that Heather had bought her as a little Christmas extra. It was fun making a fuss of him, getting everything just right, and showing him what a wonderful housekeeper she could be, if she made the effort. She gave a five-star performance as the ideal wife, and Dan excelled as the ideal husband. They washed up and tidied round together.

Best of all was the walking. Dan had made her buy a proper pair of boots and he planned a major excursion which took them up into the mountains. He was in his element, picking his way among rock-strewn paths, encouraging her on, and pointing out the surrounding peaks from where they stood. He seemed so much part of the landscape, of England. He had never seemed more desirable to her. As excited as a little boy, he explained the geography of the area, and amused her with anecdotes about Arthur Wainwright, the Lakes' most eminent walker. They sat down and pic-nicked, and laughed, and talked. The future was theirs, and everything about and beyond belonged especially to them. Ruth decided she could grow to like walking, but drew the line when Dan enthused about a coast-to-coast expedition. 'I tell you what,' she said to him. 'Take my father, since you seem to get on so well.'

'No, it's you I want,' he'd said, and kissed her right in front of two backpackers who had suddenly come into view.

During that week Ruth realised what her marriage might be like. She sensed the companionship which would be hers, and the richness of sharing a life rather than leading one. The weather was uncharacteristically sunny and she looked up nearly every day into ice-blue skies. She felt she could have carried on just as they were indefinitely.

Then the skies darkened and the rain came. The holiday was over and the real world reasserted itself. Dan began to work away from home with ever increasing frequency. Sometimes it was only for a night or two, and once she did manage to join him in a hotel in Doncaster. On other occasions he could be called away for much longer. She had to adjust to being with him for a while, stocking up on him, and then being alone. The effort of the constant adjustment drained her. Ellie was wrapped up with Adam, and so Ruth spent the evenings watching soaps and racy drama on Channel 4. This week Dan was in Bristol, and life felt barren.

She was due to go with Ellie to Adam's preview exhibition tonight. In his spare time, Ellie's boss and lover was a photographer of some standing. He took artistic shots of industrial landscapes, had won a number of prizes and had exhibited on more than one occasion. This latest exhibition was in Leeds City Art Gallery. There had been lots of publicity, and Adam's name was on everyone's lips. Reading about him in the *Yorkshire Evening Post* was decidedly odd. Ruth couldn't help but recall all the things that Ellie had told her about him, from his difficult relationship with his wife through to his love of role-play in the bedroom. From reading the paper you would think that Adam Eastwood had it all; in fact he had more than he could handle.

Since PR was Adam's speciality, he'd made sure that the preview was going to be a substantial affair. He'd invited press, some local VIPs and there had even been rumours of a BBC television crew who wanted to film the event for the local news. His guest list included his colleagues, his friends in the art and photography worlds, his daughters, his wife, and Ellie. At first she and Adam had both agreed that she had better not be there; then Ellie had felt second-rate at being excluded, and pointed out that many of his best shots in the exhibition were her ideas. They discussed the issue interminably. Although they both concluded it would be agony to be together and yet not be together, they decided to opt for the agony, Ellie had told Ruth.

Ruth assembled a cheese sandwich and glanced at the clock. The do was starting early, at seven, presumably so people could go on straight from work. She had opted to come home first and change. She'd seen some difficult clients today and felt she needed to make a transition from work to leisure. Adam's preview seemed a world away from her clients with multiple personality disorder. Or perhaps not. She poured herself some Diet Coke and downed it swiftly, and made her way to the bathroom.

She was not particularly looking forward to the preview. Her clients' problems had left her feeling a little contemptuous of the arty set to which Adam, and even Ellie, belonged. The fact that Dan was away also affected her. In addition, she cringed at the thought of seeing Ellie and Adam and his wife all together. It was a difficult and horrible situation. Sometimes she was all set to tell Ellie in no uncertain terms to extricate herself from the whole silly mess, and find herself a man she could have all to herself. At other times she recognised that Ellie had chosen, quite deliberately, to have these complications; it meant she never had to make a commitment, and she could relish the drama of an illicit union. With herself and Dan the climate was mostly temperate; Adam and Ellie were either lost in the tundra or battling through jungle heat. It was never boring. While she and Dan . . .

She stepped into the shower. It was funny how when you knew somebody really well you could never bring their face to mind. She couldn't visualise Dan now, and so instead she tried to imagine what he was doing. She guessed he would still be at work, bent over a desk, or glued to a computer screen. Poor old Dan. She was having all the fun. No, she wasn't. She would far rather be there in the office with him, then go back to his hotel for a comfortable night in. The effort of the preview seemed too much. She would have to make conversation, ooh and ah at the photographs, mix and mingle. Quite frankly, she had lost the knack of doing all that since meeting Dan again.

She scrubbed herself and wondered what she should wear. It was the sort of occasion where almost anything would go as long as it was different – outrageous, even. One could get away with designer wear, she supposed. Ruth had a smart work wardrobe culled from Next and Jigsaw, quite a bit of casual wear from French Connection, and some dresses she wore for parties. Most of them were dedicated evening wear and wouldn't do for tonight. She slipped into her towelling dressing gown and went examine the contents of her wardrobe. Just as she thought. The only thing that would do would be the old standby, the little black dress. Its scoop neckline was a shade revealing and it was just an inch shorter than it should be. It was both demure and wicked and Ruth was rather fond of it. It would do admirably.

She sat at her dressing table and quickly applied some make-up. It seemed pointless without Dan there but then she reminded herself of the truth about make-up, which was that women wore it for tribal reasons. Through the amount of make-up they wore, women sent out signals to other women. There was a time when successful women at work wore none; these days you had to wear just a little to be taken seriously. So Ruth blacked her eyes with kohl, put on a coat or two of mascara, and chose a lipstick with a metallic tint. She wiggled into her dress, decided she would be cold if she wore just that, so teamed it up with a black three-quarter length jacket. Deciding she looked a bit severe, she allowed her hair to flow loose. She examined the finished product in the mirror, and was pleased with what she saw. She wondered whether to wear the earrings Heather and Ken had given her, but rejected them in favour of some long Turkish ones Ellie had brought her back from a holiday in Istanbul. Round her neck she put Dan's pendant.

Now she was in her finery the preview seemed a more attractive proposition. Since Dan was away, it was a shame just to sit at home every evening. It was important to have a life of one's own. And the evening would be a pleasant escape from the pressure of the wedding. By the telephone she had scrawled the number of the hotel Dan was staying in, and on impulse she rang it, in case he was back in his room. The receptionist answered but confirmed he hadn't arrived back. Thwarted, she decided to try the office. She was too late; her call was answered by an answering machine. For a moment she felt bereft; then she decided that Dan had probably been taken out for dinner and was enjoying himself. An expression of her mother's came to mind: what's sauce for the goose is sauce for the gander. She would enjoy herself too. She sprayed on some Issey Miyake perfume Dan had bought her, then found her coat.

Chapter Fourteen

It was a chilly evening, and the sky was a velvety, luminescent blue as Ruth walked briskly down the Headrow in the direction of Leeds City Art Gallery. It was quite a trek from Vicar Lane, but Ruth had decided on the bus rather than her car as she guessed she would be drinking. Her father had instilled in her from an early age that alcohol and driving was always a bad idea. The fresh air was invigorating and Ruth began to feel a faint stirring of interest in Adam's exhibition. For all she knew, his photographs might even be good. Or Ellie might introduce her to some interesting people, people who didn't work in hospitals. An interlude from her own life might be just the tonic she needed.

Both the town hall and art gallery were floodlit, and seemed all the more imposing as she crossed over the road towards them. The cream-coloured stone softened the grand, square outlines of the buildings, and contrasted favourably, Ruth thought, with the Gothic extravaganza that was Manchester town hall. Self-important civic buildings always made her feel like laughing; it was the incongruity of all that pretension and pomposity and the ordinary-sized people who inhabited them.

The art gallery was the smaller of the two buildings, and was hip to haunch with the Henry Moore Institute. Both interiors were lit up as it was Wednesday, late opening night. Ruth glanced at the black marble figure of a reclining woman, with one thigh preposterously larger than the other, the doorkeeper and guardian of the art gallery. In the foyer she was greeted by a Rodin, a male figure cast in bronze, his shapely beauty frozen in time forever.

Ruth studied him for a moment, appreciating the freedom of just being able to stop and look. She remembered how much she used to enjoy visits to galleries and recalled going with Dan to the permanent Hockney exhibition at Saltaire, and the more avant-garde shows at Manchester's Cornerhouse. Since their engagement they had stopped going to things like that, and it was a shame. Ruth had no training in art but loved the way that pictures slowed you down and made you see things you would otherwise pass over. Art gave you eyes.

She paused in the gift shop, attracted by the postcards and books, then began to look for Adam's exhibition. A notice directed her through the gallery, past the double staircase to the rear. There, on the right, was the room where the preview was being held. A commissionaire stood at the door, and Ruth fished in her handbag for her invitation. The commissionaire glanced at it, nodded, smiled, and let her through.

The room was a stark white gallery, with photographs displayed along two walls and on a panel in the centre. Groups of people were examining the photographs, or talking animatedly in the centre of the room. Ruth quickly surveyed the faces and saw with disappointment that Ellie was not among them. Slowly she moved through the guests and made her way to the bottom of the gallery where a doorway led to a cafe. Here was a table laid out with glasses of champagne, but still no sign of Ellie. Feeling a little uneasy, Ruth debated what to do. The best thing, she decided, was to pass the time by looking at the photographs, then check for Ellie again, and if all else failed, ask someone. But who? She would face that problem later. She selected a large glass from the table and took it with her back to the gallery, hoping the alcohol would sharpen her appreciation of the photos.

This first exhibit she looked at was a portrait of the underside of a bridge over a canal, wet bricks glistening, debris on the bank. The shot was taken in black and white and depended for its effect on the interplay of shadow and light. It was quite good, Ruth thought. It had a certain immediacy. She sipped at her champagne, then moved on to the next shot.

This was of a landscape, a moorland hill topped by a row of tiny, blackened cottages, with lines of washing hung out in the street. A woman was pegging a sheet out, and the move-ment of her hair and of the sheet gave the impression of a strong wind. It was a cold, rather depressing shot, and there was something forlorn in the stance of the woman, although she was only an incidental figure. Ruth read the notes by the photograph which talked about the rape of the land by the early industrialists, and the deliberate contrast of the undulat-ing, feminine hills and the harsh line of jagged workers' build-ings like a serrated razor's edge cutting into the fecundity . . . *Oy vey!* she almost said. She had always had a fairly efficient crap detector and it was sending out loud signals now. Clearly Adam was not averse to snapping that poor woman hanging out the washing for his own artistic purposes, which was just as bad as nineteenth-century mill-owners snapping up cheap labour. Had he bothered to ask her permission before taking the shot? Probably not. Just as he hadn't bothered to ask his wife's permission before taking Ellie. What did it matter whether it was art or sex or business? Adam was as exploitative as the old Yorkshire industrialists.

She looked around her. There seemed to be even more people, all clutching glasses, all familiar with each other. Ellie had still not arrived. Ruth took in affluent-looking men with flamboyant ties and witty socks, women with masses of hair pinned up with deliberate carelessness and people of her own age, serious, intense, underdressed in denims and down-at-heel trainers, clearly stating their contempt for material values. Yet they had style, and the older guests had style, vast quantities of style and self-assurance, bulk-bought and piled high. Ruth glanced down at her simple black dress, was conscious of her friendless state, and felt most decidedly out of place, as if she had no right to be there, plain old Ruth Collins from Crumpsall, among all these arty movers and shakers.

Her sense of dislocation subtly transmogrified itself into critical detachment. If she felt out of place, it wasn't her fault. She was real; here were images. Adam and his ilk were raiding working-class culture for so-called Art, impressing people who were self-created too. She looked around her again at the other guests and read their poses, then loathed and envied their *faux* self-possession. They knew nothing, she thought; they knew everything. Their unconventionality was in its way just as rule-bound as convention itself. One had to wear bright clothes, designer clothes, had to dress to be seen, had to express appreciation of photographs that were one step removed from holiday snaps.

'Ruth!' Ellie had materialised at her side, like a raft in front of a drowning man. They air-kissed in the prescribed manner.

'Have you just arrived?' Ruth asked her.

'No. I've been in the loo.'

Ruth realised Ellie looked rather red-eyed. 'Are you all right?' she asked anxiously.

'No. But I'm not going to let it show. I just can't stand watching him play happy families. Look. Here he comes now.'

Ruth drained her champagne, then very nonchalantly turned her head where Ellie had indicated. Adam was the distinguished-looking, tall man with a small goatee beard, in an Armani suit and black tie. Holding his hand was a small child in a flouncy, Laura Ashley-style dress. His daughter? The woman talking to him wore a red satin blouse and a long, black skirt which sat unevenly on her hips. She looked tired and her short hair was slightly dishevelled. Ruth could see she was a good-looking woman, with strong features and large, expressive eyes, but she seemed strained and tense. Did she know about Ellie?

'They don't look very happy to me,' Ruth remarked.

'His daughter Florence isn't feeling well. She's been clingy with him all evening.'

At that point Adam picked the child up and held her to him. Ruth watched Ellie flinch and she suffered with her.

'He hasn't slept with his wife for months,' Ellie said. 'He doesn't find her attractive any more.'

Ruth could think of nothing to say in reply.

'I can't stand this,' Ellie said. 'Let s go and get another drink.'

Ruth followed her into the cafe and they both took another glass of champagne. Ellie smiled at some people and began to regain her composure. They re-entered the gallery and stood in front of a photo of a line of pylons leading into an infinite distance.

'He'll never leave her, will he?' Ellie's face had a haunted look.

Ruth shrugged. 'I can't say.' She couldn't stand seeing Ellie look so bleak. She simply had to cheer her up. 'But, hey, even if he did leave her, would you want him around you *all* the time? Just think. You're with him from nine to five every day anyway, and if he lived with you you'd have no rest from him. Then once he's installed in your place, he'll come over like a proper husband and expect you to do all the wifey things like his washing and sewing on his buttons.'

Ellie managed a smile, and Ruth was encouraged.

'So there you'd be, thinking what to cook him for dinner and he'd come back to your flat and moan about his workload, whinge about the office, burp when he thinks you're out of earshot and leave the toilet seat up.'

Ellie laughed, then turned on her. 'You've changed your tune. You're the one who's supposed to be all for marriage.'

'Yes, but . . .' Ruth floundered for a moment. 'I'm all for marriage with Dan. Adam's older and a different generation to us. Men of his age might be feminists in theory but never in practice. Dan is a genuine New Man, the real thing.' As she said this she was dimly aware that she was lying. Dan would do anything for her, that much was true, but in the Lakes she had cooked and washed and made the beds, and he had appreciated it. The truth was his mother had spoiled him. He was used to domestic bliss. Could she keep it up? Domestic bliss was as alien to the Collinses as counting a rosary.

'Dan, Dan, the perfect man,' Ellie scoffed, restored to her usual cynical self. 'You're right. I think I prefer Adam just as he is.'

Ruth glanced at him again and saw him pass his daughter to his wife, and straighten his suit. She saw him look longingly at Ellie, who was dressed simply in a cream cashmere polo-neck sweater and brown woollen trousers. She'd left her hair loose and had swept it to one side. Ruth thought she looked more gorgeous than ever. At that moment they were descended upon by two women of their own age.

'It *is* Ellie,' one of them said. She embraced her. 'How super to see you! We thought you might be here. Do you know, it's been six months since I've left the firm and it feels like years!'

'Ex-colleagues,' Ellie whispered. Ruth was enveloped in a fog of French perfume and found herself glancing down a Wonderbra-assisted cleavage.

'Adam is so talented,' the other woman said. 'He has . . .'

'Vision,' said the other. 'A super shot of the Cow and Calf Rocks. Oh my God! Have you seen who's just come in?' All heads turned, and Ruth recognised an actor connected with the West Yorkshire Playhouse. Did Adam know him? She was impressed.

'I saw him in *Hobson's Choice*,' the woman continued. 'It was super. Dare I go over and tell him how much I enjoyed it?'

Ruth watched, fascinated, as people drifted over to the actor. Only one or two ventured to speak to him; the others kept at a respectful distance, just giving him the occasional glance, ready to move in for the kill should the opportunity arise. Then a press photographer materialised, extricated the actor, and someone had fetched Adam. Time for the publicity shots. Adam and the actor stood together by a big blow-up shot of a mill chimney rearing up into a cloud-tossed sky. The phallic imagery was not lost on Ruth. The photographer took some pictures, then moved back and began to pull some more people into camera range. He selected Ellie and her two ex-colleagues, passing Ruth over. Her pride was momentarily wounded and she retreated to a safe distance, from where she watched Ellie sneak up to Adam, who looked a little flustered. She noticed the actor give Ellie an appreciative glance, as well he might. The flash went again. Photographs of photographs. Images of images. False, false.

Adam whispered something to Ellie, and her face immediately brightened. Ellie's friends approached her then, clearly begging for an intro to the actor. Ruth gave an inward shrug. She'd known the whole thing was not going to be her scene. She began to wonder how much longer she needed to stay before she could make her exit. Yet it was a shame. The champagne had made her feel potentially quite sociable, ready for an evening out, only not this sort of evening out.

She looked around the room again. It was fuller than ever with beautiful people. She felt rather claustrophobic. Everyone knew everybody else. Well, not quite everyone. There was a young man in creased leather trousers standing near a shot of a derelict mill, looking as detached as she felt. He was good-looking in a frowsty sort of way. He needed a shave, true, and his hair was a mess, but it was a welcome contrast to the plasticity around her. There was something about him that appealed to Ruth; he was almost the sort of man she would have been attracted to in the old days. Pictures at an exhibition, she reminded herself. Pictures at an exhibition. She smiled to herself, glanced at him for a final time, and to her consternation saw him looking at her. Immediately she moved off in Ellie's direction. In fact, she discovered Ellie was coming towards her.

'Guess what?' she said. 'She's gone. The kid had a temperature and had to go. Adam's got the mobile so he'll be in touch. But we're going on somewhere after this. I'm sorry. I feel I've let you down. Do you mind?'

'I was going to have an early night anyway,' Ruth said.

'I'm sad she's ill,' Ellie said, flushed. 'And I'll make sure he gets back early. But we need to talk.'

The painful cliché irked Ruth. Ellie was about to say more but another of her many acquaintances arrived, and Ruth felt herself being gently edged out of the ensuing conversation. Now, she realised, was the time to go. She took a last glance around the exhibition, then looked at her watch. It was only quarter to eight. She felt a little disappointed. It was very early to call it a night. Perhaps there was time to have a look around the rest of the gallery. The Henry Moore Institute would still be open and there were some interesting sculptures there.

She indicated to Ellie she was leaving and slipped out of the back of the gallery, finding herself in a corridor with glass-cased exhibits of tiny figures. She paused before moving on, attracted by what looked like a red marble pineapple, entitled 'Strange Fruit'. Guiltily she ran her hand over the surface of the marble, wanting to feel the undulations in her palm. It was cool to the touch, smooth hills and valleys

She looked at the figures behind the glass, admiring the intricacy of the work, yet wanting to find something more substantial, something life-sized. She walked on to the main sculpture gallery and found what she was searching for. Here were human figures captured in stone, in marble, in bronze. She stood for a while regarding Epstein's vision of maternity, a woman with a proud stone stomach and two symmetrical, threatening breasts. It said nothing to her. She glanced at four masks of men wincing in agony. She ascended a short flight of steps and looked up at the figure of a man hanging almost crucified on the wall, except there was no cross. He hung suspended, his body marked into sections like an animal's carcass about to be butchered. It was by Antony Gormley, the sculptor responsible for the Angel of the North. She observed the similarity, admired the workmanship, and yet failed to be moved. She looked down, and saw another black marble figure, a woman this time, prostrate on the plinth, her knees bent, arms akimbo, as if she was either in pain or attempting to relax, Ruth couldn't decide which. To resolve the issue, she stepped over to examine her face. She noticed then that the woman seemed to be pulling her own skin over her face – but, no, it wasn't her skin, it was a veil. She was pulling a veil over her face, distorting her features, dehumanising them, expressing an exquisite agony. 'The Veiled Venus', it was called. Like me, she thought, remembering her wedding dress.

'D'you like it?' came a voice. Ruth started, and turned to

discover the man she'd seen earlier, the man in leather trousers, smiling at her, seeming utterly at ease.

'Well, I . . .'

'Poor kid,' the man remarked. 'She doesn't look very comfortable.'

Ruth laughed now. There was something about this man's voice that was familiar to her, but she couldn't for the moment say why.

'I thought the veil was her skin at first. She looks like she's suffocating herself.'

'Yeah. You're right. Painful, isn't it?'

Ruth knew now. He had a Mancunian accent. He was from her neck of the woods. That was why she felt at home with him.

'I can't stand representations of women as victims,' Ruth went on, glad to have someone to share her thoughts with. 'That's what I don't like about this.'

'Have you seen the Epstein?' he asked. 'She's more powerful.' Together they walked to the lower gallery and Ruth took up position in front of the stone monolith.

'No. There's something . . . It's still a man's version of a woman.'

'So you prefer female sculptors?'

Ruth laughed again. She couldn't understand why she was laughing so much, and put it down to the champagne and her nervousness. 'To tell you the truth, I know sod all about sculpture. I can't even name any women sculptors. But I'm interested to learn.'

'Have you heard of Kathe Kollwitz?'

'No.'

'A German artist.'

'Oh, German.' She had the Jewish distrust of anything German.

'Yeah. I was in Berlin last week and saw her work. She was a painter too, and she lost a child in the war. I'll tell you what got to me. It was this figure she did, it was on the top floor of the museum, a figure of a mother protecting two children. She was, like, crouching down, and these two kids are surrounded by her, like she's protecting them from something, and you can't tell whether she's strong enough to do it. Yeah, that was good.' He looked serious for a moment, then he smiled at her.

Ruth was intrigued. He looked a scruff, a layabout, and yet here he was talking quite happily about being moved by art. She allowed herself to study his face for a moment and then that breathless, laughing feeling returned. His eyes were a deep brown, his features regular, his chin jutting. Yet his designer stubble was dated and his clothes looked at if he'd slept in them. He smelt of stale cigarettes. He was thin, too thin, wiry but fragile.

'Why were you in Berlin?' Ruth asked.

'It was partly a holiday, but also I'm working on a book. I'm a freelance photographer. My interest is architecture.' He laughed now. 'I did begin by studying architecture, but . . . Let's say I wasn't cut out for study. So I changed to a photography course, which was cool, but, yeah, what I want to do is get this book together about architecture and urban aspiration. Like how buildings reflect the way we see ourselves. In Berlin they're rebuilding like crazy. So I went to have a look. They've put a little dome on the Reichstag.' He laughed.

The word 'Reichstag' chilled Ruth, and she looked askance at her new friend. She'd better clear the air immediately.

'I'm Jewish,' she said, a little severely.

'Are you? Yeah, I suppose you look it.'

'That's why I think I'd never want to go to Berlin.'

'A pity. It's one of the world's great cities. The Berliners hated Hitler — the true Berliners, that is. He wanted to raze the place to the ground and rebuild in his image. No, Berlin's got nothing to do with Hitler. It's the city of the Bauhaus and Brecht and the Wall. And Christopher Isherwood. Have you seen *Cabaret*?'

Ruth had. She remembered half-longingly the sleazy decadence in the film. She looked at the man talking to her, and suddenly he became part of that decadence, slightly dangerous, slightly desirable, tempting and disgusting all at once.

'It was a good film,' she said, treading water, considering him.

'What's your name?' he asked her. There was a hoarse note to his voice; it rasped, not unattractively.

'Ruth,' she said.

'I'm Nick.'

The intimacy of first names exchanged, Ruth began to feel awkward. It occurred to her now that she might be being chatted up. Having been part of a couple for so long she had almost forgotten the rules. It was true he had not flirted with her, not overtly, but there was something in his manner that made her wary. The very fact that he had approached her, sought conversation, and asked her name was a prelude. The conversation had been impersonal, but that meant nothing. No; she had better mention her engaged status at the earliest opportunity.

'What are you doing here, Ruth?' Nick asked her.

'Oh, I was at the photography preview.'

'Adam Eastwood? Overrated. Industrial landscapes have been done to death.' His contempt for Adam pleased her.

'I tend to agree. I can't stand artists who use working-class culture to make statements about the bleakness of life while living amongst all their middle-class privileges.' Ruth was pleased to get that off her chest.

'Too right. You've certainly got something there.' He smiled at her, eye to eye. She looked down immediately. He continued talking. 'D'you come from round here?'

'I work in Leeds.' She thought of introducing the existence of Dan at this point, but decided that might sound awkward or even rude or presumptuous. *I work in Leeds but I'm engaged.* 'I work in Leeds but I come from Manchester.'

'I thought you did. Yeah, I'm from Manchester as well. Leeds is finished now. There's more investment going on in Manchester than anywhere else in the country. And more building too. I haven't been around for a bit, but I'm back now. I want to do research for my book. There's going to be a section on Manchester. Victorian stuff, and all the new build-ings.'

'So your book – is it like a thesis, or . . .'

'No, it's mainly photographs, looking at developing build-ing style, and its relationship with civic image. I'll probably end up publishing it myself.'

'So is that why you were invited to Adam's preview?'

Nick smiled. 'Who said I was invited? You're not going to tell on me, are you?'

'Oh, no!'

'Do you know Adam?'

Ruth reddened slightly. 'He's a friend of a friend. But I don't much care for him.'

'Good for you. Are you coming for a drink?'

Ruth was momentarily stunned. 'Er, no. I've got to be getting back.'

'Someone waiting for you at home?'

'No. I live alone. I mean – I'm engaged.'

'Congratulations,' Nick said. 'So are you coming for a drink?'

Ruth knew she was scarlet with embarrassment. Drowning in self-consciousness, she was trying to work out whether it would be OK to go out for a drink with him. His repeating the invitation proved, didn't it, that his suggestion was inno-cent – they were two expatriates with a shared point of view, that was all. Of course she would tell Dan. But then again perhaps it was better not to tell Dan, in case he got the wrong idea. Which meant that there was a wrong idea to get, and she shouldn't go at all. If she hesitated, she was lost. She observed herself hesitating. Meanwhile Nick stood at ease observing her. She noticed she was twisting her engagement ring.

'It's just that they'll be closing soon, Ruth.' He spoke her name caressingly, even proprietorially. This was all wrong.

'No. I'd better not,' she said.

'OK.' Nick didn't seem bothered. 'What do you do for a living?'

'I'm a clinical psychologist,' she said.

'Neat. Where are you living?'

'Chapel Allerton.'

'And where do you work?'

'I'm based at Chapel Allerton Hospital.'

'Don't know it. I'm staying with mates in Headingley, but I'm going back to Manchester tomorrow. I've got access to Longsight Baths. Have you been there?'

'No.' He made her feel ignorant.

'They were built at the turn of the century. It's a huge building. From the outside it looks like one of those late Victorian town halls. Inside there are three swimming pools, one for gentlemen, one for ladies, and another one for the workers.'

'How cheeky is that!' said Ruth, amused and horrified at the class distinction. They both laughed.

'I know. That was the Victorians for you. You should see the tiling on the walls – oriental emerald green – and the lido-style changing huts. There's a stained-glass window too, as impressive as in any cathedral. They're closed now – the pools are full of pigeon droppings – but we're campaigning to open the baths. You must come and have a look.'

'We'd like to.' Ruth felt it incumbent upon her to slip in the 'we' word.

'There are Turkish baths too and all sorts of weird contraptions like the aerotron, a sort of early sauna. I live near there.'

'Do you?'

'Yeah.' He put his hand in his pocket. 'Here's my card. If you change your mind about that drink.'

Ruth took it. 'Thank you.'

'And can I have your card?'

'Mine? Sorry, I don't have one.'

He gave her another card. 'Write your telephone number on the back of that.'

Ruth knew she ought to refuse. But on what grounds? *I'm sorry, I don't want to see you again?* That was rude. *I can't, I'm engaged.* Little Miss Prissy. *I don't have a telephone number.* Transparently ridiculous. Meanwhile he was waiting and observing her. This was getting sillier by the minute. She told herself he was a freelance journalist and therefore kept details of stray acquaintances in case they turned out useful. She was coming on like some repressed neurotic, thinking every man she met had designs on her. She took the biro he offered her and wrote on the back of his card, 'Ruth Collins, Chapel Allerton Hospital', and added her work number. He took the card back, glanced at it, and smiled.

She looked at her watch. 'My bus leaves soon.'

'I'll run you home,' he said. She looked up at him and their eyes met. He studied her inquiringly and she felt herself quake under his gaze. 'I wont bite,' he added.

'I know.'

'I like you, Ruth,' he said. 'I hope we meet again.' Then he turned on his heel and walked off.

Slowly Ruth began to breathe again. Yes, she'd done the right thing. It would have been wrong to accept a lift from him. She didn't know him from Adam. From Adam. That was funny. She felt more laughter rising to her lips. She was glad he had found her attractive – she was certain of that, he had found her attractive. He had said so. He'd said he liked her. He was interesting, and it was flattering to have the attention of an interesting man. Nick. She tried the shape of his name in her mind. Yes, he was interesting, not a stereotype. Cultured but utterly down to earth. She'd not met anyone quite like him before. He'd blagged his way into the preview. He had a cheek.

Nervously she made her way out of the softly lit lower gallery back to the entrance. She couldn't help talking to him; it would have been rude not to talk to him at all. As he'd implied, just because she was engaged, it didn't mean that she couldn't talk to other men, only that she wouldn't get involved with them, or find them attractive. Now Nick, he was attractive, he had a sort of animal magnetism . . . As she admitted this she felt something stirring – then she screeched to a halt. This was a path she was not to go down. Forbidden. *Verboten.* Then she tried to be a little gentler with herself. It was not her fault, she reasoned, that she found him attractive. She had done nothing wrong, nothing to be ashamed of at all. Besides, he was scruffy and he smoked. He wasn't her type. And good-looking, that mass of brown, tousled hair, his bone structure, those eyes. Any woman couldn't help but respond to him. But now the episode was over, well and truly over. Reality and wedding receptions beckoned.

She found herself in the foyer again, paused by the Rodin, and once again let her eyes rove over the contours of the male nude. She liked the rise of the chest and the shape of the calves. Perhaps she should get a taxi home, rather than walk down the Headrow again. No, the walk would do her good and help her to get what had just happened into perspective. Because it was nothing – just a stray conversation, a chance encounter. It was nice to know she hadn't lost her touch, and that was the only reason she was feeling somewhat enervated. Vanity, she told herself. Just plain and simple vanity.

Feeling vain, she left the building.

Chapter Fifteen

The organ played its final note. Heather picked up her handbag from beneath the pew and prepared to leave the church. She felt relieved the service was at an end, and guilty at her relief. She knew she had not been concentrating on the sermon, the prayers or the hymns. She had sung familiar words with her lips while her mind was busily engaged on a number of questions. Ought she to give in to Tim and invite his friend Samantha to the wedding although they had never met? And if she invited the vicar, she ought to invite his family too, and that meant four more guests in addition to the quota she had agreed with Sylvie. And what about Richard? The wedding was unthinkable without him at her side. And what would she do if she couldn't find a hat? And if she did ask for extra guests, ought she to offer a sum of money to help with expenses? Or would Sylvie and Ivan be offended?

Christian theology was irritatingly silent on all of these points, and John Foster's rather bland sermon on our relationship with the environment wasn't much help either.

However, being in church had calmed her, she had to admit. Just being able to do nothing, to let the familiar cadences float over and around her, to let her eyes rest on the flowers, the white altar cloth and the stained-glass window afforded her a temporary respite from the whirlwind of the wedding.

Then there was always the chance of catching John Foster and bending his ear. Vicars had a wonderful way of seeing right through one's problems and knowing just what to say. A brief chat about the wedding with him would do her the world of good. She wondered if it would be possible to speak to him, and deliberately dawdled as she left the pew and greeted other members of the congregation. Sunlight poured into the vestry as she made her way towards it. There was John, already surrounded by those pathetic women who had virtually adopted him. Really it was quite disgusting the way some people treated the vicar as if he was their own personal property, or as if they couldn't stir a step without his advice and support. Poor lamb! She wondered how he put up with it. She approached the group, waiting for him to catch her eye. He didn't notice her, so she moved nearer his little fan club. He was deep in conversation with Mrs Dyer, whose husband was chronically ill. John's eyes were lambent with concern and Heather told herself to be patient.

Eventually he saw her and smiled briefly, then turned back to Mrs Dyer's tale of woe. It would be necessary to wait a little longer. Then Heather realised she was no longer alone. Maggie Bowden appeared by her side, and they both shook hands in a Christian spirit, then inquired politely after each other's health. Keeping one eye on the vicar, Heather followed her outside, glimpsed the crocuses studding the lawn and the less spiritual sight of various members of the congregation getting into their cars on the main road.

Maggie asked after Ken's health, then Tim's, and then Dan's. Heather answered briefly, glancing occasionally at the vicar.

'And your young man,' she added. 'The one you found from the St Jude's project. I hope he's all right?'

'Yes, thank you,' Heather said.

'And is he proving useful?'

'Very.'

'I'm surprised you've managed to keep him employed over the winter,' Maggie said.

'There's plenty for him to do,' Heather said frostily. There was something odd in Maggie's tone. What was she implying?

'I've noticed him coming and going.'

She would have. Maggie lived a few doors away and was a one-woman neighbourhood watch scheme. Heather resented her interest and drew herself to her full height.

'I've been showing him how to propagate seedlings. He wishes to start up his own nursery. Rather than just employ him, I think it's important to pass on skills that he can use himself. Once a teacher, always a teacher.'

Maggie persisted in looking suspicious. Not for the first time Heather thought how unattractive she was. Buck teeth were so unbecoming on a woman – privately Heather thought of her as Bugs Bunny. Yet there was something about Maggie's manner that was disconcerting. Perhaps it was her silence. Heather felt drawn to justify her situation even further.

'He's helped me convert the attic into a nursery,' she said. 'It's a regular little greenhouse up there. I give Richard a free hand, of course. We've been looking at horticulture courses on offer at college and—'

'What do you know about his background?' Maggie asked.

'A lot,' Heather replied. 'There have been a number of difficulties — told to me in confidence, of course.'

'Of course.'

Heather bristled with dislike. Crabby old spinster, she thought. She's jealous. As well she might be. Maggie was withering away, eaten up by suspicion, while she was burgeoning with vitality, thanks to her friendship with Richard, and the little plants in the attic. And if people thought there was a little more to her relationship with Richard than that, well, let them! Heather felt girlishly defiant. Perhaps he did have a soft spot for her — a kind of crush. It was flattering, and fed her vanity. Centuries ago, this kind of relationship was sanctioned by society in countless courtly love poems. He was her troubadour, and sang to her with seedlings and by the light of overhead fluorescent tubes.

'Maggie, Heather,' said the vicar and shook hands with them both.

'John,' began Heather. 'I wanted to have a word with you—'

'Vicar,' Maggie declared simultaneously, 'I wanted to know what you decided—'

The vicar made as if he wasn't sure which one to attend to first, and smiled at both of them.

'Decided about what, Maggie?' he said.

Oh, thought Heather. So that's how it is. She gave a small,

cold smile and retreated, greeting a few stray members of the congregation, stopping to coo at a baby and finally walking down the steps to her car. She was irritated with the vicar. He was losing her respect. Always at the beck and call of she who shouts the loudest. No discernment. None of the wisdom an older man would have. Or maybe a younger man who had seen more of the world. Like Richard. She used to think that education conferred wisdom but she was not so sure any more. Sometimes Richard's insight surprised her. Increasingly she was beginning to value him, to pay attention to his views and to shed her old preconceptions about class and culture. He listened to Classic FM with her, and she had lent him *Captain Corelli's Mandolin*, which he had read, and understood, at least as much as she did. She started up the engine and prepared to drive home. Really she was so busy perhaps she would skip church next week.

She passed large houses built in creamy yellow stone and reflected that the roads were as busy now on a Sunday as they were the rest of the week. Within a few minutes she turned into her drive and saw Ken's silhouette at the window, leafing through the Sunday papers. If the vicar had been unable to answer her questions, perhaps Ken might. It was worth a try. On matters of protocol she respected his judgement. Anticipating a glass of wine before lunch, she quickly locked the car and made her way inside.

'I'm home.'

Ken wandered out from the front room, greeted her and murmured that he would open a bottle of wine. Heather followed him into the kitchen to check on the roast.

'Church OK?' he asked.

'Yes. Ken, listen. I've been thinking. Ought we to invite the vicar and his family to the wedding?'

'As you wish.'

'I can't decide. Given that Dan and Ruth aren't having a religious ceremony, we ought to have someone there to represent God. Oh, I don't know. And what about Tim's new acquaintance? He's asked if she can come.'

'The more, the merrier. Here we go.' Ken passed her a glass of Soave.

'And Richard. I'd like him to be there.'

'To help?'

'As a guest.'

'A guest?'

'Mmm.' Heather sipped at her drink, deciding to ignore Ken's doubting tone. 'Yes, I think so. But we've already exceeded our invitation quota. And I need to find out about arrangements for the top table. I really think it ought to be just Dan and Ruth and the parents, because if we include *all* the family then they outnumber us, so we would have to import Dilys, and then they might want their grandmother. Should we offer to pay for the extra guests? What do you think?'

Ken stood at the door looking gently bemused. 'You decide, dear,' he said.

'Shall I ring Sylvie?' she asked. 'Perhaps if we talked these things over . . .'

'Good idea, good idea,' Ken said.

Heather watched him return to the Sunday papers. He naturally left all these matters to her. Sometimes she wished he would take more responsibility for the wedding, but then, if he did, that would leave her with nothing to do, so it was just as well. Heather rifled through the address book by the phone and dialled Sylvie's number. It would be good to get the guest list finally sorted. She listened to the phone ring with satisfaction.

'Are you having a hot flush?' Ivan remarked as Sylvie came in from the hall, vermilion.

'Hot flush, my foot! Do you know who that was on the phone? Dan's mother. And do you know what she wanted?'

'Not until you tell me.'

'Ten more bloody invitations for the wedding, that's all. Ten! *And please could I tell her who will be sitting on the top table.* Top table! I haven't even thought about the bloody top table! For all I care, she can have the bloody top table all to herself. *Will Sharon and Rachel be on the top table?* Yes, they bloody well will, and Rachel with her nose ring too, if she wants!'

'Calm down, Sylvie.'

'Whose side are you on?'

'Nobody's taking sides here. Just tell me what all this is about.'

Sylvie pushed her hair back from her forehead, sat down, and began again.

'She wants to invite the vicar and his family, her gardener and her other son's girlfriend and her mother. And she had the cheek to offer to pay.'

'Hmm,' Ivan said.

'So I was a bit short with her and then she said that she could manage without the vicar's family. Big deal! What is this wedding? A spectator sport?' Sylvie's anger exploded in spurts like a dying firework. 'So in the end she just asked for four extra. Fine, I said, and we'll foot the bill.' Sylvie then smiled cunningly. 'I also told her we'd have four extra guests, just to balance things. I'm not having her playing the grand lady of the manor.'

'Who else are you thinking of inviting?'

'Linda, of course, and her family. So she had to agree to that, and then she starts with all this top table business, because she was concerned we had to balance sides, and . . .'

Ivan listened with the patience of a trained counsellor to Sylvie explaining the situation. He waited until his wife had run out of accusations.

'You're right,' he told her. 'But I tell you what. Let Sharon and Rachel sit where they like and we'll only have the six of us on the top table.'

'And what about my mother?' Sylvie said ominously.

'Do you really want her next to you all through the meal?'

'I suppose six is an even number. Sometimes, Ivan, you make me sick. Trust you to find a solution. Why won't you let me hate Dan's mother?'

Ivan chuckled.

'With her just-so ways and all this putting on an appearance and have I decided on the colour I'm wearing yet. Pale green actually – but I wouldn't tell her that. And then we haven't seen hide nor hair of Ruth for ages and I have to ask her about table decorations. I ring her flat and she's never there. Did you get the bagels?'

'They're in the kitchen.'

'And smoked salmon?'

'In the fridge.'

'Hmm. I'm beginning to feel peckish. That woman!'

Heather returned to the front room smiling to herself. 'I've just had a word with Sylvie. I think it will be all right. I made my views clear about the top table and I hope she took my point. It was rather awkward offering more money so I decided to compromise, and so I only asked for invitations for Tim's friend and her mother, the vicar by himself, and Richard.'

'Reasonable,' Ken said, from deep inside the papers.

'And she said she'd balance things up by inviting four more guests too. A friend of hers. Someone she met at her reading group, apparently. And her family. A son, daughter and a baby. It'll be nice to have a baby at the wedding.'

'Someone she met at her reading group?'

'Yes. I think Sylvie said she's run up the wedding dress or something.' She finished her wine. It seemed a reasonable compromise.

'I don't think that's a very good idea,' Ken said, reflectively.

'Really? Why not?'

'We hardly know them.'

'Yes, but the Collinses don't know Richard or the vicar and none of us knows Samantha.'

'Then I think we shouldn't invite any of them.' Ken folded the paper deliberately. 'The whole thing's getting out of hand.'

'But I don't see that eight extra guests—'

'Heather!' It was his headmaster's tone of voice. It quailed her into submission. 'Ring the Collinses after dinner and tell them we've changed our minds.'

'I can't do that! Besides, it's up to the bride's family to send out the invitations. I can hardly tell her not to invite her own friends. I mean, all things considered, she was perfectly sweet about Richard and the others.' She glanced at her husband, a little puzzled by his reaction. Ken was deep in thought. She saw a muscle jump at the side of his mouth.

'I suppose there's not much you can do now. It just seemed to me that the wedding is getting a little bit out of hand. The world and his wife, that sort of thing. We'll manage, I suppose.' He smiled at her from over the top of his bifocals. Heather felt the tension in the room subside.

'I'll see to lunch now,' she said. 'Tell Tim to come down.'

She retreated to the kitchen. For a moment she had thought that she and Ken were about to come into conflict. She had been quite nervous. She had a terror of conflict, and always gave in to him. He had a way of disapproving of her that made her feel utterly negated. There seemed to be an understanding in their marriage that she had to live up to his standards. He was the headmaster, after all. From the moment they had met, he was the one with the status and she was simply a suitable mate for him. She showed her gratitude by caring for him, and his contentment was a measure of her success, his anger a marker of her failure. The boundaries were clear. It was a very British sort of game. For fair play, her rewards were security, a good income, the freedom not to work, respectability – oh, she was a lucky woman, no doubt of it. He had the right to lay down the law once in a while.

Or did he? she thought, almost for the first time. Why make a fuss about the size of the wedding now, when he could have made his views known months ago? On a day when she had been snubbed by the vicar, she was snubbed again by her husband. He had wanted her to make a fool of herself by ringing Sylvie Collins and saying she'd changed her mind. It was a bit much. It was unfair – and it was inconsistent of him!

'Not that he's often inconsistent. If anything, Ken's the one who takes a firm stance and doesn't deviate. It's important to do that to establish authority. It's also why he has such a distant manner. As a Head, you can't be too friendly. It doesn't do. People take advantage of you. Or they think they can bend your ear. I think it's all dissolved now. I'll just give it another stir. I haven't heard of this fertiliser before. Where did you get it from, Richard?'

'The garden centre. It won't increase the acidity of the soil so much. No! Don't pour it over the leaves. You're better off spraying it. Do you have a spray attachment?'

'It's in the greenhouse. Shall I run down and fetch it?'

'I'll do that,' he said.

'Hold on. I have another idea.'

Heather left the attic and ran downstairs to her bedroom. On her dressing table was a perfume atomiser, never used. It had been a gift from Ken. She had demonstrated pleasure but was secretly annoyed that he didn't know that all the perfume she bought already came in atomisers. Lucky she had never used it – it would be perfect for Richard.

'Will this do?' she asked him as she re-entered the attic.

'Excellent.' He smiled at her as she handed him the atomiser. 'A present?'

'Just from Ken. I've never used it.'

'I thought you wore perfume. You always smell so nice.'

Heather laughed. 'Thank you. I like to leave a fragrant impression. Perfume is a woman's signature.'

Richard was misting the leaves of the plants with little puffs of fertiliser solution. 'What scent do you wear?'

'It depends on the occasion. Beautiful, or Eternity. I like a simple cologne too. And lavender.'

'Lavender is relaxing.'

'Yes. I think so too. Could we grow lavender up here? As well as tomatoes?'

'Eventually. There we go. That should do it.'

'Has your friend been able to find out what the seeds were yet?'

'He's certain they're a herb — sage, he suggested, or dill.'

'I don't think so. I grew dill once and it was nothing like — but I don't mind. It's such fun not knowing what's coming up.'

'It adds mystery.'

'Absolutely. Here. Let me.' Heather took the atomiser and continued to squirt it at the leaves. She was in her element. It was so lovely to have a companion while she was attending to the plants. She and Richard got on so well, she found she could speak whatever was on her mind, and he would respond. Sometimes they worked in a friendly silence; today she felt talkative.

'It's a sea of green up here,' she commented, sighing happily.

'It certainly is.'

'I must say Ken hasn't complained too much about the electricity bill. Anything that keeps me quiet suits him!'

'Come on. You're not being fair to yourself. Your conversation's always interesting.'

'I don't think Ken thinks so. Of course he's used to me, and sometimes we can almost read each other's mind. There's no need for conversation.' Heather put down the atomiser and eased herself on to the floor. Richard squatted down to join her, and took his tobacco pouch out of his jeans pocket.

'Mind if I . . . ?'

'No. Go on. I like the smell.'

'You were saying – about Ken, and the fact that he doesn't talk to you.'

'No, that's not fair. He does talk to me, as much as most husbands, I suppose. Then again, he's away a lot. He's always been a workaholic. When I met him, he was head of the history department at the grammar school. I was teaching, but not in his school - I taught the little ones. Mutual friends introduced us. Did you know he was eight years older than me? It was partly because of that I was so flattered when he asked me out. He was so sophisticated and we went to concerts and art galleries and out for dinner. My parents were delighted because they liked him enormously. I think they saw me in a different light because of Ken. Yes, I was very lucky. He was always determined to get on in teaching, and that's why he worked so hard. It was understood we would have to put his career first. We married in church and had a lovely white wedding. He was keen that everything should be just as I wanted it, even down to the choice of buttonholes. It was the best day of my life, but do you know, when I look in the album now, at all the photographs, it seems so two-dimensional. At the time it all felt so momentous. We were living in Beverley then. Am I boring you?'

'No way. Go on.'

She believed him. He looked genuinely involved. Hardly stopping to draw breath, Heather continued. 'It's quite strange thinking back. Ken and I have changed so much.' She laughed. 'I remember giving a dinner party for his deputy head and fretting over the baked alaska. I think I must have already been pregnant with Tim. We hadn't been married very long when he came along. Naturally I gave up work and around the same time Ken was offered a deputy headship. We moved here when I was pregnant with Dan. Just before house prices rocketed. I've always felt we had luck on our side. I know I'm privileged, Richard. Not many women these days can devote themselves to their children and have the time to pursue their own interests.

Heather heard her voice trailing away and was aware of Richard's eyes upon her. His wise gaze made her aware that she had given a very partial account of her marriage, an official statement, which bore as much relationship to the truth as a press release to a cabinet scandal. Ought she to say more? The silence was warm and inviting. She could step out of her social corset just for a moment.

'Richard, it's hard work, caring for all three of them and cushioning the edges of things. Harder work than people think. There's so many little things to think of – little, but they all add up. A house doesn't run itself, you know. And someone has to keep peace between the three of them. Perhaps it wouldn't be so bad if it wasn't for our public position. The Blakes are quite well known in the community – Ken has taught so many boys. They keep popping up when we go round Waitrose. We always have to be prepared for that. I'm Mrs Blake, you see, the head's wife.'

'Not to me, you're not.'

'Thank you, Richard. And sometimes I look at Dan and Ruth and I feel quite jealous. She insists on having her own life. But can you do that? Can you have your own life and make a marriage work? I've made sacrifices and—'

'Sacrifices?'

'Maybe that's too strong a word. As a wife and mother you put yourself second, perhaps that's all I mean. I'm sure that's the way it ought to be.' Heather glanced at Richard to see how he had taken this. His level gaze made her feel as if her sacrifices had been in some way her choice, that she could have chosen to do things differently. She was suddenly nervous and looked longingly at the glowing tip of his roll-up. 'I used to smoke, when I was younger,' she said.

'Have a drag.'

'No! I wasn't suggesting that! I'd hate to start again. When my father found out he was livid. There was such a scene and my mother was distraught.'

'Did you get on with your parents?'

'I suppose so. They had to scrimp and save. I was born just after the war, and there was rationing still, and utility furniture — I don't suppose you know what that is! My parents had to be careful if they were to make ends meet and I was always aware of that. Do you know, I can remember my mother bringing home some Fry's chocolate once, and dividing it into seven pieces for me, one for each day of the week. We had to make things last. My father fought in the war and that made him feel as if my generation took everything for granted. He had a dreadful temper. The first time I wore a mini skirt he exploded. He said I looked like one of those girls who hung around under lampposts. I didn't know what he meant for ages. I know you're thinking I was a teenager in the sixties, but to tell you the truth I didn't even know I was supposed to have enjoyed myself in the sixties until they were over. It was partly living in a small town in Yorkshire, but also my parents. They liked to listen to *Sing Something Simple* on Sunday afternoons, with the King's Singers . . .' She smiled at Richard. 'That's why I was glad to get married. Very glad. I loved having my own house and doing everything my way. I suppose I'm very grateful to Ken, and I still am.'

'He's a good husband, then?'

'He's generous and fair-minded and a lovely companion.'

'But you don't talk very much.'

'We've been married a very long time.'

'You leave each other to your own devices.'

'We do, Richard.'

'So you're free now, to do the things you want.'

' Yes, I am.'

'What do you want to do?'

'Well, I . . . I wouldn't like to work again. I'd like to travel. I . . . I suppose I'm quite happy.' This wasn't entirely true either, only she couldn't say what it was she wanted. Life could be a strain. And lonely, though she was less lonely since she had Richard.

'Are you close to Ken?'

'Close?'

'You know what I mean.'

Heather did know what he meant and blushed in acknowledgement.

'Sometimes,' she said, and looked away. This was an area she didn't wish to talk about. She felt a little ashamed that she and Ken rarely made love – not that he seemed to mind. He never said anything to her. On the odd occasion he reached out for her, their lovemaking was brief and lacking in something. She tried as hard as ever, but he was lost in himself and for all the arousal she felt, she could have been scrubbing his back in the bath. Embarrassed at the direction of her own thoughts, she glanced up at Richard and saw him looking intently at her, a roll-up between his lips. His hair fell softly on to his shoulders, and his eyes were large and gentle.

'Go on,' he said.

'It's private,' she said evasively.

'Does he make you happy?'

What a strange question, Heather thought. She frowned in concentration as she absorbed it. There was a buzz from the fluorescent lighting and a slight exhalation from Richard as he enjoyed his cigarette. He was sitting cross-legged now, and Heather saw his jeans were almost threadbare at the knee. She hoped he had a better pair at home.

'I shouldn't be talking to you in this way,' she said.

'No. I think you should. Is Ken the only man you've been to bed with?'

Heather's cheeks burned. 'Yes. I suppose I must sound very old-fashioned to you.'

'No. Do you regret not sleeping with anyone else?'

'I don't think so.'

'But you don't know.'

Buzz from the lighting. Richard's inhalation. Her own heart thudding. Richard's hand on her sleeve. His long, tapering fingers with soil-encrusted fingernails, the tips of his fingers yellow with nicotine. Her arm trembling. Richard edged a little nearer.

'You're shaking,' he said. 'Relax.'

There was a sharper, shriller buzz.

'The doorbell!' Heather said, alarmed.

'Leave it.'

'No, it could be important.' She got to her feet and ran down to the landing, then down again to the hall. She saw the silhouette of a man. She attempted to tidy herself before answering the door. It was a man with a parcel which was for the Ingrams next door. Hastily she signed for it and put it in the porch. She bade him goodbye and shut the door.

Her thoughts flew to Richard upstairs in the attic. Had he been offering himself to her? Her heart was bumping against her ribs. Yes, of course he was. Heather tried to steady her breathing as she tried to imagine what it — what he — would be like. Gentle, attentive, and young. Very young. Dan's age, in fact. Oh dear, no!

Now what should she do? What was he doing in her attic now? Would he be getting undressed? Should she call him down and make some tea and open a packet of shortbread? She had to remind herself who she was — Heather Blake, a headmaster's ex-wife — no! An ex-headmaster's wife. Mother of the bridegroom. Tim's mother. Organiser of the Flower Committee at church. Women like that didn't have toy boys! Respectability mattered, because if it didn't matter, then nothing mattered, and you would have to start making up your own rules. If she gave in to temptation, chaos would follow. Richard, she told herself, was a substitute son, not a substitute lover. As she thought that, she glimpsed another Heather as if through the wrong end of a telescope, being loved and caressed by—'

'Richard! Now I'm down here I'll put the kettle on. It was only a delivery for next door.' Her voice sounded shrill and reedy. She heard some thumps from upstairs — was he putting his clothes back on? Did he understand that she wasn't rejecting him, but the whole thing was so unthinkable and impossible? Ought she to say something?

Richard appeared at the head of the stairs, fully clothed and cheerful.

'I could do with a brew,' he said.

'Oh, good. I'll open some biscuits although really I shouldn't because I am trying to lose a few pounds for the wedding, naturally. The photos, that's the thing. All one's indiscretions, caught for posterity.'

'It's OK to be indiscreet sometimes,' Richard said, smiling lazily at her. 'Long as you're not caught out. No sweat. We're still friends, aren't we?'

'Of course we are!'

'And like I said, relax. You get so tense sometimes. It doesn't matter what other people think. It's what you think that matters. Not Ken.'

'*I* think we ought to have our elevenses and discuss the college prospectus.'

'That's OK by me,' Richard said.

Chapter Sixteen

Her patient closed the door very gently. Ruth listened to the receding footsteps, and sat back in her chair. There was a tightening in her temples that was a sure-fire indicator that a headache was on its way. She had been aware of it while she was listening to her patient pour out all her woes and help herself to the strategically placed box of tissues on the desk. The act of empathy with her patient had left her drained, so while she massaged her temples she tried to focus on something cheerful.

Six weeks to go to the wedding. Yet at this moment the thought only induced panic. There was the final fitting of the dress, the impossibility of finding fashionable but comfortable shoes, they had to deliver notification to the registrar, and now Heather was pestering her about wedding insurance. Then there was the honeymoon, and Dan was waiting for her to say how much he should order in travellers' cheques and the plane tickets hadn't arrived — no, the only way to fend off the headache was not to think about the wedding at all. In the short time that remained before lunch she would stay in the consulting room and catch up with her notes.

She pulled the file towards her then jumped as the phone rang. It was plugged into an extension by the window. She walked over to it and picked up the receiver.

'Ruth Collins.'

'Call for you,' announced the switchboard operator.

Ruth waited, bracing herself for more complications, work or wedding, it was all the same.

'Ruth?' came an unfamiliar voice.

'Who's that?'

'Nick. Leeds City Art Gallery. I met you about two months ago.'

Ruth was disorientated for a moment, then swiftly remembered Adam's preview and the photographer she'd met. Her little fling. She recalled giving him her work number. She was puzzled, apprehensive and pleased.

'Yes. I remember you.'

'Cool. I'm ringing on the off chance you know how to get in touch with Adam Eastwood. I'm working on a feature for a magazine.'

Ruth felt obscurely disappointed. 'Sure. I mean, I don't know his private address but I know his firm's number. Hang about and I'll get it.' She put the receiver down, found her Filofax and rifled through the pages until she found Ellie's work number, then read it out to Nick. As she did so, a thought struck her. Why ring *her* to find out Adam's number? There were other ways to find it.

'Cheers,' Nick said. 'I'll give him a ring.' There was a brief pause. 'So, how are you doin'?'

'Great,' she said. 'You?'

'So-so. Let's meet again.'

Ruth stiffened. She knew it would be wrong to see him even once more. This was an invitation she would have to turn down.

'I'm awfully sorry,' she said. 'I'm busy with the wedding. It's only six weeks away.'

'So you've got a lot to do.'

'It's horrendous. Dress fittings and hair styling and hundreds of people to phone.'

'Hundreds?'

'OK. So I'm exaggerating. But it feels like hundreds.'

'Sounds like you need a break.'

'Too right.'

'So when shall we meet?'

She'd checkmated herself. She would have to refuse his invitation more assertively.

'I'm sorry. No.'

'Give me one reason.'

Ruth felt herself getting flustered. She decided to lighten up, make a joke of it.

'Hey, I can't be seen with you! I'm almost married.'

'But not actually married – yet.'

As he said that Ruth saw her wedding as a kind of gateway she was hurtling towards, and once she got there it would slam shut behind her. She would be married. Spoken for. Out of bounds. But not yet. When she spoke to Nick again, her voice lacked conviction.

'I'm as good as married.'

He laughed, a deep chuckle that made Ruth feel foolish.

'So, Ruth, when are we going to have lunch?'

'I told you. I'm otherwise engaged.'

'Pity,' he said, 'after I've come all this way.'

'What do you mean?'

'Look out of the window.'

Hastily Ruth rose and did as she was told. Spread out in front of her were the grounds surrounding the hospital entrance. Well-manicured lawns were divided by a driveway that ended in front of the hospital. Several cars were parked there, including a battered Ford Capri. Leaning against it, mobile phone held against his ear, was Nick. He looked up at her and grinned.

She would have recognised him anywhere. He was heart-stoppingly familiar. He wore a brown leather jacket and denims; his hair was tousled and wild. She couldn't properly read the expression on his face but he was smiling, she was sure. He had been watching her all this time, while she had been speaking to him on the telephone. He had come all this way from Manchester to see her. She couldn't disappoint him.

No. He probably just happened to be in Leeds and decided to call her on a whim. Her knees felt weak and she put a hand on the windowsill to steady herself.

'So are you coming out for lunch?'

Ruth knew she wanted to. She knew she shouldn't.

'Sorry,' she said, knowing he could hear the hesitation in her voice. 'I'm, er, I'm meeting someone in the canteen.'

'No, you're not,' he countered. 'You're just scared to go out with me.'

'Don't be silly.'

'I won't bite,' he said.

'You said that last time.'

'So where's the harm? I know you're engaged. I promise to sit the regulation eighteen inches away from you. We won't talk about anything except art and culture and you can leave whenever you say.'

Would Dan understand? Should she tell him? Of course she should tell him, and Ruth vowed to. It was ridiculous to suppose that just because she was engaged she could no longer have contact with fifty per cent of the world's population. If her forthcoming marriage had any validity, it would withstand a friendly lunch with a fellow Mancunian.

She laughed. 'OK. You win. I'll be down in five minutes.'

'Top!' he said. She was pleased he sounded pleased.

It was utterly innocent and she had been foolish to suppose otherwise. If he became a friend she could invite him round to Dan's house – her house – after they were married. He was so much more interesting than the accountants and healthcare professionals they usually teamed up with. Nick was quite a catch. And if he was a little scruffy and bohemian, so much the better. He would show them a thing or two.

Though what he would show them, Ruth did not stop to think as she picked up her bag and dashed to the Ladies, running a brush quickly through her hair and putting on some lipstick which hinted at scarlet without actually being scarlet. She looked OK, though a bit formal for a lunch, with her charcoal-grey jacket and silver-grey blouse. She needed to be back for a meeting at two, which gave her just an hour and a half. Not much could happen in an hour and a half.

When she left the hospital she saw he had got into his Capri and was waiting for her. She hesitated briefly. It was a risk, getting into a car with a man she barely knew. She dismissed her reaction almost instantly; she had an instinct she could trust him. She went round to the passenger side and got in.

'Where are we going?' she asked.

'I know a pub,' he said.

The pub he knew was past the Mexboroughs. It wasn't the sort of place Ruth would have chosen for herself. It was an everyday pub, not a cafe-bar, and all it had in the way of customer bait was a poster in the window advertising pub grub. Uncertain, Ruth followed him in. The interior was shady and reeked of cigarette smoke. In the saloon off to her right Ruth noticed a pool table with a triangle of snooker balls. She followed Nick to the bar, where they examined the menu and Ruth ordered a toasted cheese sandwich.

'My treat,' Nick said, and before she could protest, he handed the barman a ten pound note. 'Do you like beer?' he asked her. She nodded. 'Good. A pint and half of Timothy Taylor's.'

They said nothing as the bartender fetched their drinks, and Ruth luxuriated in the sensation of feeling like a student again. Nick pointed out a table by the fireplace and they took their drinks there. It was a small, round table, just big enough for two. They sat opposite each other. Nick pushed the pint towards Ruth.

'I can't drink all that!' she said, taken aback.

'I'm driving,' he said. 'The half pint's for me.' He took a slug from it to establish ownership. Ruth stared at her pint in dismay, hating to waste it. There was a time when she would have managed a pint, but not now. Besides, she rarely drank at lunchtime. Not to upset Nick, she took a sip from her glass and enjoyed the creamy bitterness of the beer – Timothy Taylor's was the Dom Perignon of the brewing world.

'So?' he said, smiling almost to himself. 'What shall we talk about?'

'That's a terrible way to start a conversation,' Ruth told him.

'OK. What's been happening to you lately?'

'Like I said, wedding preparations. What with my parents in Crumpsall and Dan's parents in York and the fact we're getting married in Leeds, I know the M62 better than anyone living.'

'Dan's your fiancé?'

'Yes. I met him at university. He works for KPMG in Leeds.'

'An accountant.' Ruth didn't know whether she imagined the hint of mockery in his voice. She took another sip of her beer and discovered she was thirsty. 'So he's Jewish too?'

It interested her that he'd remembered she was Jewish. 'No, actually he's not.'

Nick was silent, but looked at her. It was a disconcerting look. His eyes appraised her in a way that made her breathless. They were intelligent, knowing eyes, dark and fiery. He was good-looking, Ruth conceded, despite the fact he looked as if he hadn't combed his hair this morning. She watched him take a box of Marlboro from his jacket pocket and extract a cigarette. He didn't bother to ask her permission to smoke. Instead he offered her one. She declined.

'You said your parents live in Crumpsall,' he continued.

'Yes. Like Bill Bryson says, somebody has to.'

'You don't like Crumpsall?'

'What is there to like? Crumbling Victorian tenements, council residential homes, Netto supermarkets – no, thank you.'

'And Leeds is different?'

'I know there are parts which are just as slummy but more is happening in Leeds.'

'Not true.'

Ruth wasn't used to being contradicted except by her mother. 'How so?'

'Have you been in the city centre lately? There are cranes, scaffolding everywhere. The city's being rebuilt. There's the Printworks, the—'

'Yeah, right. And Europe's biggest Marks and Spencer. It's just shops, shops and more shops.'

'You think that's all there is to a city?'

'Well, I—'

'Forget the shops. When you want to get to know a city, look at the detail, and then use your imagination. It's the detail that matters. A place I like is on Quay Street, opposite the opera house. The Hospital for Skin Diseases. The lettering is still there. Hospital for Skin Diseases. None of your modern euphemisms there. But the patients had to use the side entrance. Appearances must be maintained. If you had a skin disease, you had to sneak in round the corner. I can just imagine it. That sums up Victorian Manchester. On one hand, amazing prosperity, and on the other, workers living in stinking slums, cholera epidemics, crime, pollution—'

'That's what I mean,' Ruth said. 'It's an ugly place.'

'No you haven't let me finish.' But Nick seemed in no hurry. He took a long drag of his Marlboro.

'It was ugly last century, sure. When Manchester was at its most triumphant, the workers were made to live like pigs. Of course there were the philanthropists who built model villages and good old Mrs Gaskell and – have you ever been in the John Rylands Library?'

'I've walked past it.'

'But you've not gone in. Not many people do. Now that was built with cotton money, by John Rylands' wife, Enriqueta. Weird name or what? He left nearly three million pounds. Three million pounds! So what does she do with it? Build a Gothic extravaganza and buy books to fill it. It's a mausoleum of dead culture, books only scholars read, statues staring each other out. It's like a cathedral in there. It's got as much to do with Manchester as the Taj Mahal. She wanted to bring culture into the city but Manchester's not about high culture – it never has been. That's its beauty. It's low. It's dirty. It's working class. Mancunians are about mass culture. There was the Messiah in the Free Trade Hall, Coronation Street, the Smiths, and now Oasis. That's why it's the most alive city in Britain. The workers came through. They always do.'

'You sound like a Marxist.'

'Nah. I can't be bothered with politics. Anarchy has its appeal, though.' He grinned at her, and she wasn't sure whether he was having her on. His smile was infectious, so she smiled back.

'But you're left with this problem. Manchester has the most impressive Victorian heritage of any city. Do we spend money on keeping it intact? Is it worth it? Personally, I think yes, it is, just to expose hypocrisy. I can't stand fucking hypocrisy. You've got to keep that contrast alive, just to show people. Take Gorton, for example. You know Gorton?'

'Yes! That's where I bought my wedding dress.'

Nick didn't hear. He was intent on his argument. 'Yeah, right. Basically it's a shithole. But go down Gorton Lane. There are your usual terraced houses and council maisonettes. Then there's a church, but not just any church. The Monastery of St Francis. Yeah, a monastery in Gorton. The building's incredible. The flying buttresses are at the front and they're, like, so elegant. Thin, tall, soaring. They're beautiful. Designed by Pugin. It's disused now, but what they're doing, right, is trying to reclaim it – for the people. Like the Victoria Baths. But meanwhile the cathedral's rotting away. Come and see it before it gets any worse. I'll take you when you're next in Crumpsall.'

'Dan and I would be delighted.'

'I didn't say Dan. I said you.'

Ruth felt as if she had been punched. He held her gaze again, and for a moment or two – no longer – their eyes met. She felt as if she had known him a very long time. She felt soiled by the knowledge and enervated by it. He was very familiar. Then he smiled and broke the spell.

'Drink up, lass,' he said.

Obediently she took a gulp of beer. She could feel it taking effect on her. A woman came from the kitchen with her sandwich and a burger and chips for him. The arrival of the meal defused the tension. Yet when she attempted her sandwich she found she had no appetite.

'You're not eating,' he commented.

'Yeah, well.'

'I've done enough talking. Now you talk to me. I want to get to know you. Tell me the most important thing about you.' He bit into his burger. It looked horrible, Ruth thought, dripping with grease and relishes.

'Go on,' he said.

Ruth was flummoxed. Was it that she was getting married? It should be. Or that she was Jewish? But what sort of Jew was she? Most definitely substandard. That she was a clinical psychologist? No.

'I'm very driven,' she said.

'By whom?'

'By me. I want to make something of my life.'

'Cool. What are you going to make of it?'

'The usual things. Marriage, a career, children maybe.'

'And what unusual things are you going to do? What about the detail?'

'I don't . . .'

'I'm a detail. Have me.'

Ruth swallowed hard.

'So don't have me. Have a chip.' He picked up a chip and held it between two fingers and it advanced towards her. Her lips parted.

'Open your mouth,' he said.

She did. She bit at the chip and her lips brushed against his fingers. It was like an electric shock. What the hell was going on here? He wasn't her type at all, and yet she found him fascinating. He was intelligent, but careless. Dirty, and sexy. He wore a navy roll-neck sweater. There was stubble on his chin. She ate his chip, then tore a little bit of the crust from her sandwich and put it in her mouth experimentally.

'Why aren't you hungry?' he asked.

Ruth shrugged. She drank some more beer.

'Is it because you fancy me?'

Ruth laughed.

'I can still eat,' he said, 'even though I'd like to go to bed with you.'

'I think I'd better go.'

'Don't worry. I'm not going to touch you. It isn't a crime to want someone, and like I said, I'm no hypocrite. I lay my cards on the table. It's your decision.'

'I made my decision when I got engaged to Dan.'

'You didn't know me then.'

He was so cheeky. Ruth was furious and mesmerised. She was angry with herself too, for he had made all the running, dominating the conversation, dominating her. She drank some more beer.

'Look,' she said, 'I'm not denying I find you attractive, kind of, but I am engaged and that means a lot to me. I wouldn't be unfaithful. I know I shouldn't have had lunch with you but you surprised me, coming to the hospital like that. And I suppose I am finding the wedding a strain. I thought a wedding was a celebration and acknowledgement of a relationship, but it isn't. I'll tell you what it is. It's an ordeal. It's a rite of passage, and rites of passage have to include an element of ordeal. Young Aborigine males have to go on a walkabout, and Jewish boys have a Bar Mitzvah. And Jewish girls have the wedding. I have to dress up and be inspected and then there are both of the families and they couldn't be more different. And it's not going to be easy. Dan's mum is so bloody patronising all the time and my mum can't stand her. And my mum's on a diet and she's in a foul mood and carps at me. And Dan is so bloody unaware of it all and goes on about everything being all right in the end. It doesn't bother him because he's away most weeks working and it's me who has to make peace and liaise with the confectioner who's making a fruit cake that nobody will want to eat. I shouldn't be telling you all this.'

'Yes you should.'

'There's no one else I can talk to. My friend Ellie, she's always there for me, but she's got problems of her own. She's having an affair with Adam Eastwood — oh, shit, I shouldn't have said that — and he's married so she's the last one who could help me. I'm not saying I have cold feet, but what I'm trying to say is that this wasn't what I expected — that being engaged is supposed to be nirvana and it isn't. And then you think, with so many marriages failing, is this sensible? Do I just want to play happy families? And I haven't been sleeping at night. I fall asleep OK and then I wake about three and have to read for a bit, as there's so much going round in my mind. Why do people put themselves through this?' Ruth finished her pint.

'Relax. Don't take it all so seriously.'

'Relax?'

'Just live for the moment. I do.'

'No you don't. You're interested in the past, aren't you?' Touché, Ruth thought.

'And you're too interested in the future.'

'You have to be.'

'Says who?' He reached across the table and lifted a lock of her hair. He held it between his fingers and she could feel just a slight pull on her scalp. 'You have lovely hair.'

'I'm wearing it up for the wedding,' she said in a small voice. 'My sister, Sharon, she's a hairdresser, she's doing it.'

'Lovely hair.' He let it go. 'If you don't want your sandwich, I'll have it.'

'Do.'

She watched him eat it in silence. It had been her sandwich, about to go in her mouth. It was now in his. She envied her sandwich. She wanted to know what it would be like to be close to him. How would he kiss her? Would he be slow, experimental, light? Or hard, urgent, insistent? Where would he put his hands? Alcohol made her unable to focus on anything except him right now. She knew reality would intrude soon enough, so for a few more minutes she would lap up his presence and his wiry body and expressive mouth and just imagine . . .

'I'd better be getting you back to work,' he said.

'Yes.' She made no move.

'Come on.'

Reluctantly she got up from her chair and followed him back to the Capri. In the car she was more aware than ever of his body and as he drove back to Chapel Allerton it took every atom of control she possessed not to put her hand on his thigh. She did not. Instead she spoke a little bit about her job, and he talked of his photography. Their conversation was desultory, impersonal. He drove her to the hospital entrance.

'Well, thanks for lunch,' she said.

Getting out of a car, she always had an impulse to kiss the driver. It was deeply ingrained in her. She always kissed her father whenever he took her anywhere, and if Dan dropped her off, she would kiss him. Not kissing Nick was the hardest thing she had ever done.

' 'Bye,' he said to her.

' 'Bye.' Why wasn't he saying anything else? Had he gone off her?

The car slid forward. Then he wound down the window. 'Gorton Monastery,' he said, and drove off. It was their next assignation.

After work Ruth drove to an Italian deli near the hospital and bought some pre-cooked pasta and tiramisu. The plan was to take it to Dan's house as he was coming back from Hull that evening, and they could eat in. The food in the deli looked totally unappetising. Usually Ruth loved to eat Italian. Now she thought she could never eat again. She bought what she thought would be suitable for her and Dan, and then proceeded on her journey.

She had been busy all afternoon and had not had time to develop her thoughts. She had been attacked by stray pangs of guilt, moments of ice-cold panic and then pure lust got her in a half-nelson and wouldn't let her go. Now, driving off to the Lyntons, she had the time to review the day, analyse it, and decide where to go from here.

She examined her own behaviour. She told herself she had done nothing wrong. In fact she had done nothing. Going out to lunch with him was not a sin. She didn't touch him, not once. But she had said she found him attractive. She hadn't made an arrangement to see him again. So why did she feel so filthily guilty?

She would expiate her guilt by telling Dan everything.

Everything, except for her feelings. She would just fight her feelings. Which were natural. He was an incredibly attractive man. How could she help what she felt? But if she really loved Dan, Nick would never have attracted her in the first place.

Or would he?

She stopped at a red light. She glanced at the occupants of the car that had drawn up beside her, a man and a woman, and envied them the apparent simplicity of their lives, sitting together in the front of their car.

I did nothing wrong, she told herself. Thought is not a crime.

As she approached Dan's house she saw his car was already in the drive. She parked hers in front of his and felt herself propelled forward into the rest of the evening. No more time to think, to sort out, and to reflect. Back to reality, or one reality.

She let herself in with her key.

'Dan?' she called.

No reply. The lights were on so she guessed he was upstairs.

'Dan?' she shouted more loudly. Still no reply. She made her way upstairs and as she did so she could hear the sound of the shower running.

'Dan!'

His voice was muffled by the sound of the water.

'I'm home,' she said. 'I'll warm up dinner.'

Glad of a reprieve, she slung her jacket on the banister and took the food into the kitchen. The normality of Dan's kitchen did not soothe her; in fact she felt as if she was in a play in which Dan's kitchen was simply a set. Intimate with the set, she lit the oven, found a dish, spooned the pasta into it, acting all the time. It was really remarkably easy to play this part, and if she played it well enough she might even be able to convince herself that nothing had changed. She placed the dish with the pasta in the oven, adjusted the dial to number 5, and put the tiramisu in the fridge. There was a bottle of wine still wrapped in a green Thresher's bag. Alcohol had no appeal. Ruth was still muzzy from the pint of beer at lunch.

In the sink she saw a coffee mug, and decided to wash it. Today had been an accident, and she resolved never to see Nick again. Then none of this would matter. As she watched the dregs of Dan's coffee swirl round and down the plughole she banished Nick and her lunch with him. It was history. A blip. He was right; she had a habit of taking herself too seriously.

'Hi!' Dan said.

'Oh, hi!' She turned around. Dan had come down wet from the shower, a towel wrapped round his lower half, his shoulders and chest still glistening with damp. His hair was slicked over his head. 'You haven't dried yourself properly,' she commented

'Couldn't wait to see you,' he said, smiling at her in a way that made Ruth certain that she knew what was going to happen next. She was right. He approached her, put his arms around her and nuzzled her hair.

'Missed you,' he said.

'Mmm.'

He began to massage her back. 'It'll take some time before dinner's ready, won't it?'

'I guess.'

She felt him getting more aroused.

'Hey,' he said. 'You smell of smoke.'

'Yeah. I went out for lunch. To the pub.'

'Who with?'

'Just a friend of Ellie's. She was supposed to come, but couldn't make it. A photographer.'

'Interesting.' At that moment his towel slipped off and slid to the floor in a heap.

'Not here!' she said. 'The blinds aren't drawn!'

'In a minute,' he said. As his mouth met hers she was conscious of her clothes as a barrier. Dan was naked, and she was covered up. He let her go, and led her by the hand to the lounge.

'I'll draw the curtains,' she said.

She did so, her heart bumping against her ribs. She hadn't anticipated this. They were going to make love now, while the image of Nick and the sound of his voice still danced around her. There was nothing she could do. Dan approached her, and helped her to remove her clothing, gently, almost reverentially. It was easy, then, to give herself to what was happening; it was easy, too, to become aroused herself and to long for each advance to complete intimacy. She wanted it to be quick, for a climax to come, and then for it to be over, and for them to resume their fraternal relations. They lay on the floor now, and he entered her very gently, and she tried to blank out her thoughts and just *feel*. She forced herself to concentrate on every single sensation and to wait for the moment when he would pause, as he did, for a moment, quiver, and then sigh, slowly, luxuriously . . .

Dan sighed.

'Was that too fast for you?'

'No, no. It's fine.'

'Ruth! You're crying!' Dan propped himself on one elbow so he could wipe away her tears with his finger. 'What's wrong?'

'I don't know. It just affected me this way tonight. I love you, Dan.'

'I love you.' Dan said the words easily because they were so true. Resting like this inside her was so wonderful, and purged of his insistent desire he felt cleansed and pure and utterly at peace. He loved to lie like this, their bodies still linked so closely. He felt as if every time he made love to Ruth they grew a little closer, more inseparable. The wedding was an absurdity to him. Nothing could bring them any nearer than they were now. Nothing could make him love her any more than he did now. She was beautiful, and real, and perfect because of her imperfections. One of her breasts – the left – was just a little smaller than the other. He loved that. He loved her bad moods, loved her when she was irritable, loved the way she left the books she had read under his bed, collecting dust. It bothered him that she was crying.

'Are you sure there's nothing wrong?'

'I'm sure. I suppose it's just the wedding getting to me.'

'We'll have a great day.'

'I know. Did you remember to ring the travel agent?'

'The tickets'll be sent out ten days before the flight.' He

came out of her and rolled on to his side and grinned. 'Don't give yourself a hard time.'

She sat up, folding her arms over her chest. 'I won't. You've made me feel better.'

'Glad to hear it. So next time you feel tense, you'll just have to ring me and I'll come straight over and make love to you immediately.'

She laughed, but he thought her laughter seemed strained.

'Are you sure there isn't anything else?'

'Oh, Dan, leave off! You're as bad as my mother!'

'I thought you told me your mother didn't care enough about how you felt.'

'Well, all right, *a* mother. You're as bad as *a* mother.'

'So shall I make you some chicken soup? Isn't that what Jewish mothers are supposed to do?'

'Chicken soup would be lovely,' Ruth said. 'With *kneidelach*.'

'Excuse me?'

'Dumplings, but made with matzo meal rather than flour. And chicken fat, not suet. When you come over for *Pesach* you'll have some.'

'I can't wait.'

She smiled at him, and again he noticed lines of tension round her eyes. Perhaps the wedding really was taking its toll. He felt a little guilty, as he had not been around to help with arrangements, but he couldn't do anything about it. It would be suicide to refuse to take on jobs because he wanted to be at home with his fiancée. His guilt pricked at him, and made him want to make things better, even at the risk of irritating her again.

'Look, Ruth, you must say if there's anything you want me

to do. I don't want you shouldering the whole burden of arrangements. Perhaps you ought to ask for a week off before the wedding, to give yourself some breathing space. Or would you like my mother to come over and stay?'

'No! I mean, perhaps I do need a break from the wedding. It's like sand on the beach. It gets everywhere. I just want to forget about it.'

'OK, we'll forget about it. And now for something completely different. How do you fancy a trip to Robin Hood's Bay? Have you ever been there? It's a tiny village that looks like it's been split at the bottom of the cliff. All very nautical, with cobbled pavements and teashops and second-hand bookshops. Then we could drive up to Whitby.'

'Whitby? What's at Whitby?'

'Count Dracula's Castle, no less, although the local church is dead set against advertising the fact in any shape or form.'

'*Dead* set?' Ruth managed a faint smile and Dan was encouraged.

'It's quite spooky there. I remember going with the Scouts. Hmm. You have a tasty neck.' Dan bared his teeth and Ruth made as if to move away.

'Dan,' she suddenly asked him. 'What do you think about architecture?'

'Think about it?'

'Do you have a favourite building?'

'That's a difficult one. Let me see. OK. It's a toss-up between the Bridgewater Hall because of its space and light and the way its function marries its design, and York Minster, for obvious reasons.'

'What about Victorian architecture?'

'Dark, forbidding, gloomy, pretentious. I always feel intimidated by the scale of it. And grimy Victorian buildings are downright sinister. Why are you asking?'

'Nothing. No reason. It's just something else to talk about.'

'Are you worried we're running out of things to say?'

'No.'

'Hey, listen. When we're on honeymoon we can do all the churches and other sites of architectural interest in Cyprus. I'll start swotting up.'

'It seems such a long way away.'

'I know, and then when we get there it'll seem all too short. There are only a few weeks to go now. If we keep busy we'll soon be there. It's just stress that's making you feel down.'

He saw a shadow darken her eyes. He could tell she had wanted something else from him, and he wished he knew what it was. Her shoulders were hunched, and she had made no move to dress again.

'Shall I check the pasta?' he asked.

'It's OK. I'll do it.' She got up and pulled on her underwear. He listened to her run upstairs. He was tired now, and hoped Ruth didn't mind if he let her see to the meal. Luckily she liked playing around in the kitchen. What she needed, he thought, was a night just doing nothing. They would eat, share some wine, watch TV and relax.

Ruth's head popped round the door. 'Here, Adonis,' she said. 'Put on your bathrobe.' She flung it at him and he ducked to avoid it. He was pleased she was joking again. Perhaps his lovemaking really had de-stressed her. He put on his robe and followed her into the kitchen to open the wine.

'Special offer,' he said. 'A Bulgarian Chardonnay.'

'Nice,' she said, taking out cutlery from the drawer.

'What did you get?' he asked, realising now that he was very hungry.

'Cannelloni,' she said. It smelled good. He took the wine and two glasses back to the living room, and Ruth brought in the plates.

'I was at an interesting firm today,' he told her between mouthfuls of cannelloni. 'They make devices for projecting computer screens on to a wall, so you can conference. They're hoping to sell mainly to educational institutions. You can download from the Internet and share the results with a teaching group, the MD told me. But the question is, with the education system so cash-strapped, will they get the quantity of sales they need to break even? Even university departments have fallen on hard times. He was telling me – I'm not boring you, am I?'

'Do we have to talk about work?'

Dan felt a little nonplussed. 'I just thought it was interesting.'

'Yeah, well, it's just that we talk too much about work. There's other things to talk about.'

'Like?'

'Culture, and stuff like that.'

Dan laughed. 'You haven't done anything cultural for ages.'

'*We* used to,' she corrected him. 'Can't we go to the theatre or something?'

'Sure, if there's anything decent on. This photographer you had lunch with – is she the arty sort, does she have her own studio? Or what?' He wished she'd bought some salad with the cannelloni. He didn't think there'd be enough to fill him up.

'It's a he, actually. He shoots freelance photo features and he's writing a book. Nice bloke.'

Dan felt himself bridle at the idea that Ruth had gone out with another man. Then he schooled himself. He trusted her absolutely. Their relationship was far beyond jealousy. For that matter, he worked with a number of women, and often had lunch with female clients. There wasn't a problem.

'Good,' Dan said. 'So that's what's whetted your appetite for culture. I'll ring the West Yorkshire Playhouse tomorrow. Don't you want your cannelloni?'

'No. I'm not hungry.'

'Do you mind if I . . . ?'

'Be my guest.'

Dan happily accepted the plate she pushed over to him. He ate with her spoon; there were no barriers between them. He looked up for a moment at Ruth beside him on the settee, saw her absent expression, and caught her fiddling with a strand of her hair. It was one of her nervous habits. Perhaps it was that distant expression in her eyes, but for a moment he felt alone. It was a feeling he didn't care for. He moved closer to her and hooked his foot round hers. Her foot was unresponsive.

She's in a mood, he thought, but she'll probably be fine tomorrow.

Chapter Seventeen

———◇◇◆◇◇———

The envelope came with the rest of her mail, and when Ruth opened it and saw the contents were only a leaflet, she was about to bin it. But there was a note attached to the leaflet with a paper clip, and it read, 'I'm here on Saturday, April 9th, about 2. I'll show you round. Nick.' The leaflet advertised the monastery at Gorton.

She had not seen his handwriting before and scrutinised it closely. It was a feminine hand, uncontrolled, loopy, careless. After a few moments she could have reproduced it blindfold.

Well, this was silly, because there was absolutely no way she was going to be at Gorton Monastery to meet him. Although, it occurred to her, she would be in Manchester that weekend, it was *Pesach*. And so it began again: she was weak with desire for him, then sickened and shocked at her own response. She told herself her feelings were the product of a slightly obsessive-compulsive reaction to stress, then tried to focus on Dan, but her picture of him faded, blurred and dissolved, to be replaced by Nick. She felt slightly nauseous. In the last ten days she had lost four pounds. At this rate her wedding dress would hang on her.

She had thought she was getting over him. Each day she was able to go for longer without replaying their lunch in her mind. She had been on the verge of confessing all to Ellie, knowing that Ellie's laughter would break the spell and she could go back to being the everyday Ruth Collins again. His note to her had set her recovery back light years. She felt as bad as ever, but also as happy as the alcoholic breaking her vow of abstinence – she could see Nick again.

She took the leaflet and placed it in her desk, under some pay review papers. There was a clinic this morning, and she would have to shelve thinking about all of this until then, although she knew she would not be successful. Her obsessions were her personal limpets; they stuck.

Ruth knew what she had to do. She lifted the telephone, got an outside line, and dialled Ellie's number. After a few moments she heard her voice.

'Ellie? It's just me, Ruth. Look, can you do lunch?'

'Today? We've got a deadline to meet and I'm working through.'

'I need to talk to you.'

'I'd like to talk to you.' Ellie's voice sounded serious.

'I've got the car,' Ruth said. 'What if I drive round to your office and we have a sandwich in my car?'

'Yeah. Yeah, I'd like that.'

'See you around one fifteen.'

'*Ciao*.'

*

There was a small car parking area at the back of Ellie's building. Although it was full, Ruth navigated carefully into it and drew to a halt in front of a Mercedes. She turned off the engine and waited.

Rain peppered the roof of the car, beating an irregular rhythm like Morse code. Ruth sat there waiting. The back wall of Ellie's offices was red brick, and in one corner were three large waste disposal bins in olive green. This rear courtyard was a dead end, an afterthought. It was nothing like the frontage of Eastwood's Consultancy, with its minimalist reception area in chrome and black leather. Soon Ruth could see very little as the rain sluiced down the windscreen. She had thought herself blank. She was in stasis until she saw Ellie and told her everything. Ellie would give her a perspective on things. At the very least, she would share her problem.

And Ellie might, suggested a little voice, give her the permission she craved to see Nick just once again. Ellie took things lightly. She had always been the perfect antidote to Ruth's seriousness. Ellie was good at laughing. She was also good at finding justification for doing precisely what she wanted. It was a skill Ruth wished to acquire.

Here she was now, picking her way through the parked cars, a blue and white striped umbrella above her head. Ruth opened the passenger door and she slid in, shaking out the umbrella and closing it swiftly.

Ruth kissed her on the cheek. 'Good to see you.'

'And you,' Ellie said. 'So what's with the dash across town to see me?'

Ruth shrugged. She didn't trust herself to speak.

'Mind if I smoke?' Ellie asked.

'I haven't seen you smoke for years.'

'So I've started again, OK?'

'Why?' Ruth persisted.

Now it was Ellie's turn to shrug. The rain increased in intensity.

'Shit,' said Ellie.

'Are you all right?' Ruth asked her, apprehensive.

'Not really. No. Delete that. I don't know yet. I mean, I've made a decision.'

'What decision?' Ruth felt guilty that she hadn't contacted Ellie in a while, and was out of touch with her life.

'Re Adam. I'm giving him an ultimatum. He leaves his wife or I leave him, and the firm.'

'You're really going to do that?'

'Tonight. When we've finished our work on the Giller account.'

'But you always said you were happy with sharing him. You said you liked your independence.'

'I lied.'

'To me?' Ruth asked.

'No. To me.'

Ruth was silent. It occurred to her that her problem was that she had two men, but Ellie had only half a man and therefore was in a worse plight than she was. The mathematical formula seemed for the moment to simplify things, and demonstrate that it was Ellie who needed support, not her.

'What kind of existence is it when the one person who's most important to you can only give you a corner of his life? I'm fed up with the drama, with the secret assignations. Hell, I *want* to wash his socks. I'm fed up with living on the margins.'

'You'd give up your job?' Ruth asked, appalled.

'Sure. I'd move to London and find work there. It wouldn't be difficult. There's nothing holding me here.'

'What about me?' Ruth reminded her.

'You've got Dan.'

'Yeah. Right.'

Ellie did not pick up the clue. 'I've planned it all out,' she said, her voice barely audible above the drumming of the rain. 'We're staying late tonight, and we'll be locking up together. I'm going to tell him in the office, which keeps it impersonal. I'm only giving him twenty-four hours to make up his mind.'

'Ellie—'

'Don't sound so sorry for me. I've bulk-bought the Prozac. And hey, you've disappointed me. I thought you'd approve. You've been on at me for ages to have a real, committed relationship, like you and Dan. So who knows? I could move to London and meet a nice insurance broker and settle down and live in Purley.'

'You sound as if you're expecting Adam to finish with you.'

Ellie stubbed out her cigarette and started another. 'Yeah, well, I'm a realist.'

'And you're prepared to risk losing him?'

'Jeez, I don't know. It's like — you have to weigh up the happiness you get, and the unhappiness. And recently I've been spending longer unhappy, turning myself into some sort of tragedy queen on his behalf. But I'm Ellie — I'm funny, I'm smart, I'm a winner. To be myself, I have to walk away from the situation, so I'm undergoing an Adamectomy. Painful, but necessary.'

Ruth found the tension between Ellie's flip manner and her haunted expression almost too much to bear. She began to talk about herself more as a distraction than anything else.

'My life's not so simple either.'

'Have you still not found a decent pair of bridal shoes?'

'No. Oh God, how am I going to say this? I think I've — well, I've sort of developed a crush on someone else. Crazy, isn't it? I guess it's all related to the pressure of the wedding in a way — the crush is a kind of safety valve. That's all it is.' Put like that, there was nothing to get into such a state about. Ruth was pleased with her rational assessment of the whole business. She glanced quickly at Ellie to see how she had taken this revelation. Ellie didn't meet her eyes.

'Who's your crush on?'

'Actually, someone I met at Adam's preview. A freelance photographer. He's doing a feature on Adam.'

'Oh, yeah. I know who you mean. Nick something or other.'

Ruth nodded. 'I've seen him once since the preview. He came up to the hospital and took me out for a drink. Nothing happened. Now he's invited me to look round a monastery with him.'

'A monastery? Well, it doesn't sound as if you'll have anything to worry about there!'

'The monastery's in Gorton, in Manchester. It's disused now. A Grade Two listed building. What do you think I should do? Shall I go?' Ruth knew that Ellie would give her the push she needed. It was why she had chosen to speak to Ellie rather than anyone else. It was low of her, but that was the truth. Yes, Ellie would be bound to tell her to go.

'Don't go,' Ellie said.

Ruth was startled. 'Why ever not?'

'Just don't. It's not worth it. You don't need complications like that in your life.'

Yes, I do, she thought. You don't understand. 'But I'd like to see the monastery. He made it sound interesting. I've told Dan about him.' She tried to sound slightly offended.

'What did you say to Dan?'

'Just that we'd been out for lunch. I said he was a friend of yours — I said you were going to come too but called off at the last minute. OK?'

'Cheers. Next time tell me first.'

Ruth was contrite. Now it seemed selfish of her to have implicated Ellie. She touched her shoulder. 'I'm sorry. I really am. It kind of slipped out when Dan asked me. I lied because I didn't want to hurt him, or make him think there was anything in it.'

'But there is something in it. You have a crush on this guy.'

'Right. A crush. A temporary, immature thing. But what do you think I should do? See him again and give myself the opportunity to go off him, or just leave it and wonder for ages what would have happened?'

'I think if you see him again you're asking for trouble.' Ellie's voice was considered and deliberate. 'I'd drop the whole thing if I were you.'

Ruth took a deep breath to steady her emotion. It was all very well for Ellie to take the moral high ground now, when for years she had been happily having an affair with a married man. She was being hypocritical. Nick said he hated hypocrisy. Yet now was hardly the time to argue with her.

'If I see him one more time,' Ruth said lightly, 'it can be to tell him that our friendship's at an end. Hell, I think if I see him again, I'll take one look at him and freak! He's not my type at all. He's aggressively working class, and grubby, and smokes like a chimney, and—' Ruth couldn't hold them in any longer. The tears came unchecked. Ellie squeezed and hushed her.

'He's disgusting,' Ruth concluded. 'Just like me.'

'Well, you are pretty disgusting right now. Crying does nothing for you, Ruth. You'll end up with a red nose and puffy eyes. And you've got a streak of mascara just . . . here.' Ellie wiped the edge of Ruth's eye with her finger.

'I'm so sorry. This whole business has turned me into a self-absorbed wretch. I'll get over it. It has helped to talk. Just ignore me. What about you? If I were you, I'd talk to him now. Don't wait. You'll only increase your own agony. Be gentle on yourself, but do what you have to do.'

'You're sounding like my Ruth again.' Ellie allowed herself a small smile. Then suddenly she turned and hugged her hard. 'D'you know what would solve all our problems?' she said. 'If we were gay. Then we could walk away into the sunset and leave all of them behind.'

'I wish,' Ruth laughed, and hugged her back. Yet for one infinitesimal moment Ruth tried to imagine it, and thought if she had been gay, she wouldn't choose to have a relationship with Ellie. She was tremendously fond of her, but she didn't trust her. Strange.

'I'd better be getting back now,' Ellie said. 'Perhaps I'll ring you this weekend.'

'I won't be in Leeds. It's *Pesach* on Thursday. I'm taking Thursday and Friday off work and I'm going to Manchester. Try me Sunday night.'

'Sure. What's *Pesach*?'

'Passover. We have a big family meal. Dan's coming for the first night.'

'Well, enjoy!' Ellie said.

Enjoy?

'Sylvie!' called Ivan. 'We're waiting for you.'

'I'll be a few minutes yet,' came her voice from the kitchen. 'If I'd had help, maybe I'd have finished earlier.'

'But, Mum,' whinged Sharon. 'You always say to leave you well alone on *Pesach*.'

'You can help me and still leave me alone!'

The three girls exchanged exasperated glances. Ruth enjoyed the moment of sisterly solidarity. Sylvie's temper never truly bothered them; it was almost part of the order of service. She couldn't imagine a Passover supper without a hysterical outburst. In fact, she thought to herself, playing with her fork, as Moses was hurrying the Jews out of Egypt, there were probably thousands of Jewish mothers laying into everyone, right, left and centre. No wonder Pharaoh was so keen to let them go.

Ivan had pulled out the table from where it usually sat by the wall, had extended it, and laid the white tablecloth upon it, covering years of red wine stains with strategically placed table mats. All the chairs in the house had been commandeered for the occasion – four authentic dining chairs, two kitchen chairs and Sharon's dressing-table chair. In the centre of the table sat two boxes of Rakusen's matzos, two bottles of Palwin's No. 10 *kiddush* wine, and two candlesticks with candles not yet lit. Ivan's *yarmulke* was attached to his sparse hair with a silver clip borrowed from Sharon's selection. Sharon, who sat opposite Ruth, was wearing all the relevant jewellery — her Star of David, a *chai* from Eilat from a past boyfriend and a gold chain Renie had bought her. Rachel linked arms with Renie who was saying that in the olden days they always started on time, as soon as the men had come back from the synagogue. Ruth thought how fragile was the bond that held them all here, and yet how irresistible it was. Her eyes rested on the *Seder* plate, with its burnt chicken bone, the leaves of lettuce, the burnt egg, the bitter herbs and the sweet herbs, the *charoseth*. She could see Dan looking at it curiously. She dreaded him asking what everything symbolised.

'What are those things on the plate?' he asked.

Before Ruth could answer, Sharon butted in. 'That bone is really supposed to be a shank bone. It's a sign the Angel of Death passed over the Jewish houses.'

'Don't be so daft,' Rachel said. 'It's to represent sacrifices in the temple.'

'So why do we still have it if we don't have a temple?' Sharon spat.

'I don't know. I'm not a rabbi,' Rachel declared. 'And the lettuce is instead of parsley and the burnt egg is, like, life, or something, and that white stuff is the bitter herbs which taste gross and—'

'I happen to like them,' Sharon said.

'You're not supposed to *like* them, Shaz! That's not the point, is it? It's to make you think about bitterness, like being a slave.'

'I should know about being a slave,' Sharon said, 'when I think of the way I'm treated at work. I haven't told you about the new manageress, Ruth. She's changed our hours and we have to sign in. Have you heard anything like it? Only Fliss was saying she's had a silicone implant — no, honest! Well, two implants, obviously. I mean, you wouldn't just have one, would you?'

'How can you tell?' Renie asked.

'It's interesting, you can't—'

'Sharon!' Ruth had had enough. 'This is the *Seder* table you're sitting at!'

'Oh, really? I hadn't noticed!'

Renie reached over and held Dan fast by the wrist. 'This is probably my last *Seder*,' she told him.

'Why?'

'I didn't think I'd live to see this year's. Next year in Jerusalem, they say. I hate to think where I'll be next year. When I think of the family who aren't with us any more – your Auntie Sadie, Walter, Solly—'

'It's supposed to be a happy occasion, Grandma,' Rachel said.

'Happy? I'm Jewish, what do I know about happy?'

Ruth leant over to Dan. 'Basically we're celebrating the Israelites' escape from slavery in Egypt, and we eat matzo because there wasn't time for them to bake proper bread. And this,' she indicated the badly printed paperback prayer book in front of him, 'is the *Haggadah*. It tells the story of the Exodus and has all the prayers in it.'

'Right.' Dan picked his up and began to leaf through it. Ruth smiled to herself. It was obvious he'd been brought up a Christian. They actually followed services. Jews dipped in and out, paddling their own canoes. Still, following his example she, too, began to turn the pages of the book. The shapes of the Hebrew letters pleased her; some were fat and maternal, others lithe and shapely. Some stood like ancient gateways; others waved like reeds on a riverbank. It was the pictures they made that helped Ruth remember their pronunciation when she was small. Now only the most familiar words were still decipherable to her.

She closed it and placed it back on her table mat. Earlier today, not for the first time, Nick had rung and asked if he would see her on Saturday. She'd said she wasn't sure. She felt colour steal into her cheeks and hoped no one had noticed.

'I'm hungry,' she said suddenly.

'I'll pour the wine,' Ivan said. He unscrewed the Palwin's and began to fill Elijah's cup. At that moment Sylvie emerged from the kitchen, hot, dishevelled, untying a paisley apron.

'I hope you weren't waiting for me,' she muttered.

'We weren't. That's why Dad was pouring the wine,' Ruth explained.

'I slog my guts out in the kitchen and you start without me!'

'Mu-um!' cried Ruth, Sharon and Rachel in unison.

Silently Ivan handed her the matches, and then began to pour a small amount of wine into everyone's glass. At last there was a hush.

Sylvie mumbled the Hebrew prayer that brought in the festival and lit the candles. Ruth felt herself fill with anticipation. There was a magic about all of these arcane preparations. Perhaps it was all mumbo-jumbo, perhaps it wasn't. Whichever, Ruth was drawn into the occasion and felt an absurd bubble of excitement.

Ivan gabbled through the prayers and Ruth suspected that his speed was a cover up for ignorance. Yet he was never more their father than when he was rushing breakneck through the *Haggadah* swaying slightly, like countless forebears.

'My turn!' cried Rachel.

The youngest child present traditionally read the four questions that kicked off the account of the Exodus. As the eldest, Ruth could not remember a time when she had been allowed to read them, although one year they did let her read the first and Sharon read the second, but Rachel had sobbed her way through the meal until she'd made herself sick. Thereafter they were Rachel's province.

The candle flames flickered and Ivan read on. Rachel took a surreptitious sip of her wine, and Sharon began to examine her nails. Sylvie was having a hot flush, and was using the *Haggadah* to fan herself. Only Dan and Renie seemed to be following the service. Then Ruth realised that once she was married she would always have to come back home for *Pesach*; Dan could not take her father's place. Perhaps she ought to learn Hebrew again, but the apparent enormity of the task defeated her, even in her imagination. She felt very, very sad. She was about to lose something. She glanced at Dan who was wearing Ivan's spare *yarmulke*; it looked strange sitting on his blond hair. Yet Ruth rather liked it.

'*Dom*,' intoned Ivan, and everyone repeated the word, each dipping their finger into their glass of wine. '*Tsfarday-ah*' – dip – '*kineem*' – dip – these were the ten plagues. Ruth glanced at the English translation. Blood, frogs, vermin, wild beasts, pestilence, boils – charming! she thought. If only the Old Testament God wasn't so revengeful she might have a little more time for him.

'We'll skip to *Dayenu*,' Ivan said, losing his confidence with the Hebrew.

They joined in the chorus to the song, Dan doing his level

best to keep up with them. That was when Ruth decided that she would not go to Gorton Monastery on Saturday. There was too much to lose. Yes, she would summon the resolve not to go.

'I'm sorry,' Ivan said. 'The Hebrew's too much for me. I think my brain must be shrinking - every year I remember less.'

'That's because you never go to *shul*,' Renie told him.

'*You* never go to *shul*!' Sylvie said.

'I go to the Friendship club, which is more than you do. No wonder your daughter is marrying out.'

'Grandma!' Sharon sounded indignant and delighted. Ruth wondered how she managed to pack so much meaning into those two syllables.

'When you were little,' Renie said to Sylvie, 'I used to change all the crockery and cutlery and pots and I scrubbed out the house.'

'You're supposed to do that on *Pesach*,' Ruth whispered to Dan.

'Let's carry on,' Ivan said. He read, 'In every generation one must see oneself as though having personally come forth from Egypt . . .'

Why? Ruth wondered. To keep the miracle fresh? Or maybe to give hope that there are miracles, that you can escape. She imagined *Seders* that must have taken place on immigrant ships on their way to America, on trains en route to the coast with families escaping from pogroms, in concentration camps. She was moved. You could even take the line on a personal level. We all have our own Egypts. We are all enslaved to something. To the pursuit of success, to money, to . . . to Nick, she thought, and for a moment she saw him as clearly as if he was sitting in front of her. How could she *not* go to the monastery?

Please God, she began silently, but could not continue. She didn't know how to pray, didn't believe it worked and didn't know what to pray for. Did she want to learn to forget about Nick, or did she want God to part the waters of the wedding preparations and let her through to the other side, unwed and free? Did she want to feel what she once felt for Dan again, or did she want permission to see Nick again? The whole thing was an ungodly mess. She smiled a bitter smile to herself. Here she was, in the middle of *Seder*, coldly debating an infidelity, even contemplating calling the wedding off, and no one had the slightest idea. She suddenly felt the urge to laugh. She was aware of Dan next to her with his skullcap, like the brother she never had. Last night she had lied to him; she had said it was that time of the month, and had got out of making love. He had been apologetic, extra attentive, and she was short with him, then apologetic too, and they had watched Newsnight, contrite, holding hands. By Sunday, she told herself, it would all be over, one way or another. But no — she was not going to the monastery.

Ivan began to pass round the matzo, and the table erupted into conversation again, with cries of 'The matzo gets smaller every year', 'I can't stand it without anything on it', and Ruth smiled bravely and accepted her piece. Then Ivan mischievously gave Dan a more than generous helping of the bitter herbs and Dan began to cough and splutter and his eyes watered, much to everyone's amusement. The *charoseth* was sampled and pronounced a success, and Ivan closed the *Haggadah*.

'Now let us partake of the repast,' he said.

Collins family *Seders* always ended with those words. They

had come from the *Haggadah* they'd used years ago, and Ivan would recite them with a dramatic flourish.

'This is amazing,' Dan said.

'What?' asked Ruth. 'That we've actually reached the end of the service?'

'No – the whole thing. How long have Jews been keeping Passover for?'

Ruth shrugged.

'Since the Exodus,' Sharon said.

'No. Not as long as that,' Rachel chipped in. 'It's from Roman times. I remember from *cheder*.'

'That's what I mean,' Dan continued. 'That's nearly two thousand years of Passovers. And Jews all over the world are having the same service in their homes tonight. It's awe-inspiring. It makes you feel that people can make a difference.'

'Make a difference?' Ruth was puzzled.

'Sure. Most of the time the world seems chaotic, right? But when you impose a pattern on it, it seems safe again. That's what religion and ritual do. Just the fact that the Jews have survived so long is unbelievable in itself. The Romans, the Nazis, the Spanish Inquisition.'

'Nobody expects the Spanish Inquisition,' quipped Ruth.

'You're lucky. You're Jewish so you make light of it. But I think . . .' Dan made a gesture with his arms indicative of his speechlessness which Ruth thought was almost Semitic.

'I'll tell you,' Sylvie intervened. 'This Jewish family isn't going to survive much longer without its dinner. Come on, young ladies. I need help!'

Ruth rose immediately and followed her mother into the kitchen. She couldn't sit still for a moment longer.

Chapter Eighteen

—◦◦◦—

The second night of *Pesach* was always a washout. As usual, all the family had been invited to Lila and David's, where it was done properly. Lila was catering for nine already, and would have happily extended to fourteen; in fact she wanted to cater for fourteen. There was quite a competition in Lila's circle about who had the biggest *Seder*. One never-to-be-forgotten year she scored twenty-one if you counted babies too, and everyone in Lila's circle knew it. Sylvie and Ivan could not stand *Pesach* at Lila's. David read all of the service, and everything Lila cooked was fat-free and sugar-free because of David's digestive problems. This year they declined their standing invitation, although it had caused an argument.

'I told her,' Sylvie said to Ruth as they washed up, 'that I didn't see why we should celebrate two nights. Apparently in Israel they only have one night. In the Diaspora they have two as no one used to be sure when the *Seder* actually started, but this is the twentieth century, for goodness' sake!'

Ruth wiped a glass carefully. The familiar rhythm of her mother's invective was soothing.

'So she said to me, what was this? Was I turning Reform? What's so wrong with Reform? I asked her. Huh, she said. In Reform, they have women rabbis. You should have heard her contempt. I said, so maybe women rabbis are a good thing. She said to me next thing I'd be defending gay marriages. I said to her I couldn't see why two people who love each other shouldn't get married whatever sex they are. She said those ideas were anti-Jewish. I told her anti-Jewish was being as intolerant as she was being. I said the worst thing a Jew can be is intolerant. We were the victims of intolerance, I said to her.' Sylvie had stopped washing up and turned to Ruth with rubber-gloved hands outstretched.

'So she said, what was I suggesting? That she was as good as a Nazi? So I laughed, and she said, how dare you laugh at me! I wouldn't have you at my *Seder* if you paid me. I said, I have no money to pay you, the wedding's cleaned me right out. She said, don't expect to see us at your daughter's wedding. I never approved of her marrying out, anyway. I told her that Dan was going to make a much better son-in-law than her son-in-law, and that was when she put the phone down.'

'So she's not coming to the wedding?'

Sylvie turned back to the washing-up. 'She'll come. Lila's curiosity is stronger than her animosity.'

Ruth stacked the plates neatly on the dresser. Instead of an evening with Lila and David, the five of them had had a brief *Seder* in which they simply recited the most important prayers and ate the leftovers. Ruth had driven Dan to the station first thing that morning, as there was an important meeting at work. She was staying on for the second night, and possibly, she told him, Saturday as well. She would drive back to Leeds on Sunday. There were wedding details that needed seeing to. At the station she had got out of the car to get his bag from the boot, and he had kissed her lingeringly. She had just blanked him out.

Tomorrow she did not know what she was going to do. She needed to do some shopping in town, at least in the morning.

'I think I'll pop into Kendal's tomorrow, Mum.'

'Kendal's?'

'To look at the make-up. I told Sharon I want to do my own make-up. I thought I might treat myself to something.'

'Good idea. Do you want company?'

Guilt felled her like an axe blow. 'No, I . . . No. It'll be boring for you. And I don't know how long I'll be.' It seemed worse deceiving her mother than deceiving Dan. For a moment she wanted Sylvie to guess at the truth and relieve her of her burden. 'I might have a walk around, see how Manchester's getting on without me.'

'As you like.'

Ruth swallowed hard. What would happen if she told her mother about Nick? She could introduce the subject very casually, and gauge her mother's reaction. She took a deep breath, began to form the words, then stopped. It was point-less. Sylvie would be appalled. For all her theoretical free-thinking, Sylvie Collins was a stern moralist. To coin an old-fashioned phrase, she was a good woman. Whereas Ruth was bad, very bad indeed. No one in the world knew how bad.

Every night, before falling asleep she had been fantasising

about him. It had begun because she had decided the fantasies would be a substitute for seeing him again, so she could get him out of her mind. It didn't work. The fantasies grew in intensity and frequency. They now constituted a series of interlocking fantasies, a lurid novelette of steamy bedroom scenes and unbridled passion. They occupied all her spare moments. She couldn't believe she was behaving in this way.

'You know,' Sylvie interrupted, 'you've been looking a bit peaky. Anything worrying you?'

'Well, you know.'

'The wedding? It doesn't need two of us worrying about the wedding. You're supposed to enjoy it. I'm supposed to suffer.'

Ruth laughed ruefully.

'And suffering I am. Heather rings me every other day with silly questions and requests, and I can't zip up the skirt I bought. If I let it out, I'll never forgive myself.'

'That's silly,' Ruth said, shaking the water off a saucepan and drying it.

'I know it's silly, but it's hard to get rid of the habit of a lifetime. For as long as I remember I've been trying to lose weight. Now Linda, she's my size and she really doesn't give a damn. I told her she'll have to stand next to me in all the wedding photos.'

'How is Linda?' Ruth asked absently.

'Linda? Fine. Business is slow. Did I tell you she's having an affair?'

'An affair?' Ruth swung round.

'Yes, and it's been going on for years. A married man,

apparently. Not that I've met him, and she doesn't say much about him, but he exists all right.'

'Does that put you off her?'

Sylvie stopped washing up, as she did whenever the conversation interested her more than the job in hand. 'No. I have to say I surprised myself. I always used to think there was no excuse for a woman like that. What woman would let herself be attracted to another woman's man? But somehow it's different when you know only the woman. You tend to see things from her point of view. She doesn't want him to live with; he just visits from time to time. I know it's wrong, but then you end up telling yourself that sometimes wrong things work out all right. Who's to judge? What if this man's wife wants him out of her hair? What if she's having an affair herself?'

Ruth was flushed. 'Mum,' she laughed, 'You're turning into a moral relativist.'

'What's that when it's at home?'

'Someone who doesn't believe in moral absolutes.'

'Perhaps I don't. Life is complicated.'

'Ellie has left Adam, you know.'

'Has she?'

'Yes. She told him he had to choose between his wife and her, and he chose his wife.'

'How is she? I have a soft spot for Ellie.'

'Not too good. In hiding. Feeling sorry for herself. Why is life so messy?'

'You'd be out of a job if it was simple. My back is killing me.'

'Sit down.'

Sylvie eased herself down on to a chair. Ruth badly wanted

to hug her but didn't. If she hugged her, she knew she would end up telling her everything. She was also digesting her mother's words: sometimes wrong things work out all right. It was the permission she craved. She was aware of her mother looking at her.

'Wedding nerves are quite natural, you know,' Sylvie said.

Wedding nerves. If only. Ruth shrugged, she could not trust herself to speak.

'A month before marrying your father I was – what am I saying? *During the ceremony* I thought I couldn't go through with it! I was thinking, this is for life. For life. A life sentence. And I was innocent!' Sylvie laughed at her own joke. 'If you weren't nervous, then you wouldn't be taking it seriously enough. Come here.'

Ruth did as she was told. Sylvie kissed her briefly on the cheek in an unaccustomed gesture. Tears stung Ruth's eyes.

'He suits you,' Sylvie said. 'You're going to be very happy. Now put the kettle on because I'm parched. And tell your sisters to turn the television down. And tell your father to come in here and take out the rubbish. Nobody would ever think of doing anything in this house if it wasn't for me.'

If Ruth hadn't known it was there, she would have missed it. From the distance Gorton Monastery was just another massive Mancunian redbrick monstrosity, like Strangeways or the McVities' factory. The bus stopped just in front of it and she got off, walked to the front and looked up. Three slender flying buttresses in red brick and sandstone soared upwards to a figure of Christ stretched out on the cross. Above it a green spire pierced the sky. The sheer height and scale of the building amazed her; it really was a cathedral after all, despite the way it blended in with Gorton Lane and looked at ease among the maisonettes and parked cars. Four Gothic arches led to four locked wooden doors; above them were large-nosed, staring gargoyles. The front of the cathedral was grubby and its hugeness was oppressive, yet something stirred in Ruth as her eyes were led ever upwards.

There seemed to be no entrance to the cathedral; a metal fence cut it off from the pavement. Ruth walked along the road until she came to a padlocked gate. Evidently this was the way in, and Nick had not arrived yet. She stood there indecisively. Behind the gate was an asphalt courtyard littered with debris – concrete rubble, a broken traffic cone, the dead limb of a tree with a black bin liner tangled in the branches, flapping idly in the breeze like a crow's wings. Beyond the courtyard was a low building attached to the cathedral. It seemed to be part of a cloister. To the right was an opaque glass cross set into a brick wall. Some of it had shattered. From the side Ruth was struck once again by the size of the cathedral and wondered at the incongruity of its location, on Gorton Lane, in the badlands of Manchester.

She did not see Nick emerge from the cloisters, and he was already halfway across the courtyard before she spotted him. Her pleasure was such that she felt physically ill. He was dressed in his brown leather trousers and jacket, and a camera was slung round his neck. He began to unlock the padlock, treating her with what felt like casual indifference.

'Hi. I had to keep the gate locked, security and all that. I've been taking some shots inside. What do you think of it?' Nick glanced up at the cathedral.

'It's huge,' Ruth said. 'It seems incongruous. I always associate cathedrals with mellowed stone and grassy lawns and choirs and stained-glass windows and all that tourist-book stuff.'

'Yeah. But this is different. It was built by the locals, did you know that? They provided the money, and the labour, and this was during the cotton famine when half of them were starving.'

'Wow,' she said dutifully. She was relieved and disappointed. Nick was coming over like a tour guide; this assignation was so matter-of-fact, her mother could be a witness and it wouldn't matter. She was right to have come.

She followed Nick back across the courtyard to the entrance to the cloisters, through an arched door between rough concrete rendered walls. He shut it after them. They were in a walled garden, with a huge conifer planted in the centre. Suddenly they were closed off from the rest of the world. A secret garden.

She looked around her. On three sides were low buildings, with black cavities where windows used to be. They looked almost like stables, or a disused warehouse.

'That was the friary,' Nick told her. 'The monks left over ten years ago. Franciscans.'

'Founded by St Francis of Assisi,' Ruth said. 'The guy who loved animals.'

'That's the one.' And then he smiled at her. The monastery receded and his eyes ate up the distance between them. Ruth had to remember to breathe.

'Let's go in,' he said.

First she was aware of an overpowering smell of damp. To her left and her right stretched a series of arches. The marble floor was scuffed and ingrained with dirt. Paint and plaster were peeling from the walls, revealing bare brick and concrete. It would have been beautiful once. Now it was scabby, leprous. The glory had departed.

'What a waste,' Ruth remarked.

'I think so too. But there are plans to restore the building with Lottery money, so once again the locals will fork out for the building, in a manner of speaking.'

'What will they do with the building?'

'There'll be an inter-faith centre, exhibitions, rooms for hire.'

Ruth picked her way over some planks of wood and turned a corner. She gasped. She was at one end of a vast expanse of interior space. At the other was a high altar, grand and barren. Behind her two long, thin windows let in lines of light. Everywhere paint was peeling like a disease of the skin. She watched a pigeon fly across the width of the building. The emptiness and decay depressed her. Yet there was something else here too. The whole effect of this dilapidated cathedral was faintly subversive. Despite your aspirations, it seemed to say, *this* is what it all boils down to, this seedy grandeur, greatness going off. Don't try. What's the point?

'See those empty plinths?' Nick said, interrupting her train of thought. 'Here's a good story. When the monks went, the statues went too. Someone helped himself. They ended up in Sotheby's, ready to be auctioned as garden ornaments. They were spotted by a trustee of the building who happened to be down there. She alerted the authorities, the council bought them back and they're in storage now.'

'Awaiting restoration.'

'Yeah.'

Silence. Ruth walked towards the high altar, her footsteps echoing in the empty building. Nick ambled beside her. The floor was carpeted with pigeon droppings which disguised the marble inlay. Once again she looked up at the scabrous walls.

'So how have you been?' Nick asked her.

'OK.' She was conscious of the beat of her heart. Her nerves made her voluble. 'It's crazy, isn't it, letting a building go to waste like this? They spend millions of pounds on more shopping malls, and, I mean, this could be as amazing as York Minster.' She stopped in her tracks, remembering the last time she was in the Minster. Why did a nice Jewish girl like her always end up in churches? She felt a hysterical laugh rise to her lips.

'They're hoping to hire out the body of the cathedral for functions,' Nick said. 'Even weddings. I heard they were applying for a licence.'

'Weddings,' Ruth echoed.

'When's yours?'

'Soon. In a month.'

'Why aren't you looking at me?'

'I can't,' Ruth said.

Nick took off his camera and placed it carefully on the floor. He came to stand directly in front of her.

'Look at me,' he said.

Ruth raised her eyes. There he was, a smile on his lips, his eyes holding hers. Yes, she wanted him. She felt as if she could barely stand any longer. She knew he was waiting for her to make the first move. He was so confident.

In fact it was his confidence that prevented her from doing anything at that moment. She couldn't bear the idea that someone knew her better than she knew herself. Then Ruth became aware of the vast, empty space around them, and longed to be somewhere different. She walked over to the side of the cathedral where archways led to a recess.

'These used to be confession booths,' Nick said.

They stepped inside together.

She was away from observation. No one would ever find them. She could not think of a reason to stop him when he came close to her, cupped her face in his hands and kissed her very gently on her lips. Pigeons cooed above them. Suddenly she clung to him and they were kissing greedily, she desperate for something, hating herself, hating him, unable to stop. She was an animal, intent on gratification. She could feel the beat of his heart and the pressure of his hands on her back, moving downwards, pulling her to him. She closed her eyes and saw the face of the gargoyle, staring, grinning.

She opened her eyes. There was a bucket in a corner. Why a bucket? Was it here when the monks were here? It didn't matter. The bucket did the trick. It reasserted reality. She gently disentangled herself from Nick.

'Can you imagine what the monks would think if they could see us now? I mean, they took a vow of chastity!' Her voice trembled.

'They'd be jealous,' he said, unbuttoning her jacket.

She removed his hands. 'It's too spooky,' she said.

'Come on. You're not the sort to believe in ghosts.'

'I feel . . . it feels sacrilegious.'

Nick shook his head. 'No. This is just a building. What's more, we have it to ourselves.'

To Ruth it was more than just a building but she couldn't say why. Or perhaps it wasn't the building. She couldn't hide from the fact that everything she did related in some way to Dan. But how did Dan fit into this? She couldn't say; she couldn't, wouldn't think of him. Not now – maybe later.

'Kiss me again,' Nick said. 'No. Let me kiss you.'

She did not stop him. Being kissed by him felt like drowning. She clung to him, feeling the shape of his shoulder blades under his leather jacket. He tasted of cigarettes and she liked that. Her body was betraying her as she found herself responding swiftly to his every move. It was right that she should come to this – a quick grope in a disused church in Gorton. Lust and disgust battled within her.

'Let's go now,' he muttered. 'Come back to my place. It's not far.'

She could do that if she wanted. Did she want?

'I don't know,' she told him.

'Come on,' he urged her. 'No one will ever know.'

'I'll know.'

'That's all that matters, Ruth. Come on, take pity. I really want you. I wouldn't take this risk either if you didn't mean something to me.'

'What do I mean to you?'

'I don't know exactly what yet. I want to find out. Come back to my flat.'

'Look. I'm getting married in a month. This whole thing is ridiculous. If I sleep with you, it means I can't go through with my wedding. I just couldn't do it. Then what? My mother and my father would find out. They've spent all that money. Jilting used to be punishable by law, and I can see why. And with that kind of beginning, what sort of relationship would we have? Don't you see? It's impossible.'

'You worry too much. You're too serious. Lighten up.' His fingers reached out for her hair and he began to play with it. It was tantalising to feel his fingers and yet not feel them. 'Just take one step at a time. Step one: answer this question. Do you want to sleep with me?' He stroked her cheek lightly. 'Tell me the truth.'

'Yes,' she said.

'Then do it. And then you can take the next step.'

Ruth was silent.

'It's your life,' he said.

'I'm not ready,' she said, although she couldn't honestly say what she wasn't ready for.

'I can wait.' He kissed her lightly on the cheek and was the first to leave the recess. Ruth followed him. The cathedral seemed utterly unreal and out of place. They made their way out of the main building through the cloisters and Nick pushed open the door that led into the garden. It was warmer outside than inside, Ruth discovered. She was pleased to be outside, and yet felt cheated.

'I've still got some more shots to take. Are you OK getting back?'

'Sure,' she told him.

'Have you still got my card?'

'Yes, I have.'

'So you know where to come.'

'Yes.'

He kissed her once more, tenderly, as Dan would have done. 'I'd better let you out.'

She walked with him to the padlocked gate and he opened it.

' 'Bye,' he said, and went back inside.

Ruth began to walk rapidly down Gorton Lane the way the bus had brought her. She hoped that movement would stop her thinking. No such luck. First she remembered that she'd told him she wanted to sleep with him. What an admission! Then she recalled the feel of his kisses – and could have cried to think how badly she wanted him. It was a nightmare, ghastly, unpredictable and all being played out here in Gorton, as cars rushed past and a woman pushing a stroller with a toddler eating Monster Munch approached her and then crossed the road.

No, she could not walk any further. She was completely drained; her legs could not carry her. There was a bus stop over the road, from which she could get back to Piccadilly. No one was standing there, which seemed to suggest a bus wasn't imminent. She was surprised to discover she was still capable of logical thought with her life in such ruins. Looking both ways, she ran across the road, and took up position at the bus stop.

For the first time, she was glad for the ordinariness of Manchester. It was soothing to be somewhere so prosaic and mundane as a bus shelter on Gorton Lane. It reassured her. Life would go on, wedding or no wedding, Nick or no Nick. Lorries would rumble past, people would get on with their lives, buses would turn up. Or not. In this case, most definitely not. There was no sign of a bus. She panicked a little. She didn't want Nick to come out and find her. That would be farcical. She decided she would try to get a taxi back into town, and then she could walk around the shops a little, have a coffee somewhere and decide what to do next. She just had to keep moving.

She strained to see if there was such a thing as a taxi, and of course there wasn't. There was neither a taxi nor a bus. Ought she to try to walk into town, although it was a good couple of miles? She looked into the distance again. Yes — there was a black cab. Filled with relief, Ruth stepped off the kerb to hail it.

The 'For hire' light was on, and as the cab driver saw her he slowed and indicated left. She watched it approach and read the number plate. G463 NVU. Oh, no.

Chapter Nineteen

Ivan had been working the Asda at Longsight. The Professor had been off that week and had tipped him that the Asda at Longsight was always good for a few jobs. Ivan looked up to the Professor. While other cabbies hung around the ranks doing crosswords and listening to the radio, the Professor had taken a degree in history and was lecturing part-time at the university. Ivan's handle was Ivan the Terrible, which was a joke, as his reputation was for being a bit of a softie. He had a stash of supermarket carrier bags in the front of his cab in case any jobs had bags that split, and he'd been known to help old ladies carry in their purchases even when he didn't have the time to do so.

He knew if he cruised more and chatted less he'd bring in more money, but money wasn't everything. For Ivan, job satisfaction counted, and driving a cab satisfied him. He was independent but belonged to a community. At the end of each day he had cash in hand. If they were hard up, he could put in a few extra hours. He could plan his own holidays. It was true that being a cabby wasn't as safe as it used to be, and there were stories of knives being drawn, and even an occasion when Harry the Rag had a gun pointed at him, but a good cabby began to have a sixth sense about doubtful jobs. Ivan had had the odd drunk throw up in the back seat, but seats were vinyl, washable, and since he rarely did a night track it didn't happen too often. He always had some paper towels soaked in Zoflora under the back seat, although Sylvie said they stank to high heaven.

Now he decided to head back to town and work the stations, until he saw the girl at the bus stop hailing him, a girl that reminded him for a moment of Ruth. He slowed and indicated left. It was Ruth. Ivan was surprised and delighted. Ruth's presence was always a tonic to him and he felt himself brighten. But what was she doing at a bus shelter in the middle of Gorton Lane? In the time it took him to draw to a halt beside her, he recollected that she'd said she was going into town, but she hadn't mentioned Gorton.

He leaned over and wound down the window. 'Ruth! What are you doing here?'

'Can I get in?' She opened the door and sat herself on the back seat. Ivan turned round as far as he could.

'Something to do with the wedding dress?' he asked.

'No. Nothing like that.'

A father's instinct told him something was wrong. 'I'll come round to the back and we can have a chat.'

'No. Just keep driving. Please.' Her face was white and drawn. Since he could see no harm in doing what she had requested, he revved up the engine, turned off the 'For hire' sign, indicated right and moved out on to the road. He turned off the Mantax radio so they should not be disturbed. A glimpse in the rearview mirror showed him Ruth's face deep in thought. He waited. They reached the junction.

'Where shall I go?' he asked her.

'Oh, anywhere. No. Not home. Just drive, please.'

Ivan went straight ahead at the lights, past ICL until he stopped at the lights opposite a used car showroom. Ruth had still not spoken. She was staring out of the window, biting her nails.

'Come on,' Ivan said. 'You can tell me about it.'

'What if I didn't go through with the wedding?' Ruth asked him.

Ivan felt himself stiffen yet for some reason he was not surprised. Perhaps it was because Sylvie had said more or less the same to him that morning when she'd tried on her suit and it still didn't zip up. Last-minute nerves, that's what it was. He constructed a scenario where Ruth had gone shopping in town, began to panic, took a bus anywhere, ended up in Gorton, got off the bus, and Fate had conveniently arranged to send him to her.

'Cold feet?' he asked her sympathetically, turning on to the Manchester Road towards town.

'A bit more than that. I've met someone else.'

A jolt went through him. This didn't make sense. Ruth was besotted with Dan. Ivan had even admitted to himself that Dan probably loved Ruth almost as much as he did. Reprehensible as it was, he felt pleased for a tiny moment that Ruth could not fix on Dan; she was his first and most special daughter, no one was good enough for her, not even himself, except he knew he would go further for her than any man living.

'Are you shocked?' Ruth asked.

'You could say that.'

'Can I tell you about it?'

'Yes, tell me.'

There was a long queue of traffic at the lights by the flyover, and Ivan watched Ruth leave the back seat and take the fold-up seat behind him. She positioned herself at a right angle to him, so he could only glance occasionally at her profile. A curtain of dark hair concealed her face. With the security grille separating them, Ivan almost felt like a priest in a confession booth. It helped him to steel himself to hear the worst.

'I went to an exhibition with Ellie – Dan was in Bristol. I met him there. We only talked like anyone would, but then he found out where I worked – or I think I must have told him – and he came over and took me out for lunch. The only other time I've seen him is today, because he invited me to look over Gorton Monastery with him. He's a photographer.'

Ivan circled slowly round UMIST, scratched the back of his neck and absorbed this. 'Well, that doesn't sound so terrible to me. Just because you're engaged you don't have to live like a nun.'

'I know, but it's the effect it's had on me. That he's had on me. We haven't done anything, although the offer stands.' Ivan sensed Ruth's embarrassment, he was embarrassed too. 'But I can't stop thinking about him. I suppose it's a sort of obsession. His name is Nick. He's not my type at all. Scruffy and in your face and arty. But since we went out for lunch everything has changed for me. I can't forget him for a moment, at work, discussing the wedding with you and Mum, even when

I'm with Dan. No one knows about this – oh, except Ellie, and even she doesn't know everything. I'm either obsessed because of my strength of feeling for him or because I'm shocked at my own response, or my guilt. I just can't think straight any more.'

Ivan felt helpless. He was stuck in the front of the cab and could not comfort her. There was nothing he could do or say. Not that he felt he needed to say anything. Ruth's words almost sounded rehearsed, as if they had been stored up for a long time and had been waiting for an audience. She had this analytical bent, he knew. He hoped she wasn't using it as a smokescreen for getting her own way. He passed Piccadilly Station on his right and drove down Ducie Street. What could he do to cheer her up?

'Ruthie. Look. Remember when you were small?' He saw he had her attention. He turned the cab right into Jutland Street. The road was level for a few feet, then looked as if it came to a sheer drop. When Ruth was small it delighted and terrified her to be driven down Jutland Street, off the edge of the road then down the bumpy cobbles on the other side to safety. Ivan revved up the engine, and they went hurtling down. Since Ruth wasn't strapped in, it threw her about a bit, but the ride had the desired effect; it stopped her tears. Ivan slewed round to the left and drove on.

'Stop for a minute, Dad.'

He did so, by a building site just before the humpback bridge. He turned off the engine and waited.

'You don't mind me talking, do you?'

'Talk away.' Normally he loved listening to Ruth. He remembered when she was small she would sit on the doorstep and prattle at him while he cleaned the cab. The other two never did that much, but Ruth, like her mother, could entertain all-comers. He used to love the way her little life was so important to her – the rows with friends at school, the forthcoming geography test. As her father, he prided himself on his ability to navigate a route out of her problems. Could he still do that?

'I blame myself, not Dan. What's wrong with me that I should be so affected by another man? I mean, am I ready to get married? It's like, you grow up, have serial relationships, and then you can't stop having them. Even being engaged hasn't stopped me from wanting someone else. It's crazy. Maybe you and Mum should have kept me locked up until you found a suitable *shidduch*, and then I wouldn't have known any different.

'And then I think, surely it can't be all me; is there anything that Dan doesn't give me that I need? Otherwise why should I be interested in someone else? But how can I criticise Dan? It's not his fault he has to work away from Leeds. He loves me, he's kind, he's thoughtful, we have a good - I mean, the physical side of our relationship is OK – we can talk, so it can't be him and it must be me. So despite everything, my career, my degree, my diplomas, I'm just disgusting, low and disgusting and ungrateful.'

'No,' Ivan said. 'You're just like a lot of people.'

'But I wanted to be better than a lot of people. I wanted success at work and marriage and respectability and security, and daily I see the messes people get themselves in, and I thought that was all the warning I needed, and now look at me. I'm a fool. I'm sabotaging my own shot at happiness. Why?'

Ivan watched a lorry carefully edge under the humpback bridge. 'Don't be so hard on yourself.'

'How can you say that? I'm contemplating being unfaithful to Dan. I really am. Nick asked me back to his flat and I wanted to go.'

'But you didn't.'

'I still might.'

Ivan was silent. He wanted to start up the engine and take her home, ring Dan, and stop her from doing anything that would harm herself. But Ivan had been a father too long, and he knew that you had to let children work out their own problems. It cut you to the quick, but there it was. So he remained silent. He was shocked at what he had heard, but like so many things in life, you have to swallow them whole and adjust. His anger was directed at the man called Nick; he could have cheerfully run him over.

'Perhaps I ought to see him again, just to follow this thing through to its conclusion.'

'I don't know if that's a good idea.' Ivan decided to apply a little pressure.

'So what is a good idea? Marrying Dan and knowing how I feel about Nick? Telling Dan about Nick and destroying him? I can't stand sitting here staring at the wall. Can we go somewhere else?'

Ivan started up the engine and drove on, over the junction, past Argos, through Ancoats until the two big cooling towers loomed up on his right. Would Sylvie know what to do? He was out of his depth, that was for sure. Hoping Ruth wouldn't notice, he turned in the direction of Crumpsall. He had to get her home.

'I always believed the most important thing was being honest. I've never been able to stand hypocrisy. Now look at me. Dishonest, deceiving, disgusting. I used to believe Dan was too good for me, and I've proved myself right.'

Ivan came to the Junction Inn and was about to turn left towards the Bury Old Road.

'No, don't go home yet. That's it. I've proved myself right. That's why I'm so compelled to go after Nick. He's my self-image.'

'You're losing me,' Ivan said. He was always a bit overawed by Ruth's grasp of psychology.

'But if he is my self-image, my alter ego, then what am I doing marrying Dan?'

Ivan proceeded up the Rochdale Road. 'Because you love him?'

'What's love? If it's sexual attraction, then right now I feel more for Nick. If it's based on shared experience, then I still don't know Dan well enough yet to be sure I do love him. I used to believe in romantic love, but it's just for kids, isn't it? It's just two people agreeing to be thoroughly selfish together. Maybe life is just desire, gratification and boredom. Then the cycle repeats itself. I sound like Ellie.'

'You sound like you need a cup of tea and some matzo.'

'Matzo?'

'It's still *Pesach*, remember?' Ivan turned into Victoria Road, heading for home, whatever Ruth said to the contrary.

'But I still can't bear the thought of upsetting Dan. Does that mean I do love him? Only I don't see how I can love him and be obsessed with someone else. I'm going round in circles, aren't I?'

Ivan moved out to overtake a cyclist. 'No, you're not. You're going home.'

'Don't tell Mum any of this.'

'Your mother is good in these situations, especially after all the literature she's been studying.'

'I don't want her to know. I'm not sure I should have told even you. This is my mess, and I've got to find my own way out of it.'

'Look, whatever you decide is fine with me.'

'You remind me of Dan sometimes. That's just the kind of thing he would say. It's infuriating. Sometimes I just want someone to lay down the law and tell me what to do.'

Ivan laughed. 'I don't think you do, Ruth. Not if you're anything like your mother.'

'I'm nothing like my mother,' she said

That's what you think, he thought.

Chapter Twenty

———◦◦◦◦◦———

Dan glanced down at the clock on the treadmill. Four more minutes to go. He pounded harder, sure that exercise would relieve his mind. He liked to push himself on the treadmill, edging up his speed a little more each time. This evening his legs refused to go any faster and he knew it was to do with his state of mind. He was worried about Ruth. He would not think about that yet, not until he had finished his run.

For distraction he looked around the gym, at the several TV monitors tuned in to a variety of stations, to the elderly man on the treadmill next to him, in dusky pink shorts, to the sweaty woman in front of him climbing endlessly uphill on the stepper. Then he glanced at the girl weight-training in front of the mirror, dressed in a black leotard and tights. She had a good figure and Dan's eyes lingered on her just a little longer than he knew he ought to let them. He glanced down at the clock. Two more minutes.

Ruth hadn't been herself lately. She wasn't smiling as much. A light had gone out in her, and the darkness had spread to him too. Dan brought his attention back to the gym. Two of the fitness trainers behind him were sharing a joke. One minute, thirty seconds. A few months ago she would have insisted he stay with her for the whole of Passover. She'd seemed quite happy for him to go back to work this morning. And she had not been eating – he had noticed that. Fifty seconds, forty-five. He wiped the sweat from his forehead. Thirty, twenty-five. Nearly there. The treadmill slowed and Dan adjusted his pace accordingly. Again he wiped his forehead and enjoyed the feeling of having come to the end of his run.

Some sit-ups and then he would be finished. He lay on the mat looking up at the polystyrene tiles on the ceiling. It would be lonely when he went back home tonight without Ruth. It was a shame it was too late for him to drive over to Manchester. He recalled her message on his answerphone which said that she wouldn't be back in Leeds till Sunday evening – she had some shopping to do. Why, he wondered, didn't she shop in Leeds? She preferred the shops in Leeds and loved wandering around Harvey Nichols. He was free and he would have gone with her.

He would think about that later. Concentrating on his stomach muscles he commenced his sit-ups, counting in his head to still his thoughts. Between each set he lay on the mat, telling himself that he would think through this business with Ruth logically, once he'd finished his work-out. Back to the sit-ups. He started counting again.

He could tell from the tension in his back that he had done enough. Now he lay still for a short while, wondering whether to extend his time in the gym with a session in the hot tub. No, he wasn't in the mood. He had come here tonight to work off his anxiety; relaxing was something he could only do when his mind was clear.

Perhaps now was the time to be logical about Ruth. Something was wrong, he was certain. Why? Because she wasn't eating, she was uncharacteristically quiet, because she wanted to be alone. What could it be? That she was stressed about the wedding? A distinct possibility. In that case, why hadn't she shared her stress with him? Or was she having second thoughts about marrying him? The possibility was too awful, and Dan shied away from it. In his world, bad things like that didn't happen. He and Ruth were far too much in love. With the memory of the Passover supper in his mind, he wondered whether she was concerned he wasn't Jewish? This was something that Dan had begun to think about lately. He had been surprised at his own enthusiasm for Judaism. At first he had put it down to his love for Ruth but just lately he'd begun to wonder if there wasn't more to it. Since adolescence he'd always had a feeling that there was more to life than . . . well, life. Call it spirituality, if you will, although he hated the label, which reminded him of New Age gurus, yoga and feng shui. What Christianity he'd experienced at home always seemed to him form rather than substance. With the Collinses he sensed something different, a faith that believed in them rather than one they subscribed to. It had power. Dan felt himself enriched by it. He, the thirsty traveller in the desert, had come to his oasis. Lying on the mat in the gym he began to wonder about what it would be like to convert. How difficult was it? Most religions encouraged new recruits.

Much of what he had seen of Judaism through Ruth

appealed to him. He liked the emphasis on family life and was warmed by the vitality of the Collinses. Their arguing, he could see, was a logical result of their closeness; in his family everyone was insulated by acres of space, left to their own devices, lost. He loved his mother, his father, Tim even, but wanted something different now. He wanted to be part of the Collins clan and warmed by their energy and life and colour.

He could also see that when he and Ruth had children it would be so much easier if they all practised one faith. When he thought about it, perhaps it was the Jewishness in Ruth that he loved so much. It was as good a place to start as any, though there was the painful question of circumcision. He hoped that at his age it wouldn't be necessary. He considered that his link with Christianity was slight, and only still in place because of the respect he had for his mother. She would be dismayed, of course, but his first loyalty was to Ruth now. Yes; she was unhappy he wasn't Jewish, and that was a problem he could solve.

The girl in the black leotard walked past him. She had good legs. They were more toned than Ruth's, and in some strange way less attractive for that. He wondered if Ruth noticed other men in the way he still rated other women. He supposed she did, it was only natural. What if she had seen someone she preferred to him? The thought chilled him as he quickly rearranged the facts of her cooling to fit that inter-pretation. No; impossible. He banished the thought and eased himself up off the mat.

Brooding like this didn't achieve much. He liked action. The prospect of a weekend alone was unattractive. Perhaps he would drive over and see his parents. If the moment was right, he might even have a word with his mother. It was possible she would have some insight into Ruth's state of mind. For all he knew, all women had jitters before their weddings. Besides, he could do with some home comforts.

His mind was made up. Feeling in control once more, Dan strode over to the changing rooms ready for a long, hot shower.

Dan hugged his mother and began to take off his jacket.

'Where's Dad?' he asked.

'Away again,' Heather said, taking Dan's jacket from him and straightening it before hanging it neatly on the coat rack. 'An inspection in Manchester took longer than planned and he's staying there.'

Dan glanced at his mother to check her reaction. He had never quite been able to work out her feelings about Dad's jaunts from home. He used to think she was lonely, then when he was older he guessed she might even be glad to have him out from under her feet. When Dad was away, he had always tried to be a good companion to her. Tim was never much use. Now both of them were deserting her. This sudden fellow feeling made him warm towards her and he gave her an unexpected kiss on the cheek. He was glad he'd decided to come over to York.

He followed her to the kitchen as she explained that lunch needed some final touches. At the thought of lunch he realised he was hungry.

'What is there?'

'Just quiche and salad, darling, because you rather sprung this visit on me. But there is some fruit cake for dessert.'

Dan stood against the pantry, watching his mother get the meal together. He felt almost too big and clumsy for this dainty kitchen, and was conscious suddenly of how far he had moved on. His house in Leeds was home now; at least, it would be home when Ruth and he were married. He gazed around the kitchen and saw it as if it was already in the past. It was a manifestation of the life Heather had created with Ken. The kitchen was clean, ordered and tasteful. The table was already set for lunch with three flowery place mats arranged at precise right angles to each other. There was, in his old home, a feeling of structure and serenity. Dan found it mocked him today, as it seemed to take no account of his creeping anxiety about Ruth, who had not rung last night, nor this morning. But worrying about it wouldn't help.

'Tim at home?' he asked, realising the significance of the third place mat.

'He's working at the university today,' Heather explained. 'In fact I'm glad he's not here, Dan, because I did want to have the pleasure of telling you all about his girlfriend myself.'

'His girlfriend? Tim?'

'Yes, Tim. I did mention it to you but you seem to have forgotten. It's someone he met on the Internet – Samantha.'

'Isn't she coming to the wedding?'

'Yes. It took me some time to get adjusted to this new way of romance – meeting people through a computer! – but I can see now that it's not very different to meeting someone in a public place, except you're less swayed by appearance, and Tim feels that they're soul mates, you know. Really!'

Dan was intrigued, but stopped listening for a moment as he thought he heard the radio on somewhere in the house. It puzzled him, as it wasn't Classic FM but a rock station.

'Apparently she's an expert in computing too, and they play bridge together. They meet in something called a chat room, and they've exchanged photos. She's blonde, nothing like Ruth at all. He spends hours in front of his computer. She's not been at work recently because she's been ill with glandular fever, which is a great pity as Tim was hoping to travel down to Hull to meet her before the wedding. Only glandular fever is very infectious and naturally she doesn't want to meet him not looking her best. I can understand that.' Heather shook the salad dressing vigorously.

Dan was amused by the story and it cheered him.

'Good old Tim. Hey, can I hear a radio?'

'Yes. Richard is upstairs. He's joining us for lunch.'

Dan strolled over to a bowl of crisps on the table and began to help himself. He would have preferred Richard not to be there, but he could hardly blame his mother. He had rung at nine last night, too late for her to put off her gardener. Since he was on the premises, she could hardly banish Richard to another room in the house to eat.

'Could you cut some mint, Dan? There's some growing on the windowsill. I'm so looking forward to the wedding,' Heather chattered on. 'There's still a hundred and one things to do. I'm driving over to the hotel next week to discuss flowers. I'm going to see to the buttonholes too. To be honest, Sylvie doesn't seem very interested in those sort of details, which is just as well. I so want to feel part of things. I think there's a danger that the bridegroom's mother can be sidelined in weddings.'

Dan watched his mother slicing quiche. She seemed a little nervous – flustered, even. Perhaps it was the fact he had only rung last night to say he was coming over. For Heather that was very short notice; she liked to plan ahead and feel in control of things. Perhaps that was why she was chatting at him so hurriedly, and why she didn't notice the bottle of olive oil to her left which she knocked over, then quickly picked up. On the other hand, having spent the past couple of weeks watching Ruth's every move, maybe he was just transferring the same sort of hyper-vigilance to his mother. He might simply be over-interpreting her behaviour, just as it was likely he was over-interpreting Ruth's low spirits.

'Darling?' Heather interrupted his thoughts. 'Would you go and tell Richard that lunch is ready?'

'Sure. Where is he?'

'In the attic.'

Dan made his way upstairs. Once on the landing, he found the door to the attic was closed. He tried the doorknob. The door was locked.

'Richard?'

'Yeah?'

'Lunch is ready.'

'OK. I'll be down in two ticks.' Dan was puzzled. Why lock the attic door? He tried it again. It was definitely locked. Then it opened suddenly, to reveal Richard. They both looked taken aback to see each other.

'How are you doing?' Dan asked.

'OK.' Richard turned to lock the door again.

'What's with all the security?' Dan asked.

'There've been several break-ins round here lately,' Richard explained, putting the key in his pocket. 'We've been told to get into the habit of locking interior doors.'

Dan was not satisfied but decided to think about it later. There were more pressing things on his mind, though with Richard sharing their lunch he could not speak frankly to his mother. He had to admit that he resented his presence.

Lunch was a strained affair. Richard kept his head down and his knife and fork in motion. Dan glanced at him occasionally, a little taken aback at how comfortable he seemed to be. Heather, naturally, did most of the talking. Like most women, she found it easy to talk and dress up trivialities. It provided a background to Dan's troubled thoughts. He noticed Richard fill his plate from the array of salads as if accustomed to helping himself.

'There's mint in this, isn't there?' Richard asked.

'Yes,' Heather said. 'From the pot in the nursery. I brought it down earlier.'

'The flavour's developed well.'

Dan saw them smile at each other. He felt excluded. What on earth had been going on here in the past few months? Richard seemed not so much a domestic help as a close friend. Heather seemed completely at ease with him, and attentive to his needs, refilling his glass with orange juice, asking him if he wanted more quiche before she asked Dan. Dan felt supplanted. He had to remind himself that his mother, who was probably lonely, had every right to choose her own company, and he ought to be grateful to Richard, but still . . .

He made an effort to be civil to them both.

'So you've both been busy up in the attic,' he began.

'Oh, yes!' Heather seemed eager to talk about the nursery.

'Do you know, we're even making a profit! Richard has found a garden centre in – where did you say? Selby?'

'Selby,' he confirmed.

'And they're buying our seedlings! We're giving fifty per cent of our profits to charity. The vicar is so pleased. We're hoping to buy some furniture for St Jude's, too.'

'And the other fifty per cent?' Dan asked.

'We plough that back into the business – oh, and I insist Richard keeps a little as he does most of the work. We need quite a bit of equipment and we might upgrade the hydroponic kit you bought me for Christmas. We're kept ever so busy. It's lovely to have an interest again, Dan.'

Dan felt even more guilty. His mother did seem happy, and it was only right she should have a hobby to keep her mind and body active. Without entirely being able to make peace in his mind with Richard, Dan vouchsafed him a smile. Richard responded in kind.

'Can I have a look up in the attic later?' Dan asked his mother.

Heather glanced at Richard. Richard shot her a warning look.

'Sorry, darling. There's something we . . . People who are getting married in a few weeks ought not to ask questions!' she declared.

These were the words Heather had always used when he and Tim were approaching birthdays, and it meant that there was a surprise in store. 'A boy who is having a birthday in a few days ought not to ask questions!' Maybe she and Richard had moved a wedding present up to the attic. He would not force the issue. He was only mildly curious about the attic. It was more important to him that Richard should push off back there and leave him alone with his mother. Dan increased the pace at which he was eating, in order to get lunch over as quickly as possible.

In fact, after coffee Richard went to work in the greenhouse. Dan offered to help Heather clear up, but she declined and told him to go and relax in the front room. He could not relax. He paced up and down, occasionally glimpsing Richard watering plants. He happened to be looking at him when Heather stole into the greenhouse and they exchanged a few words. Again Dan felt a little ruffled. It was childish of him, but he had come back to York expecting once again to be loved and cosseted and put first. Obviously this was not going to happen. Both Ruth and his mother seemed preoccupied.

He felt a little low, and wondered whether he should have come to York at all. Maybe he ought to have just driven to Manchester for some straight talking with Ruth. If anything, he had been a bit of a coward. He despised himself. He knew also at that moment, watching his mother in the greenhouse, and hearing the distant thrum of a motor mower, he could not speak to her about Ruth. Firstly, it would be an act of betrayal. His loyalty lay with Ruth now. Secondly, there was no precedent. His father never discussed his feelings, because that was a sign of weakness. Tim never discussed his feelings, but that was presumably because he didn't have any. Dan had learned to suppress his so as not to trouble his mother. It was only since he'd met Ruth that he'd begun to explore the possibility of talking frankly about himself — at least to Ruth. When he had done so, it was intoxicating. His mother still occupied the old world order where people were brave and coped and kept up appearances. He didn't rate that world any more, and wanted to be with Ruth where you could kick your shoes off, relax, and tell it like it is. Only Ruth herself was keeping something back from him now, he was sure of it. He determined to find out what it was. Immediately he made his way to the telephone in the hall and dialled her number.

Sylvie answered. 'Dan? She's out shopping . . . To be honest, I expected her back ages ago, she was only going to look at some make-up. I think she's not going back to Leeds until tomorrow, didn't she tell you . . . ? I'll let her know you rang.'

He replaced the receiver. This was not good. He wondered how soon he could get away from York. Probably not for an hour or so, and then he wouldn't be in Manchester until the evening. Perhaps he ought to wait until tomorrow. Just then Heather came into the hall and looked at him inquiringly.

'I was just ringing Ruth,' Dan said.

'Of course. How is she?'

'She's out shopping. Otherwise, fine, although she might be a little stressed. You've spoken to her on the phone recently, haven't you? Do you think she sounded stressed?'

'I don't think so. Not particularly. Though it is difficult to pick up someone's mood on the telephone. Especially on these mobile phones. They distort your voice awfully. Richard has a mobile, and once when I rang him on it I thought he was crying! Really I did! But it was just distortion.'

Dan brought the subject back to Ruth. 'Look, I think I might drive down to Manchester to see her.'

'Now?'

Dan checked his watch. It was quarter to three. It would be rude of him to eat lunch and then leave. Perhaps he was over-reacting. Driving down to Manchester was impulsive and unwise. They could hardly have a frank talk with Sylvie and Ivan in the next room. He would see her tomorrow and talk then.

'It is a bit too late,' Dan conceded.

'Good,' Heather said, 'because I want you to see my outfit and give me your opinion on some shoes.'

'I know nothing about shoes,' he said, smiling.

'You don't have to know anything to know whether you like them,' she said, rallying him. 'Come upstairs and help me choose. You see, I bought both pairs — well, actually, and don't tell your father this, I bought three, because I really couldn't decide if the colour matched as I didn't have my suit with me, and the last pair did have a reduction, and . . .'

Dan arrived back at his house in the Lyntons at seven. As soon as he got in he went straight to the answer machine to see if Ruth had rung. The red light winked at him gratifyingly. Relieved, he pressed the play button and listened.

'Hi. It's Ellie. Are you with Dan, Ruth? I've tried your flat but you're not there. Or maybe you're not back from Manchester. Hey, I need you. Come round. I'm in all evening. We can both talk — it'll do us good. See you later, maybe.' Click. Then two short pips as the answer machine delivered itself of its burden. Dan frowned, puzzled. He played the message again, listening particularly to Ellie's final words. 'We can both talk – it'll do us good.' There was an emphasis on the word 'both'. So Ruth did have a problem, and Ellie knew what it was. Come to think of it, it was highly likely. Ellie, after him, was Ruth's chief confidante. Apparently she was in this evening.

It was the work of a moment to dial Ellie's number and to explain that Ruth was still in Manchester but he wasn't doing anything and would quite like to come round and see her. They were old friends. She asked him if he'd eaten, and he admitted he hadn't. 'OK,' she said. 'I'll rustle something up as long as you don't mind risking salmonella – I haven't cleaned out my fridge for ages.' Ellie's acerbic humour brightened him and restored his sense of normality. It didn't take him long to freshen up, change, and leave the house once more. It felt good to be on the move.

Ellie's flat was on the top floor of a large Victorian house in the Mexboroughs. Dan walked down the path of the long front garden and rang the top bell on the panel. Ellie was down in a moment to let him in. She was dressed in black – black leggings, a black sweater, and her hair was loose but pushed behind her ears. She seemed unusually pale to Dan, and he couldn't work out whether that was due to the clothes she was wearing or her lack of make-up.

'Come on, you,' she said.

He followed her up the stairs and entered her living room. He liked its bohemian atmosphere. A large skylight revealed a black slab of sky. What light there was came from several carefully placed standard lamps and candles. There was a brown velvet throw over her sofa, and Dan made himself comfortable there. He could smell the incense she had burning, and looked round appreciatively at the unusual ornaments, the tiny clock in the shape of a robot and the wind chime made of translucent shells. On one wall was a familiar Andy Warhol print; on the other were blank, pale spaces where pictures used to hang but did so no longer.

'A drink?' she asked him. 'I've already opened some red.'

'Red would be fine.'

He watched Ellie leave for the small kitchen, from where he could smell something spicy. She returned almost immediately with two large glasses of red wine, one of which she handed to him. She sat herself on a tapestry pouffe close to the settee. She seemed poised, if a little quiet. Dan was aware that she had finished with Adam — Ruth had told him. He was sorry for her, but was sure she would find someone better. He was fond of Ellie.

'So,' she said.

Dan saw it would be up to him to make conversation. 'Are you having a good weekend?'

'Terrible.'

'I'm sorry about Adam.'

'Don't be. He's a bastard. I'm better off without him. It's just that, you know, there's something missing. I feel like an amputee who's just got rid of a diseased limb. It's the pain of trying to walk again. It was good of you to come round. Like the song says, two lonely people.'

'What song?'

'Some old Frank Sinatra number that my mother used to play. Which reminds me. I'd better put some music on.' She got to her feet a little unsteadily and Dan wondered if she'd started drinking before his arrival. It was likely.

Ellie's choice of music surprised him – Mike Oldfield's 'Tubular Bells'. The music seemed to knit them together, and he smiled at her as she settled down again on the pouffe.

'Have you heard from Ruth?' she asked him.

'Not today.'

'She's due back tomorrow, isn't she? I knew that really, only when I rang I forgot. I must have just hoped she would be in. It was selfish of me It's funny how selfish people are – have you ever thought that? I don't think there's anything we do that doesn't have some kind of benefit for ourselves. Even do-gooders get some kind of kick out of being do-gooders.'

'I wonder whether I agree with that,' Dan said, thinking of the help his mother was giving Richard and feeling uncomfortable. 'Ruth says it's true that every action we perform has a positive intent – she took a course in NLP recently.'

'My intents aren't always positive.' Ellie laughed, and carried on drinking.

Dan had deliberately brought Ruth into the conversation, but he was no further on in his quest to find out what was happening to her. Again he was swept by that strange reluctance to speak openly and ask Ellie what she knew. It was almost the feeling he'd had with his mother, except now he was able to identify it more accurately as a sort of faint-heartedness, a cowardice. He hoped Ellie would bring up the subject of Ruth's state of mind herself. It was perfectly possible.

'What are we eating?' he asked her.

'Some sort of Thai curry, or so the Tesco jar promises me. I had some chicken in the freezer. Come with me and we can see how the rice is doing.'

Together they entered the tiny kitchen, Dan picked up a

wooden spatula and began to stir the curry. He could never resist stirring things on the hob. It was one of his habits that irritated Ruth. Ellie made no comment but tested the rice for firmness.

'We might as well eat now,' she said.

They faced each other at Ellie's dining table. The food was quite acceptable and Dan enjoyed it. Ellie, definitely rather tipsy by now, was regaling him with involved stories about her colleagues at work and some shenanigans regarding an old account. She was amusing and he was content to listen.

There seemed to be no dessert. After the meal Ellie took her wine and settled on the settee, her legs tucked under her. Dan tried the pouffe, rejected it, and sat on the floor. 'Tubular Bells' began again but Ellie did not notice.

'I'm going down to London next week,' she told him. 'I'm staying with Julie. Remember Julie? I want to look around and get the feel of what's on offer. I might get a flat before I find a job. I can't stand this place any more.'

'I like it,' Dan said.

'It's poky. It's lonely. Yeah, lonely. You wouldn't see that because you don't know what loneliness is.'

'I do,' Dan said.

Ellie smiled and raised her eyebrows. 'Come off it. You've been cosseted and pampered by women all your life. What with your cute face and athlete's body and little-boy-lost act you're a winner.'

Dan wasn't sure whether she was complimenting him or not, but had to put her right about the loneliness factor. 'I've been lonely this weekend.'

'One weekend. Big deal.'

'No. Not just one weekend. Recently I've been . . . No, it doesn't matter. You're right. I don't know about being lonely.'

'Been what ? What have you been?'

Dan took some wine to give him courage. 'I'm a bit worried about Ruth. She's not been herself.'

'Oh, God.'

'What do you mean?'

'Nothing.'

'Come on, you mean something.' He was certain she did. She wouldn't look at him. She pushed her hair back behind her ears again, then poured herself some more wine from the bottle she'd put on the coffee table.

'It doesn't matter,' she said to him. Only she was wrong. It did matter.

'Ellie, if you know anything about why Ruth is unhappy you must tell me. I'm going to marry her. I need to find out. It's up to me to make her feel better. Tell me.'

'No.'

Dan's pulse was racing with fear and desperation. 'Tell me!' He had raised his voice, and he didn't like what he heard. Nor did Ellie. She flinched slightly. But Dan had to know the truth.

'Does she still want to get married?' That was the worst thing he could think of.

'Yes, I think so. But it's not you that's the problem.'

'Not me? Then who is it?' He was talking wildly.

'No one you know. A photographer. Someone who came to Adam's preview. His name's Nick. He comes from Manchester, actually.'

Dan gripped the side of the settee hard, trying to assimilate this. Ruth had mentioned a photographer, a friend of Ellie's. He had been unutterably blind and stupid. Ruth had met someone else. He should have known. He was never good enough for her. But how far had it gone? Did Ruth's parents know? Did the whole world know apart from him? He could articulate none of these questions; he just watched Ellie, frantic to find out more.

She hung her head. 'I don't know whether I should have told you. But since I have, you might as well know everything. She's been out for lunch with him. He wanted to see her again, I know – he invited her to look round some monastery. I guess that's where she might be this weekend. She wasn't certain whether she was going to take him up on it. She still loves you – it's all a mess, isn't it? Look, she hasn't slept with him or anything. At least, she hasn't yet.'

He filled with an inarticulate rage. At the mere suggestion that Ruth might sleep with anyone else, a furnace of jealousy consumed him. He wanted to kill the other man. Still he was incapable of speech.

'I shouldn't have told you, should I? Dan, I'm sorry. Look, it might still be all right. Knowing Ruth, she will have seen him again, and come to her senses. She'll be back tomorrow and you'll have all this out and no harm will be done. These things happen. Life isn't nice and tidy like a Janet and John book. People do crazy things. You've got a better chance of happiness if you can accept the crazy things.'

He was still silent, trying to absorb all this and decide what to do next. Ellie left the settee and came to join Dan on the floor. She put an arm round his shoulders.

'Chill, Dan. It's nothing, just a crush. It happens to

everyone. Maybe the pressure of the wedding got to her and she just overreacted to his come-on. I met him in the office the other day. He could blag his way into anyone's bed; he's that kind of smooth-talker. Oh, God, I shouldn't have said that. I'm sure Ruth hasn't slept with him.'

A tear escaped from his eye.

'No, don't cry – I can't stand seeing a man cry.' She wiped his tear away. 'There are better things to do than cry. Be strong. Don't give up hope. I'm not. I'm starting over. You can too.'

He felt her kiss him gently on the cheek, a soothing, maternal kiss. She smelt of an unfamiliar musky perfume. The physical contact warmed him and for a moment he clung to her. Then she was nuzzling his neck.

'It'll be all right, Dan,' she murmured. 'Like I said, people do crazy things. You'll get it all sorted out.'

The next time she kissed him it was on his lips, and he was surprised. It was impossible not to respond; one did not reject an advance. She clearly needed him, and he needed her. Everything was all wrong, Ellie's presence, Ruth's absence. Ruth was wrong, and he was wrong, and what did it matter any more?

Chapter Twenty-one

Sylvie decided she'd had enough of D. H. Lawrence for one day. The man had sex on the brain. She'd thought she was going to enjoy *Sons and Lovers* in the beginning, when it was all mining, alcohol and wife-beating, but now that sex had reared its ugly head, frankly, you could stick it on the wall. What did she care whether the self-obsessed Paul Morel should marry holier-than-thou Miriam or the sexy Clara? He was spoilt for choice. As she closed the paperback Suzie had lent her, she heard Ivan's taxi pull up in the drive.

Seated in the kitchen by an empty cup of tea and a full ashtray, Sylvie awaited his arrival. Sure enough, he unlocked the front door, and with him was Ruth.

'Where have you been?' she asked her.

There was no reply from either Ivan or Ruth. Sylvie smelt a rat. She saw Ivan gently propel Ruth into the kitchen. Ruth's eyes looked swollen and her nose was slightly red. She came to sit by her mother, who noticed again how much weight she'd lost, and how it didn't suit her.

'Ruth has something she wants to talk over with you,' Ivan said.

'So talk.'

'I'm sorry,' Ruth said. 'I've met someone else.'

'Someone else apart from who?' Maybe it was age, but Sylvie couldn't quite catch her drift.

'From Dan. Dad found me waiting for a bus. I'd just been with him. We were looking round a monastery.'

'A monastery?'

'He was just a casual acquaintance. I've only been with him on three occasions. But it seems to be getting more serious, and I don't know what to do!'

'Steady on,' Sylvie said. Ruth was about to cry again. 'When you say serious, what exactly do you mean? And who is this casual acquaintance?'

She watched Ruth take a deep breath to calm herself. 'We've kissed – that's all. But I can't stop thinking about him. I want to stop thinking about him. I'm not even sure if I like him. Isn't this crazy?' Sylvie noticed Ivan slip away. 'Only, he wants to sleep with me, and I . . . I think I might want to sleep with him. Which means I can't get married. Except I want to get married – I can't imagine not getting married. What else do you want to know? His name's Nick, I met him at Ellie's Adam's exhibition, he's a freelance photographer, my age, and he lives in Gorton. That's it. I hardly know anything else about him. And don't tell me to give him up because I can't.'

'I wasn't going to tell you anything.'

Ruth looked uncomfortably at Sylvie, whose mind was now in overdrive. Like a female Clark Kent, she was busy turning herself into Supermum. Long ago she had learned how to dissociate her emotional response from her practical good sense when her daughters were in trouble. The process was happening again. She plonked her feelings on one side to be dealt with later. She knew Ruth was waiting for some instructions. Giving Ruth good advice was never easy. She challenged everything. Sylvie knew she had to tread very carefully.

'So what are you going to do?' she asked Ruth.

'I don't know. He's invited me round to his flat. I want to go.'

'OK. Then go.'

'But what about Dan?'

'That's for you to work out.'

Ruth pushed her hair behind her ears. 'I thought you'd tell me not to go to Nick.'

'You mean you wanted me to tell you not to go to this Nick?'

'No. Whatever you would have said, I would have gone anyway.'

'Good. Then go.'

'I will.' Ruth did not move. Sylvie was breathless and hoped it was tension and not angina.

'Because if you don't go back and see him in his flat, and you go back to Dan, and say nothing, this will always haunt you. When Dan disappoints you, you'll think of this what-do-you-call-him Nick. You'll think you could have done better for yourself. You can't afford to do that – not if you're going to make your marriage work.'

'But what if I see him one more time and I realise I love him and not Dan?'

'Then it's better you find out now rather than after you're married.'

'But I thought it was better to resist temptation. You're not supposed to examine it and decide whether you want to be tempted or not.'

'No more buts, young lady. You go.'

'Just give me some time to get my head together.'

'You said he was expecting you. You're a coward.'

'I'm no coward!'

'Come on, my girl! No time like the present. Wash your face, put on your lipstick, and see this through.'

Ruth attempted a smile. 'Call yourself a good mother,' she said. 'Sending me off to make a dishonest woman of me!'

Sylvie smiled, and thought that what she was attempting to do was precisely the opposite.

When Ruth had left she tried to explain this to Ivan. 'They call it reverse psychology,' Sylvie told him. 'If I let her think she cares about this boy, she'll realise she doesn't. If she goes to him with my permission, she's bound to go off him. When has she ever done anything I've told her to do? And he's no good for her; I can see that, you can see that, but Ruth will need to see it for herself. She will; she'll come to her senses. She always does in the end.'

'So let me work this out. You're saying she has to get him out of her system?'

'And flushed away into the sewage where he belongs. Fancy making up to an engaged woman! Not in my books, you don't. Bastard!'

Ivan raised his eyebrows at the expletive.

'There's worse in D. H. Lawrence,' she told him.

She could tell by the way that Ivan hovered in the kitchen, not wanting to leave her, that she had failed to convince him. It was possible, Sylvie had to admit, that her plan could misfire. It was conceived in haste, and on a hunch. Yet the very fact that Ruth had left the monastery and come home with her father indicated that she was having second thoughts about this boy. Ruth was difficult, contrary, slightly spoilt, determined to take what she wanted. But she was loving, she was serious and above all she was a good girl, like all of her daughters. Sylvie was cynical about the rest of the world, but her daughters she believed in. And Ivan too.

'Don't worry,' she told him. 'It'll work out.' She lit herself another cigarette. 'It's funny he should live in Gorton,' she mused. 'That's where Linda lives.'

Ruth cruised slowly along Hyde Road, oblivious of the driver behind her who was flashing his lights angrily. She was looking for 256a, the number on the card Nick had given her. Few of the shops had visible numbers and she despaired of ever finding his flat. The ultimate humiliation would be to return to her parents without actually being able to find where he lived. She would never survive the shame. On the spur of the moment she decided to turn into a side street, park the car, and complete her mission on foot.

She double-checked the car was locked properly as she didn't know the area, though she was aware that on one level she was also buying time. This whole affair was beginning to seem quite unreal to her; the afternoon in the monastery seemed light years away. She hardly knew why she was here, except in some obscure way it was to spite her mother. If you want me to get myself in trouble, then I will, she thought.

She deduced that Nick lived over a shop. One embarrassing factor which Ruth had not anticipated was that his flat must be very near Linda's bridal shop. She hoped it wasn't too near. Yet as she walked past newsagents and betting offices barricaded with metal shutters and scanned their numbers, she realised Nick's flat was very near. Next door, in fact. For the number 256a, in grubby polystyrene numerals, adorned an unprepossessing entrance adjacent to Wedding Bliss. This was an awful coincidence. Ruth almost turned tail and ran, except she was here, and knew she had to see her adventure through to its end.

Taking a deep breath, Ruth rang the bell but couldn't hear an answering chime. As she waited, she wondered if it was broken. Or if it wasn't broken, and Nick had gone out. Or if he hadn't gone out but didn't want to see her. Or if he was listening to music and couldn't hear the bell.

Neon street lights gave Hyde Road a garish feel, as did the lights of the pub opposite. Cars and lorries rushed by, on a road which cut a careless swathe through the heart of Gorton. Two youths walked past her eating curry and chips from a paper cone. The smell was thick in the damp air. Ruth hardly knew what she was doing here any more. Yet she pressed the bell again and followed it with a sharp rap on the wooden door.

She banged again, this time more violently. She wondered what the few stray passers-by would make of her. Self-consciousness made her bang even harder. Then the door opened.

'Ruth!' Nick looked taken aback to see her A light shone

in the hall and there was a muted sound of conversation. Behind Nick was a flight of stairs leading to his flat, she presumed. She took all this in instantaneously, then watched the expression on his face. It changed from surprise to pleasure.

'So you came.'

She said nothing. He reached out and stroked her face. She noticed there were breadcrumbs on his sweater.

'Here, come upstairs.' He shepherded her in front of him. As she mounted the first step with its faded, mottled green carpet and cigarette burns, she heard a woman call.

'Nick? Who is it?'

'A friend,' he replied.

'Who's that?' Ruth asked.

'Just my mum. Don't worry about her.'

'No.' Ruth stopped halfway up the stairs. 'No. I want to meet her.'

'Why?' She almost imagined he looked a little shifty.

'Because I'm not some tart you picked up. You don't just bring me in and rush me up the stairs like a guilty secret. If I matter to you, then introduce me.'

Nick laughed a little awkwardly. Ruth did not say that she needed to be assured that his mother wasn't Linda. Nevertheless, what she had said to him was also true. She didn't like being treated like a bit on the side; she deserved better. If she was going to give up Dan (and she wasn't certain she was going to give up Dan) then it had to be worth it. She wouldn't trade in her fiancé for a seedy assignation in a grotty flat in Gorton.

'Yeah, but my mum's got company. My sister's with her, and my dad's come over too.'

'OK, so I'll meet them all.'

'Are you sure?' He put a hand on her bottom, reminding her gently of why she'd come.

'Where are they? In your flat? Where is the noise coming from?'

'Don't worry, they won't even know you're here. My flat is separate from Mum's place. We converted the attic. She lives behind the shop and on the first floor.'

Ruth felt the pressure of Nick's hand trying to propel her up the rest of the stairs. She tested herself by looking at him again. His face had a flaccid, untidy look. He smelt of cigarettes and the dinner he'd been eating. It was impossible to tell there and then whether the fact she'd worked out he was Linda's son was responsible for the lifting of her obsession, but nevertheless she found she could breathe again. He seemed faintly repulsive to her now, frowsty, substandard. Once more she began to feel as if she was in control.

'I'd like to meet your mother,' she said again, her voice trembling only slightly.

'Later,' he said.

'Now,' she insisted, and pushed past him on the stairs. He followed her.

She turned down a corridor that seemed to lead to the rear of the premises, past large, dog-eared cardboard boxes and bundles of metal coat hangers. A light shone from a door which Ruth pushed open. Just as she had expected, there was Linda, comfortable on the settee with a plate of pie, chips and peas on her lap. On an armchair near her was a young woman dandling a baby. Linda looked at her, momentarily disorientated.

'It isn't Ruth?'

'It is,' Ruth said. 'No, don't get up. I was just calling on Nick to thank him for taking me round Gorton Monastery this afternoon. It was very interesting, Nick.' Ruth found her legs were unsteady so she made her way to a chair with a wedding dress hung over the back, and sat down.

'I didn't realise Nick was your son,' she said pleasantly. 'We met in Leeds at a photography exhibition.'

'Well, there's a coincidence,' Linda said.

The baby gurgled, then shouted, 'Da!'

'Do you want a cup of tea?' Linda asked Ruth.

'That would be nice,' she said, giving a sideways glance at a perplexed Nick.

'Nick,' said Linda, 'tell your dad to put the kettle on. He's out there somewhere.'

In the distance Ruth heard the flushing of a toilet. She guessed the bathroom was beyond the kitchen. She remembered her mother telling her about Linda's love life, and anticipated that she would soon meet this mysterious lover. She knew Sylvie would be immensely gratified. She composed herself, almost enjoying her bizarre situation. Nick was standing by a dresser, taking a packet of cigarettes from his jeans pocket. The baby was trying to bounce itself up and down on its mother's lap. Linda had begun a question about Sylvie when the door to the kitchen opened, and her lover appeared.

Ruth recognised him immediately.

'Oh, my God,' she said. 'It's you.'

Chapter Twenty-two

The expression on Ken's face told Ruth everything she needed to know. She had never seen him at such a loss before. All the colour drained from his face, then he became momentarily scarlet, then pale again. Ruth found herself thinking, so this is what a guilty man looks like. From a professional point of view, it was kind of interesting.

She glanced around the room. Linda looked baffled at the suffocating silence. So did Nick. It was the girl with the baby who spoke first.

'Do you two know each other?'

'Yes,' Ruth said. 'Ken is my father-in-law-to-be. I'm marrying his son.'

'You're marrying Nick?' the girl asked, even more puzzled.

'No, Dan.'

The baby laughed. The laughter seemed a reasonable comment on what seemed, for a moment, to be pure farce. Ruth tried to piece the mess together. Linda and Ken had apparently been lovers for some time, and Nick, it seemed, was his son. Nick and Dan were half-brothers. She had been on the verge of committing some sort of incest. Her mind reeled. She understood now why Nick seemed so familiar to her. He was Dan from the wrong side of the sheets. It was unbelievable.

'Ken, tell me how you're related to everyone,' she said levelly. She wanted to hear it from him.

Linda answered for him since he seemed incapable of speech. 'Suzie and Nick are his children, and Phoebe is his granddaughter. Ken and I have been together, on and off, for over twenty-five years.'

'You know he's married,' Ruth said.

'I do, love. Don't stand there swallowing flies, Ken. You always knew there'd be a reckoning. Who would have thought it would have come like this? Let me get this straight, Ruth. You're engaged to Ken's other son, Dan. And here I am, kitting you out in your wedding dress! Isn't life peculiar?'

'I think I'll pop upstairs,' Suzie said.

Ruth watched her go, then studied Nick. He smiled at her and shrugged. She noticed he didn't seem in the least upset. She had a sudden thought.

'Did you know I was engaged to your half-brother?'

'Not at first,' he said. 'Later on I put two and two together. There was a kind of symmetry about it, don't you think?'

'Get lost,' Ruth said.

Nick stubbed out his cigarette then followed his sister through a door on the right that led upstairs. It was the last she saw of him.

Ken was still standing in the doorway of the kitchen. Linda gestured to him to join her on the settee. He did so gingerly, as if at any moment something might jump out and bite him.

Ruth looked at him. There were two things she had to deal with here: Nick's unbelievable act of spite, and Ken's double life. She would start with Ken. It seemed the easier of the two.

'So you two are lovers.' Her glance took in the slatternly but snug room, Ken alert as a mouse sensing the presence of a cat, and Linda, with the poise that belongs only to the truly amoral.

'I'm sorry about our Nick, love. He's always been a bit resentful, like,' Linda said. 'I've never hidden the situation from the kids. Shall I start at the beginning? It was well over twenty years ago. I had a part-time job as a tea lady in the staff room of Ken's school. He was the one who started it. It was wrong of me to take him up, I know, but I fancied him, and times were hard, and you're selfish when you're young. Oh, I tried to finish it, several times. But you know how it is. Then I got pregnant with Nick, and I wasn't so keen to do without him.'

'Did you know about Heather?'

'His wife? Aye. I know that must seem the worst part of it to you. In the beginning I was a right terror, I admit. But after a time I began to fancy that she couldn't not know, with him spending so much time here with me. Either she wanted him out from under her feet, or she was a complete fool. Twenty-five years is a long time to deceive yourself unless it serves a purpose. For all I know she could have a fella of her own. Have you ever thought of that, Ken?'

The corners of Ken's mouth twitched in what Ruth supposed was a smile. Linda still seemed perfectly at ease.

'So our Nick made a play for you, did he? Can't say I blame

him, although he was right out of order. You haven't fallen for him or anything like that, have you?'

'No. I was coming here to tell him to get stuffed.'

'Good for you. I'm his mother and even I don't trust him further than I can throw him. I expect it's the kind of life he's led. Look, you've been sitting here for a quarter of an hour without a drink. Tea? Or coffee? Or something stronger?'

'Tea would be fine.'

Linda eased herself off the settee, pulled down the blouse she was wearing with its splashes of bright reds and blues, twisted the split of her black skirt round to the side again, and began to tidy up the plates on the coffee table. Ruth tried to fight the revulsion she was feeling for Nick, for herself, and for Ken, the author of all of this mess. There was so much she was going to have to try to understand.

'What are we going to do?' she said to Ken. She saw uncertainty and fear in his eyes. Part of her relished it. In faded cords and an Argyle sweater, Ken looked subtly out of place here, yet also infinitely more at ease than in his York home. Surrounded with Linda's jumble of knick-knacks, piles of old magazines and a crate of empty wine bottles, he looked almost bohemian. She decided to suspend judgement until she had heard him speak. It was important she remained clear-headed for Dan's sake. She needed to understand.

Ken cleared his throat. 'We needn't say anything about this.' He attempted a smile.

'What on earth do you mean?' She wasn't going to let him off the hook. There was no noise from the kitchen. The tea was obviously a ruse to let them talk alone together.

'It's better if no one else knows, don't you think?'

'I don't agree with you.'

Ken swallowed hard and his Adam's apple jerked in an ugly way. 'It would be a blow to Heather, and so close to the wedding.' He was beginning to sound like a headmaster again, eminently reasonable, stepping down from his pedestal to impress with his affability. Ruth could forgive his nervousness but not his smugness.

'If you don't tell her, I will.'

Ken stretched out the palms of his hands in front of him, apparently to examine his fingernails. 'Perhaps I ought to have a word with Dan about your friendship with Nick.'

Ruth felt herself go very hot. 'How dare you try to blackmail me! In any case, it won't work. One, I'm going to tell him myself, and two, nothing happened.'

Ken was silent and still would not meet her eyes.

'Nothing happened,' she said more loudly. 'I was tempted, but nothing happened. There was always something that stopped me. Huh! Your Nick is a bastard, in every sense of the word.' Ruth laughed. The subject of her obsession had been no more than another, seedier version of Dan. It was Dan she loved – or she had a fatal attraction for the genes of the shambling philanderer sitting meekly in front of her. She found she could now see everything very clearly. She wanted to share her new insight with Ken.

'Nick's to blame, mostly. But it wasn't all Nick. I have to take some of the responsibility. Dan was away a lot, and I was lonely, I guess. Nick's attention and insistence flattered me. And it became a way to avoid the enormity of the wedding. When I think about it now, the commitment you make when you say you'll marry someone – for life! – is awesome. I was scared. And there was Nick, offering an easy way out, a continuation of that shallow, take-it-while-the-going's-good relationship. It was a big temptation. I have a habit of getting obsessed with things; I became obsessed with him. And I always had this belief that Dan was too good for me; I undervalued myself. Nick was just a reflection of my own low self-esteem. That's over. From now on I'm going to be worthy of Dan. I feel nothing for Nick now. Not because of you. It happened before then. I love Dan, you see. I can't even explain why. When I'm with him, things feel right. Not perfect, but just right. I *have* to marry him. And when I do, no one and nothing will come between us. I've been lucky to learn that now. So, like I said, don't think you can blackmail me by threatening to tell Dan. I'm going to tell him all about my mistakes myself. They concern him and he has a right to know. Are you going to speak to Heather?'

Ken addressed his fingernails. 'Are you?' he asked.

Ruth was silent. Then she said, 'It's not up to me.'

Their eyes met for a moment, then Ken looked away. There were sounds now from the kitchen, spoons being clinked against cups and the trickle of running water. Ken no longer looked the headmaster; instead he recalled to Ruth the boy in the headmaster's study whose football has just smashed through the study window.

'I can't explain,' he said. 'It's just that I think things are better left as they are.'

'I don't,' said Ruth. 'I think we both have a deal of explaining to do.'

*

The M62. Ken knew every inch of it. He remembered the motorway being built, the excitement of it opening, the gradual increase of traffic until now when even on a Sunday morning there was a steady volume of cars and lorries thundering uphill from Manchester to cross the Pennines. The motorway widened into four lanes but Ken did not move into the outside lane, as he was accustomed to do. He stayed at a steady sixty. He was thinking.

The line he would take was that it was all history. Linda, he would suggest to Heather, was in the past. Young men did reckless things, which came to haunt them in their later years. It was wrong of him to start an affair when Heather was pregnant with Tim; he admitted that. He would stand in front of her with his head bowed and accept the blame. He would tell her that much. He would not tell her how Linda's provocative glances affected him, and how her gentle ridicule of his pretensions excited him. It was even better when she insulted him, then punished him. That was something Heather would never do, and something he needed. Because he was bad, and he had to be punished.

That part he couldn't tell Heather. He would put it all down to a young man's fancy. He would say that, true, it was careless that Linda should fall pregnant twice, but that was hardly his fault as he'd trusted her to take precautions. Since there were children, he was obliged – Heather would see this – to make occasional visits back to see them and support them. Children needed the guiding hand of a father.

He would not tell Heather the relief it gave him to enter the back of Linda's shop and slough off the straitjacket of respectability. He loved to follow her bouncing, ample body as she moved around the room. He relished the takeaway pizzas consumed greedily in front of the television, and thought longingly of Linda's bedroom, with her underclothing, and other necessaries, strewn carelessly around. He liked to imagine the school's governing body appalled at his other governing body (but he was wicked and must be punished until it hurt).

What he would miss most, however, were these trips across the Pennines, moving from one life to another, from the sweaty, steamy, disgusting life with Linda to the decent, ordered, respectable existence he shared with Heather. He was most himself when he was moving between them, completely in control, and controlling one while being controlled by the other (until it hurt). He admired himself for his double life while craving the abasement of serving Linda. He had functioned in this way for so long he couldn't imagine having to change. Each woman threw the other into relief, and made him appreciate her other half more. It was arrogant and silly of Ruth to think that by the exercise of honesty anything could be made better. He needed both lives, and both women, his whore and his Madonna.

He would explain to Heather, who did what he told her, that he still felt obliged to see Linda, although of course there was no more passion there, if there ever was. He wondered, overtaking a line of slow cars, if they could get to know each other and perhaps agree to share him. They would meet, at the wedding. Linda had insisted on accepting Sylvie's invitation. At first the idea had shocked him; now he hoped it might provide him with a solution. He had read in the Sunday papers time and time again of artists and writers who chose the most interesting way of arranging their domestic affairs. Why should an ex-headmaster be any different?

Although, he had to admit to himself, having Linda out in the open would change everything. In the beginning his ability to cope with a double life gave him an illicit thrill, akin to shoplifting, he supposed. The terror he felt at nearly being discovered was exquisite. At one time he took to leaving clues for Heather. He remembered bringing one of Nick's toy cars, a model T Ford, back to York. Dan began to play with it and Heather didn't bother to think where it came from. Every time he saw the car, his heart bumped against his chest and he could hardly breathe. Managing his double life took military precision, and his success in doing it gave him the confidence to take on his first headship. If he could run two homes without one suspecting the existence of the other, he could manage five hundred adolescent boys and a staff of fifty. It gave him a sense of power, too. He loved to stride on to the stage in his gown, to address the school, preaching about the virtues of hard work and fair play, while revelling in the knowledge of his Gorton life. He was above such rules. His staff was acquainted with his textbook family but no one guessed about the scrawling in the margins, Nick, Suzie and Linda – and what she made him do for her. (He was wrong, he knew, but he suffered for it – oh, how he suffered!)

Since he had retired, he had relied on his domination of Heather to give him that sense of power. She was his school, and he wanted her to look up to him. She did. She was a good wife. He did not want to hurt her. She was the mother of his sons. He would beg for her forgiveness. He had no right to expect it. She would be devastated. Devastated and angry. Very, very angry. His lips were dry and he moistened them with his tongue. He hoped she would be very angry indeed.

The M62. Ruth knew every inch of it. Until today relief had always coursed through her as she left the untidy, rock-strewn moorland of Lancashire behind and escaped to Leeds, new financial centre of the North, solid, wealthy, where she was a professional and behaved liked one. This Sunday it was different. She was proud to take Manchester with her.

Her parents had been great. Returning late last night to Crumpsall, she poured out everything to them. She would never forget the look of astonishment on Ivan's face, nor the way her mother was, for the first time, lost for words. As Sylvie slowly regained the power of speech, she comforted Ruth, cursed Nick in colourful terms, and expressed solidarity with Heather. Ivan was made to promise that he had only one family, because who knew what he was up to when he was out in that taxi of his. Luckily, he'd managed to convince Sylvie that four wayward females were more than enough for him. Importantly for Ruth, her parents were fully behind her in her decision to tell all. What moved her most was their capacity for accepting everything that had happened to her without judgement, without criticism. Never had she felt closer to them. With lessons like this in how to love, she felt more and more certain her marriage was bound to succeed too.

The gentle hills of West Yorkshire rose in front of her. She would be in Leeds by eleven, and it was her intention to go straight to Dan's house. There was no point in putting off their meeting. She wanted to clear the air; she wanted everything to be fresh and open and straight between them. He would feel pain when he heard of her involvement with Nick, she knew. She hoped he could understand and forgive. As much as she quailed at what lay ahead of her, she knew she had to tell him; how could she offer him less than the truth?

She couldn't imagine how he would react when he found out the facts about his father. She suspected Dan and Ken enjoyed – if that was the right word – a formal and distant relationship, and this morning it seemed to her that Dan would not be dealt a body blow by her revelations. In fact, she hoped it would distract him from feeling too sore about Nick. At their age, they were insulated from the misdeeds of their parents because of their own adulthood.

What would matter to Dan, she knew, was her obsession with Nick. It didn't help that Nick had deliberately tried to bed her as an act of historical revenge. What mattered was the way she had fallen right into the trap. She would have to explain that to Dan. She would account for it as a temporary madness, which it was. She would tell him it was entirely over, which it was. She prayed Dan could understand and accept her, imperfect and flawed as she had turned out to be. If there was something she could do to atone for her guilt she would do it. She wished she could be purified and reborn unsullied so she was fit for Dan again.

Ruth pressed down on the accelerator. More than anything she wanted to be with Dan, in his arms, forgiven, and starting over, as if none of this had happened. Their wedding was four weeks away. She yearned for it now, though she and Sylvie had wondered whether the Blakes would be able to keep up appearances on the day. In truth, Ruth did not care. Dan's name was like a drumbeat in her head. She was getting closer to him all the time. How disgusting she had been! How she wanted to make herself clean for him!

The motorway was relatively quiet. She was soon in Leeds, heading towards the Lyntons. Dan's house was a fairly non-descript, modern, two-bedroomed semi not too far from the shops. She imagined Dan reading the papers, wondering where she was, feeling anxious. She had to get to him as quickly as possible.

His car was not in the drive. Ruth was not troubled; he could have have put it in the garage, or gone to the gym or the shops. She had her key; she would let herself in and wait for him. She parked her own car in front of the garage and got out. It was a bright afternoon but a keen wind was blowing, and Ruth's hair whipped about her face. She pushed it back impatiently. As she felt in her handbag for the house keys, she heard a car engine slowing and stopping in the street.

She turned and saw Dan get out of his car. She was about to run to him but something stopped her. He looked lustre-less and defeated. Had he shaved? She thought she could detect a shadow that said he hadn't. Had he already found out about his father? Bad news travelled fast, her mother always told her. Concerned, she waited for Dan to approach her.

'I'm back,' she said.

He smiled at her, but it was an unconvincing smile. Puzzled, and a little alarmed, she unlocked the front door and went in. The Sunday papers were still on the mat. She picked them up and took them with her into the front room. He fol-lowed her.

'Where have you been?' she asked him.

'Where have you been?' he replied.

'Oh, Dan, I don't know where to begin!' She ran to him and hugged him. He didn't respond. He knows about Nick, she thought. How, she could not fathom. She let her arms fall.

'You're not all right, are you?' she said.

'Not entirely.'

'Shall I begin at the beginning?'

'If you like.' Dan looked haggard.

'Listen to me. I love you. I haven't been unfaithful to you. I met someone – quite unintentionally – at Adam's preview. I had a drink with him and he offered to take me round Gorton Monastery. I shouldn't have gone. I know that now. I made a mistake. But nothing happened, except I realised I want you. That's the important part. Do you understand?'

'Not exactly.'

'I know. I'm sorry.' Ruth took his hand and began to massage it gently. 'Dan. Nothing's changed. It's OK. Where have you been? Shopping? You didn't bring anything back with you.' She looked at him directly. He hadn't shaved. It almost looked as if he'd been out all night. He had not picked up the papers. 'Dan? Where have you been?'

'With Ellie.'

'With Ellie? Why?'

'I was lonely. I didn't know where you were.'

Panic gripped Ruth. 'Did you talk about me?'

The question was unnecessary. Ruth was sure that Ellie had told him all about Nick. She had no right to do that. Ruth could imagine how it had happened. Dan would have been worried about her uncharacteristic behaviour, would have asked Ellie if she knew anything, and bit by bit it would have all come out. Then he would have been devastated, and Ellie would have regretted it instantly, and tried to comfort him. Then he stayed. All night.

'You were with Ellie all night?'

'Yes,' he said.

Ruth felt as if someone had punched her. Dan had spent the night with Ellie. She knew what that meant. He was a man, wasn't he? He was weak, weak. She had always known it. He couldn't truly love her. He was like his father, fundamentally amoral. She let his hand fall. She had resisted Nick, but he had succumbed to Ellie. That was the difference between them. How could he have done it?

Now it was over. She could not marry him. Every difference between them she could transcend, but not this. She felt for her engagement ring and began to pull it from her finger. She couldn't slide the ring over her knuckle. It caught on a ridge of skin. Was she jumping to conclusions? Perhaps he, too, had done nothing. She ought to give him a chance to explain.

'What exactly happened?' she asked. As she did so, she went to sit down by the table. She was weak with fear. Yet at the same time Nick's words came back to her. There was a symmetry here. She had nearly cheated on Dan; he had nearly, or actually, cheated on her. 'Tell me what happened,' she begged.

'No,' he said. 'You tell me.'

He seemed angry with her. He had never been angry with her before. There was something hard and assertive about him now. She realised he only had her word that she had not slept with Nick. And even then, what actually constituted unfaith-fulness? She had been unfaithful in her mind. There seemed to be nothing she could say that would make it right. Nevertheless she would try.

'I didn't mean this to happen, just like a kid who wanders out of the front garden and gets lost. I made errors of judge-ment. I was wrong. I suppose I was just so secure in your love, I thought you loved me so unconditionally, that I could do more or less what I liked. It was unspeakably selfish of me. Dan, what you've got to believe is that nothing happened. I didn't sleep with him. I only ever saw him three times. All the madness is over now. I love *you*.'

'Oh. Am I supposed to be grateful?'

'It doesn't suit you to be sarcastic.'

'OK. How do you want me to be? Passive, easy-going, the sort of guy who holds the door open for women and gets trampled in the rush? Forget it, Ruth. My eyes have been opened. I'm not at your beck and call any more.'

'So that was what your night with Ellie was trying to prove?'

'I don't need to prove anything.'

Terror consumed her. This was a different Dan, one she hardly knew. The old Dan would have taken her back after a decent explanation, tears and recriminations, but not this Dan. He was white-hot with anger. Yet she was Ruth Collins, her mother's daughter, and would not quail and submit.

'How dare you come so high and mighty with me! You're every bit as bad as I am. You spent the night with Ellie – my best friend. And if I strayed, who's to say you didn't cause it?'

'Cause it? Careful what you're saying.'

'I was fed up playing happy families. Fed up with all the prissy perfection in your life, all the rollerblind crap and table decorations and boring accountant talk and all that Blake middle-class pretension. And I was utterly pissed off with your refusal to admit that there was anything wrong with us, any inequality. It's been one heck of a strain, Dan.'

'Then you should be relieved it's over.'

'It's over?' What did he mean Was he starting something with Ellie? 'Is it Ellie?'

'Do you want to know what happened? OK, I'll tell you. She made me dinner; we drank some wine and she told me about your little fling. So, yes, when she made her move I felt like revenge. I decided to sleep with her. You're not the only one who's scared of marriage. The difference is I didn't give in to fear. I worked to make it all right. Then when I discovered you weren't making the effort, I wondered why I was.' He paused and took another deep breath. 'There was Ellie, and she wanted me. Only I found I couldn't sleep with her. I realised she was using me as you were using me. That was one thing I couldn't take. So I—'

'No. You didn't sleep with her because you love *me.*'

'Is that what you think?'

'Yes. It's why I didn't sleep with Nick. We were tested, don't you see, but we came through. We're all right. It's held, Dan. We're each as bad as each other, or as good as the other.'

'You call this a test? No one's been testing you, Ruth. You did this yourself. This is your mess.'

'No, it's our mess.'

'You deceived me — that's the bottom line. I trusted you. I thought we were rock-solid, perfect.'

'No one's perfect,' she persisted. 'Are you?'

'It makes a mockery of marriage, doesn't it? All these people kidding themselves they can be faithful. They're living in cloud cuckoo land. Why are we bothering?'

Ruth could not bear it. His disillusionment and agony seared her. She had to make things right. She could see now, more clearly than ever, that her life would be impossible and intolerable without him. She watched him turn to leave the room.

'One last question, Dan.'

He paused, his back still towards her.

'No, turn and look at me. Dan, do you still love me?'

She saw the pain in his face, but also something else that gave her hope. She sensed a yearning in him.

'I'm always going to love you. If we can survive this, we're impregnable. Dan, answer me. Do you love me?'

He nodded; she ran to him and threw herself into his arms. She felt his body jump with sobs, then felt the straining pressure of his arms round her. It was going to be all right, she knew it. But she needed to hear him say it.

'Do you love me?'

'I love you,' he said, and they kissed. She was almost euphoric – having come through this, they would come through everything. She clung to him.

'We'll make it work,' she said.

'Even if it means rollerblinds and table decorations?' he asked.

'I'll take a course in napkin arranging,' she promised him.

'*Oy vey!*' he said.

She kissed him again. It seemed impossible for her to show

him how much she wanted him. No words, no actions, were enough. They kissed so hungrily that it was impossible to tell whose tears she was tasting. The centre had held. They were still together.

After a while, she broke away.

'Dan,' she said. 'There's one other thing I need to tell you, about this Nick.'

'It's history,' he said, lifting her T-shirt over her head.

'History,' Ruth said. 'That's not a bad way of putting it. Because the whole thing began around twenty-five years ago . . .'

Chapter Twenty-three

'Ken!'

Heather turned round from the sink, astonished to see her husband. He was not due home until Tuesday at the earliest. She had just finished her lunch and was washing her plate and cutlery, and here he was, suddenly in her kitchen. It was certainly a weekend for unexpected visitors. First Dan, then Ken, although calling her own husband a visitor was perhaps a distortion.

'I thought I'd come back early,' he said redundantly.

Heather dried her hands on the tea towel and went over to give him an acknowledging peck on the cheek. She began to hastily rearrange her plans for the rest of the day. She had promised Richard she would run up to the attic and check the new seedlings. Then there were a few jobs in the greenhouse and Richard had said he might call later and they could visit a garden centre to look at some new equipment. On the strength of that she'd invited him to stay for an evening meal, and a cosy night in. She would need to ring him and let him know that Ken was back.

'Lovely to see you,' she told Ken. 'Have you eaten? Would you like me to put together a sandwich? I'm afraid I don't have anything hot and it's already two o'clock. Of course I'll put the kettle on and—'

'It's all right,' Ken said. 'I think I'll have a shot of whisky. Come and join me in the front room.'

Naturally Heather did as she was told. Ken poured her a whisky too, having apparently forgotten that she didn't drink it. Luckily he didn't notice that the contents of the bottle had decreased considerably; Richard was also partial to whisky.

They took their drinks to the Queen Anne chairs by the front window; it was a gloriously sunny afternoon, and Heather craved the warmth of the sun. There was a table nearby where she placed her glass. The whisky caught the sunlight and glowed warmly. She anticipated that Ken wanted to tell her something; perhaps a difficulty had come up with his inspection, or he'd had a thought about the wedding. She glanced at him, and thought to herself that he was beginning to look rather old. The grey had spread from his temples and his face seemed more lined and jowled than usual. His shoulders sagged a little. Heather realised that she was probably comparing him to Richard, and that was why Ken looked his age today. She had become used to the company of a younger man, she acknowledged, not without a frisson of guilt.

'Heather,' he began. His voice was portentous. She hoped she hadn't done anything wrong. She began to tremble just a little bit. 'I, um, I . . . I ought to tell you that I happen to be acquainted with some of the wedding guests that the Collinses are inviting.'

'Really?' She wondered why he sounded so uncharacteristically hesitant.

'Yes,' he continued, gaining strength. 'In fact, the woman who has supplied Ruth's wedding dress is an old friend. I never realised because the wedding dress business is a recent venture for her. She had been employed in a number of capacities before then.' His voice trailed away. Heather decided this was going to be a rather dull conversation. Still, it was thoughtful of Ken to make an effort.

'How nice,' she said, wondering when she would get a chance to ring Richard and put him off.

'Yes. I've known Linda for over twenty-five years. In fact, I still visit her from time to time. There are ties, you see.'

Ken knew a lot of people through the school. So many obligations, and contacts to keep up. At times Heather found it rather wearing.

'Now, I don't want you to think in any way that what I am about to tell you is your fault. That isn't my intention at all. All in all, I consider that you have done very well, Heather, and deserve the best. Yes, yes. I'm pleased with your performance. Very pleased.'

Heather looked at him, faintly puzzled. Ken wasn't quite himself today.

'Sometimes,' he drained his whisky glass in a single swallow, 'one finds oneself obliged to people. Linda is such a person. She's not so well off, and she has two children – both grown-up now – but there is a baby too, Suzie's baby, and I like to give her what support I can, both with time and money. I knew you would understand this. Christian charity, very important. The fifth year raised over eight hundred pounds for

Save the Children. Yes. As I was saying. As a historian, I find it best to take a broad view of these matters. One mustn't shirk unpalatable facts. If I did have a relationship with Linda that resulted in these two children, one must accept that this was unavoidable at the time, and as adults and young men about to take up our place in the world we must all shoulder our collective responsibilities and deal with the situation. Yes. I knew you would understand. Good, good. You wouldn't pour me another whisky?'

'Are you sure this is your first?' He had been talking nonsense.

'Yes. First today.'

She handed him hers. 'Are you feeling well, dear?'

'Perfectly, perfectly. So, as I was saying, Linda is an old friend of mine and what a coincidence! That she should have supplied Ruth's wedding dress! I'm sure you'll get on very well. She's nothing like you, of course. One might say she lacks refinement, but not every woman can have your grace and serenity. She used to make the tea at Broad Hills when I was senior history master. I am very much looking forward to the two of you becoming firm friends. And the boys too. It turns out that young Nicholas and Dan have much in common. Nick is a photographer and particularly interested in Victorian architecture. Suzie has a degree in English literature. All four children have done very well. I'm so pleased we have come to such an amicable agreement over this. These modern, extended families have so much to offer. Not that they are so very modern, in fact. The British monarchy has a history of such liaisons and many a Victorian captain of industry had . . .'

Heather was struggling to understand what she had just heard. That Ken had two children from a previous marriage? But if he had met this woman at Broad Hills, then that was impossible as he was already married to her at that time; in fact, she was already carrying Tim. So if these children weren't the result of an earlier marriage then . . . then . . .

'Do you know,' Ken said, 'I wouldn't mind a sandwich after all. I find that I'm suddenly very hungry. What is there in the—'

'Wait a moment, Ken. I'm just having a little trouble taking in what you've told me. Are you saying that you've had an *affair* with another woman, who made the tea at Broad Hills? And that . . . there were children?'

'In a manner of speaking, yes. So shall we see about that sandwich?'

'And you still see her from time to time?'

'From time to time.' He beamed at her over his glasses.

At first Heather thought there could be little wrong with this as Ken seemed so unbothered by the situation. Surely if he had anything to feel guilty about, he would have been shamefaced, embarrassed or apologetic. Then the facts hit her like a slap across the face. Ken had been having an affair for the past twenty-five years. With a tea lady. And he had two children she didn't know about. And a grandchild.

Heather sat utterly still, trying to decide what she thought about all this, assuming it had all happened as he had said. It was hard to believe it was all true. If it was true, then he had been deceiving her. Their life was a sham. All her effort had been for nothing. She needn't have tried so hard, nor given up so much. She needn't have been so afraid of him. She was angry, certainly angry, and felt betrayed, very betrayed, but there was another feeling too, a lightness, a lessening of tension – surely not relief? No; that was an hysterical reaction, occasioned by the suddenness of his revelation. She was very angry. How could he have done this to her and expect to get away with it?

'I won't make you a sandwich,' she said. Her first act of rebellion!

He raised his eyebrows.

'You've been unfaithful to me. I'm . . . I'm appalled.'

'You have every right to be,' he said.

'That doesn't make it better.'

'I know.'

'Oh, I don't know what to say! I feel as if I could hit you!'

'Could you?'

'Oh, no. I don't know what I'm saying. I can't take all this in. Nothing feels real any more. What will people think? What will the boys think? What kind of example have you given them?' The white-hot liquor that was filling her veins she recognised as anger. It was intoxicating. 'How could you have deceived me for so long? You set yourself up to be such a pillar of society, and you do this. Why, you're no better than a common criminal!'

She searched in her mind for more insults. The wrath of ages was finding expression. If she heard the car pulling up in the drive it did not register in her conscious mind. It was only when the doorbell rang that she stopped hurling abuse at him.

'Heather,' he said. 'I think we have visitors.'

Heather turned. Through the window of the front room she could see two young women at the front door, neither of whom she recognised. The car blocking the drive was a blue Escort. Imagine having visitors at a time like this! Etiquette demanded that she did not ignore them although she intended to send them packing as soon as possible. She hurried to the front door and opened it.

'Heather Blake?' one of them said.

'Yes.' She noticed that two casually dressed young men were standing beside the car. Surely not Jehovah's Witnesses!

'My colleagues and I would like to conduct a search of your premises.'

Heather's first thought was that they had come for Ken. Although what he had done was not actual bigamy, it was as good as – or as bad as – and might possibly be punishable by law. She was about to point out that her husband was in the front room when the two men approached the front door and stood silently on either side of the women. Suddenly Heather began to feel very crowded. Summoning all her dignity, she attempted to take control.

'Search my premises? I don't even know who you are!'

'Police officers, madam. We have a copy of the search warrant here if you would like to look at it.'

Heather glanced at it but could not take it in. Police officers? Then, in that case . . .

'Well, I suppose you'd better enter.'

Almost before she could finish her sentence, the police were inside her house, one pushing open the door to the front room where Ken was standing, astonished, and the other going into the sitting room. The two male officers ran up the stairs. She scurried behind them, outraged and bewildered in equal measure.

'You can smell it from here, Jim,' came a gruff Yorkshire voice.

One of the officers tried opening the door of the attic but of course it was locked. To Heather's horror, they didn't even bother to ask her for the key. One of them heaved at the door, it cracked, gave way and the two of them were thumping up the stairs to her nursery. Anxiously she followed them, with Ken and the two female officers at her heels.

'It's a beauty,' she heard one of the officers say.

She was flattered. The nursery was beautiful. It was a sea of green. There were exotic plants in different stages of growth everywhere, adult plants, young plants, seedlings. Richard had created an extension to the water tank so that there was a trough constantly feeding all the plants. This was to save her labour. The sweet, sharp smell of the plants was an intoxicant to her. As they stood there, however, the overheard lights switched themselves off (Richard had installed a timing device) and they were all plunged into darkness.

'Heather Anne Blake,' said one of the female officers. 'You are under arrest for growing and supplying cannabis plants. I have to tell you that anything you say . . .'

The rest of their words were lost to her. Cannabis plants! Surely not. But now that she thought about it . . . How silly she was not to have realised! Yet the whole affair struck her as faintly ridiculous. Since she never knew they were cannabis plants, of course she hadn't done anything wrong. Richard was equally ignorant, although she had often wondered how he had acquired the knowledge to become so expert in tending plants he hadn't been able to give a name to. She'd always thought he was a secret Dr Hessayon reader, but then again . . . And all the money they had been making! No wonder the plants were selling so well!

'. . . back to the station with us.'

'You can't take her to the police station!' came Ken's voice. 'Surely you can ask her some questions here. I'm sure this is all a terrible mistake.'

One of the officers laughed. 'Some mistake,' he said.

No, it wasn't a mistake, Heather thought. How could anything that grew green and fresh and flourished under her hands be a mistake? In a world in which little made sense any more, this was one fact of which she was certain. She remembered a little saying printed on one of the notelets the church had produced to raise funds for the roof: you are nearer God's heart in a garden than anywhere else on earth.

'Is Richard Dawson on the premises?' she was being asked.

'No, not at present,' Heather answered. 'He ought to be here shortly, or if you like I can contact him for you on his mobile.'

She thought she saw the officers conferring but could not catch what they were saying. In the dim light that came up from the doorway at the bottom of the stairs, Heather could see that Ken looked thoroughly discomfited. She was obscurely pleased that she had been able to distress him. He might be nurturing a secret family, but it turned out that she had been nurturing something much more dramatic. Touché.

'So you say he's on his way here?' one of the officers asked.

Heather drew herself up to her full height. 'He isn't on his way here as such. He said he would call later. He's coming for supper. As I said, I could phone him and ask him to come earlier.'

More conferring. Heather realised that they imagined that if she rang Richard, he would run off and they would never find him. Surely he wouldn't do that! Or would he? The possibility was too horrifying to contemplate. She stepped back from that dizzying precipice. No, she thought. He wouldn't do that. Richard is my friend, my best friend, my——

'Mrs Blake,' an officer began, 'we'd be obliged if you could ring Richard Dawson and ask him to get here immediately, but you're to give no indication whatsoever as to why his presence is requested. Do you understand?'

She resented the tone. No longer was she going to be treated as an imbecile. 'I am not a child.' She spoke haughtily. 'I do understand. The telephone is in the hall, and I shall make my way down there.'

They all proceeded down the attic stairs. Years of training helped Heather to maintain perfect composure, but her mind was racing wildly. She could not tell Richard to walk into this trap. It would be a betrayal of their friendship. Yet she had no choice but to ring him. To ring him, and lie. It was the lie she couldn't stomach. She'd had enough of lies. Apparently she and Ken had been living a lie. But then, did she trust Richard enough to tell him the truth? If he deserted her, that would be the final straw. She didn't know if she had the courage to take that risk. She hesitated at the telephone, trying to find some words to say.

'Come on, Mrs Blake, we haven't got all afternoon.'

The rudeness decided her.

She dialled his number. The phone was only picking up messages. 'Richard?' she said. 'Hello, this is Heather, dear. Could you arrive a little sooner today? It's just that I'm having a spot of bother with the police, who have taken an interest in our little nursery. They're here now so I would appreciate it if you could hurry. I'll pay for a taxi. 'Bye.' She put the receiver down and looked levelly at the officer who seemed to be in charge.

'That wasn't very clever,' he said.

'Perhaps not,' she replied. 'We'll see. Now, I wonder which of you officers would like a cup of tea? I have the remains of a date and walnut loaf, and I think we could all do with a little stimulant.'

There was a gratifying silence. Ken and the officers followed her into the kitchen where she began to prepare the tea things. No one spoke. Heather began to realise that she might be in some sort of trouble, but still clung to the notion that since her intentions were innocent, a court of law would find her innocent. A court of law? Would it come to that? For a moment she considered the ensuing notoriety, the column in the local paper, the comments of the women at church. She felt slightly breathless. It was the thought of the gossip that appalled her most; she imagined Maggie Bowden in conference with the vicar . . . A thought struck her.

'Could it have been Margaret Bowden who informed you about Richard?'

'All information we receive is confidential,' one of the female officers replied.

It was Maggie, she was certain. The woman's jealousy was such that she'd shopped both of them. She didn't have a friend left in the world. It seemed more important than ever that Richard should turn up. Ken had let her down, Dan was getting married, and as for Tim . . . To quell the rising tide of hysteria, Heather concentrated on the preparations for tea. She helped the officers to seats around the kitchen table, and suggested to Ken that he bring a couple of folding chairs from the cellar. She noticed that there were two more officers prowling around her garden armed with walkie-talkies, peering into the greenhouse and making notes. She felt violated. Later, when all this had blown over, she would issue a complaint. For now, she attended assiduously to the teapot, the slicing of the cake, and the arranging of plates on the kitchen table. The familiar actions calmed her. She began to wonder what would happen next. Would she be asked to make a statement?

'Will you be questioning me?' she asked.

'Not here – down at the station,' came the reply.

That jolted her. She would be taken to the police station like a common criminal. It was so unfair. She might be a criminal, albeit accidentally, but common she wasn't. If only Richard were here. She wondered if another posse of officers was staking out his lodgings. It occurred to her that they were like a latter-day Bonnie and Clyde, and the idea pleased her. Then she returned to reality. Going down to the station would be the ultimate humiliation. She would spare herself that much.

'I shall talk to you *now*,' she said.

'Listen, Mrs Blake—'

Ken arrived at that moment with the spare chairs, and there was a diversion while he unfolded them, and placed them near the table. He sat on one, while Heather put one hand on the back of the other to steady herself. She remained standing.

'You see, Richard helps me in the garden,' she explained to

the officers. 'I first met him at the St Jude's Project, and I was introduced to him by the vicar. It was Richard who suggested we could grow plants indoors which would enable me to garden all year round. I'm passionate about gardening, and I do have a lot of time on my hands – my husband is away a lot.' She paused to glare at Ken. 'As I was saying, gardening is my hobby. Then one day Richard brought some seedlings along that someone had given him and we cultivated them. I did ask what they were but he said he didn't know. I didn't insist on finding out because it hadn't occurred to me that growing plants could possibly be against the law. So, really, Ken, I had no idea until this afternoon that we were growing cannabis. Although didn't I remember reading that even Prince Charles acknowledges its uses as a medicine?' She hoped she sounded sufficiently withering.

'Ah – that was the kettle. Excuse me while I fill the pot.' Heather turned and continued talking. 'My original intentions were simply to help Richard start up his own business as he has been unemployed for some time, apart from some bouts of casual labour. I have to admit that I have benefited from the arrangement too. Apart from the delightful nursery he created, he has been a wonderful companion. In every sense. Yes, Ken, in *every* sense.' Heather started to pour tea into the assembled cups. Confession, she decided was rather intoxicating, and liberating too. She decided to continue.

'I hope Richard arrives soon to tell you all this himself. I hope he will. And if I've helped him escape well – I don't care.'

It felt wonderful to say those words.

'You see, it's been a difficult afternoon. I've just found out that my husband, Ken, who used to be headmaster of the boys' grammar school on the Selby Road, has being having an affair for the last twenty-five years – that's right, isn't it, dear? He has two other children I've never met, and it turns out they're all coming to my younger son's wedding. Now, looking at my husband, you would never imagine he could do anything worse than help himself to an extra portion of dessert at dinner. So you see, appearances can be deceptive.

'And then there's the wedding in under four weeks, would you believe. I need to order the flowers and I still haven't decided what shoes to wear, although in some respects it isn't so important as they aren't that easy to spot on the photographs. I won't be kept in gaol, will I? I would hate to miss the wedding.'

'We should be able to arrange bail.'

'Oh good. Milk, sugar, everyone?'

To her surprise she saw that her hand was not trembling as she poured tea. She felt light, light as air. Or drunk. So drunk that she cared about nothing any more. Having lost everything, she was, in an odd way, entirely free. Somewhere in the kitchen was euphoria and relief and freedom, and when all her visitors had gone she would inhale it in great gulps. She was not bound to Ken. She had thoroughly disgraced herself in the eyes of the church. She had enjoyed a liaison with a younger man, which might, or might not, be over. It hardly mattered. She was stepping out of a whalebone corset. Everything was bathed in a clear, translucent light.

Of course there were her sons to consider. No sweat, as Richard might say. Tim needed to be jolted out of his complacency, and Heather admitted for the first time that she didn't really like him very much. Bringing up Tim had been hard and unrewarding work. Dan was different. Dan was adorable. He would be hard hit by this but she knew he would stand by her. And Ruth? That would remain to be seen. She rather hoped that she would shock Ruth too.

She handed round the tea and saw the officers consult the clock. She knew they thought Richard would never turn up. She wondered what else they imagined about her. Did they think she and Richard were lovers, re-enacting a modern version of Lady Chatterley? Well, let them think that. Or did they imagine she was a sad, middle-aged lady ruthlessly exploited by a smooth-talking ne'er-do-well? That was almost certainly what they imagined.

So what was the truth? She glanced at the clock. Richard could arrive at any moment. Yes, of course he had used her, but he had every right to. She had used him too. He had become her substitute son initially, helping her cope with the loss of Dan. Then, as she opened up to him, he was her best friend, gently making her see how the people around her had subtly abused her. He had shown her that respectability was only ever a veneer, a lacy tablecloth one threw over family life. And then, a few nights ago, he had shown her something else, that she was, after all, a very attractive woman. She smiled to herself, sipped at her tea and waited. She would be able to face the future without Richard, but how much better the future would be with Richard. She willed him to arrive, and arrive soon.

She watched the large hands of the male officers fingering her dainty china. The date and walnut loaf remained untouched. One of the female officers was wearing lipstick and Heather could see that a tiny spot had adhered to her left front tooth. Bad breeding, she thought. One should always look in a mirror before going out, to check details like that. She swallowed her tea self-consciously. The clock ticked guiltily. One of the male officers reached out for some date and walnut loaf with a thief's dexterity. She had been growing cannabis. A pity, she thought, she didn't know, because she could have tried some. It would have made an interesting addition to the date and walnut loaf.

Ruth sat on the settee next to Dan, her head resting on his shoulder.

'Do you think,' she said, 'that what hooked me was his resemblance to you?'

Dan followed with a non sequitur. 'I don't want to meet him.'

'I guess one day you'll have to.'

'My mother,' he said. 'This will break her completely.'

Ruth wanted to disagree with him, but couldn't, so she was silent. For the last hour their conversation had been like this, long bouts of silence interspersed with comments floating on the surface like the detritus of a shipwreck. Both of them had avoided the big questions. Yet in their physical closeness there was hope, Ruth thought. She snuggled closer to him and he did not move away.

'You'd better go and see your mother.'

'Yeah. I will.'

The clock ticked audibly. Ruth summoned her courage.

'Do you think she'll be able to cope with the wedding?'

'The wedding?' he echoed.

'I'm assuming we're going ahead with it.'

'Right.' He seemed to think for a moment. 'When I see her, I'll be able to make a guess.'

'So we are still getting married?' Ruth needed to get this clear.

That silence again.

'What do you think?' he asked her.

'The wedding we planned – it doesn't seem to belong to us any more, if it ever did. It belongs to the old Ruth and Dan. Only, the odd thing is, I want it more than ever.'

'Me too. If only to prove to my parents that we know how to do it properly. Although we might have to take another look at the guest list – I've got family I've never met! And will my parents still want to sit together? Are they talking to each other? And your parents—'

Ruth interrupted him, a shade nasally. She could never cry in a becoming fashion. 'Does this mean that you still want to marry me?'

'Did you ever doubt that?'

She buried her face in his chest and gave in to the luxury of a grade one cry. They had been through so much already, she thought, that they almost didn't need the marriage. Hell, they *were* married. Nothing could separate them now. Not that she was averse to the occasional symbol. She took her engagement ring from her jeans pocket and slipped it back on her finger, where it belonged.

As he walked along the avenue where Heather lived, Richard could feel the bulk of his leather wallet pressing against his thigh. It had been a good deal today, and the man at Badger Hill had promised more orders. A decent bloke. A lecturer at the university. His front room was lined with books on something or other medieval. It had been a good place to sit around and enjoy some of his own skunk. Only it had made him late. Still, as luck would have it, a bus had arrived almost immediately, and he had drifted off, and hardly remembered how he got here, but, shit, was he hungry! Good old Heather would be bound to have something for him. He knew he ought to listen in to the messages on his mobile, but business could wait until after he'd eaten.

He passed the house of the old bird who looked like Bugs Bunny, but today she wasn't out trimming her hedge. Near Heather's house he saw a Fiesta – did she have visitors? – and then a blue Escort blocking the drive. He wondered idly whose cars these were. There was a local election due shortly, maybe the motors belonged to a canvassing team. Or whatever. Stupid to leave a car blocking a drive though; no consideration, some people.

He took a deep breath of air to clear his head, and peered in the Escort as he edged past it. On the back seat he saw a policeman's helmet. He paused. His head was still fuzzy so it took him a little time to work out the significance of this. Heather had a visitor who was a policeman, or . . . or they'd finally tumbled.

Suddenly he was clear-headed. If this was a police raid, then he'd better run. There was still time. He could be out of York in half an hour. He had the dosh to go anywhere. It would be easy to start over. Yeah. He was cool.

Still he stood rooted to the spot. It would be a wrench.

He'd always fancied growing his own and his crop had flourished remarkably, thanks to Heather. They had a good scene going. She was all right. And she would be in there now with the pigs. Shit.

She could cope, he told himself. Heather had class, and they'd have to believe she knew nothing about it. Walk away, he told himself. Piss off out of it.

Only he was curious. Were the pigs giving her a hard time? She didn't deserve it. He couldn't bear the thought of her being roughed up. The fact is, she wouldn't have a clue how to handle them, whereas he knew only too well. Not that he'd ever been caught with blow before. But there was this geezer he knew in Sheffield who dealt from his bathroom. He was raided and only ended up with a probation order and community service, seeing it was his first time. And with Heather on his side, he might just be able to swing it his way. Christ, he owed it to her.

Richard was surprised at himself. It felt unusual, deciding to do something for somebody else. Kind of weird. But OK. Like, she'd been a mother to him, at least, until very recently. No, he couldn't let her down. And community service couldn't be any worse than St Jude's. For all he knew, he might even be sent back to St Jude's.

He rang the doorbell. No response. He was about to press the bell again when he heard scuffling in the bushes and felt a heavy hand on his shoulder.

'Richard James Dawson? You're under arrest.'

Chapter Twenty-four

————⋄∘⋄∘⋄————

'I do *not* believe it! I do NOT believe it!!'

'I'm sorry, but that's how I feel.'

'Like, how sad is this? Your last night of freedom, and you
don't want a hen party? Look, Ruth, I came home early just for
you. I've even been ringing round to see where we could go.
There's a pub over in Irlam with some male strippers and
Rach said she'd come with us if you pay, but I told her that
might not be your scene so we could always do something a
bit more upmarket. You can't just sit in and watch telly. I mean,
you'll be doing that for the rest of your life!'

'Leave her alone, Sharon!' shouted Sylvie from the kitchen.

'I don't see why Mum shouldn't come too. All girls
together, eh? D'you fancy it, Mum?'

'Just leave me out of it!' Sylvie replied.

'Well?' Sharon stood aggressively in front of Ruth, who
had been sitting at the dining-room table leafing through the
material from the Open University that Sylvie had sent away
for. Ruth knew she was playing the part of Boring Older

Sister again; thus it ever was. She would refuse to play with Sharon, who would go whingeing off to Mum. Nothing had changed, even on the eve of her wedding.

For a moment – but only for a moment – she missed Ellie. It would have been nice to have had a friend of her own choice with her on the eve of her wedding. Ellie was no longer in the North, having left her job and all her ties. A mutual friend had informed Ruth that Ellie had a flat in Peckham and was working for a temp agency. Apparently there was a man on the scene too. Losing a friend in that way was like having an amputation, Ruth thought. She had not quite become used to Ellie's absence. She had never seen her since her night with Dan, nor did she want to. Nevertheless, she wished her well. She returned her attention to Sharon.

'Sharon, I can't go out with you mainly because Dan is upstairs.'

'Dan? Omigod! You're not supposed to see the bridegroom the day before the wedding. It's bad luck.'

'As if we haven't already had all our bad luck.'

'I know,' Sharon said, kicking off her shoes and flinging herself on the settee. 'The whole thing is so amazing. But what I don't understand is why Dan's parents are still living together. Like, they're both in love with other people.'

'It's not as simple as that. Ken doesn't know what he wants; he's in a much worse state than Heather. Besides, there's the bail conditions which make it necessary for everyone to stay at their usual addresses. That's why Dan's here. He doesn't want to be on his own tonight, but he doesn't much want to be with his parents either.'

'Oh, right.'

'So you can see that a girlie night out isn't the best idea.'

'I still think you're a sad old cow,' Sharon said affectionately. 'Anyway, I s'pose we've got to be up early in the morning. Dad reckons it'll take us at least two hours to get to the hotel. I still don't see why you couldn't have got married in Manchester. Though when I get married I'm getting as far away from here as possible. Like the Seychelles. Where are the Seychelles, Ruth?'

The sisters stopped talking as they heard someone unlocking the front door.

'I hope that's Dad,' Ruth said.

It was not. Rachel entered.

'What the heck have you done?' Sharon exclaimed.

Rachel smiled at them uncertainly. 'I like it, actually. It lets my scalp breathe. Of course I've got to be careful not to go out in the direct sun in case I burn, but I can always wear a hat. The woman who did it said I had a beautiful-shaped skull. And look, she left a little bit at the front and dyed it white. Cool, isn't it? Isn't it?'

There was an eloquent silence.

'Oh, God, what have I done?'

'Ssh, Rachel, don't cry,' Ruth soothed. 'It'll grow again, but maybe not in time for my wedding. Look, we all make mistakes.'

'Well, at least you won't have a bad hair day,' Sharon remarked.

Sylvie entered and her jaw dropped.

'Give me strength,' she said eventually. 'Rachel, you look like a concentration camp victim. What on earth possessed you to do it? And the night before your sister's wedding?'

Rachel took recourse in tears.

'At least she's got rid of those dreadlocks,' Sharon remarked. 'I hate to think what was living in those.'

'Shut up!' Rachel screamed.

'Is it too late to find somewhere that sells wigs?' Sylvie asked.

'I'm not wearing a bloody wig!' Rachel shouted. 'And I'm not going to the wedding if SHE'S there,' she concluded, pointing at Sharon.

'I wouldn't be seen dead with her,' Sharon riposted.

Quietly Ruth got up and left the room. She ascended the stairs just as Dan was coming out of the bathroom, having showered and changed.

'Can we go out somewhere?' she asked, her tone urgent.

'Sure.'

Ruth left a note pinned to the door explaining they'd gone for a walk. She winced at the sound of the screaming from the lounge. The front door snicked back into place and she was free.

It was a warm, balmy evening with only the faintest breeze ruffling the trees that lined the street. The soft sunlight seemed to mellow the brick of the surrounding houses.

'Where shall we go?' Dan said.

Ruth thought. 'It would be nice to take a walk through town. It should be easy to park now.'

'OK.'

They got into his car and headed into the centre of Manchester. Ruth wound down her window to get the air on her face. So this was it, her last night as a single woman. Yet it was quite an ordinary night. Cheetham Hill looked the same as ever, its busy Asian shops buzzing with activity, women in colourful saris selecting interesting-looking fruit from outside stalls. The traffic coming out of Manchester was as heavy as ever, a solid line stretching from the city centre. They passed wholesale factories and converted warehouses, and arrived at the Arena.

'Where now?' Dan said.

Ruth directed him down Deansgate. It was as good a place as any. Since the explosion of cafe-bars along the street, the whole area had become a magnet for those hell-bent on having a good time. She thought perhaps there was somewhere they could have coffee.

They parked round the back of Kendal's, then walked past Sticky Fingers to Deansgate itself. Manchester was as comfortable as an old, familiar duvet.

'Happy?' Dan asked her.

'Mmm.'

She didn't feel like talking. She just wanted to get her head together. As close as the wedding was, she couldn't quite believe it was taking place tomorrow. Of course, she had been nagged about it for the past fortnight, and her parents had been pestering her about the ring, and the arrangements with the registrar, and where to put the presents. It was exciting, but she still couldn't rid herself of the bizarre feeling it had nothing to do with her, or with her relationship with Dan.

Dan had said to her that he felt as if he had been blown to pieces and then reassembled according to the old pattern, except some bits were missing. One of those bits was respect for his father, she knew. And he was distinctly uneasy around Richard, and furious with Tim, who had refused to speak to

Heather for a whole week as she had threatened his standing at the university. Dan said he felt as if he had gone back to school to learn about life from the beginning. He said the only thing he felt certain about were his feelings for her. With this as a background, the wedding, she thought, seemed like an empty frippery.

They crossed the road and stopped to look in the window of Waterstone's. They almost went inside but the pleasant evening tempted them to walk further. The city was emptying now, and seemed to pause, holding its breath, before Friday night proper and the mad, materialistic rush of the weekend. She linked her arm in Dan's as they crossed John Dalton Street and strolled on.

The sky was a pure blue, with only the faintest smear of cloud in the distance. The day of their wedding would be beautiful, as no doubt everyone would be reminding them. Yet just now Ruth felt more able to relate to the tired old buildings of Manchester and thought for the first time that when they had got used to being married they might move back here. Should they have children, it might be important to be near Mum and Dad.

'We could wander up to the town hall,' she said.

She guided Dan up a side street that led to Albert Square. She recognised immediately the building on her right because she had been there once. It was a synagogue – the only synagogue in the city centre. It was brick-built, square and substantial, but like most synagogues it did not draw attention to itself. There was a flight of stone steps leading to a double door, one of which was open.

'That's a synagogue,' she told Dan.

He stopped to look at it. 'It seems to be open,' he said.

'Yeah. It's Friday night. I guess there's a service on.' She pulled at his arm to urge him to continue their walk.

'No, wait,' he told her. She waited. 'Could we go in?'

'Go in?'

'Yes. I've never been in a synagogue before.'

Ruth felt decidedly awkward. She wasn't sure if anyone could just walk off the street and into a service, especially them, a non and a lapsed Jew. Dan seemed to expect her to know what was going on when really she didn't have the foggiest. She had only ever been to *shul* for weddings and Bar Mitzvahs and the odd festival when they were small. She had faded, sepia-tinged memories of men clad in prayer shawls in pews around the *bimah*, while all the women were herded upstairs into the gallery where they exchanged gossip and eyed each other's outfits. She would have to explain to Dan it was impossible, they would never fit in, they—

It was too late. He was already crossing the road and walking up the steps. She followed him into the lobby, acutely embarrassed, and working on plans for a rapid exit. Dan was looking about him, like a tourist, she thought, reading the notices, looking at the lists of founders engraved on stone tablets, and a panel commemorating those who fell in the wars. A caretaker stood at the entrance to his cubbyhole, watching them but saying nothing.

'Shall we go now?' she said to Dan, tugging on his arm.

'Can't we have a look inside?'

'Not if they're having a service. You can't just go in and gawp.'

Dan ignored her. He walked to the door of the synagogue itself, and peered in.

'It's empty,' he said.

The caretaker approached them with two prayer books. 'They're in the room at the bottom,' he said. 'You're all right. The rabbi's not down yet.'

Dan took the books, helped himself to a *yarmulke*, and to Ruth's horror entered the synagogue. Powerless, she followed him. The *shul* itself was grander than she'd remembered with a *bimah* at the front, and an ark surrounded by grey marble. It was closed now, the scrolls hidden by a blue velvet curtain and ornate gilded gates. A red carpet led to a room at the far end of the synagogue and they followed its path between the pews. Ruth thought how churches seemed to take one outwards, towards God; they soared, whereas synagogues did the opposite. They hemmed you in.

The door at the far end was ajar, and Dan pushed it open. About a dozen people were seated round the perimeter of the room and they all looked curiously at Ruth and Dan. Was it still OK to turn tail and run?

'Hello,' Dan said. 'We were just passing. My fiancée's Jewish – I'm not. Is it OK to stay for the service?'

Ruth managed a tight smile in response to the ready welcome they received. What was it with religious people that they always seemed so happy and damned pleased to see you? Was it an act? They were a motley crew, she thought, a black man, a slim, older gentleman in the corner, and a mother and daughter both wearing *yarmulkes*! Women wearing *yarmulkes*! What was Judaism coming to? There were also two couples of her and Dan's age, with whom she exchanged shy smiles.

Up in the left-hand corner of the room a small ark had been built, with a blue curtain concealing the *torah*, and a small red light burning above it. At the front was a table with a silver goblet. On a shelf by the window was a bottle of Palwin's No. 10 and a few glasses with wine already poured out. Apart from these indications of the purpose of the room, the surroundings were bare. Yet once again she had the sensation of being closed in, pulled in, and forced to relate to the group of people she was with. She swallowed nervously and glanced at Dan who had begun to leaf through the prayer book. She noticed he had begun to read it back to front, and she hastily explained to him that Hebrew books opened left to right, and the script was read right to left.

As she finished speaking, the rabbi walked in. Now there was no escape. The rabbi beamed at them, acknowledging he had not seen them before, but happy, apparently, that they were there. Ruth experienced a faint shock that he looked reasonably young, did not sport an impossibly old-fashioned beard, and reminded her more of a favourite tutor at university than an implacably kosher man of God.

He announced the page the service began on. Again Ruth was taken aback. In her experience, services were long, incomprehensible, and a men-only affair. In this place, you were supposed to follow what was being said, and women joined in lustily, almost too lustily, she thought, listening to the slightly tone deaf woman in a *yarmulke* beside her.

She scanned the English translation of the prayers and decided that had she felt less self-conscious and out of place, she would have appreciated the words. Covertly she watched the people around her, all of whom seemed intent on the proceedings. She wondered what on earth they were getting out of it. Did they even understand the Hebrew? Did they believe in everything that was being said? Just for professional reasons, she would be interested to know. For it was acknowledged in the courses she had attended that religion helped reduce stress and aided recovery from depression. Yes; it was a kind of spiritual Prozac. She hoped the service wouldn't go on too long; what a way to spend the night before your wedding! If Sylvie knew she was here, she'd have a fit. Ruth smiled to herself and moved closer to Dan.

Looking at the exotic Hebrew lettering in his prayer book, Dan felt like a child again. He could dimly remember a time before he could read, when he gazed at words in books and they seemed like magic spells to him. The Hebrew letters created the same effect. He wondered how long it took to learn to read them. He dutifully perused the translations of the prayers and relished the tang of the ancient they still possessed. In this plain room with its simple furnishing there was a promise of something out of the ordinary. Jews, it seemed to him, were foreign, but at the same time not foreign. They had something special; in a way, they were indeed the Chosen people. He could see that. Ruth's Jewishness was something very exciting, and he had never understood why she made so little of it. The arcane rituals, the mellifluous cadences of old tunes fascinated him.

He had lost his place in the service. It didn't matter. It was soothing just to sit here and let the sound of the prayers fill the room. The people who were sitting round the room seemed like a charmed circle to him, and he longed to be part of that. The Family of Israel, he thought to himself. Nice. Then everyone stood and faced the door and Dan did too. He was getting the hang of this!

This was one of the things that annoyed Ruth about Jewish services. It's like a game of Simon Says, she thought. You have to follow the leader and stand when everyone else does or bow, or face in a certain direction. A religion for the illiterate.

She sat down again and realised she had lost her place in the service. So she began to leaf through the prayer book, pleasantly aware of deliberately misbehaving. Obviously this *siddur* had been updated; there were quotations from people she had actually heard of. She recognised his words and found herself having a silent colloquy with the author. Yes, real love *is* more than just a powerful emotion, she told him. Yes, she said to him, you're right to state that love is a decision and a promise. It feels like that for me. Loving Dan is a commitment, and one I choose to make freely. And publicly. And like you say, there's judgement involved too. I believe I can love Dan for ever.

She was moved, overwhelmed, by the seriousness of the moment and swallowed hard to prevent her tears.

Dan joined everyone as they stood to face the ark. He liked the fact that there were just a few people in a small room; it suited him more than the formal gatherings at his mother's church. Tonight there was a definite air of informality. In fact he was certain that the rabbi lost his place at one point, as there was a moment of uncertainty in the congregation, and the mother and daughter next to him exchanged amused glances.

Now he sensed an air of seriousness. What was it behind the curtain that drew these people? Just a scroll? Why was it so important? He ached to know. Calmly he acknowledged to himself that he would come back here and try to find out.

I don't know if I believe in God, Ruth thought, but I believe in this. She read again the quotation she had found. She resolved to show it to Dan after the service; perhaps they could include it in their ceremony tomorrow.

It would be a fairly plain ceremony. The vows were basic and simply about commitment. She would be married in a country house hotel between Leeds and Harrogate, a place that held no particular significance for her. She regretted that, in a way. Perhaps they should have put more of an effort into making their marriage ceremony more individual.

When she was younger she had assumed automatically that she would get married under a *chuppah*, and they would stamp on a glass, and everyone would cry *Mazeltov!* That was not going to happen. It was a pity; there was something to be said for the old traditions. Suddenly, she wished she'd never set foot in this synagogue; it was unsettling her, making her feel as if she had lost something, whereas in fact tomorrow she would be gaining something, she would be augmented, not diminished. Only she wished that her wedding was in some way more serious. She was beginning to realise just how serious marriage was.

The pattern of her thoughts was disturbed as the service paused and wine was handed out for *Kiddush*. To her delight Ruth found she was able to join in the blessing for wine — she hadn't lost everything, after all.

They all sat down. The rabbi put down his book and began to address them about the festival that was coming up. But then, in the Jewish calendar, when wasn't there a festival coming up? It was *Shavuot*, apparently, which celebrated, among other things, receiving the law at Mount Sinai. The rabbi read to them:

> I betroth you to Me forever.
> I betroth you to Me with integrity and justice,
>   with tenderness and love.
> I betroth you to Me with faithfulness . . .

Dan nudged Ruth. He wanted to say to her, that's how I feel. The nudge would have to do. He wondered if it wasn't too late to include those words in their ceremony tomorrow. He wanted their marriage to mean more than just becoming a legal and taxable unit.

As it was, his parents had successfully upstaged them. All eyes would be on them tomorrow. What's more, Richard would be there, and Linda, and his half-sister and half-niece, not to mention Tim's blonde bimbo. His heart sank. He had made light of his misgivings to Ruth, but now they hit him full force.

He tried to listen to the rabbi's lecture but could not concentrate. Instead he looked around the room and observed the two couples of his age. They, he presumed, would be having a

Jewish wedding. He had to admit he was jealous. Jewish weddings, he knew, took place under a canopy. He liked the idea of that. But to do that, both partners had to be Jewish.

It was over. Everyone closed their prayer books and shook hands, saying *Shabbat shalom*. Ruth joined in, a little embarrassed by the open friendship. She deftly fielded inquiries as to who they were, and agreed when the rabbi said it would be nice to see them there again. In a few moments they were out of the synagogue and back on the street. Ruth walked briskly forward, taking Dan with her.

'Well?' she asked.

'It was good,' Dan said. 'Not what I expected.'

'Me neither.'

'It makes you feel part of a community.'

'Yeah. I guess. D'you fancy a drink?'

'Wouldn't mind.'

It was warm enough to sit outside, and they did so, facing the town hall, nibbling on tortilla chips and drinking red wine.

The feeling she had had in the service would not dissipate. That claustrophobia she experienced, that sense of being hemmed in and being forced to relate to people affected her still and pulled her back to thinking of the service. Being Ruth, she tried to intellectualise what she had felt. Maybe the point of Judaism was that you had to learn to relate to other people. That claustrophobia was necessary. Religion shouldn't be about feeling good in isolation but connecting and identifying with others. Like marriage, really. Her thoughts drifted as she watched some office workers walk past, talking loudly. Yes, maybe one day they ought to go back to that synagogue and experience a service again. Meanwhile, tomorrow they would get married in a civil ceremony.

Civil. That said it all, really. Civil. Polite, respectful, well-behaved. No. She wanted more than that. Much, much more.

'Dan?' she said.

'Ruth?' he began simultaneously.

'You first,' she insisted.

'I've got an idea,' he said. 'It's been there in my mind for a little while but what happened tonight has crystallised it. I think it might still be possible.'

'Are you thinking that—'

'Shut up and listen. This is what we could do.'

She listened, nodded, then nodded even more eagerly. Then her eyes widened in astonishment. Then she laughed.

'You're on,' she said. 'But we've got a hell of a lot to do and it might not be possible to sort it all out in the time we've got left.'

'We'll have a damn good try,' Dan said.

Chapter Twenty-five

The Three Tuns Country House Hotel was just visible peeping out from behind a row of close, confidential conifers. A good view of it could only be obtained by driving over the cattle grid and on to the gravel lane that led to its imposing front. Pale stone steps led to a modern, glass entrance which had been added seamlessly to the older post house behind it. On either side of the original building were extensions, in newer, creamier stone. In the warmth of the May sunshine, all looked positively bridal.

Ivan stood in the lobby of the hotel, conspicuous because of the newness of his grey suit, and the brilliance of the royal blue tie that Sharon had insisted he wore. He greeted the wedding guests, shaking the men's hands vigorously, kissing the ladies shyly, and accepting presents on Ruth and Dan's behalf. He shepherded his charges through an archway to the hotel's conservatory, where the ceremony was to take place. Already some of the guests had taken seats there. Lila and David sat erect in the second row, with Renie by their side in the gangway. Her stick had fallen and threatened to trip up the bridegroom and bride. Ken sat alone at the end of the front row, glancing at the door nervously from time to time. He kept his line of vision well away from the surrounding garden.

The Three Tuns' garden comprised a series of terraces, laid out with rockeries and flowerbeds. Beyond it was an expanse of lawn, where several peacocks had congregated. A small stream meandered through the grass, with a miniature bridge crossing it at one point. It was on the bridge that Heather and Richard stood. He inhaled occasionally on one of his roll-ups, at one point passing it to Heather who took a quick drag too. Richard's hair was scraped neatly back in a ponytail, and the suit Heather had hired for him fitted perfectly. She was in a dusky pink costume, her scarlet hat relieved by a confection of decorative beading and wisps of lace

'Ought I to go and join Dan now?' she said.

'Yeah. Do that. I'll have a gander at the bedding plants. I reckon we could have a display like that in the back.'

Heather kissed him on the cheek and picked her way back to the hotel, avoiding the conservatory and entering through a side door that brought her into the dining room. She surveyed it appreciatively. The displays of flowers she had created looked superb, and together with the balloons and menu cards everything was suitably festive. They would have a lovely day after all. She was a little nervous, not so much at what people would whisper about her, Richard and the paragraph in the *Yorkshire Post*, but at the enormity of the occasion itself. Dan, her own little boy, was finally getting married. It was, in its way, a kind of liberation.

He was waiting in her room now, and when she joined him

they would go down together. She would have liked Tim to help him prepare but Tim had deserted them both and was stalking up and down outside the hotel, awaiting Samantha. Ruth was changing into her bridal dress with her mother, sisters, and the Linda woman. She had not yet been able to catch a glimpse of her.

Leaving the dining room Heather passed some friends of Ruth's dashing into the Ladies to adjust their hats. She had not met any of them before; apparently Ellie, the only friend she did know, could not come to the wedding after all. Heather did not miss her. She still recalled the way she ate up Richard with her eyes at the engagement party. Nothing was so unbecoming as a predatory female or rather, a young, predatory female.

In the hotel lobby Ivan stood by a table full of presents, mopping his brow. He grinned at her. She had to admit she rather liked Ivan.

'Not long to go now,' she said.

Ivan checked his watch. 'Just over half an hour. The registrar's cutting it a bit fine.'

'I expect he'll have been at another wedding. Glorious weather, isn't it?'

'It is,' Ivan agreed, and Heather went through the fire doors up to the room where Dan was waiting.

'Are you ready for the dress now, Ruth?' Linda asked.

'Hold on a mo. Let me just pop to the loo first.'

'You can't,' Rachel announced. 'Mum's in there and I'm next.'

'OK,' said Ruth, quite unbothered.

'You've put your lipliner on crookedly,' Sharon said. 'Here. Let me.' She bent over Ruth, wielding a lip pencil with the concentration of the true artist. Ruth sat there passively while her sister worked on her lips.

'That's better,' Sharon said, glancing at her sister in the mirror.

Sylvie came out of the bathroom. 'You mean to say you're not in your dress yet? *Oy vey!* Do you realise the ceremony's in half an hour? What on earth are you playing at? And Rachel, take off my hat! Sharon, don't sit on the bed. You'll knock over the flowers.'

The bridal posy was on the bed, together with Sylvie's jacket and handbag. When her hot flush subsided she would put on the jacket. Or maybe it wasn't a hot flush she was having at all. Her nerves were in a dreadful state; she was in a much worse way than Ruth, who looked as unconcerned as if she got married every day of her life. Always the mother suffers most, she thought. Because a mother is responsible, responsible for everything. And life now was like chicken soup just about to reach boiling point. The last twenty-five years had been leading up to this moment. Ruth was born, brought up – or rather dragged up, kicking and screaming – went away to university, met Dan, and got engaged, although such an engagement she wouldn't wish on anybody. Yet it hadn't put Ruth off and now she was about to tie the knot, except that just sitting dreaming at the dressing table in a petticoat wasn't going to help anyone and these registrars worked to a tight timetable. Daughters! Who would have them? Me, thought Sylvie, and *kvelled* with pride.

*

Twenty minutes until the ceremony. It seemed to Ivan that most of the guests had arrived. He had just welcomed Heather's vicar, complete with dog collar. That made Ivan a little uneasy. Having come to terms with the fact that Ruth was marrying out, a vicar at the wedding seemed a little excessive. But where was the registrar?

Ivan walked over to the front door, shaded his eyes, and looked out to the lower car park. Someone was getting out of a car now. A blonde woman in her thirties, by the look of her, but – no, not the registrar, because she had a boy with her. They did not belong to the wedding party, they were both in jeans and T-shirts. He watched them make their way to the hotel. She looked harassed; the boy, who seemed to be about twelve, was reluctant to be there, as far as Ivan could tell by his body language. A baseball cap obscured his face.

To his surprise, the woman approached Ivan.

'Excuse me. Is Tim Blake around?'

Tim, who had been standing at the bottom of the steps, hurried up them to meet the new arrivals.

'Tim,' said Ivan. 'People to see you.'

Ivan watched the woman look Tim up and down.

'Samantha?' he said hesitantly.

'No. I'm Doreen. *This* is Samantha,' she said, pointing to her son who was studying his trainers with exaggerated attention. 'Go on, Sam. I told you. You'll have to explain. Go on. Or you'll be getting another damn good hiding.'

'I was pretending to be Samantha,' the boy mumbled. 'Sorry.'

Doreen addressed Ivan. 'That's the trouble with this Internet business. You never know whether people are who they say they are. I thought I just had to be careful he wasn't logging on to these porn sites; little did I think he'd provide the porn himself! Filthy little bugger! Samantha, indeed! I doubt I'd have found out – our Sammy's very close, you see – except I discovered your wedding invitation tucked between his boxers in his bottom drawer. Not what you'd expect to find, you'll agree. And folded inside it was a note from this Tim Blake that made my hair curl. That afternoon I confronted my lad and we had it all out. I made him show me his mailbox. Apparently this affair's been going on for months. Well, honestly, I don't know where the little ratbag gets it from. Not his father, I can tell you! So there was nothing for it except for us to come over to explain in person, so to speak. Are you Tim's father then?'

'No. I'm the bride's father.'

She turned to Tim. 'I admit he led you on, but you're disgusting, you! The things you wrote to him – you ought to be ashamed of yourself. Though to look at you, you don't seem the type. Well, appearances can be deceptive, that's for sure. Fancy writing all those things to a twelve-year-old boy! But to be fair, I suppose you didn't realise. Samantha, he called himself! Would you believe it? His dad's livid – he clobbered him when he found out. Well, we won't be staying for the wedding. What have you got to say, Sam?'

'Sorry,' the boy repeated from underneath his baseball cap.

'Where have you come from?' Ivan asked.

'Hull,' Doreen said.

'You can't go all the way back without some refreshment. Tell you what, why don't you stay and see my daughter get married, have a bite to eat, and then get back? Is that all right with you, Tim?'

Tim was stony-faced and Ivan wondered whether his offer of hospitality had been a mistake. Still, it was a harmless prank, he supposed, and on his daughter's wedding day he wanted no disharmony. Tim turned on his heels without saying a word and marched back into the hotel. Ivan showed Doreen and her son how to get to the conservatory. He checked his watch. It was twelve minutes before the ceremony was due to begin. Where on earth was the registrar?

'Dan!' Heather exclaimed.

He grinned at her. He was wearing an impeccably smart, dark suit, but a waistcoat embroidered with bright red hearts. Heather put her hand to her mouth.

'You like it?'

'Well, I . . . Yes, I do like it. Why didn't you tell me?'

'A little surprise for you. I'm more or less ready. Does Tim have the ring?'

'He did, the last time I spoke him, which was about half an hour ago.'

Dan's tie was at a slight angle, so she straightened it. As she did so, she had just the faintest sense of the little boy she used to guard and fuss over. Then the boy vanished, to be replaced by this bridegroom, this adult male, ready to be a marriage partner. There seemed to her something faintly absurd about the whole thing, and suddenly she had to fight hard not to laugh. She sincerely hoped there had been nothing in the cigarette Richard had shared with her.

'I'm ready to go down now, Mum,' he said. 'I ought to have a few words with Dad.'

'Poor love,' she said. 'He's all on his own.'

Dan tucked Heather's arm in his and they left the room.

Five minutes to go! This was ridiculous. You'd have thought the registrar would have rung if he'd been delayed, Ivan thought. The horrific possibility occurred to him that there could have been an administrative error and the man was not coming at all. As the bride's father he ought to find out what had happened.

Not wanting to worry the bride and groom or, worse still, Sylvie, Ivan explained the situation to the receptionist who told him that she had never known of a case when the registrar had been late except once, when his car had broken down. Ivan rang the number she gave him, hoping the office was manned on a Saturday lunchtime.

'No,' said Ruth. 'No. I just don't feel comfortable in it.'

'But you look beautiful,' Linda said.

'It's just nerves,' Sharon joined in.

' 'S wicked!' said Rachel.

'I'm warning you, my girl,' said Sylvie.

Ruth twirled round again in front of the full-length mirror. 'Linda, you've done a grand job. It fits perfectly. But I feel silly in a churchy long white dress, I always have done, and since we're in a hotel, and it's going to get hot later on, I think I'll just get married in my sun dress. Lucky I have one with me.'

'Ruth . . .' Sylvie's voice was menacing.

'I'll see to the money side of things, Mum. You won't be

out of pocket.' Quickly Ruth slipped out of the dress. 'Here, Rach, pass me the dress I came in. Yes, the pale lemon one with the thin straps. Ah – that's better. I don't want to be uncomfortable on my big day.'

'What will your father say?' It was a toothless threat. Sylvie knew it, and knew that Ruth knew it.

'He'll be surprised, and then get over it. Oh, wow, look at the time! We must go down now. The ceremony should have started five minutes ago. Do you think I'm fashionably late, Sharon?'

'You're stupid, you, having a beautiful wedding dress and not wearing it.'

'Come on, ladies,' Ruth declared. 'Into the fray.'

Sylvie was livid. So livid that all her nerves, all the sentiment that had been about to overwhelm her vanished completely, leaving her not just furious but furious and impotent. What game was that girl playing? Always so determined to have everything her own way. She could gladly strangle her. She hurried behind her daughters with Linda, who looked as puzzled as she felt.

They turned at the bottom of the flight of stairs into the lobby where Ivan was on the telephone. He beckoned Sylvie over.

'Syl, I don't want to worry you, but there's no—'

'Come along, Dad. We're late as it is,' Ruth declared, pulling her father into the conservatory. 'Sorry!' she called to the receptionist. 'Can you put the receiver down for him? Thank you.'

My God, thought Sylvie. This is how the Collinses make an entrance, bursting in through the doors in any old order, and Ruth not even in her wedding dress. It was the ultimate humiliation. All the assembled guests turned to stare at them. And there was Dan – what would he think? He left his place in the centre of the front row and came to kiss Ruth. Before the ceremony? Sylvie was numb with disbelief, and as for his waistcoat . . .

She felt Ruth's hand on her shoulder pressing her down into a seat. What was going on? She felt very, very suspicious.

Dan and Ruth faced the assembled guests. There was a deathly silence.

'First of all,' said Dan, 'welcome to everyone. We're glad you could make it.'

'Yes,' said Ruth. 'Although we're not actually getting married today. We've cancelled the registrar. We've – ah – sort of changed our minds.'

'But not about getting married. In fact, weddings are so much fun, we thought we'd do it twice.'

'Don't joke, Dan. Look, sorry, everyone, but we found we couldn't go through with it. It's like . . . if you really thought about what getting married entailed, well, then no one would ever do it! I'm sorry if I'm not making much sense but I don't quite know how to put this.'

Dan took over. 'We want to get engaged again. We're not ready to get married yet, at least not in the way we want.'

'So there isn't going to be a wedding after all – not today. But there will be another engagement. Dan and I want to begin all over again, and now is as good a time as any. We feel that we need – we want – to get to know each other all over again. And prepare for our marriage. We're going to pay for the do today ourselves, and we'll return all your presents. We haven't exactly cancelled the honeymoon, but we've transferred it to my mum and dad – don't look like that, Mum, I'll help you get organised. And it isn't *that* hot in Cyprus at this time of year. Is it? So really that's all the explaining done.' Ruth felt herself drying up. There was a stunned silence in the room. She dared to look at her mother. Sylvie was clutching Ivan's hand as if she intended to break every bone in it. Sharon was open-mouthed; Rachel was smirking.

'But first, Dan and I want to read some things.'

'To plight our troth,' Dan added. 'Apparently people used to do that. It's a little more binding than an engagement, but not as final as a marriage.'

There was an unearthly screech from the garden, like a cat being strangled. The peacocks had wandered up to the conservatory, and one of them now displayed his tail feathers in a blaze of green and mauve and turquoise eyes. They glittered and rippled in the sunlight. A couple of peahens glanced up, then carried on pecking at the lawn in a desultory fashion. The attention of the wedding guests returned to Dan and Ruth, who had turned to face each other. They gazed straight into each other's eyes. They had memorised the words they were speaking:

> I betroth you to me forever.
> I betroth you to me with integrity and justice,
>   with tenderness and love.
> I betroth you to me with faithfulness . . .

*

It was all right, getting pissed on champagne. The high kicked in pretty early, and lasted well as long as you kept yourself topped up, Rachel thought. But now she was knackered, and just wanted to find somewhere where she could chill out. Everyone was hanging out in the gardens, except for Heather and Linda who had retreated to the hotel bar. She would have joined them, except they seemed to be getting on so well it seemed a pity.

Rachel re-entered the hotel through the dining room. The hotel staff had begun to clean the dinner debris away. One of the waiters, a cute guy with an earring, winked at her, and she smiled back. She hoped he didn't notice her stumble slightly as she edged past the tables. It was those damn stupid stilettos Sharon had made her wear. Impatiently she kicked them off, took them in her hand, and made her way to the entrance of the hotel.

It occurred to her she could go and have a nap in her mum and dad's room. She pushed open the fire door and climbed the stairs. She walked along the tastefully decorated corridor, then sniffed the air. Hmm. She knew what *that* was, else she'd been wasting her time at uni. Blow. Draw. Cannabis, or whatever. So that was where Richard had got to.

Not wanting to compromise herself, she left her stilettos outside her parents' room and crept back down the stairs. Yes, she'd definitely go back later and have a chat with that waiter, only first she had to get her head together. Through the archway she could see that the conservatory had been restored to its usual state, with yucca trees, rubber plants and easy chairs. It looked empty. Rachel entered it, and found an inviting chaise longue in a shady corner. She eased herself on to it, stretched herself out, and closed her eyes.

A mistake. The darkness seemed to spin dangerously out of control. She opened her eyes again and tried to focus on the ceiling with its stippled white paint. Better. Like, this had been the strangest wedding she had ever known, except it hadn't been a wedding. It was romantic, really, Ruth and Dan saying their own vows. But the big shock was discovering Dan wanted to convert. How weird was that? But it was dead nice that he wanted to do it for Ruth. Ruth was lucky. Rachel thought that she wouldn't mind getting married one day to someone like Dan. But not yet. Not while there were thousands of blokes to work your way through, and gallons of alcohol to drink. There was a time to get married, but it wasn't her time. Nor was it Ruth's. No, what Rachel wanted now was just to have a quick nap so she could start partying again later on. Carefully she tried shutting her eyes again. This time the darkness seemed more stable. The afternoon sunshine warmed her limbs and dissolved her last few random thoughts. Rachel drifted off into a peaceful sleep.

SHERRY ASHWORTH

A MATTER OF FAT

At the Heyside branch of Slim-Plicity, the women are struggling valiantly with their waistlines. Stella, the sylphlike group leader, is very encouraged. They are going to be the slimmest group in the north-west and qualify for a celebration buffet. Meanwhile, in a nearby pub, members of the Fat Women's Support Group agree that dieting is a tool of women's oppression used by men and the media. It's time to change the public perception of fat by being proud to be big.

Sandra, an English student at the university, is torn: she wants to be slim, but she doesn't want to be oppressed. Helen wants to be slim but eating is the only thing that relieves the boredom of her life. And Stella herself is discovering that thin does not always equal perfect bliss . . .

As the various members of Slim-Plicity and the FWSG try to find happiness, the question is: to diet or not to diet?

HODDER AND STOUGHTON PAPERBACKS